A double murder le[...] a web of internationa[...] gripping novel by the [...] of *The Jury.*

The Arraignment

The verdict on *The Jury* was unanimous. Larry King in *USA Today* called it "a cracklin' good read" and *Publishers Weekly* proclaimed it as "one of Martini's best novels to date." Now, *The Arraignment* takes lawyer Paul Madriani into uncharted territory—into the minds of men whose murderous greed knows no bounds . . . and onto the front lines of the South American drug war.

"Good fun."   —*The Washington Post*

"Martini's legal maneuvers, dialogue and quirky secondary characters are imaginative and enjoyable."

—*USA Today*

"Expect Martini's trademark plot twist at the end."
—*New York Daily News*

"Sprinkling his tale with violence and intrigue by putting Madriani at risk on the streets and in the boardroom, Martini keeps the story building to a deft, visual climax."
—*The Boston Globe*

"One of his finest . . . Martini shows a deepening talent for character and description."   —*Publishers Weekly*

continued . . .

Titles by Steve Martini

THE ARRAIGNMENT

Steve Martini

JOVE BOOKS, NEW YORK

This is a work of fiction. Names, characters, places, and incidents either are the product of the author's imagination or are used fictitiously, and any resemblance to actual persons, living or dead, business establishments, events, or locales is entirely coincidental.

THE ARRAIGNMENT

A Jove Book / published by arrangement with
SPM, Inc.

PRINTING HISTORY
G. P. Putnam's Sons hardcover edition / January 2003
Jove international edition / June 2003
Jove edition / September 2003

ISBN: 0-515-13595-X

A JOVE BOOK®
Jove Books are published by The Berkley Publishing Group,
a division of Penguin Group (USA) Inc.,
375 Hudson Street, New York, New York 10014.
JOVE and the "J" design
are trademarks belonging to Penguin Group (USA) Inc.

PRINTED IN THE UNITED STATES OF AMERICA

10 9 8 7 6 5 4 3 2 1

In memory of Ralf

CHAPTER ONE

Nick's office is on seven, the bottom floor of Rocker, Dusha and DeWine, better known to the legal set as RDD. It is the largest law firm in town, with more than three hundred lawyers and offices in four cities.

Nick has been here only two years and already he has a corner office and two young associates assigned to him. Like a mini–law firm within a firm.

His office has been sharply decorated by Dana, the new Mrs. Rush. Her touch is on everything, from the Persian carpets and artistic earthen vases that adorn the alcoves behind his leather-tufted chair to the gold stud in his right nostril.

Nick may have a new sassy-looking wife, but he is the same man I've known for more than ten years. A cigarette dangles from his lower lip as he talks, dropping ash on the expensive leather blotter of his desk. Nick may not look the part, but people tend to listen to him when he talks.

He sweeps the ash away with the back of his hand and examines the burn mark on the new leather.

"If she sees that, she'll kill me," he says. He's talking

about Dana. He tongues a little saliva on his finger and tries to fix it.

"I have to smoke here. Dana doesn't like it at the house. She says it leaves a smell on the furniture and her clothes. I don't smell it. But then, my smeller's gone."

He takes a good drag from the cigarette and immediately has a coughing jag.

"First one of the day." He says it between fits of trying to catch his breath, cigarette hanging from the corner of his mouth. "She's right." He holds the cigarette out looking at it, then puts it back in his mouth. "This shit'll kill you. That'll teach me to marry an interior decorator."

He says nothing about the fact that he's older than his wife by twenty years. He looks at me to see if I am offering any sympathy. That particular bank is closed at the moment.

My own practice, Madriani and Hinds, is small, no rival to RDD. My partner Harry Hinds and I staked out a quiet bungalow office lost in the foliage of a courtyard across from the Hotel Del Coronado two years ago. Looking for a cooler climate and a fresh start, we had relocated the practice from Capital City on the financial wings of a large judgment in a civil case. Since then Coronado and the environs around that city have become home for me and my fifteen-year-old daughter, Sarah. Sarah has no mother. Nikki died of cancer several years ago.

What takes me to Rocker, Dusha today is a phone call from a friend. Nick is in his fifties. Prime earning years for a trial lawyer. Old enough to have judgment and young enough to do the heavy lifting in court. He considers the move to Rocker, Dusha to have been a good one. I'm not sure I agree. To look at him, Nick has aged ten years in the last twelve months.

The firm recruited him with assurances that they would move him into civil litigation. Instead, he has been buried in white-collar crime. Along with business bankruptcies, it is one of the growth sectors of the law, both areas being driven by the aroma of corporate book-cooking that took place in the last decade. The "me generation" of the 1960s is not faring well.

Nick's corporate criminal skills have been honed over more than two decades, first in the U.S. attorney's office, then in his own solo practice before coming here. There are rumors that Nick has been recruited elsewhere but has chosen to stay with Rocker, Dusha. I suspect if you chase these rumors down, you will find Nick residing under the rock from which they crept.

What the firm wanted was somebody to pick up the respectable businessman who occasionally slips and falls through the cracks, your friendly financial adviser who decides he'd rather invest you in his new yacht than in the bonds he told you about and then prints his own securities so you'll have something to put in your safe. To Nick, this doesn't even qualify as crime.

"They were supposed to groom me for the civil side, but as you can see it hasn't happened." He points to the files on the floor lining one wall three feet high.

"They can't bring filing cabinets in fast enough. We've generated more revenue in the last two months than any other division. I told 'em I need help. They tell me to work my people harder. If I could bill a fifty-hour day I'd do it. Chamber of commerce crap," he calls it. "Consumer fraud. Junior league crime. They should have to give you a plastic ring and a special decoding button before they charge you with any of this shit. I swear, half the stuff in those files I didn't know was illegal until I came to work here."

"Why don't you leave? You could probably write your own ticket."

"Too much invested. Two years. I'd have to start all over someplace else. Too old for that. I've got a wife who wants me to wear argyle silk socks to court and sue insurance companies so she can tell her friends over dinner that her husband's a corporate lawyer and not have to lie. I know you think I'm out of my mind for being here. Getting divorced, getting remarried."

"I didn't say anything."

"Your silence is deafening," he says.

"I'm not your therapist."

"I know that. He tells me when I fuck up."

"OK, so maybe I made some stupid moves. *Stupid* is the word that comes to mind, isn't it?" He assesses my expression one more time, then adds, "OK, there's no maybe about it. But it's done. Over. How do you un-ring a bell? The personal side of life for me is cooked. But the law practice, the career, that's a work in progress."

This is more optimism than I've seen in Nick in a while, on any front. He's the kind of lawyer who thrives on a full caseload.

"I wish you were my therapist," he says. "You ought to see this guy. I go to him once a week. It's like going to the dentist to have my brain drilled without Novocain. I tell him I'm feeling pretty good, I'd like to move on with my life. He tells me I need to find closure with Margaret now that the divorce is over. I tell him I got all the closure I needed when her lawyer drove a pike up my ass in the support hearing, you know, the alimony. If that wasn't enough, she took every dime I had. I tell him I've got plenty of closure, I could sell him closure. Then he says, catch this, he says I need to deal with Margaret to get over my feelings of guilt. I tell him I have no feelings of guilt. He tells me I should, that if I don't I must have problems empathizing. And for this he hits me for a hundred-and-a-half an hour."

"Stop going to see him."

He looks at me through cigarette smoke, gives me a face, something you might see from De Niro. "Then I'd probably feel guilty," he says. "My old man used to say pain is good for the soul. I know, that makes as much sense as my joining this fucking firm. But you make your bed and you sleep in it. And if it happens to be next to a twenty-six-year-old woman with an incredible ass, what can I say?" He laughs. The price Nick pays for lust.

He looks at me over the top of his cheaters, half-lenses for reading. He is wearing a three-thousand-dollar suit but has dandruff on his shoulders and cigarette ash on his tie along with a wrinkled tan forehead that ends in baldness he is trying to hide under dying wisps of black hair.

"People grow apart. Call it a midlife crisis. Call it a second childhood. Call it what you want. I got an itch. So I scratched it."

This is how he describes a two-week binge in the Caribbean with Dana. And this wasn't the first itch for Nick.

He took Dana from Nevis to St. Lucia, then down to Belize and back to the Bahamas, half a jump ahead of the investigator Margaret hired to track him down. What Dana told her employer I don't know. Maybe she took vacation time or figured she had her hook set far enough into Nick that she could quit.

The investigator caught up with them in Nassau. All the while Nick was supposed to be at a trial lawyer's seminar in New Orleans, paid for by the firm.

"You ever done it with a twenty-six-year-old?" he asks me. This comes out of nowhere.

"When I was twenty-six."

"No. No. I mean now?"

I know what he means, but knowing Nick I figure the question is rhetorical. I have seen him do this in front of juries for money, lots of it, pleading a client's case, boring holes through them with those beady little eyes over a smile you know is not being driven by humor.

When Nick asks a question like "How can you be sure the sky isn't green?" he is never looking for an answer. What he wants is the surrender of your rational thought process. Once he has you questioning your own logic, it's a simple act of illusion before he has you buying into the fable his client is going to spin on the stand.

In this case it's an exercise in absolution by silence from another lawyer. Even if I haven't done it recently with a twenty-six-year-old, Nick can comfort himself with the thought that I would like to.

"So Margaret has to go hire herself this prince of darkness," he says, "some fucking divorce lawyer out of L.A. to stake me to an anthill. Hey, do I complain?"

The fact that he is doing so now doesn't slow him down.

"No. I just pay the tab and figure this is the price of moving on with my life."

If the dark circles under his eyes are an indication, getting on with life would appear to be killing him. Nick's face is a declining graph of sleep deprivation. Whether he's working too hard to meet the alimony payments or playing too hard at night with Dana, I can't be sure. One or the other, or both, are killing him.

"If you had an itch like this," he says "wouldn't you scratch it? Any guy with a normal sex drive . . ." He continues talking as if I'm not here.

Nick suspects I have had my own dalliances, perhaps in a former life before becoming widowed, though I have never shared any of this with him. It's the reason he calls me from time to time. I'm cheaper than his therapist, and he can more easily ignore whatever I tell him since I have no training in the occult. Being outside the loop of his partnership, I am a safe shoulder to cry on.

As he sits across the desk from me, his brown eyes look like they belong behind wire mesh in the dog pound. There are basset-hound bags under each.

Dana, the new Mrs. Rush, is sleek and blond, four inches taller than Nick. She has the fresh look of a model on her way to becoming a movie star. And unless I have completely lost my judgment of character, she knows how to climb the rungs of life. I have met her three times, and on each occasion she parted with looks that made me wonder if she wasn't trying to come on to me. But then, I suspect with Dana most men might foster this illusion, feeding it regularly, in hopes that it might grow into reality.

Dana possesses a kind of style that screams TROPHY. Tall and tan with a smile that glows like a nuclear reactor, she can stoke the coals that fire most male egos with a single fleeting glance across a crowded room. And for all you know she might be looking at the clock on the wall behind you, worried that she is late for an appointment to have her nails done.

The first time Nick met her was at a political fund-raiser.

He left his brains on the table along with the tip and began doing his thinking with his dick. He hired her to decorate his office and the rest is history. He has been on this particular treadmill now for almost two years and is beginning to show serious signs of wear.

"You would scratch it. Right?"

"What?" I look at him.

"This itch? Tell me you would," he says, "otherwise I'm gonna start thinking you misplaced your libido."

I give him an expression that is noncommittal.

"Fine, then tell me you wouldn't scratch it."

"She's your wife," I tell him. "I wouldn't scratch it."

"But if she wasn't my wife?"

"I don't think I have your stamina."

He laughs. "The secret is to pace yourself."

"You'll have to show me sometime."

"Yeah, well. I admit it can be a problem." He looks at me. Wrinkles an eyebrow. Wrinkles on wrinkles. "All the same, if you gotta go, what better way?"

It's the kind of expression you could get from Nick just before he told you what your fee was going to be—and always up front. Nick has made a religion out of tracing the source of his clients' money to make sure that it will not be confiscated by the government as the fruits of some illicit deal.

"She wants me to quit," he says.

This catches my attention and Nick notices.

"Not the practice," he says, "just the heavier criminal stuff. So I'm getting it from both ends. Screwed over by the firm and Dana putting pressure." He grabs a bottle of antacid tablets from the desk, unscrews the cap, pours some into his hand without counting, and slings them into his mouth, chewing and swallowing, then follows it with something in his coffee cup.

By the time he swallows and comes up for air, he's back ragging on Dana. "She's angry that they haven't come through on their promises. She wants me to talk to Tolt.

Press him to get the big civil cases. Like he's gonna turn these over to me. He hates my ass."

"Why?"

"I don't know."

"There must be a reason?"

"Hey, you know me. Even-tempered. Easy-goin'. I get along with everybody. I'm learning how to climb the corporate rungs. You may not believe it, but I'm becoming discreet, diplomatic, political," he says.

"Lose your knife in somebody's back, did you?"

"There you go again. This dog's tryin' to learn new tricks and you keep running me down."

"No, I know this dog. He may be calling it a bush but he's trying to pee on my leg."

"How can you say that? There's talk that some of the partners want to put me on the management committee."

"I take it these are some of the partners whose pictures are on the walls out there in reception with brackets around the dates under their names?"

"I'm serious," he says.

"I know you're serious. It's their mental state I'm worried about. If they're serious, they're in the grips of dementia."

"You think so?"

"Nick, putting you on any committee would be an act of anarchy. The only administrative position for which you're qualified is emperor, and that would only work in hell and then only if there were bars on the windows."

He laughs. "Well, they're thinking about it. Tolt's the only one standing in the way. From what I hear, half the partners in the firm are ready to walk." He says it with a little glee as if burning his own place of employment to the ground is his ultimate objective. Nick gets off on blood, especially if it's somebody else's.

"Don't say you heard it here, but they're pissed at him." He's talking about Tolt. "Rumor is there will be no year-end bonuses. He wants to plough everything into a new branch office in Chicago. They're already overextended. That's what happens when you grow too fast," he says. "I stay here long enough and Tolt starts doing some creative accounting, I might pick him up as a client."

Nick is having fantasies. Adam Tolt is the firm's managing partner, for all intents the CEO, Yahweh, the higher power of what is now Nick's universe. He chairs a management committee, but according to anyone who knows Tolt, he's the man who makes the decisions. He is on a dozen corporate boards, two of the companies that make up Dow-Jones.

"So what did you tell Dana?"

"I told her I'm working on it. Have a little patience. Everything comes to those who wait."

"Is that something else your father told you?"

"Read it on some guy's toe tag at the morgue. He was sitting on the tracks when a train hit him, and all they could find was his foot."

I know the story to be true. Coroner's bedside manner.

"Besides, I've got a few irons in the fire."

"What?"

"Can't talk about them right now." With Nick, it's always the big mystery. The next major coup in his life.

"Hell, at least with Margaret she didn't care," he says. "Whatever I wanted to do was fine, as long as we could pay the bills."

"Sounds like you regret leaving her."

"Only once a month," he says. "When I'm making the support payment." Then he thinks for a moment. "No. That's not true. Sometimes I see her in my dreams," he tells me. "Coming at me with an ax." Nick's laugh at something like this is always the same, a kind of shrill, pitched giggle you wouldn't expect from a man his size with a barrel chest. It was a bitter divorce.

"There's an old saying," says Nick, "that the truth shall set you free. I'm living proof. I told her the truth, and she divorced me. But at least I left her with a song in her heart."

With this he smiles. Nick's parting was not exactly a class act. It was talk all over town, gossip at all the watering holes.

A man possessed of a tongue gilded with enough silver to waltz embezzlers and corporate confidence artists out of court couldn't figure out how to tell his wife he wanted another woman.

Even after she caught him with Dana, Margaret was prepared to forgive him. But Nick thought of a way to save her from herself; with the lyrics to a piece by Paul Simon— "Fifty Ways to Leave Your Lover"—playing on an old turntable and a farewell note propped above it on the shelf.

Margaret had her revenge in the divorce and the support hearings that followed. Nick is likely to be practicing well into his eighties to pay the bills, though I suspect his annual income before taxes is into seven figures. I can imagine he might now be in a financial pinch.

"You're probably wondering why I asked you to come over." He cuts to the chase.

The hair on the back of my neck goes up. Nick wants a favor.

"I want you to understand it isn't me asking; it's really Dana."

"That makes it easier to say no," I tell him.

"Be nice. She likes you. She's the one who suggested I come to you."

Now I am nervous.

"She has a friend. This guy sits on the county arts commission with her. Seems he got himself involved in some kind of grand jury probe."

I'm already shaking my head.

"Listen, don't be negative," he says. "Hear me out. The guy's just a witness. He may not even be that. He hasn't even been served with a subpoena yet."

"Then why does he need a lawyer?"

"Well, he thinks he will be. I know. And I wouldn't ask you to do it, except I got a conflict. I can't represent him. The man's in business."

"So is the Colombian cartel. It's nothing personal," I tell him.

"As far as I know, he's clean. No criminal history. He's a local contractor."

Knowing Nick, the guy is probably drilling tunnels under the border crossing at San Ysidro. Nick would tell a jury his client was drilling for oil, and they'd probably believe him.

"So why would the U.S. attorney want to talk to a local contractor?"

"They got some wild hair up their ass on money laundering. That's all I know. Probably one of their snitches got into a bad box of cookies. The feds go through this every once in a while. It's like the cycles of the moon," he says. "One of their snitches has a bad trip, starts hallucinating, and half a dozen federal agencies go on overtime. From what I gather, it's the people down in Mexico they're looking at."

"What people down in Mexico?"

"You can get all the details when you talk to the guy."

"That assumes I'm going to talk to him."

"Dana's friend's name." He ignores me. "Actually he's not even a friend. She just met him a few months ago. Apparently his name was mentioned by another witness in front of the jury."

"How did that happen? More to the point, how do you know what a witness said in front of a grand jury? Last time I looked, they lock the door and pull all the blinds inside grand jury rooms."

"Don't ask me things I can't tell you," he says. "Hell, if I was subpoenaed in front of a grand jury, I'd probably end up mentioning your name."

"Thanks."

"No. I mean it. If I told 'em 'I went to lunch with my friend Paul,' the FBI would start sifting through your trash. They do this all the time. They'll spend two years doing an investigation, dig up your garden, talk to all your friends, tell your boss it's nothing to worry about, they just want to look in your desk for heroin, and then they stop. Nobody gets indicted, and nobody ever knows why. Of course, all your neighbors drag their kids in the house, draw the drapes, and chain their doors every time you walk by. But that's life in a democracy, right?"

I'm still wondering who's down in Mexico.

"Listen. All I'm asking is that you talk to the guy. It'll probably just go away. I doubt if they'll subpoena him."

"They were sifting my garbage a couple of seconds ago."

"Yeah, but you're not as squeaky clean as this guy. Listen, all he needs is somebody to hold his hand."

"Sounds like a perfect case for you, to turn over a new leaf," I tell him. "You said he was a businessman."

"I would if I could. But we've got a conflict. The firm did some work, a civil case against his company a few years ago. You know how it is? Dana did this big buildup on her husband the lawyer. She's new on the arts commission. She wanted to make a good impression. So when this guy tells her about his legal problems, she says 'I'll have my husband talk to you.' Now she can't. What do you want me to do? You want her to lose face?"

Knowing Dana, the guy was probably trying to come on to her. I don't share this thought with Nick.

"She's trying to make an impression," he says. "Besides, the man's a big giver. He digs deep for all the right causes."

"So if he's into so many good works, why does the grand jury want to talk to this Brother Teresa?"

"It's probably nothing."

I begin to waffle and Nick can smell it.

"You'd be doing me a huge favor. I'd owe you my life," he says. "Well, maybe not that much."

"What you mean is I'd be doing Dana a big favor."

"Same thing."

I can already see him edging her toward the sack tonight whispering in her ear about how he took care of her friend, put him in good hands, all the while looking for a little sweet reciprocity.

"What's his name? This client?" I got one of his business cards and my pen to make a note.

"Gerald Metz. I'll have him give you a call."

"No drugs, Nick. I don't do drug cases. You know that."

"I know. It's not drugs. Trust me. As far as I know, the guy's clean. His name is being dragged into it because he had one business deal with some people. You know how it is?"

"I know how it is." I hold up a hand and cut him off before he can start all over again. Chapter two, Rush on civil rights.

"Listen to his story, tell him not to worry, and charge him a big fee," he says.

"What if the grand jury calls him to testify? Does he understand I can't go into the jury room with him?"

"You're borrowing problems. Hey, if he gets called, you advise him of his rights. Tell him to take the Fifth."

"I thought you said he was clean."

Nick gives me one of his famous smiles. "Why would anybody need a lawyer if they were totally clean?" Then he laughs. "I'm only kidding," he says.

"Nick!"

"Listen, I gotta go. I got a client waiting outside. I'm already late. But we'll talk," he says.

"I thought you were going to spring for lunch."

"I know, and you said yes. But you said it too easily," he says. "Next time make it a challenge." He's around the desk, his hand on my arm, ushering me toward the door. "Next week. It's on me. I promise. We'll do it at the club. You haven't seen the club. It comes with the partnership," he says. "That and a window."

Nick has what he wants: me on the hook. "Dana told him you'd give him a call to set up an appointment."

"I thought you said he was gonna call me?"

"Did I? You better call him. He might forget. I told Dana you'd understand."

I was wrong. Nick has already gotten his treat from Dana.

"Listen, I'm sure this guy's clean. I mean, my wife doesn't run around with felons." He looks at me over the top of his half-frames. "That's my job."

He's got me by the arm now, guiding me toward the side door, the one that leads to the hallway outside instead of reception where he has clients stacked up like planes at La-Guardia.

"How well does Dana know this guy?"

"Listen, I gotta tell you a story." Nick changes the subject. He's good at that.

"A couple of weeks ago, Dana takes me to this exhibit. The guy who gets the blue ribbon. Catch this. His piece of art is a cardboard wall painted dark blue with all this glitter shit on it. It's covered with condoms, all different colors, glued on like deflated elephant trunks. The artist calls the thing 'Living Fingers.' I ask Dana what it means. She says she doesn't have a clue."

"Maybe it's in the eye of the beholder," I tell him.

"Something's in somebody's eye," says Nick. "Because later that night this particular Picasso sells for twenty-seven hundred bucks to some old broad wearing a silk cape and a felt fedora with a feather in it. I guess she figures the fingers will come to life when she gets it home. Don't get me wrong," he says. "I like art as well as the next guy."

This from a man who in college took art history early in the morning so he could sleep through the slide presentations in the dark.

"You didn't answer my question."

"What's that?" he says.

"How well does Dana know this guy?"

"Who, the guy who did the painting?"

"Gerald Metz," I say.

"Oh, him. She doesn't know him at all. They meet once a month. Give him a call. And next week we'll do lunch," he says. He looks at me with those big brown eyes, the last thing I see as I find myself standing just across the threshold of his door, watching the walnut paneling as it swooshes closed in my face. Chalk another victory up to Nick Rush.

CHAPTER TWO

"It's bullshit. I don't know what Rush told you, but you can take my word. I never been involved in anything illegal. Check me out if you don't believe me. I never even been arrested."

Gerald Metz is fit, tall, and tan. He has the look of a man who works out-of-doors, except that he doesn't do this with his hands. His nails are manicured and his palms uncalloused, causing me to suspect that the only thing they've grasped recently are the drivers and irons from a golf bag.

His speech is a little rough, hints of the self-made, up from what may have been some rough streets in another life. He is not what one conjures when thinking of the arts and those who patronize them. He wears a polo shirt under a blue blazer.

"That's why when this stuff came up, I was surprised. Why the hell would the grand jury want to talk to me?"

It has been two weeks since I met with Nick, and Metz

is in my office, a thin leather folio in his lap and a lot of nervous chatter on his lips.

If I had to guess, I would say he is in his mid-forties. He is angular, with a high forehead and receding hairline slicked back on the sides.

He hands me a bunch of papers from his briefcase, then leans back in the chair, trying to put on an air of confidence like someone putting on a suit of clothes that doesn't quite fit. The fingers of one hand tap a cadence on the arm of his chair, one leg crossed over the other, while his eyes dart nervously around the office, trying to find something to settle on besides me. Beads of perspiration pop out like acne on his forehead.

"Mind if I smoke?" he says.

"Prefer it if you don't."

He exhales a deep breath. If he is called before the grand jury, the man is going to sweat a river.

I read through the papers he has handed me.

"Didn't even know these people. Met 'em once," he says.

"Uh-huh." What I'm seeing are a lot of first names on the salutations of their letters to him: "Dear Jerry."

From the left sleeve of Metz's blazer pokes an expensive-looking gold Rolex. He keeps sneaking peaks at it as he talks.

"Do you have another appointment?" I ask.

"Hmm. No, no." He tugs the sleeve down to cover the watch and puts his hand over it.

"I'm just wondering if this is gonna take long."

"That depends. Are these all the papers you have?"

He nods. "That's it."

There's a hint of an accent, nothing strong. I'm thinking Florida by way of New Jersey.

"We didn't even do the deal," he says. "The whole thing fell apart." Comes the flood of nervous talk. "Can't figure why they'd be interested in me. Maybe you could just call 'em and tell 'em that."

"What are you talking about?"

"You know, tell the attorney I don't know nothin'."

"The U.S. attorney?"

"Why not?"

I look at him and smile. "If I did that, they would sub-poena you for sure."

"Why?"

"Trust me."

"Fuckin' government always on your ass. Last time it was an audit."

"When was that?"

"I don't know. Few years ago. Screwed me around for over a year. IRS demanding every scrap I had. Fourteen months they couldn't find a damn thing. Now this. You ask me, I think it's retaliation."

"For what?"

"Cuz they're pissed that they couldn't find nothin'. All I know is my name keeps coming up in this grand jury thing. Word gets out, it's gonna kill my business."

"What do you mean, your name keeps coming up?"

"People called to testify, former employees of my com-pany. They call and they tell me that they're being asked all kinda questions about me and my business—you know, with these people down in Mexico." He nods toward the letters on my desk.

"These witnesses, did they call you or did you call them?"

"Hell, I don't know. What difference does it make? One of them called me; I called somebody else. After a while they're all telling the same thing. This attorney. This federal guy."

"The deputy U.S. attorney."

"That's the one. He keeps bringing my name up asking questions." He thinks for a second. "I didn't do anything wrong by talking to these people. The witnesses, I mean."

"Probably not."

"What do you mean probably?"

"They're free to talk to you about their own testimony. If they want to. You say they're former employees? What type of work did they do?"

He gives me names. "One was a secretary; the other was my bookkeeper."

"How did you find out she had appeared before the grand jury?"

This stumps him for a second. He can't remember. He tells me he heard it on the grapevine. The construction industry being a small community.

"So it sounds like you called her, this witness?"

"I probably did. It pissed me off. Can they do this? Some government lawyer asking a lot of questions about my business. Can they do that?"

"A prosecutor in front of a federal grand jury can ask almost anything he wants. What did he want to know?"

"Mostly financial information, from what I was told."

This would make sense if the feds are investigating money laundering.

"What kind of financial information?"

"The business thing down in Mexico. They seemed to be interested in the one deal."

"Tell me about that." I look at the letter on the desk in front of me, the signature block at the bottom. "Tell me about this man Arturo Ibarra."

"Two brothers. Arturo and Jaime. Arturo was the brains. I don't think Jaime can write," he says.

"Then you do know them?"

"Not really. Met 'em a few times. Just that Jaime's got the slanted head. Know what I mean? What do they call 'em, 'Anderthals. Caveman."

"You mean Neanderthal?"

"Whatever."

"What about the other one, Arturo?"

"He was business. Educated. The brains. You know, I don't like to ask. But I got one question. How much is this gonna cost me?" He's looking at his watch again.

"That depends how long we take."

He fumes, looks up at the ceiling. "Is there any way I can get my legal fees back on this? I mean if I'm not involved, why should I have to pay legal fees?"

"Unfortunately, that's the way it works."

"Can I take it off on my taxes?"

"Talk to your accountant," I tell him.

He looks at me, as if to say "fucking lawyers." "So whadda you want to know so we can get this over with?"

"Whatever you can remember."

"These two brothers, they owned some property with their father."

"What was the father's name?"

"Hell, I don't know, Mr. Ibarra. I never met the man. All I was told he was a big-time developer down in Quintana Roo. Southern Mexico," he says. "On the Yucatán. You ever been there?"

I shake my head. "I've heard of it." In the press it's been called the first Mexican narco-state. Bordering Guatemala and Central America, it's a pipeline for drugs.

"How did you find this job?" I ask him.

"The two brothers came to me. Said they wanted to develop this property into a resort. It was on the coast, beach-front. Mostly swamp land. South of Cancún on the highway, down toward Tulúm, what they call the Mayan Riviera. The two brothers took me down to their property, a few hundred acres of cactus, swamp, and mosquitoes, probably snakes and alligators if you wandered out that far. I took their word for it that there was a beach out there somewhere."

"Why did they come to you?"

"My company's got heavy equipment. We were the closest. Just across the border. Most of the work down there is done with hand labor. Pick and shovel stuff. Labor being cheap."

"Why did they want your equipment?"

"They wanted to move fast. A window of opportunity in the permitting process. All I know is what they told me."

"Go on."

"I figured they probably crossed a few official palms with some gold. Way of life down there." He says it as if graft doesn't exist north of the border.

"How were they going to pay you?"

"Some cash up front and then a piece of the ownership."

"How big a piece?"

"Ten percent. They were gonna develop the property, get it in shape where foundations could be poured, then spin it off to some hotel chain to build the resort. We were all supposed to cash in at that point."

"You say the deal didn't go through?"

"No. I was told the old man pulled the plug. He controlled the funds. There was some kind of falling out and the deal collapsed. That's it. Long and short of it."

"Everything?"

"Pretty much. You gotta remember this was a while ago. You can't expect me to remember all the details. The whole thing lasted a total of a few months. It never got beyond some letters and telephone calls."

"But you said you went down there?"

"Well, sure. They paid my way. Why not?"

"How long were you there?"

"Shit, I don't know, a few days, maybe a week. This was two years ago."

Well within any statute of limitations for money laundering, though I don't mention this to Metz.

"Did any of their agents or employees meet with you in this country?"

"No. Not that I can remember. No, wait a second. There was one guy. I can't remember his name. We met once and talked on the phone a couple of times. I may still have his card." Metz pulls out his wallet and starts picking through the contents—rat-eared receipts, licenses, a social security card that looks like it's been around since the Civil War, a collection of business cards. Finally he finds the one he's looking for.

"Here it is." He holds it out at arm's length as if glasses might be in order for reading. " 'Miguelito Espinoza.' Mexican labor contractor."

He hands me the card and I make a note—an address in Santee with a phone number. On the other side of the card, everything under the name is printed in Spanish, including a title *notario publico*. In this case it means the man holds a license as a notary public. He can verify documents and put his seal on them. The designation is often used north of the border to give a false implication to those not speaking English that the holder is a lawyer, as the title would signify in Mexico.

"Anything else?"

He shakes his head. "No."

"You're sure?"

"Yeah."

"There are a few things you should understand. The fact that you haven't been called to testify is not necessarily a good thing."

"Why's that?"

"Have you received any correspondence from the U.S. attorney in connection with this matter?"

"Like what?"

"Perhaps a letter?"

"No."

"That's good. Because if you're a target of their investigation they will be sending you a target letter. It will tell you about the proceedings, warn you not to destroy documents, tell you about your right to confer with counsel outside the jury room and your right not to testify."

"Why the hell would I be a target?"

"I'm not saying you are. But the fact that they haven't called you to testify and that they're questioning former employees is not good."

This puts a look of anxiety on his face. Metz is no longer looking at his watch.

"How many telephone conversations did you have with these people?"

"I don't know. How the hell am I supposed to remember something like that?"

"You can be sure the DEA or the FBI will know the answer," I tell him. "If they're investigating you, they may already have your telephone records. They'll know how many times you talked to the brothers in Mexico and how long each conversation lasted. They may know about this man Espinoza. They'll have that at a minimum, unless of course the Mexican authorities tapped into the brother's phone lines down there, in which case they're likely to know a great deal more."

I can tell that this is a sobering thought.

"Did you send them anything in writing, any letters?" All I have before me are letters from the one brother to Metz, nothing going the other way.

"I, ah. I don't think so."

"You do keep copies of your business correspondence?"

"Yeah. But you know how things are. Sometimes they get away from you."

"What do you mean?"

"That's everything I could find."

"You mean you may have written letters to these people, but you can't find them?"

"It's possible. I can't remember."

This is not looking good.

"What if the prosecutor subpoenas them?"

"I'll give them what I can find. What the hell else am I supposed to do? If I can't find 'em, I can't find 'em. Right?"

"You said one of the witnesses was a former secretary to your company. How many office employees do you have?"

"One. Sometimes I don't have any. People quit, come and go. Stuff gets lost. I told my gal in the office to get whatever was in the files, like you asked. That's what she got." He points to the few letters on my desk.

"And what if your secretary is called to testify. What will she say?"

He gives me a steely-eyed look. "That she gave me everything she could find," he says.

"And that this is it?"

"Yeah. Sure. I'm not trying to be difficult," he says. "It's just that I can't give 'em what I don't have."

"Of course."

"That's all I can tell you."

"Tell me, did you sign a contract on this business in Mexico?"

"We never got that far."

"Did they pay you anything, compensation?"

"Like I said, they paid for my trip down there. Traveling expenses and the like."

"How much?"

"I don't know, maybe four thousand, forty-five hundred dollars. And there were some consulting fees."

"Consulting for what?"

"The location, difficulty of getting heavy equipment in and out of the job site."

"How much did they pay you for this?"

"I can't remember exactly."

"An estimate?"

"I don't know."

"More than a thousand dollars?"

"Oh, yeah."

"More than five thousand?"

"Uh-huh."

My eyes are off my notepad now, looking at Metz. "How much?"

"Somewhere in the neighborhood of two million," he says.

"Dollars?"

He nods.

I sit there staring at him, the gaze of an animal in front of a speeding locomotive at night.

"For consulting fees?"

"Well, no, no, it was . . . actually, it was a security deposit."

"Security for what?"

"My equipment. Hell, you don't think I'm gonna take heavy equipment across the border without some security up front. This is expensive stuff. A front-end loader, a big one, the kind that articulates, can set you back a quarter of a million dollars. What if it disappears? I mean, this is not Nevada we're talking about. If they greased somebody's palm for permits and the sky falls in, a fuckin' swamp without a permit to drain it ain't worth shit," he says. "The first thing the Mexican government does is grab my equipment."

"So what was the understanding as to this money, this security deposit?"

"I'd hold their money until the job was done. Then I'd get my equipment back and get paid. They'd get their deposit back."

"But you never signed a contract and you never sent any equipment across the border?"

"No."

"And they gave you two million dollars on a handshake?"

"That's right."

"So what happened when the deal went bust?"

"They got their money back."

"All of it?"

He makes a face. Scrunches up his mouth a little. "Everything except the ten percent," he says.

I look at him.

"For my time."

"What time?"

"You know, puttin' the thing together. Talking. Goin' down there?"

"But you said they paid for your trip?"

"Yeah. But my time's worth something, ain't it? Like I say, consulting fees."

"But you had no contract or written arrangement for these fees before you went down there?"

"No."

"A week of your time in Mexico, not considering traveling expenses, which they paid, is worth two hundred thousand dollars?"

"I could have been doin' other work," he says.

"You lost a big job because of this week in Mexico, did you?"

"I might have. I mean I could have. I don't know."

By now I am scribbling furiously, trying to get Metz's

story down on paper before the ludicrous logic of it disappears like a vapor.

"And what did you do with the two million deposit money? Did you put it in a bank in this country?"

"Not right away," he says.

I stop writing and look up again. "What do you mean?"

"I mean, I brought my money up here after the deal fell through . . ."

"Your money?"

"The two hundred K. Over a period of time," he says.

"Stop. Did you maintain a foreign bank account?"

"Yeah."

"Where?"

"Belize," he says.

"Why Belize?"

"I don't know."

"Did you report this account on your taxes for that year?"

"I don't remember. Have to talk to my accountant."

"Is this the accountant who's already been called to testify before the grand jury?"

"Yeah. I suppose so."

"And the ten percent you kept. What did you do with that?"

"I transferred it here."

"To a U.S. bank?"

"That's right."

"But not all at once?"

"No. Like I said, over a period of time, as I needed it."

"Let me guess. Ten thousand at a time?"

He nods.

This is the legal limit for cash coming into the country. I don't have to ask how he got it all here. Metz is not going to wait twenty years to move two hunderd K into the country at ten grand a year. No doubt he's used mules, friends, or employees on junkets down to Belize to carry it back whenever he needed cash.

"I'm hesitant to ask, but was this money paid to you or your company?"

"It's confusing sometimes to keep track of what income is payable to my corporation and what is payable to me. For services."

"I'll bet. Especially when it's consulting fees, is that it?"

"Yeah." His eyes light up, thankful for the suggestion.

"Mr. Metz, I don't think we're going to be able to do business. But I will give you some advice since you're paying for my time, at least for this visit."

He looks at me, the first glimmer of surprise.

"If you were my client, which you are not, and you were called to testify before the grand jury, I would advise you to take the Fifth."

CHAPTER THREE

It's late April, and Nick stands out on the sidewalk with his hands thrust into the deep pockets of a belted trench coat he has worn on cool mornings ever since I've known him. He is out near the curb, fifty feet from the sign over the door, big gold letters, each one larger than a tombstone, spelling out: EDWARD J. SCHWARTZ UNITED STATES COURTHOUSE.

Rush is the only lawyer I know who has never carried a briefcase. It is against his religion and might dispel the impression that he can do anything on the fly and off the cuff.

As I approach, he expels clouds of warm breath into the chilly morning mist. He sees me a block away and smiles, gives me a nod like "what's up," rocking forward and back, heel to toe to keep warm. It is cold for San Diego, the season of early morning fog. By afternoon people will be on the street in shirtsleeves.

Eight-thirty. We are meeting for a quick briefing over coffee so that I can hand off Metz. Nick is to meet with the client at nine. If I am lucky, I will be out of here before it happens. I have no desire to be drawn into this thing further. Nick will then have half an hour before he has to appear with Metz in front of a judge. Nick's instincts were right on one point. Metz was never called before the grand jury. Six days after our conversation, he was indicted on multiple counts of money laundering and international currency violations. He is scheduled to appear for arraignment in federal district court this morning. My guess is that the feds are just warming up.

It is vintage Nick Rush, surfing the lawyer's version of the pipeline in a typhoon, standing out on the tip with all ten toes over the edge. Doing everything at the last minute is a test of the man's deftness and a measure of his ego.

He has operated his entire career on the notion that any lawyer who needs more than twenty minutes to get ready for anything in court should find another line of work. I have seen him kick the butts of ambitious young prosecutors who spent a year building a case only to watch it get flushed like Tidy-Bowl when Nick got loose in front of the jury.

It is the reason he is double- and triple-booked on his calendar. If you've embezzled a few million from your company's accounts or you have half a ton of white shit under the floorboards of your house and get caught with grow lights sucking energy from the grid while a jungle of Mary Jane sprouts in your basement, the man to call is Nick Rush. Whether you're cooking amphetamines or corporate books, his soothing words uttered in tones of divine confidence will ease your anxieties faster than a handful of Percocet.

Nick decided it wasn't necessary to spend a lot of time with Metz as long as I'd prepped him. I warned him that Metz was dynamite on a stick with a short fuse up his ass, but Nick saw only the challenge. Besides, he told me it doesn't matter what they have, Nick is pleading him not guilty and sorting it out later. According to Nick, he has disclosed his conflict with Metz over the phone, and Metz has signed a waiver that they have sent back and forth.

As I approach, he smiles broadly but doesn't take his hands out of his pockets to shake. "I can now confirm Hemingway's thesis—the sun also rises," he says. He looks up at the fog-shrouded sky. "Though you wouldn't know it from standing here."

"Hemingway was too blitzed in the morning to know it himself. He took it from the Bible," I tell him.

"That's what I like about you. You know all the trivial shit you know."

"It comes in handy when I have to deal with people like you."

"And what kind of people am I?"

"People who deal only in the big picture," I tell him.

He laughs, but it's true. Nick doesn't waste energy on details that aren't essential to the grand picture, the task at hand at any given moment. He has an intellect like a vacuum. He can suck up the minutest details of a trial in three minutes, organize them in the order of importance, and march them out like an army to do battle in court while his opponent is still trying to get his briefcase open.

"I thought all the while you were doing these early morning court calls," I tell him.

"That's why God invented young associates," he says. "If Dana wasn't involved with this prick, he'd be dealing with the federal public defender."

I warn him that after he hears what I have to tell him, he might want to reconsider taking the case. I suggest the cafeteria in the courthouse. Nick says he favors a little coffee shop around the corner and across the street, so he leads the way.

This is federal territory, the few blocks around the two United States courthouses—one reserved for bankruptcy proceedings, and the other for more serious stuff. Like the Indian nations of old, this part of town has different rules and a culture of its own. Here the cops are the FBI, IRS, DEA, and a dozen other alphabet empires, each striving to showcase their indispensable primacy in the public-safety pecking order.

The federal courts are realms of limitless marble and gray-haired marshals in blue blazers standing like men in livery. It is more refined and genteel than anything at the local level. It speaks of limitless budgets and the boundless tax reach of the federal government whose hands are in everyone's pockets and moving now from the elbow up to the shoulder. It is a world I do not often frequent; instead I confine myself to the lowly and somewhat disheveled state courts where those who set policy cannot print their own money.

Nick thrives in all of this. He will go toe to toe with the most austere members of the local federal bench and on occasion walk the fine line of contempt.

As if to reinforce this, he takes me to the seedy coffee shop at the street level under the old Capri Hotel.

"I've been having coffee here for twenty years. Every morning," he says. He leads me down a flight of stairs, chipped plaster and peeling paint. The handrail on one side is missing. Some vagrant must have borrowed it.

"I used to know the guy who owned the place," Nick says.

I follow him through the door to the coffee shop. We get inside and I stop. The place is a dump.

"I didn't know you were so well connected," I tell him.

"It looked better back then," he says. "It's gone downhill in recent years."

"You're kidding. I would never have known."

The walls in the coffee shop are that dingy brown color you know is not paint. The stainless steel hood over the grill in the kitchen is impregnated with enough grease that the cook could open his own tallow works.

"Best of all, it's quiet."

"I can see why."

I'm afraid to ask him about the hotel upstairs. Any little shake, and it may visit us while we're sitting here.

"The owner's name was Wan Lu Sun. Chinese," he says. "Good businessman. But he died a couple of years ago. His kids have the property now. Not like the old man. The new generation. They have no sense of values. Americanized," he says.

"If you say so." I'm still taking it all in, trying not to inhale for fear the dust particles floating in the isolated ray of sunlight that's managed to penetrate one of the encrusted windows might be asbestos.

"The developers are lined up like vultures ready to whack the place with their wrecking balls," he says.

"This isn't the place you're . . ."

"Yeah." Nick smiles at me.

"Tell me it's not true."

"It's true," he says.

I've been reading about it in the papers for almost a year. A group of community preservationists have launched a campaign to save some downtown structures they claim are historic. Every few months Nick's name pops up in print, leading the charge.

"Take my advice," I tell him. "This place needs a good wrecking ball."

"Stick around. It'll grow on you."

"That's what I'm afraid of. You must have better things to do than this?"

"I do, but I figure I owe it to the old man," he says.

"What old man?"

"Lu Sun," he says. "Hell, if he was around, developers wouldn't get near this place. Not unless they posted their first born as collateral. The old man would have gotten an arm and a leg for the land."

Nick has tilted at a few windmills in his time, but this is a stretch even for him.

"I knew you were stirring the embers of discontent," I tell him. "But this is a side of you I've never seen. Your passion for preservation."

"I've come to it late in life." He smiles, then winks at me. "Actually, between you and me, I just like to stir the shit."

"I would have never guessed."

"The firm gives us time to devote to community activities. I had to find something to do. Besides, I don't like walking two more blocks down to Starbucks just to make an executive decision on what kind of beverage I want in the morning. Here I got the place to myself. Have a seat. The booth over there in the corner is mine. It's the one without holes in the Naugahyde," he laughs.

Nick knows the waitress by her first name. She looks as if she's worked here since the hotel's grand opening.

"Two coffees, Marge. We'll take them at the booth." He passes on menus and grabs some Equal from what appears to be a private stash under the register.

"Hate the Sweet'n Low," he says as he waltzes me toward the booth. "It leaves a taste." We sidle into the bench seats, something out of the fifties, probably the last time the place was remodeled.

"You have to admit it has a certain ambiance," he says. "All it needs is some drunk to drive a Cadillac with fins through the front wall, and it would be chic."

Marge comes over with her glass pot and pours. He asks her how she's doing. They chat.

No doubt my senses are colored by the odor of smoldering grease from the kitchen, where nothing in particular is being cooked unless the cook is eating it, but the coffee seems to slide out of the pot, instead of pour. Some of it is fluid, but there are a lot of black lumps like tar.

"You know, on second thought," I tell her, "I think I'll have tea."

"All we got is Earl Grey," she says.

"That'll be fine." As long as I can see the bottom of my cup through the hot water.

She leaves to get it.

Nick catches me looking at his cup as he loads three little packets of pretend sugar and stirs in cream. "What's wrong?"

"I just don't like to use purification tablets this early in the morning."

"Hey, this is the real shit," he says.

"That's what I'm afraid of."

"Actually, if you want to know, the real shit is in London. I was reading this article the other day." This is vintage Nick.

Everything reminds him of a story, even on a deadline with a case in less than a hour.

"They've got this stuff over there they call Crappuccino. People pay through the nose. It's brewed from some kind of coffee berries that pass through monkeys."

"Nick. I haven't had breakfast yet."

"You wanna eat? I'll have her bring a menu."

"No!"

He laughs.

"Yeah, I'm not kidding. Five hundred dollars an ounce and you have to use toilet paper as a filter. They say it has a very earthy taste."

"No wonder the Brits drink tea," I tell him.

"Really, the coffee here is fine," he says. Still, he's looking off in the distance as if maybe he'd like to try this Crappuccino someday.

"Time is getting short," I tell him. "Do you want to know about Metz or not?"

"Not to worry. The arraignment's only a first appearance. You know," he says. He's looking around again, taking it all in, his private dining room. "You have any idea what this place is probably worth? I don't mean the building. I mean the location?"

I shake my head. "But I'm sure you're going to tell me."

He takes out what looks like a cell phone. Lately Nick has been playing with this gadget. I call them all PalmPilots. He calls this one a Handspring, every electronic device imaginable in a package the size of a deck of cards.

He slides the little stylus out of its holder on the side and starts tapping the screen.

"What, you're not going to call somebody now?"

"Just working the calculator."

"Nick, listen. I've got work waiting for me back at the office."

"Keep your shirt on. Relax. Why are you so uptight all the time?"

"I'm not uptight. I just have better things to do."

This is the Nick I know, putting me on the defensive

while he kills my morning musing about downtown real estate prices.

"Figure you can get it for eight million, maybe eight and half," he says.

Metz is probably wearing out shoe leather right now, out in front of the courthouse, wondering if he will be sleeping in his own bed tonight or in one of the bunks at the federal lockup.

"And it's outside the corridor, the approaches to Lindbergh Field. That's important," he says. "You wanna know why?"

"Not really, but you're going to tell me, I'm sure."

"Because outside the corridor, you can go as high as you want, as long as you get a variance. You know, get around the current height restrictions."

"Are you becoming a realtor?"

"No, but I ought to," he says. "Some developer's gonna come in here, buy the place cheap, go to his friendly planning commissioner or a county sup, and multiply his investment by a factor of four overnight. All he has to do is get a variance to go up higher. He wouldn't even have to do anything with the property. Just turn it over. Make a cool what, twenty, twenty-five million? And these assholes call our clients crooks."

"That's business," I tell him.

"Yeah. The business we ought to be in." Nick smiles. "But we're too honest," he says. He's back to bullshit. "And besides, I like to preserve the past. Dana has her causes; I have mine."

"Now can we get back to Metz?" I ask.

"Are you sure you wanna give this thing up?"

"What?"

"Metz." He looks at me as if I've been off on some other track. "I mean, it could be an opportunity."

"I'm sure."

"We could do it together," he says. "After all, you are the only person I've ever shared one of the few true secrets of my life with."

"What's that?"

"Laura." Nick is stone serious when he says this.

I had almost forgotten. I thought Nick was too far into the sauce to remember the night he let it slip over drinks after a bad day in court. He was feeling a failure, even with a sassy new wife. Laura is the mystery in Nick's life—and probably the only female he will ever truly love.

"Have you seen her lately?"

"Last week," he says. "Only for a few minutes. Listen to me. Metz is good for a sizable fee." Nick is good at changing the subject. Especially if it's something he doesn't want to talk about. "He wouldn't be involved with the arts if he didn't have money."

I laugh.

"It's true. I've never seen one of those people yet didn't have money. Lack of taste, maybe, but they all have bucks. It's a precondition. Otherwise they don't get into the fraternity. You don't get on the A-list for the auctions and fundraisers. Get your face on the social sheet in the *Trib* and the *Times.*"

"Is that how you did it?"

"I did it through my wife. She has class and taste," he says.

"And your checkbook."

"That too." He drinks some coffee, and I have to divert my eyes. "What else are you gonna do for fun when you get old and flatulent?"

"I've never viewed art auctions as that much fun," I tell him.

"I wasn't talking about art." He's talking about Dana. "Come on. Why not? You can hold Metz's hand and I'll do the trial. We'll lift him by the heels and shake him, see what's in his pockets."

"You might not be prepared for what falls out," I tell him.

"That bad?" he says.

Nick and I haven't talked since our conversation four days ago. I played telephone tag with him for a week before I finally caught him in his office, and then he didn't want to discuss the details over the phone. It's the nature of Nick's practice. You can never be sure whether your phone is tapped.

"You want my honest opinion?"

He nods.

"All of the pieces are in place, including the transfer of large sums of cash and the laundry fee." He listens as I fill him in.

"If your man's to be believed, he took two hundred thousand dollars while he parked two million of his partner's money in an account in Belize."

None of this unnerves him. "Go on."

"He calls his part a consulting fee, but it never shows up on his company's books."

"So we have an accounting error," says Nick.

"He tells me the money was actually intended as security on heavy equipment he was supposed to ship south to do a job. Except that none of the equipment was ever moved. According to Metz, the deal never got off the ground. He took one trip down to Mexico that lasted maybe a week, and for this he charged a two-hundred-thousand-dollar fee."

"Maybe his time is valuable," he says.

"And maybe his two Mexican partners wanted to cleanse some revenue from illicit activities?"

Nick clears his throat. "Doesn't mean he knew about it."

"On top of all of this, unless I misjudge the man, I think you're going to find currency violations and probably tax evasion."

Nick lifts one eyebrow, rubs his chin, and looks at me with the kind of expression I might expect from an appraiser who's being told the diamond ring he just told me to buy is melting ice.

"If you check, I think you're going to find that he used friends and neighbors to move his fee back into this country in order to do the limbo under the currency limits. And if he did that, I suspect he may have gone just one baby step further in forgetting to report any of it on his tax return."

"You didn't ask him?"

"I thought I'd leave that one to you."

Nick nods, his knowing and understanding nod. This is practiced, refined from years of listening to sordid deeds, so that by now nothing particularly arouses or discourages him.

"What did he say about the account in Belize? Why did he set it up?"

"I didn't ask that either. I wouldn't want to cut into your options for maneuver."

He laughs, tips his cup to me.

I have often suspected that Nick is not above performing surgery on the facts in a case once the curtain is pulled and he and his client are safely behind it. It is the reason I have refrained from getting into these details with Metz, so that I don't end up as Nick's scrubbing nurse.

"Did you ask him why he kept the money? The two hundred K?" Nick is hoping beyond hope.

"Unfortunately I did, and his answer was not encouraging, or believable."

"What did he say?"

"Consulting fees."

"That sounds fair to me," he says.

"Especially if you can get your hands on it for legal fees," I tell him.

"See, you're learning already. Let's start looking at the upside." Nick would have to be a stone monument to optimism to find even a tin foil lining in this particular cloudburst.

"None of the major money came into the U.S., right? I mean the two million. It went from Mexico to Belize and back again, is that correct?"

"Except for Metz's fee."

"Forget about that for the moment. What we have here is perhaps some financial sleight of hand. But it all takes place outside of U.S. jurisdiction. Right?"

"That's one way to look at it. The other way is that you have a U.S. citizen facilitating currency violations in two foreign countries."

"So? Let them charge him there. You and I aren't licensed to practice law in Mexico. That's somebody else's problem."

"Ask Metz if he wants to take his chances on serving the next millennium in some dung heap in Mexico."

"You think the Mexican government would actually bring charges?"

"I think that if the feds are trying to squeeze your man to find out what he knows, they may well threaten him with extradition south. They could probably get the Mexican government to lend their cooperation. The last time I looked, the two countries had a treaty."

Nick ponders this problem, scratching his chin with the back of his fingers while he grins at me from across the table. "I guess I'm gonna have to talk to my wife about the company she keeps."

"Answer one question for me," I say. "Tell me you didn't suspect this was drug related."

He looks at me and hesitates only a second. "Sure. I still don't," he says.

The words are there, but they are not convincing. The fact that he says it with a smile undercuts the effect even more. If Nick didn't know, his demeanor tells me that he had strong suspicions. He thanks me for taking the time as he finishes his coffee and I study the water in the little stainless steel pot. Nick looks at his watch.

"I guess I'm gonna have to go," he says. "Unless of course you want to do a favor for a friend."

"Don't push it," I tell him.

"I understand," he says. Then slides out of the booth. "I'll give you a call this afternoon. Let you know what happened."

"Not unless you want me to bill you for my time," I tell him.

He laughs, then heads for the door. "Marge. My friend will catch the bill. Put a good tip on it," he says.

Before I can turn to say anything, he's out the door.

It's the thing about Nick. He can screw you twenty ways

from Sunday, but he lives on the sunny side of optimism so it's hard not to like him.

I give him a good head start, playing with the tea bag, not because I want to drink it. I have no desire to run into Nick with Metz out in front of the courthouse on my way back to the car.

Marge comes with the bill, slaps it unceremoniously on the table, and takes Nick's coffee cup away, the sludge still in the bottom. Two minutes later, I get up from the booth, peel some singles from folded cash in my pocket, when I see it. Lying there against the worn red plastic of the bench on the other side of the table is Nick's little handheld device. For a man with a cerebral vacuum, who can suck up the most abstract details in a courtroom, Nick is missing the gene that keeps him attached to physical possessions. As long as I have known him, he has left things behind. Like my teenage daughter, if he owns it, he'll lose it.

I pick it up, slip it into my coat pocket, and pay the bill.

Outside I make tracks. Maybe I can run him down before he finds Metz. When I get to the corner, I look down the street toward the courthouse where Nick is supposed to meet his client. There is a mass of humanity between me and the front of the building, people walking on the sidewalk, but I don't see Nick.

I cross over and start down the other side of the street, hoping I catch his eye before he hooks up with Metz. I'm a third of the way down the block before I see him. Nick's hands are again buried in the pockets of his coat as he hustles down the sidewalk a hundred feet ahead of me, with four lanes of traffic between us. I cup my hand over my mouth to holler, but a city bus gets between us. Belching fumes, its engine drowns any hope of being heard. By the time it passes, it's too late. Nick is standing on the sidewalk in front of the walkway leading to the courthouse. He is talking to Metz.

I take my hand from my mouth, pat the little device in my pocket, and continue on toward my car a block away. I'll have to call him later and make arrangements to get it to him.

As I walk, I can't help but toy with the possible angles he has been playing. I suspect that he knew all along that Metz was up to his ass in laundering money. If so, he also knew I wouldn't take the case. So why would he try and refer it? One possibility, he wanted to shield himself from a close-up inspection of the particulars until I had filtered them for him. My interview with Metz. This way he could shade his eyes, take a more artful approach at sculpting the facts in his initial discussions with the man. In this way Nick could lead Metz to tell him stories that would be more helpful while avoiding a flat-out suborning of perjury. It is the kind of Machiavellian mental coil I might expect from Nick.

But there is another possibility, one that is more likely. This one involves Dana. From what Metz told me, if I believe anything, it is that Dana knew the broad outline of his problem, that it could be drug related. If she is, as Nick says, hot to clean up his practice, Dana wouldn't want him handling this, particularly with a client in her own social orbit.

Knowing Dana, her first concern would be that it could splash on her, that some enterprising reporter from the society section might pick up on the fact that Metz served on the commission with his lawyer's wife, all of this while she was striving to steer Nick toward more genteel clients and climb the social rungs of the city's arts community.

She could have told Metz to take his problems elsewhere, but that wouldn't prevent him from calling Nick on his own. Supporter of the arts he may be. But knowing Dana, she was looking for a sure way to sidestep a possible embarrassment. Nick's story of a conflict with Metz and the ease with which he disposed of it seems a little too convenient to be believed. Nick decided he would refer the case elsewhere.

So who does he call? The one lawyer in town he knows who will not touch a drug case. And kazam, poof, it bounces back to him. Now he is not only able to take the case, he is able to tell Dana that he had no choice. He will take care of her friend, but she will pay the price. That brain would be doing double time with the thought that this would not only give him chits in his marriage but latitude in his practice.

How could she complain when it was she who brought this particular client to his doorstep? And after all, he had tried to get rid of it.

By the time I reach the end of the block, I am smiling to myself, convinced that I have untangled the sordid intrigue of Nick's marital machinations. I am savoring this little victory so that I fail to hear them as individual reports but instead as a continuous burst, like a loud zipper being opened. The shots resonate off the concrete walls of the buildings around me and echo off the four-story government offices that span Front Street. My arms go up, and I crouch against a wall, the instincts of survival taking hold.

It isn't until I hear the sound of screeching rubber on the roadway behind me that I turn. A small dark sedan leaves a cloud of exhaust and burned rubber as it peels away from the curb in front of the courthouse. I can hear the engine hammering on eight cylinders, the raw power of an engine pushed to the limit as the car slides through a left turn onto Broadway. The cross traffic braking, screeching to a stop to avoid hitting it, horns honking. Before I can focus entirely, the car disappears around the corner.

I look back across Front Street to the main entrance of the courthouse. Two women are crawling on their hands and knees on the sidewalk. A guy helps one of them up, only to have her hands fly up to her mouth as she screams. I can hear it, a piercing high note, even half a block away. She is looking down at something behind her on the sidewalk.

The gathering crowd has blocked my view. One of the marshals in his blue sport coat exits the courthouse door on the run. He disappears behind the small sea of onlookers, I suspect gone down to one knee.

Within seconds, two other men in dark uniforms join him, both coming out of the courthouse door on the run. They have guns drawn. One of them is talking into a small microphone clipped to the shoulder epaulet of his uniform.

Traffic has slowed on Front Street as drivers stop to rubberneck. I weave between cars, horns honking, as I cross over and make my way along the sidewalk toward the front of the courthouse. Other people are running in the same direction now, everybody with the same thought, to see what has happened.

As I come up behind the throng, I try to edge my way through, shoulders sliding sideways until I find a crevice in the crowd where I can see. There on the ground lying in a river of blood is a body. A man, dark hair, his face turned away from me on the concrete, part of it bloodied and gone. He's wearing a sport coat gone sideways on his upper body as he hit the ground. His gray slacks are soaking up blood, legs tangled as if he were trying to flee as he was cut down.

I look for Nick, but I don't see him. By now at least a half dozen marshals are assembled, trying to gain control, pushing people back, making a path for the EMTs whose ambulance I can hear in the distance. Two city patrol cars pull up in front, their light bars flashing. One of them has a semiautomatic drawn. Then he realizes it's over, and reholsters it, clipping it down with the snap strap before he starts pushing people back to clear a path.

People are stumbling, being pushed. An old woman in a long coat and bandanna, nearly goes to her knees. A guy reaches out and grabs her. A look of confusion as she has no idea where these saving hands have come from. Delayed panic ripples through the crowd as stunned silence turns to agitation and people regain their bravado. Curiosity sets in. They press in for a look, and the cops push back, holding the line.

"Did you see it?"

"No. I heard the shots."

"Anybody hurt?" One of the cops is calling out.

"Over here." A man's voice.

A city traffic cop, still wearing his cycle helmet, cuts a swath through the crowd. It isn't until then that I realize it's not one gathering but two, each orbiting like constellations around their own black hole. There on the sidewalk I see Nick, sitting, his heavy-lidded eyes fixed in a half-closed sightless stare cast at the rivulet of his own blood running down the sidewalk and over the curb. There are little dark dots seeping into the fabric of his coat, too many for me to count. The bullet holes in his chest run downward diagonally across his body, not disappearing until they reach his waist. The impact has blown him back against a concrete planter box, where his body sits slumped like some child's discarded puppet.

CHAPTER FOUR

Standing on the sidewalk, I can do nothing. Within seconds, a fire engine rounds the corner, followed a minute later by an ambulance. Two EMTs jump off the engine, and, before I can move, they are working on Nick. They hover over him, pulling equipment from their large emergency packs—needles and plasma, an oxygen mask connected to a small tank. I move through the crowd and realize that the other man is Metz. I can see the back of one of the emergency medical techs hunching over him, doing chest compressions.

In less than three minutes, Nick and Metz are loaded onto stretchers and moved into the ambulance. I can see part of Nick's face outside of the mask as they wheel him past. It is ashen, a hue of blue-gray. His eyes are partly open, a lifeless expression that you know is not good.

Before I can turn for my car, the ambulance and its cargo are gone. I would guess to the trauma center, but given the medical facilities in this town I would have better odds playing roulette. Instead of guessing, I head to the car and ply the cell phone. It takes me ten minutes of calling information before I find the right hospital, only to be told that the ambulance has arrived but no information can be given out. The nurse wants to know if I am family. I tell her no. She asks my name and phone number. I tell her I will call back later and hang up. There is nothing I can do. In a daze, I head for the office. One of those episodes when you drive, arrive at a destination, and don't know how you got there. I'm parked on the street outside my office, sitting in the driver's seat, not knowing how long I've been here.

I shake my head, wipe my forehead. For a moment I think I am imagining it. But my hands are trembling. I turn the key in the ignition halfway and turn on the radio, and push buttons for local stations. I break into one of them and hear the words:

". . . outside of the federal courthouse in downtown San Diego. At this time we don't know how many people have been injured. Again, it was a drive-by shooting."

I reach for the control and turn up the volume.

"According to confirmed reports, two men are dead."

My mind has already registered the fact, but hearing it somehow makes it real.

"The identities of the two victims are being withheld pending notification of next of kin. According to police, the motive for the shootings is unknown. There have been no arrests and police say the investigation is continuing. We'll bring you further details at the hour."

The rest of that day and the day after seem largely a haze of nightmarish images, of dark dreams that I can escape by awakening only to discover that I am not dreaming.

• • •

Fortunately, the cops do not get around to me until three days after the fact. At first, I thought maybe my name might have been on Nick's calendar. When they didn't show up that first day, I knew it wasn't.

A double murder involving a prominent lawyer in front of a federal courthouse is front-page news. The local channels and the papers are hitting it hard, the cops fanning the flames, feeding them information, none of it favorable to Nick. As a criminal defense lawyer, Nick was infamous, the kind of advocate who took no prisoners in a courtroom. It has already been leaked that there was an envelope with four thousand dollars in cash in Nick's coat pocket when they undressed the body at the morgue. That there was a name scrawled on the envelope is all that authorities are saying. It is enough for readers to draw unsavory conclusions.

The police are saying nothing about motive, though reporters have ferreted out that Metz was under indictment. They have referred to Metz only as a prominent businessman. The key clue for the press is Nick. They have dwelled on the fact that he specialized in major narcotic cases both in the U.S. Attorney's Office and in private practice, and from this they have pieced sketchy conclusions, offering just enough for readers to speculate.

As for the authorities, they are saying nothing. Under the circumstances, Nick's passing is not likely to result in the dedication of any lofty limestone memorials by civic groups.

Cameras and a steady gaggle of reporters have been staked out in front of the security gates leading to Dana's house down in the Cays. I have seen the images on the nightly news—the widow in dark glasses being chauffeured through the phalanx by friends, one in particular, a tall gentleman, slicked-down dark hair with a little gray at the temples, and wearing a sport coat and slacks that look as if they were flown in for the occasion from Saville Row.

Dana is fortunate to live in a gated community where they are not trampling her front lawn and poking through her windows on ladders with their cameras. Security has kept the media herd huddled out near the Silver Strand and away from her house.

This morning Harry is in the office early, ready to run interference when the cops finally show up. We have been expecting them. I have told Harry about Nick's electronic handheld device. As with most things electronic it is a mystery to Harry, though he thinks I should turn it over to the cops and let them figure it out. I want to know more about it, and whatever information is inside, before I do that.

I hear the voices in the outer office—some lieutenant of detectives and his partner. I miss their names. They want to see Mr. Madriani.

Harry stalls to give me time to prepare myself. In a voice loud enough to raise Nick, he asks what it's about. The police are no doubt tracking backward over the hours before Nick's death, piecing together the people he met, whom he talked to. They have either caught up with Marge, the waitress at the grease spot under the Capri Hotel, who gave them my description, or Dana. She would have known that Nick and I had a meeting that morning. If my guess is correct, and Nick was doing a head job on his wife with Metz, she would have given the cops my name. Nick would have laid it on thick, telling her how he tried to get me to take the case and how I refused.

No doubt it has occurred to her that had I taken Metz on, it might be me who was lying on the slab at the morgue instead of her husband. There has been little else in my own thoughts since the event. Guilt, alleviated by the thought of my daughter Sarah as an orphan.

Seconds later there is a knock on my door. Harry's head pops through, followed by his body, as he slides through the crack and closes it behind him.

"Two of them," he says and hands me a business card, official police stationery with the city's seal and the name Lt. Richard Ortiz, Homicide Division.

"May as well show them in."

"You don't have to talk to them," he says.

"It's either now or later. Besides, what's to hide? They probably know more than I do, at least let's hope so."

Harry gives me the look of a lawyer whose client has just refused to take good advice. Sullenly, he opens the door wide. "You can come in," he says.

A moment later, two men step into my office. One of them is tall, slender, dark hair cropped close, a face with a lot of crags and eyes set so deep that I would need a diving bell with lights to tell their color. There is a certain hungry look about him, human descendent of the vulture family. I would guess he is in his mid-thirties. From his looks, any mirth has been long since squeezed from him by his occupation.

The other guy is built like an Ohio State linebacker— short blond hair, neck like a bull, and biceps that are stretching the arms on his sport coat. He is younger.

"Mr. Madriani, I'm Lieutenant Ortiz." The tall vulture is in charge. "My partner, Sergeant Norm Padgett."

Before I can say a word, a rush of panic sets in, adrenaline high. My eyes pass over Nick's Palm device on the far corner of my desk where I'd dropped it this morning after finding it in my coat pocket. It's too late now.

"Have a seat," I say. If I reach over and grab it, they may wonder why. If Dana told them Nick had one and they didn't find it in a search of his office, they would be looking for it.

"Would you guys like coffee?" I ask.

They both decline.

"What can I do for you?"

Harry rests part of his weight on the credenza against the far wall of my office and settles in. The sergeant turns to look at him.

"I'm sorry. You've met my partner, Harry Hinds."

"We met," says Ortiz. "This is a confidential investigation," he says.

"I understand," says Harry. "We'll keep it between the four of us."

"I think my partner would prefer to stay," I tell him.

"We could do this downtown," says Ortiz.

"In which case I'll get my coat," says Harry.

Ortiz looks at him from the two dark sunken holes in his skull.

"Last time I looked, my state bar card was still good," says Harry.

"Is there a reason you would need a lawyer?" Ortiz asks me.

"You tell me."

"You're not under any suspicion, as far as we know," he says.

"That's good to hear. I'll make a note," says Harry.

The cop doesn't smile, but he says, "Fine." First skirmish to our side.

"We just have a few questions," he says. "I suspect you know why we're here?"

"Why don't you tell us?"

Every once in a while my eyes drift toward the handheld device on the desk. I'd like to reach for it casually and just sweep it into one of the drawers of my desk. But I don't dare.

"I'm sure you're aware of the shooting outside the federal courthouse earlier this week. A double homicide."

He waits to see what I will say. Maybe some lame thing like I've read about it in the paper. I don't say anything.

"From what we understand you knew both of the victims, a Mr. Nicholas Rush and a Mr. Gerald Metz."

"Is that a question?"

"Sure."

"I knew Mr. Rush. I was acquainted with Mr. Metz, having met him once."

"Good. Thank you." A pat on the head from Ortiz. "And I take it you were aware of the shooting?"

"I am."

"How did you find out about it?"

I look at him. We duel with eyes.

"I'd like an answer."

"I heard the shots."

"You were there?" he says.

"I was across the street, about a half a block away walk-

ing the other direction when it happened. By the time I turned
to look, it was over."

"Did you see the car, the vehicle with the shooter?" asks
Ortiz.

"Just for an instant. It was going the other way, away from
me. What I remember is that it was a dark sedan. I couldn't
tell you the make or model. I didn't get that good a look."

"And of course you didn't see a license number?"

I shake my head.

"You probably wouldn't," he says. "We don't think it had
any plates. They were removed by whoever stole it, before
the shooting. We found the vehicle late last night abandoned
on the other side of town. I'm sure you'll read about it in tomorrow's paper," he says.

"Did you get any fingerprints?" says Harry.

"That you won't read about," says Padgett.

"How well did you know Mr. Rush?" says Ortiz.

"We did business from time to time. Referred clients. That
sort of thing."

"Were you close socially?"

"We would get together for lunch once in a while. See
each other at bar meetings."

"We've been told that you talked with him the morning he
was killed."

"We had a brief conversation."

Padgett takes out his notepad.

"Can you tell us what it was about?" asks Ortiz.

"In general terms?"

"We can start there."

"It was business. A client who was referred to me by Mr.
Rush."

"Would that client have been Mr. Metz?" asks Padgett.

"I'm going to suggest that he not answer that," says Harry.

"I thought you were just watching and listening." Ortiz
looks at him over his shoulder.

"Sometimes I hit the ball back," says Harry.

"Fine. Why shouldn't Mr. Madriani answer my question?"
he says.

"The identity of a client, before there has been any public representation," says Harry, "is a matter of attorney-client privilege."

I smile at Ortiz. "Aren't lawyers a pain in the ass?"

"Does that mean you represented Mr. Metz?" says Ortiz.

"No. It means that I'm not going to answer your question."

"Why not? What's to hide?" says Padgett.

"The identity of a former client," says Harry.

"Who is dead," says Padgett.

"Assuming that that client was Mr. Metz," says Harry, "which is the very question you're asking, and we're declining to answer."

They run up a dead end. I can tell by the body English that Padgett doesn't want to leave it. Ortiz takes the higher road and chooses to ignore it.

"We're informed that you had one meeting with Mr. Metz to determine whether or not you would take his case, and that you declined."

They have been talking to Dana.

"Can you tell us why you didn't take the case?"

"Assuming your information is correct, which I'm not conceding, I couldn't comment. I know. It looks like we're not getting very far. But I am trying," I tell him.

"So you did talk to Metz?" says Padgett.

"Did I say that, Harry?"

"No."

"I didn't say that."

We all know why Harry is here. So that Padgett, acting as scribe, can't get creative with his pencil and notepad.

"But he did have some legal problems," says Ortiz.

"We understand he was indicted," says Padgett.

"If you say so."

"It was in the newspapers," says Padgett.

"Was it?"

"Let's cut to the chase," says Padgett. "We know you met with Rush that morning. We know the conversation was not some hold-your-dick-and-tap-it-till-it-drips pass-the-time-of-day in the men's room. We have a witness," he says, "saw you huddled over a table with the man less than ten minutes before he was shot and killed."

"Then why are you asking me?"

"Because we want to know what you were talking about."

"Your witness didn't hear enough to tell you that?"

Padgett says "No" before his partner can walk over the top of him verbally, saying: "We wanted to hear what you would say."

"Which is it, yes or no? Because if your witness did hear it, then that person would be your best source of information. Because I can't discuss it."

"So it was attorney-client?" says Ortiz.

"I thought we already established that."

"If Rush was your friend, why wouldn't you want to help us catch his killer?" says Padgett.

"Why don't you ask me if I still beat my wife?" I tell him.

"Do you?" he asks.

"She died of cancer several years ago," says Harry.

Padgett looks at me. "Sorry."

"All we want to know is what Metz told you during your initial client interview," says Ortiz.

"Unless and until I'm told by a judge to the contrary, any communications I've had with any clients are privileged."

"Even dead clients?" says Ortiz.

"Even dead ones," I tell him.

"I see, you don't make the rules, you just follow them, is that it?" says Padgett.

"You're not as dumb as you look," says Harry.

"Harry. They're just trying to do their job," I say.

"And you're not helping much," says Ortiz.

"I'm sorry. But I have to do mine," replies Harry.

"How long did you know Nick Rush?" Ortiz takes a different tack.

"Ten years. More or less."

"How did you meet?"

"I've thought about that a few times since it happened. You know how it is. When you lose someone you know. I think it was probably a conference or a seminar. Continuing education of the bar maybe. But to be honest, I can't re-member the specific event or where it was."

"Let me ask you a question. How could Metz be a client if you didn't take his case?" Padgett doesn't want to give it up.

"You know as well as I do, whether I declined representa-tion or not, whatever a client told me in an initial interview . . ." He's starting to write in his notepad. "And mind you, that's not saying that I ever talked to Mr. Metz about legal mat-ters, but if I did, it would be covered by privilege." He scratches it out, closes his notebook. As he does, he sees the device on my desk. He looks at it for a second. My heart gains ten extra beats.

"I'm told you don't do drug cases," says Ortiz.

I try to look at him, but my gaze keeps going back to his partner who is still looking at the device on my desk.

"Is that true?"

"Excuse me?"

"That you don't do drug cases?"

"As a general policy, no. I don't handle cases involving narcotics."

If Padgett picks up the device, turns it on, and sees Nick's name, we will all be finishing this downtown, probably in front of a judge where I can be charged with concealing ev-idence in a capital case.

"So maybe you have some redeeming qualities after all." Padgett forgets about the device for a moment and looks at me.

I smile at him.

"Why don't you do narcotics?" he asks.

"I have no expertise in the field."

"I take it back," he says.

"Is that the only reason?" says Ortiz.

"Any other reasons would be personal and have nothing to do with any particular client or case," I say.

"Is that why you wouldn't take the Metz case? Because it involved drugs?"

"Assuming Metz was my client, for purposes of an initial

interview, the reasons that I might not take such a case would be privileged."

"We're back to that?" says Padgett.

"That means it's none of your business," says Harry.

"You're wrong," says Padgett. "They're both dead, and that is our business. Besides, who are you protecting, a client who doesn't exist?"

"Until a court tells me otherwise."

"I think if Metz were here he might want you to help us," says Ortiz. "I sure would if somebody pumped me full of holes while I was standing on the sidewalk minding my own business."

"And your friend?" says Padgett. "I would think you'd want to help us out on that one just out of professional courtesy if nothing else. You know, one shark to another."

Suddenly I'm out of my chair. Harry is off the credenza to stop me.

Padgett is on his feet, shoulders back, hands ready.

I slowly reach across my desk and take one of my business cards from the little holder on the corner and flip it to him. Pumped with adrenaline, he has trouble trying to catch it in the air, ready for a fight when the test is one of dexterity. If I wanted to nail him, now would be the time.

"Why don't you call me next time you want to talk," I tell him. "So I can decide if I want to be in or not."

Padgett stands there looking foolish, ready for a fight that isn't going to happen. My card on the floor. He doesn't know what to do, so he bends over and picks it up.

I use the opportunity to reach for the handheld device, quietly sliding it across the desk and into the center drawer, then closing it. Ortiz is still looking at his partner and doesn't seem to notice, or if he does, it doesn't seem to register.

"Then you won't help us?" He looks back at me.

"If I could help I would, but I can't. The simple fact is, I don't know anything."

Ortiz gives me a mocking smile. He doesn't believe this. As I study the grin, I get the feeling this is as close as the man ever gets to humor.

"Without talking about specifics, clients, or cases, there are good reasons why a lawyer might decline a case," I tell him.

"Such as?" says Ortiz.

"Speaking hypothetically?"

"Hypothetically," he says.

"Perhaps a feeling that the client is not telling you the truth."

"Metz lied to you?" he says.

"We're not talking clients or cases," I remind him.

"Of course not."

Padgett smiles, still standing at the edge of my desk. Finally getting somewhere. "What did he lie about?" he asks.

I give him a look, like "do you really expect me to answer that?"

"What? You only deal with truthful drug dealers, is that it?"

I don't take the bait.

"But it was narcotics, wasn't it?" he says.

"I didn't say that."

"You said that's why you didn't take his case."

"He never said anything about Mr. Metz." Ortiz wants to hear more. Whatever I will tell him.

"Then you wouldn't have any idea who killed them? Or is that covered by attorney-client privilege as well?" Padgett asks.

"No, I don't. But if I were you, I'd start by talking to the United States Attorney's Office."

"We've been there. Like talking to a fucking wall," says Padgett.

Ortiz shoots him a look to kill. The sergeant's expression is that of a man who wishes he could inhale his words and swallow them.

The feds aren't sharing information.

I look up at Harry. We have suddenly learned more than they have.

Bull neck, biceps, and all, Padgett is going to get his ass kicked when Ortiz gets him outside.

"Have you ever heard of a woman named Laura?" says Ortiz.

"In what connection?"

"I don't know. Maybe a business associate. Perhaps a friend of Mr. Rush?"

"Just Laura, no last name?" I say.

"No. Just Laura."

I think for a moment. The envelope in Nick's pocket with the name written on it, with the four thousand in cash inside. This would set the embers of curiosity glowing at Homicide downtown. But the way Ortiz asks the question allows me to sidestep it without lying.

"You say a woman named Laura? Sorry I don't. Can't help you."

"You're just overflowing with information," says Padgett.

"If there's anything else, can we get back in touch with you?" says Ortiz.

"You've got my card."

Ortiz gets on his feet and they head for the door. Padgett is out ahead of him. At the moment I suspect he'd rather stay here, maybe hide under my desk.

"There is one more thing," says Ortiz. He's almost to the door, turned, looking at me. "Did you know that Mr. Rush and Mr. Metz were in business together?"

He can tell by the vacant expression on my face, whether true or not, that this thought has never crossed my mind.

I shake my head.

He looks at a piece of paper he has been palming in his hand. "Something called Jamaile Enterprises?" There's a little uptilt in his voice as he says the word "enterprises." He looks at me, waiting for a reply.

"Nothing? Nothing?" he says.

I am speechless.

"I was just wondering," he says, "whether Mr. Rush, being a friend, might have mentioned it to you."

CHAPTER FIVE

Though I cannot recall Nick ever having darkened the door of any church, his funeral is held at the old Mission San Luis Rey, a few miles from the coast near Oceanside.

It has been ornately choreographed with three gleaming black funeral trucks hauling enough floral arrangements to look like the Rose Parade behind Nick's flag-draped coffin in the hearse. No one has explained to me what the flag is doing on the coffin, since Nick was never a veteran, though he was clearly shot in the line of duty. No doubt this is a touch demanded by Dana, who will have it folded and handed to her at the gravesite.

It is a large and hushed crowd that gathers under the hand-hewn beams of the old Spanish baroque church, its thick adobe walls magnifying every cough and the shuffling of shoes on the Spanish tile floor.

We go through the calisthenics of a Catholic service, from the pews to the kneelers and up on our feet again as the priest intones a final blessing over the coffin, sprinkles it with holy water, and swings a giant brass incense burner from a chain as it issues clouds of gray smoke.

The information from the cops has been running through my head like a ticker tape since our meeting—the name Jamaile Enterprises and the assertion that Metz and Nick were in business together.

It is possible they were simply trying to get a rise. If Ortiz and his partner failed in that regard, they did manage to plant a seed that is now sprouting suspicion. The question being: If Nick knew Metz from some prior dealings, why wouldn't he tell me? I have thought about little else for the past two nights. I have no hard answer, and this is troubling. Was Jamaile a criminal enterprise? It is possible, though knowing Nick he would never be so thick as to put his own name on the documents of formation—unless perhaps he discovered the nature of the business after the fact. This would explain why he wanted to shed Metz as a client. Which leads to another question: Did Nick see the situation as dangerous? I saw no signs of it that morning when we talked in the restaurant. I find it hard to believe he would use me in that way. I am convinced that whatever happened, Nick never saw it coming.

His coffin rests on a rolling gurney centered before the gilded altar above which plaster saints stand like stone guards in their alcoves. A large wooden crucifix bearing the figure of Christ dominates this picture. The odor of incense and burning candle wax hangs thick in the air as if suspended from the rafters.

Harry and I have arrived late and stand in one of the pews near the rear of the church. There are a few political figures here, people Nick knew and worked with over the years, two judges from the federal courts and a city councilman. A few pews up, there is a former state legislator for whom Nick beat a narcotics rap years ago. Nick was sufficiently slick that even the voters acquitted the man at election time, leaving him in office until term limits finally tapped him out.

Senior partners from Nick's firm take up two rows in the

front, right behind Dana, who is decked out in black complete with a veil and flanked by friends handing her Kleenex.

I have looked for Margaret, Nick's first wife, but if she is present I don't see her. It is one of those things you think about, even with all the acrimony of the divorce, would she make an appearance? If she has, she has burrowed into the crowd quietly.

The wheels of the gurney, one of them squeaking as if in protest, rumble over the ancient Spanish tiles, as the pall-bearers slowly roll the coffin down the aisle toward the door and the waiting hearse. Interment is to be at Eternal Hills a few miles away, a private affair for family and close friends.

The casket rolls by, followed by Dana, her face covered by the veil. By her side is the tall gentleman I had seen on the television news driving her to and from the house—austere and slender, dark hair with just enough gray around the temples to offer the image of authority. He steadies her, a hand on her elbow, the other around her shoulder. An older blond woman is on the other side, probably a sister as there is a clear family resemblance.

The mourners file out behind them from the front of the church, so Harry and I are almost the last to leave. As we make our way to the great plaza in front of the mission, the hearse is already loaded. The undertaker's staff scurries about trying to get the family into the limos and the floral arrangements back onto the trucks for the ride to the cemetery.

The limo carrying Dana is pulled up tight behind the last gleaming black truck, its windows darkened, its rear door on the other side open.

"Mr. Madriani." I hear my name before I see where the voice is coming from. When I turn, standing in front of me is the man who had been holding up Dana as she walked down the aisle.

"We've not met," he says and extends a hand. "I'm Nathan Fittipaldi, a friend of Mrs. Rush."

We shake.

He wears a dark striped Italian suit and silk tie, an expensive linen shirt, and hand-burnished calf-leather black loafers with tassels poking from beneath pant legs pressed to the sharpness of a knife's edge. Everything has the sartorial pedigree of being worn once and discarded.

"She's asked me if I would talk to you. She's not really in any shape right now."

"I understand."

"She would like you to stop by her house. She would like to talk with you. I told her I was sure you wouldn't mind."

"Of course not. When?"

"Whenever it's convenient. I wouldn't do it today," he says.

"Sure."

"You might call before you drive out, just to make sure she's in. I'll give you the number."

I tell him I have it. He tells me it's been changed. It seems Dana has been getting phone calls from the press.

"Mr. Rush had given it out to some clients," says Fittipaldi. "We suspect one of them was probably the source for the press. These people have no sense of respect for those in grief." It is unclear whether Fittipaldi is talking about Nick's criminal clients or the fourth estate, though I suspect he would lump them both in the same social set. I suspect that Dana was not alone in her low opinion of Nick's clientele.

He jots the new unlisted number on the back of a business card and hands it to me.

"Good to meet you," he says. "Dana tells me you are a good friend. She will need us all in the weeks and months ahead."

I smile but say nothing.

Then before I can ask why she wants to see me, he is gone, around the back of the limo. He disappears into the open door on the other side, it closes, and the procession pulls away.

"What's that all about?" says Harry.

"I don't know." I look at the business card in my hand,

expensive velum with a watermark no less. I turn it over to the printed side. It reads:

FITTIPALDI ART & ANTIQUITIES
Nathan Fittipaldi, Owner
Agents for Acquisition by the Discreet Collector
London, New York, Beverly Hills, San Diego

There is no phone number, only a fax and a web address, "Discretion.com".

Home at night with Sarah is not always a quiet time. She does her homework, one leg folded under the other in one of the sofa-style armchairs in our living room, with the television going full bore, watching *Star Trek*. With this she gets straight As. How she does it, I don't know.

Her hair, thick as a pony's tail, brunette with flashes of auburn like spun copper whenever sunlight hits it, is put up in cornrows tonight, something new. She says it makes it easier to handle in the morning.

She is becoming a young woman, not only in the way she dresses and cares for her appearance, but in matters of judgment as well. Sarah is her own person. When peer group pressures seem to slay other kids, my daughter has demonstrated a maturity that at times embarrasses me in my more exuberant and rash moments. We have played board games of conquest in which she has demonstrated a kind of strategic thinking I would never have credited to someone her age, with an element of compassion for those lesser competitors, protecting them from my native male aggressions, until she crushed me. This, at fifteen. I shudder to consider the heights to which this may take her, but feel more confidence in that generation knowing there are people like her in it.

Tonight we are left to our own thoughts. Sarah to her science and history, and me to the little Palm device that belonged to Nick. So far I've figured out the screen and the little green button at the bottom that turns it on. But I've been afraid to do much beyond this without instructions, afraid that given my ten thumbs for all things computer, I will lose the data stored inside. It is one thing to walk off with possible evidence in a capital case. It's another to lose it.

At the top of the screen, each time I turn it on, is an image of a battery. It appears to be draining slowly. The black shaded area of energy sliding a little more to the left each day. When it disappears, I suspect I will lose whatever information is stored inside.

I lift the tiny battery cover in the back. Two AAAs are housed inside. I study these for a moment.

"Sarah?"

"Emm?" She doesn't look up from her schoolwork, her focus riveted on the book cradled in her lap.

"Do we have any batteries, triple As?"

"The small ones?"

"Yes."

"I think so." She goes to the refrigerator where she keeps these, mostly for the walkman she listens to constantly in the car.

"Like this?" She holds one up.

"That's it."

"How many do you need?"

"Two."

She brings them over to me. "What's that?"

"I think they call it a handheld device."

"Shuur. I know that. But what's the little thing on top?"

"It's a cell phone."

"Cool. Where'd you get it?"

"It belonged to a friend."

"He let you borrow it?"

"Sort of," I tell her. "Do you know anything about them?"

"Some of the kids at school have them. Theirs aren't that nice." Sarah's looking over my shoulder, big brown eyes checking out the device. "What do you want to know?"

"How to change the batteries."

"Oh, Dad. Here, give it to me." She reaches for it, but I hold it away.

"I can't take a chance on losing the information stored inside."

"Maybe it has a bubble memory," she says.

I've heard of bubble gum and bubblehead. But bubble memory is a new one.

"If it does, then everything's stored inside, on a chip or something. We learned about it in technology. Even if you disconnect the power it stays there."

"How do I find out if it has one of these memories?"

"You could look online. Something that cool must have a site. How much does it cost?"

"I don't know."

"My birthday's coming up," she says.

"I'm buying you batteries," I tell her.

She gives me that look of mock exasperation, something of her mother's to remember her by.

"Can I see it? I won't break it. I promise," she says. Reluctantly I hand it over.

"Hey, this little button on top. It's the cell phone."

"I know. Don't touch it."

"Relax," she says. The same thing Nick told me before they shot him. "Why can't we just turn it on? See if it works."

"Because it may drain the batteries." I don't tell her that the cops have probably landed on Nick's cell phone account by now. If so, the service provider will have a trap on the line so they can isolate the cell by location if any signals go out from the phone, even if it's just looking to go online.

"If there's a site on the Internet, do you think you could find it?" I ask.

"I don't know. I could look."

It takes her less than five minutes. Sarah works her nimble fingers over the keyboard and rolls the mouse, using Yahoo! to check sites. On the fourth one she hits pay dirt, a logo that matches the one on the device, two curved crossed slashes with a dot between them at the bottom, Handspring.com.

We scan the page for half a minute or so.

"I don't see anything that looks like directions. Do you?" she says.

"No. So what do we do?"

"Gimme a second." She punches the button on the page for customer support. An e-mail message screen pops up.

Sarah types out a message, telling them that we've lost the directions and need to know how to change the batteries. And asks whether we'll lose any stored data.

Ten minutes later there's a reply. Attached are a set of instructions for operation. The e-mail message itself advises us to sync the device to a desktop computer and then change the batteries. It tells us that if we can't do this, we have only one minute once we start removing the old batteries to replace them with new ones. After that the device will crash and we will lose any data inside.

"Looks like there's no memory inside," she says, "unless there's batteries."

Without the hot-sync cradle to attach to the computer and the software to run it, we can't back up the device by syncing it to the desktop.

"You want to do it or do you want me to?" Sarah's talking about changing the batteries.

"I'll do it."

Armed with the two new batteries and the printout from the Internet, I lift the battery cover off the back once more with my fingernail. My hands are shaking as if I'm defusing a bomb. I pull one battery and quickly slide a fresh one into the slot. I pull the second. I pop the other one in, then realize I've gotten it in backward. I almost drop the device on the floor. Sarah grabs it before it can hit the carpet. She holds it while I turn the battery around and slip it in the right way. Then I look at her. "You think we got it?"

"I don't know. Turn it on."

I snap the battery cover back in place, flip the device over in my hand, and hit the green button on the bottom. When the screen pops up, the battery indicator hasn't moved. It's still where it was before, near empty. Oh, shit. An instant later it flickers. The shaded area suddenly slides across the image of the battery, all the way to the right. It is now fully charged. I let out a sigh.

"Gee, Dad, you really ought to calm down. This stuff really gets you uptight. It's just a little computer," she says.

"Yeah. Right."

"Here, let me see it."

I hand it over and try to catch my breath.

Sarah starts tapping the screen with the stylus. "You can do graffiti on it too," she says. "Do you want me to show you?"

"No. No graffiti," I tell her.

"Dad, it's not the kind of graffiti you think. Look," she says. "You can write letters on this section of the screen to call things up. See?" She orders up Nick's address book and makes the letter "c" in a small window at the bottom of the screen. Suddenly the book jumps to the section with names starting with "C."

"Got it," I tell her.

She shows me how to call up the calendar, the To Do List. "This one even has e-mail, but you have to turn the phone on," she says. "Why don't we do it? The batteries are fresh."

"Not right now."

"Oh, gee," like I ruin all her fun. "This is really cool. The kids at school would go nuts."

I'll bet. Calling people in London and leaving messages for Joe, then calling them back and telling them it's Joe and asking if there's any messages.

"Can I take it to school tomorrow?"

"No. And do me a favor. Don't tell anybody about it."

"Why not?"

"For the moment it's our secret."

She looks at me like "why would I want to do this?" Something this cool and she can't tell anybody about it. Then she shrugs and says "Sure," and hands it back to me. She returns to her homework, settles into the chair with her book and the *Star Trek* reruns, the endless generations.

"Sarah."

"What?" She looks up at me.

"Thank you. I couldn't have done it without you."

She fights it, but finally there's a beaming smile that slips out. "Anytime," she says.

I settle back into the sofa and look at the small device. I'm wondering if Nick had software and a cradle and whether he downloaded it onto his desktop at the office or home. If he did, the cops have it. They have seized his computers at both locations; with the firm I'm sure going toe-to-toe with them over client information that may be stored on the hard disks. If he didn't sync it, the only copy of whatever the device holds is in my hand.

I put my feet up on the coffee table and start to surf using the stylus.

It takes several minutes to scan the address book. There are forty-three names and phone numbers, not nearly as many as I would have thought, knowing Nick and the contacts he had. Most of these are just names, without any addresses or other information.

Some of the area codes are San Diego. I recognize the 415 as San Francisco. The phone book tells me that the only other two area codes for names in the address book are for Manhattan and Washington, D.C.

I recognize a few of the names as lawyers at RDD in San Diego. Nick has made entries under "Title" for some of the people in the other cities. Most of these involve one-word entries: "Litigation," "Licensing," "M&A," "Govnt. Affairs." I don't recognize any of the names attached to these.

Except for an entry made by the vendor who sold the device to register the warranty, there is nothing on the To Do List.

But the Memo Pad has what appear to be street addresses, three of them, followed by letters, SF, NY, and DC. Three of the four cities listed in the address book. There is also an entry under a separate note, something called Antiquities Bibliotecha, with what look like a series of numbers following it, what could be an overseas or international phone number. I make a note.

By midnight, Sarah is long since in bed, and part of the mystery is solved when I call a few of the numbers and confirm my suspicion, all the numbers ring at Rocker, Dusha offices in the cities listed.

What is puzzling is why the device doesn't contain more numbers. Nick knew a thousand people in San Diego alone. None of them are in the address book. There is nothing for the courts in any of the four cities, no addresses, phone numbers, and no court appearances in the date section, just meetings with some of the lawyers in the firm's various offices.

The first of these shows up in early April in San Francisco. There are several meetings, in New York and Washington in the early summer. These continued through the summer. The last meeting was in San Francisco nine days before Nick was killed.

At first I suspect that Nick was only practicing with the device, unwilling to toss his Day Runner in the trash until he had mastered all of its functions. But its true purpose surfaced with the discovery of another name. A single cryptic entry marked on the same day, repeated each month, the twenty-fifth at eleven A.M. Next to the time and the notation—"Money for Laura"—is an icon for an alarm so Nick wouldn't forget. Next to this is another tiny icon, like a dog-eared piece of paper. I tap it with the stylus and a note opens. Laura's name, first and last, along with her mother's. There is an address and phone number.

This is not something Nick would have ever committed to a written calendar or address book in his office, where prying eyes might see it.

Laura would be almost four now, the result of a brief liaison with a young secretary Nick met outside the firm in the months before Dana, when his marriage to Margaret was crumbling. It was a tryst with an unhappy ending. The night Nick told me about the child he was drunk. His eyes filled with tears of regret for what might have been. He had asked the mother to marry him, but she declined, telling him he had no obligations. They kept their secret. She never sought support. Still, Nick visited the child several times a week at night after work. And each month there was an envelope with cash. He told me his daughter knew him only as Uncle Nick. He never told Margaret or Dana.

Why he told me I don't know. Maybe it was the booze, the blinding clarity of failure offered by drink. Whatever it was, that night I became Nick's confidant. It was like so much of Nick's life, a talented gamester full of risk and hell bent for leather on a rocky road paved with luckless choices and a lot of pain.

CHAPTER SIX

In combat it is called "survivor's guilt"—the fact that people who have witnessed a traumatic event, and lived to talk about it, will often embrace guilt rather than confront the more agonizing reality that matters were beyond their control, that they were helpless.

Since that day, the moments leading up to Nick's murder have played in my mind like an endless loop of videotape. But the one I focus on, the most unfathomable, was the result of a momentary social impulse.

It is not the fact that I kicked Metz and his case back to Nick. Metz lied to me about money laundering and probably other things as well. I suspect Nick knew what he was shipping over when he sent me the case.

What bothers me is something far more innocuous. It is the fact that I didn't make more of an effort to call to Nick out on the sidewalk that morning. I have thought about it at night before I sleep and in those endless hours before dawn, seeing my movements, analyzing them as a choreographer might review the sequence of steps in a dance.

To anyone not carrying the burden, hearing the shots or seeing the images of carnage on the street that morning, it might seem inane. But not to me.

I had yelled to Nick, only to be cut off by the bus as it drove between us down the street. I suppose I could blame the driver and his diesel engine, the transit authority, or the traffic. But after the bus passed, when I saw him standing there on the sidewalk next to Metz, I stopped. I could have called out again, but I didn't. If I had and if I'd held up the device for him to see, Nick would have crossed over. He would have been standing with me on the other side of street when the shooters came by. But for my failure to act, Nick would be alive.

So why didn't I call out? I've asked the question a hundred times, and every time I get the same answer: for the same reason we all dodge people we don't like, the petty desire to avoid an uneasy moment, this one with Metz. Having spurned his case, it was more comfortable to avoid him and to return Nick's handheld at a later time. So I slipped it into my pocket and walked away. I could not have known at that moment that a seemingly inconsequential omission—my failure to follow up, my distaste for Metz—would cost Nick Rush his life.

I'm sure any psychiatrist would tell me I was faultless. But a lawyer, a man trained to sharpen the point on guilt, might view it otherwise, as I do, as a proximate cause of death.

Survivor's guilt, maybe. But it trumps all the other reasons for Nick's death that I know, because it was the one *I* could have controlled. And until I know who shot him and why, it is certain to eat at me.

I wait a few days before I contact Dana, a respectful period, and place the call late in the afternoon. It is May, and the number may be new, but the phone system isn't. It's one of those voice-programmed things that give the caller options. "If you want to talk to Nick, press one. If you wish to speak to Dana, press two." The eerie part is that the voice used to program it is something from the grave. It is Nick's voice.

I press the number for Dana and wait for her to pick up.

It is answered by another woman, I assume a maid as Nick told me that Dana had hired one. There are intonations of a Mexican-Spanish accent.

"I will check to see if Mrs. Rush is in. Who is calling?"

"Paul Madriani."

"One moment please."

The phone goes to chamber music, a little NPR, as she puts me on hold. A few seconds later, the strings of Mozart are broken.

"Hello, Paul. It's so good to hear from you." Dana's voice comes over the phone a bit breathless. I can visualize her flipping her pixie-style blond hair out of her eyes with a wag of her head as she speaks.

"I did want to talk with you, but I'd rather not do it over the phone. I wonder if you have time to come by the house?"

"Sure. When?"

"Can you make it this evening, say about six-thirty or seven?"

I look at my calendar. "Why not."

"Good. I'll look forward to it." She hangs up.

From my office, the Cays are a skip and a jump, just a few miles from Coronado, down the Silver Strand. It is one of the more desirable locations to live, your only neighbor to the north being the navy's amphibious training base, miles up the beach. It is close to the city for commuting. Some of the newer houses, mostly renovations, tip the scales at five million dollars a pop.

What makes it pricey is not only the vistas across the bay, but the fact that it is one of the few places left in California where you can own a private dock in your own backyard. The Cays offer direct access to the harbor and from there to the open Pacific, and some of the private pleasure craft moored here rival small cruise ships.

Dana has left my name on a list at the security kiosk out

on the Strand, so when I arrive I am waved through the gate.
Her place is situated on Green Turtle Cay. I have been here
on a few occasions for social outings, the last being a bar association fund-raiser for some cause I do not remember.

I drive over the bridge and hang a left. The house is sheltered from the bay behind another man-made island called
Grand Caribe Cay. As I pull up in front of the house, it is
dusk. The view is a display of lights from across the water,
the brilliance of the setting sun reflected off shimmering
skyscrapers, an image of the mythical City of Oz, with the
twinkle of houses in the hills behind it. I suspect it is part of
the reason Nick bought the place, that and the fact that Dana
tanned so well in her bikini out on the flying bridge of his
boat in summer. He once told me he would lull under the
giant aircraft carriers moored at the naval base on the north
end of the island and watch as Dana untied the top to her
bathing suit while she sunned herself lying facedown on the
deck of his boat. Nick got a charge watching the sailors drool
over the railings. Why have a trophy wife if you can't enjoy
it?

I step from the car, slam the door closed, and lock it.
When I turn, I see Dana framed in the open doorway of the
house, waiting for me. She is shoeless in dark nylons and a
black dress that at the moment is well above her knees as her
arms are stretched above her head bracing her lithe figure in
the open door as if framing a picture.

She turns it on me as I walk up the path toward the house.
Her hands remain on the doorframe as she tosses her head
to one side to flip her hair from her eyes.

"God, I'm glad to see you," she says. "I saw you at the
funeral, but I just couldn't deal with all the people."

"I understand."

She takes me by one hand and pecks me on the cheek. "I
don't know what I would do without friends," she says. "You
and Nathan."

"That would be Mr. Fittipaldi?" I say.

"Emm." She nods. "You wouldn't believe how good he's
been."

"How long have you known him?"

"I don't know. A year maybe. He's on the arts commission with me."

"He's a member?"

"Emm. Very influential." She leads me into the house and closes the door behind us. "Nathan has galleries all over, in Beverly Hills, New York, Europe." She guides me toward the living room.

"I saw his card," I tell her. "What is it exactly that he does? I mean besides being a friend."

She looks over her shoulder at me, the kind of sultry grin that tells me I could get on that list too. Be her friend.

"He's in art acquisitions, for important clients. Private collectors, large museums, that sort of thing."

"It sounds impressive."

"He is," she says. "But let's not talk about that right now."

So I turn to another topic. "How are you doing?"

"You can't imagine. No one could," she says, "until it happens." Then she looks at me, hand to her mouth. "Oh, I'm sorry."

"What for?"

"I forgot you lost your wife." I don't know if this is her ham-handed way of reminding me that I am available. With Dana you never know.

"Nikki died some years ago," I tell her.

"Nikki. That was her name?"

I nod.

"Still, it was thoughtless," she says. "What was I thinking? Of myself obviously. My mind. It's not all there. Nick told me about it. What did she die of? I forget."

"Cancer."

"That's right. And you have a daughter?"

"Sarah."

"How old is she?"

"Fifteen."

"Fifteen. I remember that," she says. "What an age. And I'll bet she steals the hearts of all the boys too. You'll have to bring her by sometime so I can meet her."

"Sometime," I tell her.

"I suppose it is a little different. I mean Nick being killed and all. And your wife dying of natural causes. You must have had some time to prepare." Dana has switched gears again, perhaps a measure of her state of mind.

"Not that that eases the pain, I'm sure. But this. It was the shock as much as anything. One minute he's here, the next he's gone. And the press. You don't know what it's like until you have to deal with those people. They have absolutely no respect for anything. One of them actually rented a boat and motored up to our dock for pictures. The police had to haul him away."

"I saw a couple of them out by the gate, parked in their cars," I tell her.

"They're animals," she says. "Well, at least the TV cameras are gone. I mean I couldn't even drive out. They had the exit blocked. The homeowner's association had to call the police twice to get them to move. It's like a bad dream. I keep waiting for Nick to come walking through the door. But I can't wake up. It doesn't go away."

"You're right," I tell her. "I can't imagine."

"I don't know what to do." She looks up at me.

I have no answers, but as she steps toward me and puts her arms around my neck, resting her head on my chest and pressing her body against me, it's clear that Dana does. She's trying a new set of shoulders on for size.

The smell of perfume, odors of sandalwood and Indian jasmine, wafts up to seduce me.

"Somebody killed him, Paul. And I don't know why."

I shake my head. "Somebody killed him, but it was an accident."

"An accident." She tilts her head up and looks me in the eye.

"I'm sure whoever did it wasn't shooting at Nick."

She doesn't say anything. Certainly this thought must have entered her mind before now. The papers have been filled with the theory that Metz was the target. "I never thought of it as an accident," she says.

"Nick was just in the wrong place at the wrong time," I tell her.

I'm not sure this eases her mind, but we uncouple and she steps away, new thoughts obviously running through her head.

She leads me toward a table where a silver tray has been laid out with coffee in a china pot and two cups. She offers me some and prepares it.

"Sugar?"

"No thanks."

"Cream?"

I shake my head.

"Please sit down," she says.

I settle into the large tufted sofa. She hands me a cup, then places her own on a table next to an armchair and sits down. One leg is curled under her so that the dark stocking-covered knee is exposed, showing a run in the nylon. She sees this and covers it with a hand as she smiles—that cute school-girl grin that she has patented.

"I must look a mess." She bites her lower lip.

"You look fine."

"You're just being nice," she says, then runs her hands through her hair in an effort to straighten it. This only musses it a little more. She glances down at the bodice of her dress to make certain that everything is in place.

"I'm a wreck and I know it. I haven't been able to sleep since it happened." The redness of her eyes confirms the fact. Her dress is creased as if perhaps she had been lying down before I arrived.

"I suppose I should explain to you why I asked to you to come over. You were one of Nick's best friends."

"I was a friend."

"No," she says. "You weren't just a friend. You were a good friend. And Nick didn't have many of those. I know.

"The partners at the firm. They didn't socialize with us. Oh, they made a big show at the funeral, but outside the office they didn't want anything to do with Nick."

"That's not what Nick told me. He told me that some of

the partners wanted to put him on the firm's management committee."

"Nick was dreaming." She ignores my protest. "They were all, you know, big business lawyers, civil litigators." She slurs the word a little so that I wonder if maybe she'd had a few drinks before I arrived. "You know they made big promises to Nick to get him to go over there. And then they didn't follow through. Adam Tolt," she says. "He rolled out the red carpet to get Nick. Told him they would work him into civil cases, move him upstairs. Then Nick got there and found out it was nothing but lies. They took the money he earned, but they didn't want anything to do with Nick or his clients. But you, you were different. You were his friend."

"Maybe it had something to do with the fact that we had the same kind of clients."

"Except you wouldn't do drug cases," she says.

When she looks up from her coffee cup at me, she can see that this stung.

"Oh, I'm sorry," she says. "I didn't mean it that way. Actually I respect you for having standards. It's something Nick could never do. I told him he was better than that. But I don't think he ever believed me. I know what you're thinking. You're thinking that if you'd taken the case, Mr. Metz, that Nick would be alive and you'd be dead. You shouldn't think like that."

Obviously Dana has thought of it.

"You can't blame yourself," she says. "If anybody's to blame, it's me."

"You?"

She nods. "I was the one who brought Metz to him. I was the cause of Nick's death."

"No. That's not true."

"It's true enough," she says. "If I hadn't known him from the arts commission, none of this would have happened."

How do I tell her that the cops believe Nick was in business with the man?

"He would have gone to some other lawyer with his problem and some other poor dumb bitch would have a dead husband." She begins to cry, just a little. "Damn it," she says. "I told myself I wasn't going to do this. She catches a single tear with a napkin as it runs down her cheek. "Nick was such a sad case," she says. "All that work. That's all he had."

"He had you," I say.

"Yes. Me." Dana rises from the chair and turns her back to me. I can't tell if she's trying to compose herself or think of what to say next.

"I knew you would feel bad about what happened," she says. "And I—I simply wanted to tell you that there's no need—no reason that you should feel that way." She talks with her back to me.

"I thought he was such a nice man." She shrugs her shoulders and turns toward me, the little girl, looking down at me like a frazzled pixie. "Mr. Metz, I mean. He was always a gentleman. He talked about his family. He had grandchildren. Did you know that?"

Most of us do if we live long enough. I shake my head.

"How could someone do that to him? And to Nick?"

"I don't know."

"I keep telling myself I had no way of knowing, but it doesn't do any good," she says. "I feel responsible." She sinks down on the sofa next to me with a sigh.

I ask her if she's had any counseling, perhaps a therapist, someone whose business is to deal with grief.

"Right now I don't know if it would do any good."

"You don't know unless you try. Do you have any friends in the neighborhood? Other women?" I ask.

"I'm not going to get into that," she says. "The lonely widow."

I yearn for one of the chairs, farther away. I'm thinking perhaps all of Dana's emotional gyroscopes are out of kilter at the moment. Still, I sit here, next to her on the sofa. She holds my hand in both of hers.

"I try to put a brave face on it. Yeah right," she says. "Look what happens." She smiles, and we both laugh.

"I had to talk to you because the police said you were the last person to talk to Nick."

"I suppose that's true."

"Did he talk about me?" she says. She looks up at me, haunting eyes, seeking release from something I don't understand. Then it hits me. Stupid man. She wants to know if he loved her, and if he shared this with me.

I begin to wonder how well she really knew him. Nick might talk about a lot of things with other men, including sex swinging from a chandelier with his wife. But he would never discuss the intimacies of love. It takes me a second to get the question in focus. In that time I can see that she takes this for a "no."

"He talked about you all the time," I tell her. "You were the most important thing in his life."

"Really?"

"Absolutely."

"Did he talk about me that morning?"

"What do you mean?"

"I mean did he mention my name?"

"Sure. Several times."

"What did he say?"

"That you were the best thing to ever walk into his life." He may have said it with a view from behind, describing the sculpted round landscape of her tight little ass, but in one way or another, Nick said it.

"Really?"

I nod, raise three fingers like a scout, hoping they don't rot before her eyes and fall off.

Before I can take my hand down, she takes it in both of hers. We sit there for a couple of moments. Me looking at the table, the coffee cup, anything but Dana's blue eyes. She's looking for something, whether it's to be consoled or for information, I'm not sure.

"I'm trying to understand why it happened," she says. "You met with Mr. Metz; Nick told me you did. Why would anyone want to kill him?"

Dana's now entering forbidden territory, items I can't discuss. If I do and she repeats it to the cops, they would have me on the carpet for a good grilling, arguing that I had trashed any claim of privilege. With the client dead and no other interest to be served, it would be evidence of a waiver.

"I don't know."

"He must have told you something. I know it had to do with some business he had down in Mexico."

"He told you that?"

She nods. "Before he went to see Nick. We talked after one of the commission meetings about his problem."

"How much did he tell you?"

"Not much. He told me that he didn't do anything wrong, that he needed a lawyer, and so I told Nick. What was it about? I have to know."

"I can't tell you."

"Why not?"

"Listen, you'll know soon enough. The police will find the people who killed Nick. Then it'll all come out. Be patient."

"You tell me to be patient. I've lost my husband," she says. "I want to know why. Was he involved in something?"

"What makes you say that?"

I can tell in this instant she wishes she hadn't. "Nothing," she says. "It's just me. I haven't been myself."

That's not true. This is the Dana I know.

"It's just that it's hard to be patient. To wait, not knowing what happened."

"Yes. I know."

"Then he didn't tell you anything that would give you a clue. Metz, I mean?"

I shake my head. It's a lie, but at the moment it's the best I can do. Whether she believes me or not, she accepts this.

"There was another reason I called," she says. "I needed to talk to you about something else."

"What's that?"

"It's—I'm afraid this is going to sound awfully crass," she says.

"Try me."

"It's the insurance on Nick's life."

I look at her quizzically.

"I mean if Nick had a policy of life insurance, at the firm, the fact that he was shot, murdered—I'm not—I mean I'm not sure what to do."

"You want to know whether that would affect your ability to recover on the policy?"

She nods. This is Dana the helpless, blue eyes and silky skin, the veiled complexion. Sitting here holding my hand.

"Was there a policy?"

"I think so. Nick told me about it once. Something I think he called a key policy."

"Key man?"

"That's it. Do you know what it is?"

This is something a firm like Rocker, Dusha might have. Hefty life insurance on each of the partners, so in the event of death the firm wouldn't be strapped to buy out the partner's interest.

"It's not exactly my field," I tell her.

"I know, but I trust you. You were Nick's friend." Dana now wields this like a sword.

"Do you have a copy of the policy?"

She shakes her head.

"Did Nick have a safe, a safety deposit box?"

"The police took the safe," she says. "We had a safety deposit box at the bank, but it's sealed until they can go through it. I can't even get the papers to the house. The mortgage," she says. "To see what we owe. How much equity I have." She may be helpless, but she's not stupid.

"So, no policy?"

She shakes her head again, looking at me sort of breathless, waiting for answers.

"This must sound heartless," she says. "The grasping widow."

"If there's a policy and you're the beneficiary, then you're entitled," I tell her.

"I haven't told anyone else about this, but Nick left me

in, well, what is not exactly a good situation," she says. "Financially, I mean."

"I had no idea."

"No one did, including me," she says. "I think it was some investments he made. I read in the paper that he was supposed to have four thousand dollars in cash on him when he was killed. I don't believe it," she says. "Nick told me the market tanked, that we'd lost a good deal of money. The house isn't paid for, I know that. I'll have to sell the boat," she says. "That was Nick's pride and joy. I may have to look for something more modest. I mean a place to live, if I'm going to have anything to live on.

"You know Nick. Life on the edge is a badge of honor." She talks as if he were still alive. "And as long as he was taking care of things I never asked questions. But now," she says.

"I understand."

"That's why I called you. I knew you would. And Nick trusted you."

Dana knows how to turn the knife.

"I can make a few phone calls," I tell her.

"Oh, thank you. You don't know what a relief it is to be able to turn all of this over to somebody else."

My expression tells her this is not what I said. Dana chooses to ignore this.

"To have somebody who knows what they're doing." Suddenly her arms are around my neck, leaning toward me on the couch, her warm face planted against my chest so that I have to use my hands to keep from falling over backward on the couch. "I don't know what I'd do without you," she whispers.

My thought at the moment, given the situation, is not something I would expect. It concerns Dana's speculation regarding Sarah and boys, and the certain knowledge that Dana has been polishing these skills since she was fifteen. I make a mental note to have a conference with my daughter.

CHAPTER SEVEN

T he next morning as I come through the office door, Harry is picking through pink phone message slips with an eye on one of the morning talk shows bleeping from the television set in the lobby. His briefcase is on the floor next to his feet, his coat still on, so I assume he has just arrived or is heading out again.

There are some phone messages in my slot on the reception desk, so I grab them.

On the screen, one of the network news anchors is being interviewed, a sagging form sitting there in his suspenders sans suit coat trying to look like a regular guy in his starched $3,000 shirt.

"I think he threw his back out giving the news a twist," says Harry.

My partner has no use for what passes as journalism these days, particularly on the tube. According to Harry, they spend too much time in deep admiration for politicians who show particular skill in lying, so much so that they have now institutionalized the destruction of public ethics by elevating deceit to a statecraft called "spin." It is no longer the lie that matters but the qualitative fashion in which it is told.

We now have a receptionist and file clerk rolled into one, though she is not in yet this morning. Marta comes in six hours a day around her school schedule to screen messages from our phone mail, knock correspondence into final form, and organize files so that we don't drown in an avalanche of loose paper.

"So how did it go, the meeting with the widow?" Harry was in my office when I placed the phone call to Dana.

"Fine."

"What did she want?"

"Some advice." I thumb through my messages. There is one from Nathan Fittipaldi. Perhaps he's checking up for Dana.

"No shoulder to cry on?" says Harry.

"That too." I quickly change the subject to what little information I gleaned from Nick's PDA.

"Let's talk in the office." Harry punches the power button on the TV's remote, the screen goes dark, and we head into my office and close the door.

I fill him in on the information I got from Nick's PDA.

"I did what you asked," he says. "You know you can get most of that stuff online." Harry is talking about corporate filings with the Secretary of State's office up in the capital.

"Fortunately, Effie was here late last night so she was able to go online." Harry still won't use a computer, not even for word processing. In Harry's arcane world, keyboards are for secretaries and typesetters. No self-respecting lawyer would touch one. I tell him he's a dinosaur.

"Her name is Marta, not Effie," I tell him.

"I like to think of her as Effie." Harry has been on a kick lately, fiction noir, reaching back in time, the old mysteries of Dashiell Hammett and Raymond Chandler, relishing a time when everything was black and white. He has taken to naming our secretary after Sam Spade's girl Friday from *The Maltese Falcon*. One of these days I'm afraid I will come into the office to find the names of "Spade and Archer" in black letters across our front window.

"It's fine with me as long as she doesn't mind," I tell him. "The laws of harassment being what they are."

"She thinks it's cute," he tells me.

Marta is Latina, about five-foot-two, with a good sense of humor, an affable nature, and a work ethic that keeps her nose to the grindstone sixteen hours a day between school, work, and two kids. She is eager to learn and has taken charge of the office, even finding some available space for filing cabinets in one of the vacant cabanas two doors down from our office.

"She went online," says Harry. "She's getting good."

"Maybe she could teach you," I tell him.

Harry gives me a look as if to say "in your dreams." "We managed to run down the corporate records for Jamaile Enterprises. Like the cops said, it's a limited partnership. The stuff was filed a little over a year ago. Shows your Mr. Metz as the general partner. Nick shows up as one of the officers. It looks like Metz had control of the day-to-day operations of the business and that maybe Nick was an investor. It's not really clear."

I am wondering if maybe this was the investment that went sour, the one that Dana told me about. The reason she was broke.

"Any other names on the filings?"

"One. A Grace Gimble," says Harry. He looks at the notebook in his hand and shrugs his shoulders like this doesn't ring any bells. "She shows up on the statement of officers as the secretary."

"Where was the business located?"

"It shows a P.O. box as the address of record." He gives me this on a piece of paper.

"You can be sure the cops have already been there with a search warrant," I say.

He nods. "Maybe one of the partners knows about it?"

I continue to finger absently through my phone messages. "Anything else?"

"Just the usual. Articles of incorporation containing a statement of purpose for the business."

I look up at Harry.

"Like the cop said, import-export. That and any other lawful business they wanted to conduct. A lot of boilerplate from the form books," says Harry.

"That's it?"

"I went to the law library and had them run a Lexis-Nexis on Grace Gimble." This is not something we have bought into on the office computer yet. "We found a couple of G. Gimbles, no Grace, and without more information we couldn't tell if it was the right person."

"What are you thinking?" I ask.

"About the woman?"

I nod.

"It could be a secretary, somebody with the firm. A signature of convenience they used for formation when they put the thing together."

"That was my thought."

"You want me to check it out? Call the firm?"

"No. Let's hold off. It wouldn't do to be asking the same questions the cops are."

Harry considers this. "Why wouldn't Nick have told you about this? Good friend that he was." Harry looks at me, that cynical twinkle in his eye. "I mean if he was in business with Metz, what's to hide? Unless they were importing contraband," he says.

"Don't even go there," I tell him. "A lawyer like Nick sees a lot of people in a year. It could be he talked with Metz over the phone and signed the formation documents through the mail."

"Right," says Harry. "Nick did so much corporate work he just couldn't remember."

He has a point.

"Did you talk to her about it?" Harry is talking about Dana.

I shake my head.

"Why not?"

"The subject didn't come up."

He laughs. "What, she was too busy loosening the knot on your tie, toying with your belt?"

I look at him.

"I know, don't tell me. I have no respect for those in mourning."

I leave it as a statement of fact.

"What did she want?"

"Some information on an insurance policy."

"There was insurance?" Harry's eyebrows go up a notch.

"We don't know."

"Maybe you don't," says Harry. "But I have a feeling the erstwhile Mrs. Rush does, though it begs another question."

"What's that?"

"Why you? You do about as many insurance cases as Nick did corporate formations."

"She thought she could trust me."

"Can she?" Harry wants to know if I'm interested in more than just the legal issues involved.

"She also wanted to know what Nick and I talked about that morning, over coffee."

"Ah. Did you tell her?"

"What I could remember. Not all of it."

"And in between remembrances, this insurance thing came up?"

"Yeah."

"What kind of policy is it?"

"Like I said. We don't know if there was a policy."

"She doesn't have a copy?" says Harry.

I shake my head.

"Don't tell me," he says. "They had a key-man policy out on him at the firm?" Harry is a quick study.

"If it's in play."

He starts to laugh, the kind of laugh he reserves for foolish acts by foolish people. "You told her you'd go over there and ask them about it?"

"Somebody has to. He left her high and dry. Besides, I have other reasons for doing it," I tell him.

"I hope they involve a fee?"

"They might not."

Harry looks at me. "You didn't tell her you'd do it for free?"

"I didn't tell her anything about fees. The problem is, Nick told me some things that I can't discuss. They involve other people. Innocent people who could be drawn into this in ways that would be ugly." The thought of Laura and her mother with reporters camped outside their door is not an image I wish to be responsible for. It is the reason I didn't tell the cops, that and the fact that Nick had trusted me with his secret.

"You'll have to trust me. There is a reason. It's a good reason." I look a Harry. He glances back at me, then nods.

"Nick made some bad investments," I tell him.

"Yeah. In former wives."

"He also made some other mistakes."

Harry looks at me sensing this is the item I can't talk about.

"You feel strongly about this?"

"I do."

"All right. Fine. What do you need from me?"

"Thanks."

CHAPTER EIGHT

Rocker, Dusha and DeWine is one of the old-line firms in town. No one can remember when Jeremiah Rocker died, and James Dusha's picture in the outer lobby depicts a proper gent in waistcoat and staid collar, squinting at the camera lens through a pince-nez.

While the firm name may be old, there is nothing sedentary about their business plan. In the last few years, they have gobbled up two other sizable law firms and established other offices in San Francisco, New York, and Washington, D.C. They have moved to the power and money centers, and word is that they are on the prowl for more, always with an eye for people having contacts to corporate clients.

The firm looms large on the political scene. A few years ago RDD led the charge in Congress lobbying for a bill later known as the Corporate Lawsuit Reform Act. It carried all the right buzz words, everything people hate in the form of "corporations" and "lawsuits" and love by way of "reform." This particular piece of mischief fed a steep recession, though you wouldn't know it from the profits scooped in by RDD.

The legislation contained what is known as a "safe harbors" clause for accountants and lawyers, so they could shade their eyes from otherwise obvious fraud committed by their business clients, while taking hefty fees in the process. In this way, the lawyers and accountants could avoid both civil and criminal liability while their corporate clients stole billions from unwary investors. Within four years, mega corporations around the country began folding up like card tables, filing bankruptcy, throwing tens of thousands out of work and transforming retirement plans into piles of worthless paper. Of course RDD couldn't be touched on any of this. They had legal immunity from Congress.

RDD has become a master player in this game. They have been known to lobby for legislation creating the crime and then to represent the injured in a class action lawsuit afterward. That the victims got three cents on the dollar, and that this was taken to pay gargantuan attorneys' fees, does not even faze them.

The firm has more than three hundred lawyers and an untold number of legal assistants, secretaries, and drones, strapped to the oars and toiling to keep this great ship of commerce pointed in the right direction: always toward the bottom line. Few in the bar and certainly no one at RDD ever blanches at the notion that justice, if it exists at all, is a mere by-product of making money.

All of this shows up in the firm's address and the tasteful appointments of its public spaces. RDD occupies the upper five floors of a highrise on the waterfront, overlooking the bay. It is well known that they own the rest of the building beneath them, renting it out until they can raid enough of the competition to fill steerage and bilge.

The executive suite is up on eleven. A Persian carpet long enough to cover the runway at LAX paves the way to the reception, enough knotted wool to have gnarled the fingers and blinded a generation of kids toiling in some dim Middle Eastern sweatshop.

A large bronze sculpture of whales, mother and calf, rests on a pedestal in the center of the room, a metallic statement of the firm's sensitivity toward motherhood and the environment.

So as to cover all their bases and not offend commercial interests, oil paintings of ships, some of them under sail, dot the walls illuminated by halogen-spot museum lighting. None of this mars the uninhibited vista to the west, across the bay, an unparalleled view of the north end of Coronado Island and its sprawling naval base.

I approach the counter and drop a business card on it. "Paul Madriani to see Mr. Tolt."

The receptionist, a slender redhead in a business suit and telephone headset, sports fingernails an inch long as she picks up my card and eyes it. I tell her I have an appointment.

"Just a moment." She punches a button and calls to the back, mentions my name and the appointment, listens, smiles, then pushes the disconnect key. "Mr. Tolt's assistant will be out in a moment. Please take a seat."

I try the cushy couch under the massive oil painting of a square-rigged ship in storm-tossed seas and hope that I won't get wet. The outer office is a busy place. There is the constant bleep of telephones, three receptionists pushing buttons repeating the mantra "Rocker, Dusha," "Rocker, Dusha"— DeWine, it seems, has somehow gotten lost in the commercial flurry, every billable second being precious. Long-nailed fingers flail the buttons on phones with the speed of flamenco artists, connecting calls to the back offices and downstairs, feeding the money machine. Computerized billing devices attached to the phones will be clicking every six minutes, charging for each tenth of an hour. Slot machines in most casinos don't provide the house with this steady a take.

In less than a minute, a well-dressed woman in a dark blue business suit appears from around the corner of the reception counter. She is smiling under blond shoulder-length hair. She stops for an instant to gather my card at the counter and then, still reading it, moves toward me.

"Mr. Madriani."

I push myself up from the couch.

"Glenda Rawlings, Mr. Tolt's administrative assistant. If you will come this way."

I follow her past reception and down the corridor. There is only one large double door at the end of the hall. On the dark mahogany in gold letters is the name "Adam Tolt." She knocks.

"Come in." The voice is muted behind the solid wood.

She opens the door and leads the way. I have never met Tolt before. He appears as a gray eminence behind a massive dark desk twenty feet away. God would have such surroundings if he had more money. There are Greek vases lining a continuous shelf on three of the four walls, the other being glass. These are obvious relics of great value in earthen hues. On the wall behind Tolt's desk is a Matisse, not a copy, an original, in shocking colors, vibrant blues and greens.

The surface of Tolt's desk reveals swirls of inset bird's-eye inlaid in a delicate border around an exotic dark polished slab that spent an eon surviving on the floor in some primeval tropical forest. It is swept clear of everything except an ornate silver pen set, a telephone with a zillion buttons, and a large leather blotter. On the blotter is a sheaf of papers to which the man is giving his undivided attention. He doesn't look up as I enter.

"Glenda, I'm going to need the file on the Masery case. Tell Halston I want to see him before I leave. And call Schafer and tell him I want a briefing on the Electric Stylus matter when I get back on Friday."

With the point of his fountain pen, he scratches a diagonal line across the page he is reading.

"This memo to Wentworth needs some work." He flips it at her so it sails and she has to catch it in the air a foot off the surface of his desk.

"I don't know who did the figures," he says, "but they don't add up." By now he is already looking at the next piece of paper in the stack.

"Yes, sir. I'll take care of it right away."

He scratches the scrawl of his signature, the point of his pen like a needle over the linen letterhead, lifts the page and repeats the process. He does this four more times in quick succession, his name represented by what looks like two letters, an A with a T through it, followed by an inky squiggle. He affixes this to the paper with the staid majesty of one using sealing wax and the royal signet ring to endorse an imperial commission.

Tolt is a fixture not only in the politics of this state, but on the national scene. As a young man he is reputed to have led a trade delegation to the Orient where, within a year, rumors of bribes to foreign officials began to surface, rumors that blossomed into scandal, and led to the collapse of a government over the purchase of defense equipment. The fact that one of Tolt's clients was the supplier of this equipment did not seem to tarnish the man. That he could do this, his name never being mentioned in the press or any of the inquiries that followed, coined for him the title, in darker corners and behind his back, the "Stealth Fixer."

Tolt's political tracks have the same illusive qualities as a shadow. Shine light on them and they disappear. There are those who suspect that his fingerprints would not even adhere to the smooth leather surface of his own briefcase. Currently he sits on more than a dozen corporate boards, as well as the national committee of one of the two great political parties. Given the moral compass of the country over the past quarter century, one day we will no doubt find him on the Supreme Court or in a presidential cabinet.

He doesn't look up at me until he is twisting the cap back on his pen.

"And Glenda, hold my calls, and call the airport and make sure the Gulfstream is fueled and ready. I don't want to wait for the crew again."

"Yes, sir. Your car is downstairs. The driver's waiting."

"Thank you, Glenda."

She hustles out, the picture of efficiency, and closes the door behind her.

Tolt picks up my business card, which she has placed on the blotter near his right hand, and examines it. He wears glasses under a creased forehead. His face is well tanned, and he seems fit for a man I would guess is in his early six- ties. "Mr. Mad-re-ani?"

"Mah-dree-ahnee. The a's are long," I tell him.

"Have a seat. I don't have much time. I have to leave for D.C. on business," he says.

This makes me want to send a national consumer alert to taxpayers. He looks at his watch. "I was told you wanted to see me. Something having to do with Nick Rush."

"If it would be more convenient, we could meet when you have a little more time. Perhaps when you get back . . ."

"No. No." He would rather get rid of me now.

I take a seat. "I'm here at the request of Mrs. Dana Rush. Nick's widow. She asked me if I could look into some busi- ness matters for her."

"I see." He shakes his head solemnly. "Tragic," he says. "How someone with that much promise could be cut down in his prime." Tolt makes it sound as if the greatest loss is that Nick's fingers are no longer plying the billing machine in his office.

"Specifically the question regards insurance on her hus- band's life, the firm's key-man policy."

"Uh-huh." Suddenly he's looking for something, swivel- ing in his chair. Then he sees it: the attache case on the floor behind him, under his credenza. He wheels around so his back is to me for a second as he reaches for it.

"I don't usually get involved in these kinds of details," he says. "Have you talked to Humphreys?" Tolt is back around to face me, the attache case open on his desk in front of him. For an instant, I think maybe he has a copy of the key-man policy in this briefcase. Then I realize he doesn't. He is just packing up, getting ready to leave.

"Humphreys is your man," he says. "He's the firm's busi- ness manager. He handles all that stuff. If you have an in- surance claim, you lodge it with him."

"I talked to Mr. Humphreys yesterday. He's the one who

set up our appointment. He said there was some problem, but he couldn't discuss it. He said I would have to talk with you."

"Problem? I don't know anything about a problem. Who do you say you represent?"

"Mrs. Rush, Dana Rush."

He looks at me as if the name doesn't click. "Hang on a second." He picks up the receiver on the phone, hits one of the hot keys on the bottom, and waits for it to ring.

"Hello, George, this is Adam upstairs." He swings around in his chair, back to me again. "I have a man up here, name of Paul Mad-ri-ani. Says he talked to you on the phone about the key-man policy on Nick Rush.

"Uh-huh. Uh-huh.

"Well, why wasn't I told?

"Uh-huh.

"Well, yes, but I should have been told.

"Uh-huh. Really. Is anybody looking into this?

"Uh-huh. Uh-huh. Well that's fine but what's . . .

"Uh-huh. So what's it look like? Does Jim think we're going to be in the middle?

"Uh-huh. Uh-huh. Well, keep me posted, OK?" He hangs up, picks up my card again, taking another look at it.

"You're right. It looks like there could be a problem," he says.

"What's that?"

He puts my card down and is back to piling some papers from a desk drawer into the open attache case in front of him.

"The good news is there was a key-man policy out on Nick. The policy was taken out when he joined the firm. The firm paid the premiums and all," he says. "It's part of the compensation package for partners. In return for the insurance payout, heirs agree to forego any claim as to an interest in the law firm," he says. "The key-man policy is a good way to make sure nobody gets hurt."

"And?"

"The bad news," says Tolt, "is that the named beneficiary doesn't seem to be your client."

"What do you mean?"

"How well did you know Nick?" he asks.

"Pretty well."

"Then you knew he was married once before."

I nod.

"That's the problem," he says. "The former wife's name is on the policy. I think I met her once at a firm social function. Name of Margaret. Do you know her?"

I take a deep sigh and nod.

"She probably doesn't know her name is still on the policy. Not yet anyway." He's futzing in the briefcase, making sure he has everything. "It puts us in a difficult position," he says. "Any claim on the policy by somebody else, and the carrier is going to have to notify her. Doing insurance work, I'm sure you understand."

"I don't do insurance work."

"I thought you said . . ."

"I didn't say anything."

"Your card says you're a lawyer."

"I do criminal work. That's how I knew Nick."

"Oh," he says and stops packing. His bushy eyebrows, furry and gray, turn heavy hooded and move to the center of his forehead like two migrating mice.

He picks up my card once more and takes a closer look this time, reading it as if to himself: "Madriani. Madriani. I remember. You defended in that thing about a year ago, they found the body in her office out by the beach. What was it?"

"The Hale case."

"That's it. The old man who won the lottery. The victim was a woman."

"Zolanda Suade," I say.

"That's the one." He closes the lid on the attaché case and looks at me. "That was a fair piece of work," says Tolt. "And all that free publicity."

"And I thought nobody noticed."

"Ever do any white-collar work?" he asks.

"Some."

"Really." His eyebrows go up a notch, wondering, I'm

sure, how fast my fingers might be able to work the billing software on the unattended computer in Nick's office. He leaves the closed briefcase on his desk and settles back in his chair. "How long did you say you knew Nick?"

"We go back a few years."

He sits silent, looking over the desk at me, waiting for details. I offer none.

"Unfortunately I didn't know him all that well. I regret that I didn't take more time with the man. I suspect he resented it, but unfortunately Nick didn't understand how hard it is running a firm like this. Grumbling partners, every one of them wanting bigger bonuses at the end of the year, having to reason with them constantly in order to expand. Practicing law in a firm like this is like trying to herd cats and they're trying to fight. It doesn't help that the last two years we're down on profits."

I'm starting to bleed for him, looking at the priceless Matisse framed in gilt behind his chair.

"Too many lawyers," he says.

"From what I hear, still looking for more."

He smiles.

"Nick and I would pass each other coming and going. Talk at Christmas parties. I think we collaborated twice on cases. Client business matters that went awry."

What he means is that Nick was called in when the firm needed help cleaning up a criminal mess left behind by one of their clients whose business practices went up on two wheels cutting corners.

"And then he did a few drug cases. I don't think there were a lot of them. We tried to keep him in the white-collar area as much as possible."

"I see. That's as far down the criminal food chain as the firm wanted to go, is that it?"

"Something like that. Don't misunderstand me. I don't want you to think I would disparage what other lawyers do. Their clients are certainly entitled to a vigorous defense."

"But not here?"

"Well . . ." The answer is in his expression. "Unfortunately we're a little thin on the criminal side right now. I mean we have a couple of young associates, but Nick was the guiding light. So we couldn't afford to have him doing other things. And now we do have a problem. With Nick gone, we have to start looking for somebody to fill the void. Nick had cases. They need tending," he says. "That's your field. Maybe you could give us some recommendations?"

If I didn't know better, I might think he was offering me a job. Crisis of the moment: like men of power everywhere, Adam Tolt realizes the only problems that count at this moment are those belonging to him.

"Maybe we should wait for the body to get cold," I tell him.

"Of course," he says. "Thoughtless of me." The words may pass through his lips, but the commercial squint does not leave his eyes. Tolt is a cross between FDR and the devil. He has the toothy grin, the flamboyant hail-fellow-well-met, and the presence of command, everything but the cigarette holder and the paralysis. In fact, he seems remarkably fit and moves like a man half his age.

"I wish I could do more for you," he says. "But you understand the problem? On the insurance?"

"Yes."

"What do you plan to do now?"

"I'll go back and tell Mrs. Rush. Can I get a copy of the policy?"

"I don't see why not. I'll make a note and have one mailed to your office. Of course, they could resolve it," he says. "The two wives."

"How?"

"Agree to share the policy."

"What's the face amount?" I ask.

"Two million," he says. "They'd have to agree to each take half."

"Why would the named beneficiary agree to that?"

"Well, she could have some problems too. There could be a property settlement agreement when they divorced that could undercut her claim to the insurance."

"Is there a settlement agreement?"

"I assume," he says. "You would think leaving her name on the policy after a divorce was an oversight." He looks at me over steepled forefingers, his elbows on the arms of the chair, then sits up and clicks the snap locks closed on his briefcase. A grand an hour, a hundred sixty-five dollars every ten minutes, small talk off the clock gets expensive.

"And if it can't be resolved by settlement?" I ask.

He makes a face, looks at me. "Then I suppose the carrier will have to file an interpleader."

What he means is a stakeholder's action, a legal free-for-all in which the insurance company will throw up its hands, confess that it owes money but doesn't know who to pay. A court will have to sort it out. After a year or two of litigation, with lawyers for the insurance company and the two women brawling in open court, a check will be made out, but whose name will be on the payout line is anybody's guess. The only thing more certain than death is that the lion's share will go to the lawyers.

Harry was right. I've stepped in it. Now I will have to call Dana and give her the sorry news. The old saw is on the mark: the last people on earth to have their wills up-to-date and their affairs in order when they die are attorneys.

CHAPTER NINE

This morning Harry has information. It comes by way of a telephone call from a friend of his, a deputy D.A. he meets with on Thursday evenings in a friendly card game. Last night between shuffling and dealing, the guy let slip that an arrest has been made by federal authorities, not in Nick's murder, but according to this prosecutor there may be a connection.

Harry is standing in the doorway to my office having just bought a newspaper from the rack in front of the cigar store out on the street. He is scanning the inside pages. On the front page, which is open to me, is a picture of a crane swinging a wrecking ball through the sign on top of the old Capri Hotel, Nick's morning coffee shop. If he is looking down, or for that matter up, I can't help but wonder what he would say about this.

"Here it is," says Harry. "It's just a short piece." The headline reads:

Arrest in Visa Theft

A taskforce of federal and local law enforcement agencies led by agents of the Immigration and Naturalization Service as well as federal customs agents raided a residence in Santee last night, and an arrest in connection with the theft of thousands of border crossing visas in Tijuana last May.

The visas, issued by the Immigration and Naturalization Service, are used for short-term stays in the U.S. They were stolen from a commercial delivery van at gunpoint near the U.S. Consul's office in Tijuana on May 23.

Arrested was Miguelito Espinoza, a local labor contractor whose business involves hiring unskilled labor, mostly for work in agriculture. According to authorities, Espinoza was in his home at the time of the raid and offered no resistance.

Authorities refused to say whether they found any evidence in Espinoza's residence. The visas are believed to be worth as much as a million dollars on the black market, where they can be sold and used to enter the U.S. by undocumented aliens or by those seeking to smuggle people or contraband into the country.

Authorities have been searching for the missing visas for months. According to sources who declined to be identified, the documents represent the latest in laser identity technology and include holographs. It is feared that the hijackers who took the visas may be able to copy the laser technology in order to forge new cards.

Harry lowers the paper and looks over the top at me. "That's it."

"Why does your friend at the D.A.'s office think this is connected to Nick and the shooting?"

"What he said was, the guy they arrested was somehow involved with Metz."

"Did he say how?"

"He didn't say, and I didn't want to crawl across the table and ask him. I got the sense that he probably didn't know."

"Do you think he'd tell you if you called him and asked him?"

Harry shakes his head. "We're friendly, but not that friendly. What he did say is that the guy they arrested, this . . ." He looks at the article again. "This Espinoza, he was under surveillance by the feds for some time prior to the arrest. We're talking months," says Harry. "And I mean a blanket. Immigration wanted these visas back in the worst way according to what I heard. The D.A. wants to shake the guy to find out if he knows anything about the shooting. They're assuming he couldn't have been directly involved since the feds were watching him at the time. But they think he may know something. I didn't even want to bring it to you, but I knew you'd want to know."

"Thanks."

Harry starts fixing himself a cup of tea, hot water in a cup in the microwave across the hall. He comes back dunking the tea bag on a string. "Did Tolt have a copy of the insurance policy?"

"What?"

"The key-man policy for Rush's wife?"

"Oh. Yeah. He's sending it to us in the mail."

"Was he cooperative?"

"I suppose. As much as he could be. There's some question, a complication," I tell him.

"What kind of complication?"

"Seems her name is not on the policy as the beneficiary."

"I'd call that a complication. Who's name is on it?"

"The first wife."

Harry rolls his eyes toward the ceiling. "So what are you going to do about it?"

"I don't know."

"Let me give you some advice. Send her the policy when it comes, put a cover letter on it, and tell her to get a good insurance lawyer."

"I can't do that."

"Why not?"

"Because there are others involved."

"Who?"

If we get drawn in, I'm going to be asking Harry to give up his fee. He deserves an answer.

"There is a child. Nick had a daughter out of wedlock a few years ago, before he met Dana. Her name is Laura."

Harry looks at me. Mental tumblers turning in his head. "The envelope the cops found with the cash in Nick's pocket," says Harry.

I nod. "Nick had been paying support since the birth. No court order. Voluntarily. No one except the mother and him knew about it. It was the way they wanted it."

"And you want to get the insurance for the child."

"Unfortunately, I can't. That's going to be governed by the terms of the insurance contract. What I can do is to cut a piece out for her."

"Our fees?"

"I nod."

Harry nods. "Why didn't you tell me earlier?"

"I couldn't. If the cops questioned you, you could honestly say you didn't know anything. I wanted to protect their privacy. This way they won't have to be a party to the scramble for insurance."

"Why didn't Nick put the kid's name on the policy?"

"He probably wasn't planning on dying quite yet. And to name her as beneficiary would put her head-to-head with Dana in the claims department. I suspect it's the reason he left Margaret's name on the policy. That way it might be up for grabs. The child could get something if the mother decided to pursue it and Margaret was found to have an invalid claim based on the divorce. I owe that much to Nick. He'd do the same if I were in his situation."

"You very nearly were," he says.

"Don't remind me."

"I understand. I only wish you'd told me earlier. Have a little more faith in me."

"It wasn't a matter of trust."

"I understand." Harry is hurt. "Of course we give up our fees. No question."

Harry is looking down into the dark tea in his cup, wondering if he should just leave it there. But he can't. "Rush's death wasn't your fault," he says.

"Who said it was?"

"Nobody. It's just that sometimes I think you have some lingering doubts. Especially now that I know what's driving it. Did she know him, the child I mean?"

I nod. "According to Nick he went over whenever he could. She thought he was her uncle. You could see it in his eyes—he loved her. Told me how smart she was. How happy."

"Still it's not your fault. You recognized Metz for what he was and you opted out. You gave Nick fair warning. Would you rather it was Sarah who was without a father right now?"

"Believe me I've thought about that. I thought about what Nick might do in my situation. The four grand a month Nick was paying her mother isn't there anymore."

"And you're thinking the insurance money?" Harry is already there.

"That's what I'm thinking. And when she gets a little older, I suspect she is going to have a lot of questions about her father, who he was and how he died. It might be nice if there were some answers, something beyond the hideous speculation on yellowed newsprint about her dad doing business and dying with a client who was indicted."

"The money I understand. Looking for answers as to who shot him and why is something for the cops."

"Maybe. But I don't see them busting their hump looking."

"Could it be they figure Nick got what he deserved?" says Harry.

"One criminal defense lawyer more or less is not something high on their list."

"You think it's going to end up in the file of unsolved cases?"

"That's what I'm thinking."

"Then maybe that's where it belongs."

"And what if you were his daughter?"

"I'm not, and neither are you. Besides, what if you go looking and you don't like the answers you find? What then?"

"Cross that bridge when I come to it."

Harry shakes his head. "If it's something you're doing for Nick, you can forget it. The man's beyond sentiments of appreciation." Harry gulps a little tea.

"You know, Harry, I hope if somebody shoots me dead on the street, you would at least take a passing interest."

"Is that what you're doing? Well. God forbid," he says, "but if somebody shoots you, I'd probably shed some tears. I'd bury you in style, say some moving words over your grave. I'd do what I could to look after Sarah. Or at least see that she was cared for. I'd think about you a lot, and I'd get on with my life."

"Hard-nosed," I say.

"On things I can't control, you're damn right. We made a decision," he says, "a long time ago. We take no drug cases. We agreed. For good reason. There's too much time spent coming up to speed on the decisional law, the flow of appellate opinions on the subject being on the order of a ruptured sewer over Niagara. Besides, there are some things you just don't want to do. Like climbing up on the legal stump for organized crime. You can end up finding out about things you'd rather not know. Stuff that keeps you up nights wondering if you hooked all the chains and turned all the bolts on your doors and whether you have enough bars on your windows."

"That's why I didn't take Metz," I tell him.

"Right," says Harry. "Because we agreed. So why don't you blame me that Nick got his ass shot off? I can live with it." With this he turns and heads out the door, down the hall toward his office.

For several minutes I sit there looking at the newspaper article, the name Miguelito Espinoza, and wondering what Metz would want with border-crossing visas.

Then I go out to the reception. Marta is there catching up on filing. I open one of the file cabinets, the drawer labeled M through O.

"Can I find something for you?" Marta looks up from her desk.

"Think I found it." I pull the file on Gerald Metz.

"How's your day going?" I ask.

"Good." She smiles brightly.

Within ninety days, in her efficient way, Marta would have closed this file, there being no billing activity. She would have placed it in archives, in one of the cardboard boxes stored in the bungalow two doors down. And if she is still with us in a few years, she would toss it, have it hauled to some landfill, the ultimate archive of American culture.

Quietly I retreat to my office with the file. There isn't much in it, the few letters given to me by Metz that morning in my office, along with my notes, scrawled on some pages from a yellow notepad. There on the third page written out and underlined twice is the name Miguelito Espinoza, with an address and telephone number in Santee. It was the name on the rat-eared business card given to me that morning in my office by Metz. Espinoza had acted as the go-between with the two brothers down in Mexico on their supposed development scheme with Metz.

I haven't seen Margaret Rush in more than three years, so when she opens the front door, she gives me an expression that says she recognizes the face but can't quite fix the name.

"Margaret, it's Paul Madriani."

A moment of hesitation and then: "Oh yes." She smiles, struggles to arrange her hair with the back of one hand. There is dirt under her fingernails. She is wearing a pair of jeans with smudges of mud at the knees.

"I'm afraid you caught me gardening," she says.

"I wonder if I could come in for just a moment?"

She hesitates, caught between concerns for security and

a social blunder, then fumbles with the latch on the screen door. "Of course."

"It's been a long time," I tell her.

"It has." I can tell she is still not entirely certain who I am. She recognizes the name, the face, but can't quite place the setting in which we met.

"I think we saw each other last on that bay cruise. The county bar reception, a few years ago," I tell her.

"Oh. Yes." Recognition lights up her eyes. "You were a friend of Nick's."

"I was."

Her expression tells me she now regrets letting me in. "I really don't have much time," she says. "I was just getting ready to head out."

"I won't take but a minute."

"What is it you want?" she says. "You'll have to make it quick."

"How have you been?"

"Me? I've been fine." She stands in the entryway. "Can I ask what this is about?"

"Can we go in and sit down?" I ask.

"I suppose. But I only have a minute."

She turns toward the living room and I follow her. The room is small, on the order of the house itself, a single-story rambler on a street of well-groomed strips of front lawn, lined with established Japanese elms. There is a sofa against one wall facing the front window and the street. Feminine knickknacks of china and crystal and a small antique tea set line shelves that are high on the wall and surround the room. There is a beveled glass china cabinet against one wall and a single wingback chair in the corner next to the fireplace. She sits in this, leaving me to take the couch.

"I didn't see you at the funeral, but then there were a lot of people."

"Nick's funeral?" she says.

"Yes."

"I wasn't there. That part of my life ended some time ago," she says. "What is it you want to talk about?"

It seems we are not going to do any small talk.

Her hair has gone gray since I saw her last. Wrinkles envelope her face around the eyes. The tense expression on her face tells me that she may have washed Nick out of her life years ago, but thoughts of him still occupy dark recesses of her mind.

"How's your son, Jimmy is it?"

"James," she says. "He's fine."

"I wanted to talk to you about Nick."

"What about him?" she says.

"It's actually about his estate."

"Oh, yes. Now I understand. They called from the firm a couple of days ago and told me. It's the insurance policy, isn't it?"

"Yes, the key-man policy," I tell her.

"Did she send you?"

"Who?"

"Who," she says in a mocking tone, the creases around her eyes focusing the anger in her voice. "You know who I mean. Dana."

"No."

"Then why are you here?"

"To avoid a problem," I tell her. "To resolve a potential dispute. Maybe to do what I think is right."

"And what is that?"

"Nick is dead. He's out of everyone's life at this point, yours, hers. There may be aspects of this policy that benefit both of you."

"You sound just like Nick, just trying to make peace, fix everything for everybody. Oh, by the way, I'm screwing my interior decorator and I'd like a divorce, but it's nothing personal."

"You have every reason to be angry."

"You bet I do."

"But in your anger, you don't want to hurt yourself," I tell her.

"What do you mean?"

"You've received a copy of the policy?"

"Yes."

"And you know your name is on it as the beneficiary?"

"I do."

"You're also aware that there was a property settlement agreement at the time of the divorce?"

She looks at me but doesn't respond. She knows this is the issue.

"I take it you're represented by a lawyer in this matter?"

"Why should I have to tell you that?"

"You don't have to tell me anything. If you are, represented by a lawyer I mean, that's good. If so, I should be talking to him."

"It's a woman." She says it in a tone that makes me think male lawyers are not to be trusted.

"If you'll give me her name, I'll take it up with her and she can communicate with you."

"Her name is Susan Glendenin."

"She works for the Petersen law firm downtown?"

"That's right."

"I know her." A stroke of good luck. Susan Glendenin is a good lawyer; more important, she is a voice of reason in a bar increasingly peopled by lawyers who pride themselves on taking no prisoners and who operate on the maxim "screw reason, let's go to war."

"What's important is to understand that this is a threshold legal issue, the question of who is to be paid under the insurance policy."

"What do you mean?"

"I mean the way it's structured, the insurance company has to pay somebody. They don't particularly care who it is, just as long as they're out from under when it's all over."

"And?"

"There may be a way for both of you to win."

"What was your name again?"

"Paul Madriani." I reach into the breast pocket of my suit coat, find the small stash of business cards, pull one out, and hand it to her.

"Let me tell you, Mr. Madriani, so that you understand.

I will take two million dollars and not a dime less," she says. "You can go back to your client, that harlot, home wrecker," she says, "and tell her that as far as I'm concerned she can go to hell. Fuck her, fuck you, and fuck the horse you rode in on. Now if you'll excuse me, I have things I have to take care of." She gets up out of the chair.

"I have one question," I say.

"What's that?"

"Do you mean it when you say you'll only release your claim to the insurance policy in return for two million dollars?"

She looks at me through mean little slits, the anger of a lifetime welled up in her eyes, bitterness and betrayal. "You can bet your life on it," she says.

CHAPTER· TEN

This morning Dana is wearing a pair of silk pajamas, black and slinky, bare-footed, sitting up straight on the edge of a wingback chair in her living room, one leg curled under her, trying to explain how she found Nick's copy of the insurance policy but forgot to call and tell me.

"I swear to you, Mr. Madriani. I got busy. It slipped my mind."

"Call me Paul," I tell her.

"All right. Paul. I found it after we talked. It was up in his safe, in the study." Dana looks at me over a haggard smile, desperate to be believed, innocent, beseeching, sitting next to the fireplace.

"You do believe me?" She flashes her long lashes in my direction. The body language is good, the shiver in her voice authentic, so if I didn't know her better, I might even buy this. She sent me on a goose chase to the law firm to get a copy of the policy when she already knew what was in it.

"Please believe me," she says.

I stop looking at her. Instead, seated on the couch, I turn my attention to one of those kinetic toys that Nick had strewn around his office. This one is on the coffee table, the kind with five shiny steel spheres on strings, clicking against one another as they transfer energy through a cycle. I let her listen to this for a second or two before I ask: "How did you get the safe open?"

"I found the combination."

"Where was it?"

"It was in one of the drawers. In Nick's desk upstairs."

"Maybe we should look and see what else is inside the safe. There could be other important documents." I start to get up off the couch.

"No. That's not necessary," she says. "I've checked everything that was there. There's nothing else."

I look at her. She refuses to return my gaze. "You know, you're pretty good. You're not the best, but then you haven't had a lot of practice. At least I hope you haven't."

"Practice at what?"

"Lying."

"What do you mean?"

"You expect me to believe that Nick would go to all the trouble of locking his private papers in a safe and then leave the combination in his desk drawer where any after-school roustabout teen who broke into his house could find it? Maybe you were married to a different Nick Rush than the one I knew." I start to get up off the couch like I am going to leave.

"All right." Now the pleading tone is gone from her voice, replaced by an edge. Her posture sags in the chair, as she looks down, smoothing the soft wrinkles from the silk fabric on one thigh. "Fine. I had the insurance policy all the time." Then in a softer, weaker voice, the kind she uses for feminine persuasion, she says, looking up at me, "But I didn't know what to do. I saw her name on it and I panicked. I was desperate, broke. I had no one to turn to. You do understand? You don't know what it's like not having someone . . . Well you know. Someone to rely on."

"Someone like Nick?" I say.

"Well, yes. He handled everything. Our finances, taxes, the investments. I had no idea. I thought we were secure. I don't know anything about that stuff."

"Then how do you know you're broke?"

She takes a deep breath, sighs, looks away from me at a blank wall. "I, I had Nathan look at our finances. After Nick died."

"Fittipaldi?"

She nods.

"It's good to know you weren't entirely alone," I tell her.

She doesn't appreciate the sarcasm. "I had to turn to someone. What did you expect me to do?"

"Why didn't you turn over the insurance policy to Mr. Fittipaldi?"

"We talked about it. He didn't know what to do either."

"Ahh-uhh."

"I figured you were a friend of Nick's. I thought . . . I thought that since you'd known Nick before we were married, that perhaps . . ."

"You thought I'd go over to the firm, find out that your name wasn't on the policy, that I might feel sorry for you, and that maybe I would go over and talk to Margaret Rush, is that it?"

"Well." First she looks at the ceiling, then back to me, batting her lashes a little. "Yes. I thought you might know her. That maybe you were a friend."

"You thought I might be able to intercede, is that it?"

"Was I wrong?" she says.

"No. Maybe a little naive," I tell her, "but that was more than made up for by your seamless manipulation of the situation. I mean it was worth a try, friends being friends and all."

"Yes. I thought she might listen to you."

I laugh and click the little steel balls on the table one more time. "Actually I've only met her once. But even if we were bosom buddies, you'd have to think very highly of friendship to believe that Maggie Rush or anybody else would give up a claim on two million bucks based on that."

"So she refused?"

"In words that I wouldn't want to repeat in polite company," I tell her.

Dana is up out of the chair, turns her back to me, the nails of one hand to her mouth as if she's going to bite them to the quick. I gaze at her reflection in the mirror over the fireplace. She stands there, nibbling, pupils searching an invisible horizon as she contemplates her next move.

Suddenly she turns, looks at me, and says: "What do we do now?"

Before I can say anything, she's sitting on the couch next to me, pushing the kinetic toy out of reach so that she has my undivided attention. Silk rubbing against the worsted wool of suit pants.

"I suppose you should call Nathan and give him the news," I tell her. "I don't know what I'm going to do. Probably go back to the office and get some work done."

"You know what I mean," she says. She reaches over and takes my left hand in both of hers. "You will help me, won't you? You talked to the woman. You know how she feels toward me. She hates me. You know that Nick didn't intend to leave her all that money. They were divorced."

"That's true." I start to get up off the couch.

"You're not going?" she says. "Please don't go. You're the only one who can help me. You talked to the firm. You know they treated Nick unfairly. You would think they would want to help now."

"I talked to Adam Tolt."

"And?"

"It seems he'd rather not get involved. As far as he's concerned, it's between you and the insurance company."

This ratchets up her anxiety so that she squeezes my hand until the blood leaves my fingertips.

"You were Nick's friend. You wouldn't let them do this. I mean not to your friend's wife. Tell me you wouldn't."

"You need to get a good lawyer," I tell her. Harry would be proud of me.

"I've got one," she says. "You."

"No, I mean a lawyer who knows how to find his way around an insurance policy. Trap all those little wiggle words, nail down the exclusions, screw the definitions to the floor so the insurance company can't move them around on you. And that settlement agreement Nick had with Margaret. I hope he had a good lawyer draw it up."

"What do you mean?"

"Because that's the key," I tell her. "If that wasn't drafted properly, well, let's just say no lawyer, especially a good one who knows insurance, is going to want to waste much time on it."

"You don't think I have a chance?" I've seen people accused in capital cases with less apprehension etched in their eyes. "Have you looked at it?" she says. "The settlement agreement."

"No. But contract law is not my strong suit."

She drops my hand like a dead fish.

"Who, who should I get?"

"I don't know."

"You must know somebody. If it's money, I can pay," she says.

"I thought you were broke."

"I can get it."

"It's not just money."

"Then what is it?"

"Let me think about it for a few days," I tell her.

"Oh, good. Of course. Take all the time you need. You must think I'm awful. I mean to get you involved like this."

"What are friends for, right?"

"I knew you'd help me." At the moment the friends she's thinking about all have Grant's picture engraved on them.

"Nick must have shared a great deal with you," I tell her.

"What?" Her mind is other places.

"I mean about his work. What he did?"

"Not really."

"From what he told me, the two of you were very close."

"Well, yes, we loved each other, if that's what you mean."

"And I'll bet there was pillow talk." I look at her. She looks at me. I smile. She blushes.

"Well, a little."

"Good. Then he must have told you about Jamaile Enterprises?"

She looks at me, a quizzical expression. "No. I don't think so. What is it?"

"It's a corporation—or was until it failed to pay its franchise tax fee."

"What does it have to do with Nick?"

"He was one of the corporate directors."

"I don't know anything about it. I've never heard of it. He never said anything to me," she says.

"I thought he might have, since the only other officer in this company was an acquaintance of yours."

"Who is that?"

"Gerald Metz."

Her eyes grow dark with this news, pupils shifting as she processes the information. "What? No. He never said a thing." I can sense questions fulminating in her mind like popcorn over a hot fire. "When did they do this? Did Nick tell you?"

"Over a year ago, and no, Nick didn't tell me."

If she knows anything, you would not be able to detect it from the expression of confusion on her face. "I don't understand."

"That makes two of us. Nick told me you met Mr. Metz on the arts commission."

"That's right."

"When was that?"

"I don't know. Probably the first meeting I attended," she says. "Now that you mention it, he seemed to know who I was."

"How?"

"I don't know. He just came up and introduced himself. Said, 'You're married to Nick Rush, aren't you?' "

"Then he admitted he knew Nick?"

"No. I asked him, and he said he only knew him by name. He'd seen it in the paper. That sort of thing. With the kind of clients Nick had, he couldn't keep his name out of the papers even if he wanted to, which he didn't."

I sit there silently mulling this information. Dana's not looking at me. Instead her eyes are cast down at the carpet.

"How did you find out about this, this business thing between the two of them?"

"The police," I tell her. "We were able to confirm . . ."

"The police?"

"Yes."

"They never said anything to me."

"Maybe they didn't want to bother you with it." I can tell this weighs heavily.

"How did they find out?"

"I don't know."

There's a long silence as she thinks. "I told them that I had referred Metz to Nick," she says.

"Well, as far as you knew at the time, that was the truth. Right?"

"Absolutely."

I can tell from the stark expression this has not been one of Dana's better days. First the insurance, now the cops with information that her husband had dealings with Metz before she knew him, information that is inconsistent with what she had told them. She has to wonder what they are thinking.

"How did Metz approach you regarding his legal problems?" I ask. "What exactly did he say?"

I can tell her mind is already headed in the same direction, trying to reconstruct events. "It . . . it was at a meeting." Now she's flustered. Information overload, too much of it disturbing, or maybe she just wants me to think so.

"I think it was in March. Last spring anyway. He came up to me after the meeting and said he knew that I was married to a good lawyer and that he needed some help with a business problem he was having. I told him my husband did criminal law, and he said that—that's what he needed."

"Did he give you any details about this problem?"

"Nothing. Just that he had needed a lawyer."

"Had you ever talked with Metz before this conversation?"

"Sure. I mean there's twenty-eight people on the commission. We meet. We talk. We serve as a clearinghouse for NEA grants in the county. National Endowment for the Arts."

"Is there much money involved?"

"It depends. Some of the grants are large. We're reviewing one for a new opera house that could involve a few million dollars. Most of them are small individual grants."

"How about Metz? Did he usually show up for meetings?"

"Most of the time. We had talked socially a few times, discussed things. I can't say that I knew him well."

"Do you know how Metz got on the commission?"

"I assume the same way we all did, by appointment of one of the county supervisors."

I consider this as she looks at me.

"Just out of curiosity, who appointed you?"

"I knew you were going to ask. The cops did, and I couldn't remember. How embarrassing," she says. "But I looked on my appointment papers afterward. It was Supervisor Tresler."

"Do you know him?"

She shakes her head. "Not personally. I mean I may have met him at some function or other. If I did, I don't remember. I'm not really into politics."

I am thinking, "Yes you are, just not the kind where people cast secret ballots."

"Then how did you get appointed?"

"Nick thought it would be good for me. I think he was trying to find something I'd enjoy. It's not a big deal," she says. "I mean it's not one of the best commissions. There are some boards, advisory groups that pay a salary. There's no compensation for the arts commission. They cover some expenses. Once every year, a small group gets to go to Europe, for meetings with art exhibitors. It's on a rotating basis. I haven't had a chance." She looks down. "I guess now I may not have a chance. I mean I may have to resign and find a job. I don't know what else I can tell you. You will help me, won't you?" Dana's back to my hand again, giving it the squeeze treatment, so that when I stand up I have to stoop over to release her grip.

"I'll do what I can. I'll get back to you."

With Nick and Metz dead and the cops chasing rainbows looking for the killer, the only viable lead at the moment is the man Espinoza. For the time being, he's rotting in a federal detention facility downtown, waiting for the federal public defender to have bail set.

What I'm afraid of, given the vagaries of federal judges, is that some magistrate with a wild hair up his ass might set a figure that Espinoza or one of his associates could match. In which case, they would turn the man loose and Espinoza would disappear in a heartbeat—my last chance to get information.

So this afternoon I'm sticking my head in the legal lion's mouth, running and capping, trying to snag him as a client to keep him in jail.

As I approach the front door, I can hear a television set inside, the zany music and voices of cartoons.

Over the top of this, a baby is screaming.

I knock on the door. Whoever is inside doesn't hear it. I check the street number stenciled over the front door one more time. If Miguelito Espinoza's family or whoever lived here with him hasn't moved, it's the right address.

This time I knock louder. After a couple of seconds, a shadow moves inside through the frosted glass.

"Who is it?"

"My name is Paul Madriani."

"What do you want?"

"I'm looking for the family of Miguelito Espinoza."

All I can hear is the sound of the television and a baby crying on the other side of the door.

"What do you want with them?" The door opens a few inches, safety chained at eye level. A blue eye bounded by some straight, blond, straggly hair peeking through at the level of my chest.

"Hello." I beam my most disarming, nonthreatening smile and slip a business card through the opening. She takes it with a hand, trying to hold the baby at the same time while she reads.

"I'm a lawyer. I think I can help Mr. Espinoza."

"You've seen Michael? You talked to him?"

"Are you his wife?"

She looks at me again but doesn't answer, then checks the card one more time.

"He had nothing to do with that stuff," she says. "I know Michael. He wouldn't do nothin' like that. Besides he told me when they took him away they had nothin', no evidence." She is talking as if I am going to try the case standing here on her front steps, through a chained door.

"That's what I thought," I tell her. "Can I come in?"

"When did you talk to him?"

"I really don't want to stand out here and talk about something like this on the front porch. I have some papers for you to sign."

"What for?"

"So I can represent him."

Suddenly the door closes. I hear the chain being slid across the brass groove. It opens again, this time all the way. There in the doorway is what can only be described as a child-woman, maybe five-foot-two, a hundred pounds soaking wet. She has long, dirty-blond hair and is wearing a threadbare pair of jeans and a man's flannel shirt four sizes too large. She is bare footed standing on the dirty carpet inside the door. In her arms she is holding an infant wrapped in a blue blanket. I cannot see its face. Hers is oval, its features fine, almost birdlike, a drooping mouth that looks as if it has lost the ability to smile.

"He's hungry," she says.

From the wailing tones issuing from the blanket, there is nothing wrong with the baby's lungs.

"What did Michael say? Did he ask about me?"

I ignore her questions. "Can I come in?"

"Yeah." As I step inside, she looks behind me, out toward the street as if maybe she is expecting someone else. Then she closes the door, holds the child in one arm as she turns the bolt on the lock and slides the security chain back into place.

She turns and crosses into the living room, stepping over articles of clothing, old newspapers and empty soda cans, and what looks like a discarded disposable diaper. There are discolored stains on the carpet that cause me to suspect that pets may have been part of Miguelito's life at some point. An empty pizza box lies on the middle of the floor, melted cheese hardened like white plastic stuck to its cardboard innards.

Child-woman reaches for the button on the television. The baby stops crying for a second, then starts up again.

"He likes the noise of the television," she says. "Sometimes it quiets him." She pulls the blanket back and strokes the infant's head, cradling him in the other arm, as she tries to comfort him.

"What did he say? Can you get him out of jail? I don't have any food left in the house," she says. "Can Michael get some money to me?"

"Are you his wife?"

She nods.

"What's your name?"

"Robin. Robin Watkins. Espinoza," she says. "We were married last summer."

"Do you have some proof? A marriage license."

"Why should I have to prove it?"

"It's necessary if I'm going to represent your husband."

"Somewhere," she says.

"Can you find it?"

"Just a minute." She half runs and skips down the hall,

footfalls nearly imperceptible even on the worn pad of this threadbare carpet. I stand near the entrance to the living room surveying the litter on the floor. Against the wall is a sofa that has seen better days, upholstery that has been shredded on one arm. Signs of a cat.

I hear mother and child rummaging through things in the other room, drawers opening and slamming closed, things dropping on the floor. After a minute or so, I hear her coming back down the hall. Walking this time, quickly but more composed. She straightens her hair with one hand, conscious for the first time that her appearance may be important to her husband's welfare. She juggles the baby and an envelope in the fingers of the hand cradled under the child. She holds the envelope out and I take it.

"Can you get him out on bail?" she asks.

Inside the envelope is a single-page document. I take it out and unfold it. It's a marriage certificate issued in this county the previous July to Miguelito Espinoza Garza and Robin Lynn Watkins. Robin lists her age as eighteen. I would not want to have to verify this under oath.

"Can you?" she says. "Get him out?"

"I don't know. I need you to sign something."

"They wouldn't let me even talk to him," she says. "They got him down there in that big building. The tall white one downtown. I went inside and they won't even tell him I was there." Her right cheek has a smudge of dirt on it, Little Orphan Annie. "They told me I had to leave or they'd arrest me." More than likely they'd call a truant officer to pick her up.

"Do you know if he's represented by anyone else?" I ask. "The federal public defender?"

She shrugs her shoulders, shakes her head. "Like I said, they wouldn't tell me nothin'." She looks at me with big blue empty eyes.

"How long have you known Michael?" I ask.

"Why do you wanna know?"

"It would help to know some background."

"We met at the fair up in Pomona. Last summer. I was

working one of the kiddy rides and Michael came by. He saw me." She smiles with thoughts of love at first sight, not looking at me, but off into the distance, kind of dreamy. "We lived together for a while," she says. "But then Michael said I could get some money from the county if we were married. He wasn't here a lot so . . . Maybe I shouldn't be telling you this."

"It's all right."

"I get welfare. It's for my baby," she says. "I'm probably not supposed to. But Michael's not around. He travels. I'm getting worried," she says, "cuz I got no more money for formula. I spent it. My baby's hungry." She's back to stroking it's head, kissing the little face lost in the blanket.

Under my arm I'm carrying a thin leather folder. I open it and take out a single typed sheet I prepared before leaving the office. With a pen I print her name under the signature line at the bottom.

"This is an authorization and an agreement for legal services," I tell her. "It allows me to represent Michael. Here." I hand her the pen. We juggle the baby and I end up holding it while she takes the folder, paper, and pen.

"Where do I sign?"

"On the bottom. The line above your name." I point with one finger from under the baby. It is still screaming, pangs of hunger.

She doesn't ask why I need this, if I've already seen her husband. Instead when she looks up she says, "How am I gonna pay you?"

We exchange baby and briefcase. I put the signed paper back inside, then I lift my wallet from the inside pocket of my coat and open it. In the billfold I have four hundreds and some smaller bills. I pull the hundreds out and hand them to her.

"Here, this is for you. Michael and I will make arrangements. Don't worry about it."

Her eyes light up. "Get some food for the baby, and groceries for yourself."

CHAPTER ELEVEN

M id June and we are huddled in Adam Tolt's walnut-
paneled conference room.

"Glenda. Adam here. You can show them all in." Tolt re-
places the receiver in its cradle and settles against the high
back of the tufted leather chair as he looks at me. We are
seated against the glistening surface of the table in the executive conference room that adjoins his office. This is the
holy of holies, the place where the firm's management committee meets quarterly to chart the bottom line, where it
doles out bonuses and inducts new partners into the fold, no
doubt with secret handshakes.

"I'm gonna let you handle it," says Tolt. He's referring to
the negotiations about to start.

"I'll just make the introductions, and then if there's anything I can do . . . well." He makes an aristocratic gesture, a
sweep with the back of one hand you might expect from a
Venetian doge. His hand passes over the leather folder with
its gold corners and the black Mont Blanc pen resting atop it
like a sleek torpedo.

Tolt's eyes study the door behind me as the fingers of one hand, adorned by a gold university ring, tap the tabletop in a drumroll one might expect as a prelude to an execution.

Adam has by instinct taken the place of honor at the head of the table. It is his turf. He does not think much of my chances here today, particularly in light of the intractable positions taken by the two women, Dana and Margaret Rush. Neither is willing to settle for less than two million, the full face amount of the policy on Nick's life, though I suspect I could cause Dana to buckle if I pushed. I have not shared my arguments with Tolt. I am not sure whether I can trust him. So he will be hearing everything for the first time as I lay it out.

The door across from me opens, and I look up. Tolt's administrative assistant plays usher, shepherding them in. The first face through the door is ruddy, red with rosacea, a man about six feet tall, well built, I would guess in his late forties, with close-cropped blond hair, combed over and parted on the left like a prairie banker. He wears a well-turned dark suit, power pinstripes for whatever psychological advantage it might provide. He studies me briefly through searing blue eyes offering nothing but the confidence of his grin, the kind you get from politicians feeling their oats and business types who have climbed over other bodies on the way to the top.

According to the playbook and the descriptions I have been given by Tolt, I am guessing that this is Luther Conover, senior adjuster and vice president for claims at Devon Insurance, the principal underwriter on the key-man policy for Nick's life.

"Luther. Good to see you." Tolt gets up out of his chair. "It's been a while."

"It has. Too long. When was the last time? I think it was up at the northern regionals when our board met. When was that? Two years ago?"

"Sounds right. How's Julie and the kids?"

"Oh, they're fine. The twins are headed to college next year."

"No." Adam loads his voice with doubt.

"Eighteen," says Conover.

"I can't believe that. They were just little things." Tolt holds his hand at a level even with the tabletop. "It has been a while," he says.

"Thank God for little favors," says Conover. "It's not that I don't like to see you," he says, "but I'm not sure my wallet can handle the stress."

"Nonsense," says Adam. "We always have a wonderful time. Besides, it's not your money."

"Yes, but your hands keep stretching my pockets out of shape." Conover looks at me and laughs, the signal for me to join in. It's all very cordial, chuckles all around. I have no idea what they're talking about other than to gather that Tolt has put his own mark on Devon Insurance in the past.

"I want to introduce you to Paul Madriani." Just like that Tolt acquaints Conover with the hand aimed at his other pocket.

We shake. He gives me the same solid grin he offered charging through the door, the once-over to assess the latest lawyer trying to shake him down. He quickly turns his attention back to Adam and they talk golf, kibitzing and quizzing each other on current handicaps.

"We'll have to get you over to Temecula," says Conover.

"Seems I only get to play these days when I'm on vacation," says Adam.

"Where's that?"

"Out at de Anza."

"You have a membership?"

Tolt nods. "We bought a condo on the fourteenth fairway. We spend some time there."

"How is Margo?"

"She's good. Healthy. She keeps me in shape."

"De Anza. That's a little rich for my blood." Conover looks again in my direction. "You play golf, Mr. Madriani?"

"Sorry to say it's not one of my vices."

"Good. We'll have to get you out on the course. I need somebody I can beat. Adam here chops the legs out from under me every time we get near the greens. Whatever he lacks in his drives, he more than makes up for with his putts."

"Putz is the right word," says Adam.

We laugh again as the line piles up outside the door to the conference room.

Behind Conover, a slender guy in his thirties is hauling a briefcase in both hands, trying to lift it over Conover's shoulder as he slides in behind him to get to the table across from me.

"Excuse me," says Conover. "Like you to meet Larry Melcher, house counsel with Devon. Paul Madriani. Is it Madriani? I am pronouncing it correctly?"

"That's right." I'm shaking Melcher's hand as I talk to Conover. When I turn to look at the lawyer, he gives me the insurance eye, a play for dominance. There is much mutual sniffing here. This is well practiced by every indemnity lawyer I've ever met. He would frisk me if he thought he could get away with it. Instead he tests my hand for grip as if any contest between us will be settled by arm wrestling on the conference table.

"Now who exactly is it you're representing here today?" Melcher hasn't even taken a seat and he's plumbing for information, trying to nail down my client. It wouldn't do to be playing too many sides of the same fence.

"My firm represents Dana Rush. You may have met my partner out in the reception area?"

"I don't think we had that opportunity." He says it with a kind of fraternity grin that makes me think that whatever happened out in reception wasn't that cordial. With Dana and Margaret in the same room, they may have to chip the ice off the walls.

Dana is next through the door, followed by Harry. I had to twist his arm to get him to come. I needed somebody to referee in the event Margaret and Dana decided to do best two-out-of-three falls while they were waiting.

They come around the long way to my side of the table, Dana taking a seat between Harry and me. As I make the introductions, Conover is busy filling his eyes with my client and flashing his pearly whites. He would no doubt like to ask her a few questions, perhaps undress her, but this is not the place or time.

While this is going on, Margaret wanders through the door behind him, ogling the surroundings, the French crystal chandelier over the table and the original oils on the walls, seeing how God might decorate heaven if He had the money. She is followed by her lawyer, Sue Glendenin, a bright, cheerful blond, perky and cute. Her slight build and sometimes timorous voice have deceived more than a few lawyers into playing patty-cake with her in the courtroom only to wake up with their pants on the floor and their pockets empty. As usual Susan is smiling. Margaret is not.

Glendenin moves to the head of the line, introduces herself to Adam, and starts giving out business cards. She repeats this with Conover and his lawyer, then nods to me.

"How are you doing, Paul?"

"Tell you in a while." I wink at her.

"No need to give you one of these." She puts the little case with business cards back in her coat pocket. This does not go unnoticed by Conover, the fact that lawyers representing the two adverse parties have been talking out of school and are still smiling at each other.

Moving slowly, like a wounded animal on a predator's turf, Margaret cannot find enough things to look at. She stares at the paintings behind us, up at the clock, her eyes falling anywhere and everywhere. The only place they don't land is on Dana. The invisible woman. While there are handshakes and introductions all around, no one possesses sufficient stupidity or enough balls to fall into the social pit of introducing these two women. For their part, they try as best they can to ignore each other.

"I think maybe we should get started," says Adam. "Would anybody like coffee? Anything to drink?"

"A scotch and soda, but only after we're finished," says Conover. He and Adam laugh.

"Why wait?" I say. "Harry would be happy to pour."

More laughs, everybody but Margaret, whose fuse already seems lit.

"Please take a seat." Adam assumes the duties as master of ceremonies, while his assistant takes orders for coffee and calls them out front on the phone's com line.

There are adjustments into chairs all around the table. Since these are on wheels, I notice Margaret sliding perceptibly down the table away from us. Her lawyer stays close, right up next to Melcher, crowding him at the table, so if he wants to take notes, he's going to have to hold the legal pad against his stomach to write anything in confidence.

Adam's assistant, Glenda, has set up office at the other end of the table, taking notes in case there is any dispute later as to what is said or the ground covered.

"I suspect we all know why we're here today." Tolt sits up straight in his chair at the head of table. "Devon Insurance issued a policy of life insurance on one of this firm's partners, Nicholas Rush. Mr. Rush, as we all know, is now deceased, and there appear to be two separate claims to that policy, each laying claim to the full face amount of the policy, two million dollars. One of these is filed by Mrs. Margaret Rush. One by Mrs. Dana Rush. Please stop me if anything I say is incorrect or if there are any questions." Adam looks around the table. Nobody says a word.

"There are some details," he says. "Complications that I'm sure we can all discuss if that becomes necessary." "Details and complications" is how Adam covers the question of the marital settlement agreement between Margaret and Nick and the fact that the widow's name is not on the policy as beneficiary, issues over which some Third World nations might go to war given the sums involved here.

Adam clears his throat and takes a drink of water from a glass that Glenda had poured earlier and placed next to his hand.

"The purpose of this meeting is to see if there is any accommodation that we can all arrive at here today, in order to resolve any dispute short of litigation." Tolt looks at the two women as if to make his point. "That is, without having to go to court and have a judge make a ruling that perhaps none of us would be entirely happy with."

"I could live with it if the court enforces the insurance policy." Margaret shoots from the lip, unable to control herself any longer.

"Yes, but what if you lose?" says Adam. "There are other issues, as I'm sure your lawyer has explained to you. And none of us here today would want to see you without some recompense."

Margaret gives a mean stare and holds it on Dana, convinced, I am sure, that Adam does not speak for everybody in the room.

"The same is true with regard to you." He turns to Dana. "I honestly don't think that Nick would have wanted either of you to suffer."

This draws an audible groan from Margaret. "Oh, spare us," she says.

Tolt ignores this. "The fact is that none of us here today want to see either one of you in a position in which you are harmed. I think that if you consider the risks, and think about it for a while, you will agree with us." For Margaret to arrive at this conclusion could take a couple of lifetimes.

Glendenin moves a little toward her client, puts one hand on Margaret's arm, a gesture for her to calm down, to which she receives a contemptuous look from her own client. Then just as quickly Susan is back invading Melcher's zone of privacy, leaving Margaret to drift in her sea of scorn.

"I hope that includes us?" says Conover. "I mean the part about nobody being harmed."

"Absolutely." Adam's eyes twinkle as he gives this assurance. If nothing else, it provides a little comic relief.

"That's reassuring," says Conover smiling. "Of course we understand that we have an obligation to pay out," he says. "The only problem is who do we pay?"

Margaret is still looking at Dana, contempt welded in her pupils, so I suspect my client would like to slide under the table. It's not so much the money as the fact that Dana would get some of it that prevents Margaret from negotiating. She slides her chair back over on its wheels toward her lawyer and cups a hand to Susan's ear, whispering into the funnel. Once having stated her bottom line to me, she is not likely to give ground. Having lost her marriage to Dana, she's not now going to give up the policy with her name on it. This is written in her eyes as she whispers, so it doesn't take a sooth-sayer to read this message: "Not a dime less than two million." She glances at the door as I watch her. It wouldn't take much to cause her to bolt. She knows we won't get a second chance for a meeting with the carrier, short of litigation.

"Perhaps if we could get some movement, some direction," says Conover. He looks over at Margaret still whispering to her lawyer. "Maybe if we could get one of the ladies to break the ice. Talk to her lawyer with an offer."

Conover sits there staring directly at Margaret as he says this. She stops whispering in mid-syllable. His tactic is clear; drive a wedge between the women and sit on the two million while it earns interest at seven percent and they grind each other into dust in some courtroom.

He's about to pop the question of compromise to Margaret, the grenade in the corner. Conover wants to pull the pin and get the hell out of here. I suspect the only reason he has come to this meeting is to humor Adam Tolt. No doubt Adam, in some other life, sits on corporate boards and otherwise rubs shoulders with Conover's superiors back at the home office. Tolt is a man with an iron in everybody's fire.

"That is precisely what I was hoping for." The first words I have spoken in earnest. "Some movement," I say.

"Is your client prepared to compromise her claim?" It comes from the lawyer, Melcher, who pounces like a panther.

"She is. She's willing to give up half of it."

"There we go," says Conover. "Mrs. Rush," he gestures toward Dana using the designation he knows will infuriate Margaret Rush, "is willing to give up a million dollars to settle this matter." He makes it sound as if he's soliciting applause at a charity bazaar.

"I didn't say that. I said she's willing to give up half."

Over steepled fingers and with his elbows resting on the arms of the chair, Adam has now settled back to watch this cat fight.

"In fact she's willing to give up two million dollars," I add.

"You mean she's willing to step away from everything?" Conover gives me an incredulous look, as if to say, "then what are we doing here?"

"No. Just half," I tell him.

He shakes his head, looks at his lawyer, who shrugs his shoulders, each trying to figure what they've missed.

"Explain," he says.

"The total claim isn't two million dollars," I tell him. "It's four million."

"What are you talking about?" says Melcher.

"I'm talking about the double-indemnity clause."

"What?" Melcher looks at his boss, shaking his head, shrugging his shoulders, turning up the palms of his hands as if to say, "Who let the crazy guy in?" "Where have you been practicing?" says Melcher. "Not insurance law."

"Mostly criminal," I tell him.

"Ahh." A look like "well that explains it." "Double indemnity is only for accidental death." He says this in a kind of gentle tone as if a mild education is all that is needed here. "This was a homicide," he says. "A double homicide maybe, but not double indemnity." He smiles a little at the pun he has made. "Mr. Rush was murdered, unless there's something we haven't been told."

"That may be," I tell. "Have you read the police report?"

"Somewhere," says Melcher. He opens his briefcase and starts fishing.

"Let me save you the trouble, and so that you understand what I'm saying. Nick Rush may have been the victim of an intentional act. That we concede. But the question remains—was he the intended victim in that shooting or merely an innocent bystander—*shot by accident?*" I emphasize the last three words.

"Oh, come on," says Melcher. "You can't be serious?"

Conover's looking at his lawyer, wondering what the hell's going on. This is not what he'd planned. A quick meeting and out the door, followed by several man-years of litigation while they turned the screws on the two women.

"I couldn't be more serious. More to the point, there's case law on the subject."

Sheaves of paper, each neatly stapled, come sliding down the table from another direction. Harry is handing them out of a manila folder lying on the table in front of him like he's dealing faro from a boxed deck. Copies of these slide in front of the lawyers and Conover.

"There is also a copy of the homicide investigation report. This concludes that the deceased Nicholas Rush was not the intended victim in this case, but that his client Gerald Metz was in all likelihood the target of the attack. This is based on the physical evidence at the scene, witness statements, and other evidence in the possession of the authorities, both state and federal. I commend it to your reading," I tell them.

Harry sends copies of the police report down next so that Conover and his lawyer are still reading the first page of our legal points and authorities when the investigation report comes sliding in on top of it like a runner safe at home plate.

Now the lawyers are all flipping pages. Glendenin and Tolt are sitting back amused, as if they have no dog in this fight, while Conover looks at his lawyer, waiting for Melcher to pull a rabbit out of the fly to his pants.

"This is nothing. This means nothing," says Melcher. He hasn't had time to read past the first page but feels compelled by his boss's presence to get his sword out of its sheath. "Your man was standing next to his client. Sure he was shot."

"And your argument is?" I ask.

"His client was the intended victim. Says so right here."

"I agree. That's precisely what I'm saying."

"No. No. No. No." Melcher says it as if each time it adds to the weight of his argument. "You don't understand," he says. "The fact that your client was standing next to the intended victim doesn't mean he was shot accidentally. I mean, he was representing the man. He was his lawyer."

"What's that mean?" says Harry. "Are you saying he assumed the risk?"

"Not exactly. Well, in a way," says Melcher. "I mean this man. And no offense, ladies," he looks at Dana, then shoots a quick glance down the table toward Margaret. "No offense, but Mr. Rush represented some questionable clients."

"You're telling me?" says Margaret.

"What does that have to do with anything?" I ask.

"You figure it out." Melcher is starting to lose his cool. "You got a dirtbag drug lawyer hanging out with his client in front of a federal courthouse when the two of them get shot. Now if you want sympathy, I'll give it to you by the truckload," he says. "But not this. What do you think a jury is going to say when they find out your man's representing some drug dealer when he gets shot?" He looks at me arching his eyebrows as if he's just dropped a bomb on our case. He doesn't wait for me to answer. "I'll tell you what they're gonna say. They're gonna say he got what he had coming. Especially when your claim is . . . is . . . is . . ." his anger takes hold and he starts sputtering. "Is this," he flips the papers in front of him. "That it's an accidental death?"

"First of all, that information is never going to get before a jury," I tell him.

"What?" he says.

"In fact, I can almost guarantee you that a trial judge isn't even going to allow you to inform the jury that Mr. Rush was a lawyer, much less that he was in any way associated with Mr. Metz. It's irrelevant, and I would argue it's highly prejudicial."

Harry pipes in. "Read the points and authorities," he says. "Very illuminating."

"The only real issue here," I say. Melcher is looking back at me, knowing he is getting double-teamed. "The only issue is whether Mr. Rush was the intended victim of this act or whether he was killed by accident. Let me ask you a question."

Conover is looking down, holding his head in hands, elbows propped on the table as if he doesn't need any more questions.

"Assuming Mr. Rush was standing out in front of that courthouse alone, without Mr. Metz, would this shooting have even occurred?"

Melcher looks at me, down at the police report in front of him, back to the points and authorities. He'd rather not answer. He knows it's a question I can ultimately raise before a jury. The ultimate and unavoidable issue, but for Mr. Metz . . .

"It's a simple question. Based on the evidence in front of you, do you think the shooting would have occurred?"

"We don't know." Conover demonstrates why he is Melcher's superior. His head comes up, and he cuts off his lawyer before the man can answer.

"We don't know. We haven't had time to read through all of this." Better that than an open admission in front of witnesses, even if these are arguably settlement negotiations. Conover's had enough surprises for one day.

"If our clients have to get you in court, I suppose you can argue with the cops," I tell them.

"What cops?" Melcher can't resist.

"The ones who will testify as to the intended victim and the accidental nature of Mr. Rush's death."

These are witnesses to die for in a civil case, and both of them know it: cops testifying that a defense lawyer was shot by accident. What possible reason could they have to lie? And how can they change their testimony given the contents of the police report?

"Now I'm sure you'll be able to get them to tell the jury all about Mr. Metz and whatever sordid dealings he was involved in."

"And if we don't, you will," says Melcher.

I concede the point with a smile. "The only thing they're not going to be able to talk about is the fact that Mr. Metz was Mr. Rush's client or that Mr. Rush was a lawyer."

"Any whiff of that," says Harry, tapping the points and authorities, "and you'll have a mistrial."

"So what you have here," I tell them, "is a man walking down the street, minding his own business, who happens to be caught up in a drive-by aimed at somebody else."

There is a moment of reckoning as the reality of the argument settles in. This lasts for several seconds, until the silence is broken by Adam Tolt leaning back in his chair, its springs squeaking. He's trying to maintain a sober expression, but it's a losing battle. He finally breaks out in a full-bodied laugh.

"Come on, Luther, you have to admit I never put you in a pickle like this before." Still laughing, he says: "I have to say, it sounds like an accident to me."

"You're not exactly an objective audience, Adam." Conover's humor is being stretched to the limit.

"Come on," says Tolt. "You can take me to Temecula and get it back in the sand traps." Tolt can't help himself laughing, trying not to ridicule his friend Luther. "Listen, I'll put in a word. They'll understand." He's talking about the home office.

"It's still an open investigation," says Melcher. "Who knows what the cops will come up with?"

"If you think you can get them to change direction once they've got their noses to the ground, you're a better man than I," I say.

"We've tried," says Harry. "We know. Of course in the past they were usually after our client." Harry can't help but smile a little at this. The irony is lost on Conover and Melcher. They are starting to see a four followed by a lot of zeros on a company check.

There are reasons why the cops would not want to open too many lines of inquiry going in multiple directions, at least on paper. They would have to disclose each of these to defense attorneys once they settled on a suspect and made an arrest. Every lead pointing in another direction carves a notch of reasonable doubt into the legs of their case. If they withhold this information from defense attorneys, it is grounds on appeal to reverse a conviction. Cops are not likely to point like weather vanes with each changing current of information. At least not as long as the courts continue to tell them that a straight line is the shortest distance to a conviction.

"Of course you're free to pee on a few bushes if you think you can get them to chase some other scent," says Harry. "In the meantime, we'll expect you to tender the full amount of the policy. Not two million," he says, "but four, under the double-indemnity clause. And so that we don't forget . . ." Harry hands out the last document from his folder, a formal letter of demand to the carrier. Conover knows the significance of this as soon as he sees it.

Though he didn't want to come, Harry is enjoying the moment. Seldom do you get an insurance company in this position: bent over, holding its ankles.

"Since you've already acknowledged that you have an obligation to pay," says Harry, "if you fail to meet the demand . . ."

"You'll claim bad faith." Conover comes to the point quickly. He has seen the form letter Harry has just handed him before. It is the boilerplate setup for bad faith.

In this case the upper limit of any judgment could take a healthy slice out of the national debt. We would be able to examine their books to determine what amount is necessary to adequately punish the company for withholding prompt payment from two women, one of whom is bereft having her husband murdered and the other left adrift by an ugly divorce. These are not happy circumstances for an insurance company to circle its wagons and start shooting Indians.

Conover looks at Margaret, whose expression is leaden, even now on the verge of victory.

Still holding Harry's letter, he studies Dana, who offers nothing but a wan smile. If he glanced a little farther to his left, he would see Susan hiding behind his own lawyer. She is gazing down at the table like the mouse who just got the last crumb. It was Glendenin who managed to get Vesuvius to the meeting and keep her from erupting, so that we can now discuss in private a division of spoils between the two Mrs. Rushes.

Conover lifts his eyes toward me. From the look, it is clear. He is trying to figure how he will pull the split rail from this particular fence out of his ass before he has to call the home office and explain what has happened. I doubt if he'll be asking me to play golf anytime soon.

CHAPTER TWELVE

Miguelito Espinoza, father of an infant and husband of the child-woman, is thirty-five, hard as a diamond, a tattoo chain of black ink around his neck, and on both arms Spanish gang graffiti in blazoned letters.

He has a slicked-back do with a net over it, pulled tight around the edges covering the tops of his ears. The man is dead in the eyes, and dark in more ways than his complexion as he sits there slumped down, one leg crossed over the other, cool, his chair pushed back from the table as if he is low riding on his way to hell.

He faces multiple counts of armed robbery, the theft of federal property, as well as possession. He faces twenty-five years on each count if they can prove that he was involved in the actual visa hijacking. He faces ten years on each count of possession for the three visas found in his closet.

We are seated on opposite sides at a steel table in one of the small lawyer-client cubicles in the Metro Detention Center, the white high-rise tomb downtown. There is a guard watching from outside the glass, his eyes constantly on the table between us so that nothing passes without his notice.

The place was a skyscraping joke when it was first put up a few years ago. The contractor stiffed the federal government on the concrete used to build it, so inmates pounding on the walls hard enough could punch holes and shimmy down their bed sheets to the ground outside. Guards were reduced to listening to the hammering from upstairs to pick up the direction in hopes that they could scurry out to the street before the tenants could rappel down their bed covers and hightail it. Since then, the government has hardened the cells, so now inmates would at least need a spoon to chisel their way out.

Espinoza is not impressed that I have come here. He is filled with questions. Streetwise, he is looking at this gift horse as if perhaps there is something in the package that may bite him.

"Why don' you tell me who hired you, man?"

"I told you. Your wife, Robin."

"Listen, man. Save the bullshit for your friends. Robin don' know shit. You think I'm a fool? Robin's a fuckin' idiot. Where's she gonna find a lawyer? She can't find the fuckin' phone book. And if she could, she couldn't read it. Besides, she ain't got the money to pay you. Look at your fine clothes, your little leather briefcase." He says this in mocking tones, with the fingers of one hand idly pointed toward my case on the floor next to the table.

"Listen, man." He sits up at the table, elbows on top, and leans close to me as if he's about to explain the mysteries of life. "Look at me," he says. "I ain't talking to you 'til I know who you are. You got it?"

I shrug my shoulders. "Fine. I hope you like the accommodations." I get up from my chair, grab my briefcase, and move toward the door.

"Hey, man. Where you goin'?"

"You said you don't want to talk."

He glances over his shoulder at the guard who starts to move this way to take him back to his cell.

"Sit down, man."

"Not unless you want to talk."

"Fine, man. Fine. We'll talk. Relax." He's back, slumped in the chair, trying not to notice the guard and hoping he will go away.

"Sit down, man." He taps the stainless steel surface of the table with two fingers, an invitation for me to join him again. Anything is better than the cell inside. "Maybe we can talk about the weather," he says.

I take a seat, and the guard backs off and returns to his position against the wall outside, watching us.

"You gotta be cool," he says. "Gimme a minute." He is thinking, trying to piece together who would hire me and why. "I just wanna know who you are," he says. "That's all."

"I told you."

"You tol' me nothin'. Who hired you?"

"What difference does it make as long as we get you out of here?"

His eyes darting around, thinking about this.

"Why would you do that?"

"Call it my civic duty," I tell him.

His eyes read bullshit, but he's afraid to say the word for fear I might get up and this time walk.

So instead he says: "Can you do that? Get me out?"

"I don't know. First you'll have to trust me. Tell me what's going on."

"Can you get me out on bail?"

"It wouldn't be easy."

"Then what the fuck good are you?"

"This close to the border and you charged with taking a truckload of U.S. visas, a judge might have a problem giving you bail."

"What the fuck, you think I'm a flight risk?" He knows more lawyer lingo than half the attorneys I know.

"It's not what I think that counts."

"I don' know nothin' about it, man. Those fuckin' passes. I don't know how they got there." He is sitting up now in the chair, dropping the detached demeanor, looking at me directly, trying to focus a shimmer of honesty in those dark, beady eyes.

"They were in your apartment. On your closet floor."

"Only three of 'em, man. Where's the rest?"

"Maybe they think you're going to tell them."

"How do I know? I mean, I don't know shit." He's looking around, shaking his head, palms up and out, extended in the con's perennial disclaimer, your average honest man filled with disbelief. "I'm sleeping in my bed, man, these assholes come in, fuckin' flashlights in my eyes, put a shotgun in my face. Next thing I know, they're pulling this shit out of my closet. I'm telling you, man. You know everything I know. I don't know how they got there. Maybe somebody put 'em there, man."

"Obviously. The question is who?"

"How would I know?"

"It's your apartment."

"Lots of people come and go," he says. "Maybe they did it."

"What people?"

He thinks for a second. You can read it in his eyes. He's opened this door a crack, and now he wants to close it.

"Them."

"Who's them?"

"Fucking Immigration," he says. "They're always after me."

"You're saying the INS framed you? That they dumped the evidence onto the floor in your closet?"

"How do I know? Anything's possible, man."

"You'll have to do better than that."

He looks around, the gray cells moving at light speed now, sullen, thinking of new ways to lie to one more lawyer.

I tell him that if this were a state action, he would definitely have something to worry about. "It would be strike three," I say. "I've seen your record. It's not good. How does a lifetime behind bars sound?"

"But it ain't no fuckin' state action." He takes solace at least in this.

"Maybe it is, and maybe it isn't."

Espinoza gives me a sideways glance. "What's that supposed to mean?"

"It was federal property that went missing. But the fact that some of it turned up in this state, specifically on your closet floor, could make out a case for possession of stolen property."

"They can't do that, man. Can they?"

I make a face. Anything's possible.

He's up close at the table now. I have his undivided attention. "Tell me, man. Why would they want to do that to me?"

"Why not? You think they're going to cut you some slack? In case you haven't figured it out, they want to squeeze you, Miguel. I can call you Miguel, can't I?"

He nods. "Why?

"Because they think you know something. They want you to roll over on some of your friends."

"Who sent you?" he says.

"Are we going through that again?"

"I don' know nothin'." Just like that he's back to low riding in the chair, only this time he has a hand up to his mouth, nibbling fingernails. From the tip of his tongue, he spits out the chewed-off remains along with the black crude from underneath. I watch him for several seconds as he sits there biting and shooting looks from beady little eyes in every direction as if the walls have ears. In this case, they may. I can't be sure that our conversation is not being monitored. There are now in place what are called Special Administrative Measures. These permit federal prison authorities to listen in, even between lawyer and client in cases where national security is believed to be at issue. The fact that Espinoza is charged with the theft of a thousand high-tech visas to enter the country must have them wondering for what purpose these documents were stolen.

A tattoo across the back of Espinoza's hand reads "Sangre" (meaning "blood"), in Gothic block letters like some ethnic mural on a wall in East Los Angeles.

"Even if they don't turn you over to the state, the feds are not likely to go easy. In case you haven't noticed, scrutiny at the borders has been turned up—just a notch."

I emphasize the last few words. It takes him a beat or two to make all the intended deductions, then he looks at me. "No way, man." Then he looks away as if this puts distance between himself and his own conclusions. "I ain't no fuckin' terrorist," he says. "Maybe people once in a while. Sure I brought people across, sometimes. But, but not that shit. No way, man."

"Maybe they don't know that. We're talking some risky stuff that went missing. These were not green cards knocked out on somebody's home computer, Miguel. These were laser-etched visas with holograms. You know as well as I do they can't be traced. The little camera they use at the border down at San Ysidro to shoot pictures and send them back to Virginia." He follows my every word. Espinoza knows exactly what I'm talking about.

"You know the one, where they check to see if they're forgeries. That little camera, and those people in Virginia, they wouldn't be able to stop you if you had one of these cards at the border. They'd think you were just another honest citizen crossing over to do business. Bad people could bring a lot of dangerous shit into the country with cards like that."

"That's not . . ." He bites the next word in half.

"That's not what? That's not why they were stolen?"

All of this has him thinking of perils he's never considered, looking down at the tabletop again and then back to me.

"Why, man? I mean why would they think I'm some fucking terrorist? There's no evidence I ever did nothing like that." He thumps the table with two fingers to make the point.

"Maybe they think you're moving up in the world."

"Hey, man, you're fuckin' with my head. That's bullshit."

He turns away from me, the devil he doesn't want to see or hear. But the thought has seeped into his brain where it now sizzles like corrosive acid.

"They can't do that, man. That's fuckin' illegal. They got no fucking evidence. There are laws," he says. "I am entitled . . ."

"Of course you can make all of those arguments," I tell him. "But the people who sit on juries are a little uptight right now. If they think you might be that kind of a threat, well, they might just throw you in the can until sometime around the year when your grandchildren have children."

I can tell that this is a sobering thought, one that has him forgetting for the moment who might have hired me and thinking instead about the sky outside—and how long it might be before he gets to see it again.

He looks at me, shiny brown eyes. "Whadda you want to know, man? Tell you what I can."

"What do you mean you're representing him?" Harry is looking at me as if I'm crazy, seated in one of the client chairs across from my desk in the office.

"I met with him over at the federal lockup late yesterday afternoon and told him I'd take his case."

"Why? Did he give you a retainer?"

"We'll have to work that out. Ever hear of a drug, street slang, something called Mejicano Rosen?"

Harry shakes his head. "Heard of Maui Wowee. Hawaiian Sensimilla. It's the same stuff," he says. "Potent. And I've heard of black tar and white china, angel dust, snow, B.C. bud, baby-T . . ."

"What's baby-T?"

"Another word for crack," he says.

"Where did you hear all of this?"

"Some of us lead less sheltered lives," says Harry.

"But you've never heard of Mejicano Rosen?"

"Your Spanish sucks," says Harry. "Sound like some Jewish dry cleaner in Tijuana."

"Do me a favor? See if you can run it down for me?"

"Where?"

"I don't know. Start by asking around wherever it is you lead this less sheltered life of yours. Maybe over one of your card games on Thursday night with that vice cop and the deputy D.A."

"Oh, right. What am I gonna go over there and yell, 'Hey guys we have a client running some stuff outta Mexico and we'd like to know what it's worth'?"

"Try the library. Take Marta with you. Maybe there's something on Lexis-Nexis? An article or an appellate case that mentions it."

"You're wasting my time. Why don't you just ask your client?"

"Espinoza did the limit. He's not going to tell me anything more unless he gets awfully lonely in the jail. I get the sense he doesn't trust me that much."

"Can't understand that. Just cuz you're trying to pump him for information in a double murder involving a friend without disclosure?"

"Hey. I'm not even sure he's going to let me represent him."

"Did you happen to mention Nick? Tell him about all the blood on the sidewalk in front of the federal courthouse, the fact that Metz, who was shot with Nick, mentioned Espinoza's name?"

"We didn't have that much time."

"I see you were too busy listening."

"Lawyer's job," I tell him. "Hearing the heartache."

"Makes you wonder how they ever came up with the word mouthpiece," says Harry. "When exactly are you going to break this little tidbit to your client, the fact that you're hoping he runs in the same circles with the people who killed Nick, so maybe he can give you a reference you can pass along to the cops?"

"Look at it this way. I could be giving him a wonderful case on appeal. That's more than the federal public defender can offer. I'll tell him when it becomes necessary."

"Oh, good," says Harry. "Then maybe they'll just suspend your license instead of disbarring you. How can you be sure he didn't have a hand in doing Nick himself?"

"Your friend with the D.A. said he was under federal surveillance at the time."

"He said he thought he was. There's a difference."

"He did admit that he knew the people who pulled the number down in Tijuana, the ones who held up the delivery van and took the visas. Of course he had nothing to do with it."

"Of course."

"And he gave me a name. First name only."

"What else did he tell you?"

"Some information as to where this person might be found."

This does not excite Harry.

"It could just be coincidence. Espinoza says he was a high roller out of Mexico, flashy dresser. He says the man always had a large roll of cash and he seemed to be calling the shots. His name was Jaime."

Harry looks at me out of the corner of one eye. "So?"

"Metz, that morning in my office, told me one of the Ibarra brothers was named Jaime."

"So was Jimmy Stewart," says Harry. "Maybe they should dig him up and look for visas."

I ignore him. "It does beg the question: why he would flop in a flea house like Espinoza's apartment?"

"I've seen the place. He says this Jaime and some friends stayed with him for a few days. I tried to get a fix on when this was. He said he couldn't remember exactly, but it was last summer. It was definitely after the van carrying the visas was knocked down in Tijuana. He says these guys must have left some of them behind. Of course, then he fell into his own pit."

I can tell by the look that Harry is curious, but he doesn't want to encourage this.

"He got his stories screwed up and let slip that some of the visas were supposed to be used for getting stuff across the border. What he called Mejicano Rosen."

Harry muses for a moment. "Did you consider the fact that this man deals in flesh? A labor contractor working the Mexican border. Maybe this Rosen is a person? Different kind of contraband," says Harry. "Besides, what makes you think any of this is true? Dollars to doughnuts, he pulled the trigger on Nick."

"No. That he didn't do."

"How do you know?"

"Because he wasn't available for the shooting. He was in Mexico."

Harry looks at me.

"Sarah goes to school with a boy whose father works one of the border checks at Immigration. We got to know each other during basketball last season. I called him late last week and told him I had a client, and I needed to know if the man was in the country or not during a period of time. He told me there was no way to check, that they don't usually take down passport numbers. I told him that on this guy they might, to check anyway. He did. Espinoza used his passport, not a visa, to cross the border at Tijuana four days before Nick was killed. He didn't return until five days later."

"How would they know that?" says Harry.

"I figured if the information from your friend over cards was accurate, and the feds had Espinoza under surveillance, they'd have him on a 'watch list' at the border. They did."

I had no intention of getting involved with Espinoza until I could verify that he had no hand in killing Nick. That would have been a little too messy. As it is, I am walking the edge.

CHAPTER THIRTEEN

"I'm afraid I have good news and bad news." Adam Tolt looks at Harry and me across the cavernous ravine formed by the top of his desk.

He called late yesterday afternoon and wanted to see me this morning. Said it was important but not something he could discuss over the phone.

Harry's not letting me out of his sight if it has anything to do with Nick's death or Dana. He is still invading my private space over my representation of Espinoza.

"Why don't you give us the good news first," says Harry.

"Our friends at Devon Insurance are getting ready to make an offer of settlement. According to the signal flares they're sending up, it's going to be quite generous."

"How generous?" says Harry.

"Three point eight million."

"That's not four," says Harry.

"You didn't expect them to pay the full demand?" says Tolt. "Trust me, this offer was not recommended by their lawyers. Turn it down, and they will circle the wagons and defend the claim for double indemnity."

"And who's supposed to compromise?" says Harry. "We all know where Margaret's coming from. You tell her to reduce her demand, you better get out of the way, because she's gonna bounce off the walls like a rubber ball. The whole deal may go away."

"I agree," says Adam. "It looks like your client will have to back off. I did convince the company to forego confidentiality as to the terms of settlement."

What Tolt means is that we would be free to publicize the deal.

"Why would they want to do that?"

"They didn't, but I told them it might make their offer more palatable. Of course, you wouldn't have to publicize it, but you'd be free to. A feather in your cap," he says.

This is something most insurance carriers would never give up willingly, details as to the amount of settlement. It tends to make lawyers in other cases more aggressive, especially when the figures climb above six.

"You have to ask yourself if it is worth litigating for the next decade over such an amount," says Adam. "Two hundred thousand dollars."

"Maybe you should ask Margaret after she stops foaming at the mouth," says Harry.

"You haven't heard the bad news yet," says Tolt.

He opens a manila folder on the desk in front of him, a few pieces of paper and a folded spreadsheet.

"There's a problem. Not with the insurance settlement. Another matter. The firm's been conducting an audit since Nick's death. It's routine whenever a partner leaves." He makes it sound like Nick resigned.

"We review their cases to see what commitments the firm has, examine their client trust records. That sort of thing."

Harry and I sit listening.

Adam covers his mouth with a fisted hand and clears his throat a little. "The problem is we've come up light on Nick's accounting for the client trust fund."

It's the kind of news that tends to drain the blood from your head if you're a lawyer.

"Are we talking a minor error in math?" I ask.

"I'm afraid not. It's out of balance a little more than fifty-seven thousand dollars," he says.

"You're saying Nick invaded the client trust account?"

"Not exactly," says Tolt. "All the checks were drawn over the last sixty days."

"I don't understand."

"The checks were drawn after Nick died." He says. "It appears that someone gained access to blank checks and signed Nick's name to them. They were drawn to specific amounts in different names and deposited in several banks around town. We've checked those accounts. The funds were withdrawn, and the accounts closed all within a few days of the deposits. It appears that whoever did this gave some thought to how it should be done. We can't get information as to social security numbers for the people receiving these funds because of banking privacy laws, though with a subpoena or a search warrant from the authorities this could be made available. I suspect that whoever did it may have used false employer I.D. numbers or bogus social security numbers, whatever. Of course I can't be certain of that unless we inquire further. But we do have some of the canceled checks. None of them were endorsed since they were for deposit only, but the signature for the payor is not Nick's. We do know that. We haven't yet reported this to the police."

"But you're taking the time to tell us?" I say.

"Given the circumstances, I thought that it might be best."

"Why is that?"

"The firm has no interest in stirring up a cloud of bad publicity unless it can't be avoided. It seems your client removed a number of Nick's personal effects from his office a little over a week after the shooting."

"Dana?"

He nods. "According to one of our senior secretaries, the trust checks were in a drawer in Nick's desk before Mrs. Rush visited. They were missing after she left."

"This is a careful secretary," says Harry. "How would she know?"

"Ordinarily she wouldn't," says Tolt, "but the police had just removed their yellow tape from Nick's office door that morning. I'm just guessing, but I suspect that Mrs. Rush had called them to inquire as to when she would be able to collect her husband's personal effects. The secretary in question, at the firm's request, conducted an audit of everything in the office that morning, in preparation for boxing it up and reassigning client files."

"I see." Tolt has Dana painted into a corner.

"It's an awkward situation," he says. "Sooner or later, we're going to have to report the discrepancy to the State Bar. It would be good if the money could be restored before that time."

Harry and I look at each other, but neither of us says a word.

"The bar has no jurisdiction over lay persons, and the firm would have no reason to file a criminal complaint once the money is returned. We'd rather not get law enforcement involved unless it's necessary. Please understand I don't want to cause any more pain than is absolutely necessary." The way he says this, the conviction in his voice makes me believe he is telling the truth. If the information is accurate, he's already gone farther than he should have to protect Dana, and he's assumed some risk in doing it.

"What do you want me to do?"

"Talk to her," he says.

"Did you know this when we met with the carrier?"

"If I had, I would not have participated," he says.

"But you realize the settlement may be the only source from which she can make reimbursement?" I tell him.

"I've considered that. I would not like to put pressure on her to settle on terms you feel are unfavorable. But you have to understand our position as well. If the insurance company were to get wind of this, they would no doubt withdraw their offer."

Tolt is right. They would force Dana into court and take

their chances there. In the meantime, they know we would have to involve the cops. Criminal charges would be filed against her.

"You see the problem?" he says.

I offer him nothing but a painful expression of concession. It's one of those times when words can only make things worse.

"And then there is the one final aspect," he says.

"Which aspect is that?" says Harry, as if it couldn't get any worse.

"I prefer not to go there. I don't believe it for a minute," says Adam. "But if the police have to be told about this, given their natural suspicion, an open and unsolved double murder. Well . . ." He cocks his head to one side and shrugs that shoulder.

"They might wonder whether a woman that desperate for money might not hire somebody to kill her husband for the insurance on his life. Is that it?" I say.

"As I said, I don't believe it for a minute."

But it does add a whole new dimension. It looks as if Dana will be compromising her share of the settlement whether she likes it or not. If what Tolt tells me is accurate, I have little interest in laying my body on the blocks to push the carrier farther, even if I could.

"I would ask you to talk to your client and see what can be worked out. And to do it as quickly as possible. Of course, I'll send you copies of the trust records for your review."

I agree to talk to Dana, make no promises beyond that. There's not a lot of choice.

"Good. Now that that's done." Adam gives up a sigh. You can almost see the tension rise from his body like heat waves. "Not a pleasant task," he says, "but I had to play the cards I was dealt. I hope you understand?"

"Of course."

"Good. Have you folks heard anything more about Nick's death? The police are coming and going here," he says, "asking questions, but offering no answers."

"They're known for that," I tell him. "We read the papers.

That's about it." I don't tell him about Espinoza. For the time being, those details are best left between Harry and me.

"Same here." He shakes his head, takes off his glasses, and settles back into his chair. "You know, what I can't figure is why would a man like Nick get involved with someone like Metz?"

He's not talking about attorney-client relations now, but the partnership, Jamaile Enterprises.

Following our meeting on the insurance settlement, Adam told me that the cops were probing, questioning some of the partners and staff. They brought up the limited partnership. According to Tolt, who has now turned over every rock in the firm, this is a mystery to all of them.

"I've wondered the same thing. Let me ask you, did the cops ever mention a name, Grace Gimble?"

He looks at me, then Harry, thinks about this for a second, then shakes his head slowly. "No. Not that I know of. Why? Who is she?"

"I'm not sure. The name cropped up on the partnership records. One of the original directors."

"Probably a secretary. Somebody who was around when they put the thing together. When was this, the formation?"

"A little over a year ago."

He allows this to settle in as he calculates. "Nick was with the firm over three years," he says.

"That's why I thought you might know the name."

"I don't think anyone by that name works for us now, but I could have somebody check personnel records. Assuming we have them that far back." He makes a note to himself on a pad on his desk, then puts the pen down on top of it.

"So what we have are two points of contact, this business Nick was involved in and his wife Dana, who was on the arts commission with Metz."

"There's another aspect to this thing," I say. "Nick tried to hand Metz off to me, before he was charged. He told me the firm had a conflict with Metz, so he couldn't handle it. Something about some contracts Metz had, that Rocker, Dusha was on the other side of."

"I can check. But if we had an adverse interest, how did Nick get around it for the arraignment?" he asks.

"He told me he disclosed it to Metz, and I assume the other client, and they all waived."

"The man seems to keep turning up in Nick's life like a bad penny," says Tolt. "We don't know why or how they got together on business. Does anybody know how Metz got on the arts commission?"

"Zane Tresler appointed him," says Harry.

I look at my partner, surprised at the source of this information and how readily it comes pouring forth.

"Well, you were getting wrapped around the axle, so I just thought I'd check it out," he says. "He also appointed your pal, Fittipaldi."

"Who is this?" says Tolt.

"A friend of Dana's," I tell him.

"Dana's term is up in three years, unless she gets reappointed. Fittipaldi has a year," says Harry. "Metz had two years when his ticket got punched. Anything else you want to know? It's the same Tresler as the museum they're planning downtown. You have heard about that?" he says.

Word of the museum has been in the papers two or three times in the last year, a thirty-million-dollar museum and gallery planned for a location somewhere near the waterfront, set to start construction in the next year or so.

"Actually the museum is being named for his father. Zane, Senior." Tolt is leaning forward, elbows on his desk, smiling at the verbal swordplay between Harry and me. "A combination of some public money, mostly federal grants, and matching contributions from the Tresler Family Foundation. The old man died back in the late sixties. There's a son, grandson, and I'm told a great grandson."

"Which one is on the board of supervisors?"

"Zane, Junior, the son. He's been on the board twenty years I guess. As long as I can remember. He chairs the board's courts committee. I know that much. The judges have to grovel in front of him yearly to get their heat turned on in winter and the air turned up in summer. He controls funding for staff, desks, pens, paper clips. He has more juice with the local courts than the appellate bench. I'd bring him into the firm as a full partner. He wouldn't even have to come into the office," he says, "but unfortunately he's not a lawyer." Adam makes it sound as if this might be only a minor impediment.

"What does he do besides supervise?" I ask.

"Not much. The grandson runs the family businesses now. Mitchell Tresler. He's in his thirties. Not quite as quick as his father. I guess the genes have been watered down," he says. "I'm told there's a fourth running around out there somewhere, probably in grammar school. If I had a pretty little granddaughter, I'd send her to that school and tell her to make friends. The kid's going to be rich someday."

"Where did the family money come from?"

"Mostly real estate development," says Adam. "They do large projects, malls, major subdivisions. That and give a lot of money to charities.

"The family started in real estate back in the early part of the last century. Zane One put most of it together. I never actually met the man, but from what I've heard, you wouldn't want to get in his way if there was a land rush. The wheel ruts in your body would be deep. And he was well connected. A friend of William Mulholland, the engineer who built the Owens Aqueduct. Anyway, the family ended up owning a good part of the eastern end of the county. This was back when it was nothing but sagebrush and jackrabbits. The Treslers bought it up for a song. Then the water project came through, the diversion from the Colorado River. Suddenly old man Tresler was sitting on a fortune."

"Funny how that works," says Harry.

"Isn't it?" says Adam. "The rest is history. Zane, Junior, grew up with the county, and now he runs it. This year it's his turn to be chairman of the board. He also heads the regional joint powers commission."

"What's that?" I ask.

"The city, the county, and the port authority signed a joint powers agreement a few years ago. They formed a special regional powers entity to govern land along the waterfront and most of the commercial property downtown. They have the final word on development in that area. Tresler's the chairperson. It gives him a huge hammer. What he wants he gets."

"That's a little dicey, isn't it?" asks Harry. "I mean sitting on a county governing body that settles zoning disputes when your family's company is doing development?"

"Tresler is a careful man," says Adam.

"And if you're smart, you don't ask questions, is that it?" says Harry.

"Not if you want his vote on anything that's important," says Tolt. "And to be honest, I think you'll find him above reproach. There's nothing anybody can give him that he doesn't already have—money, power, you put it on a list, Zane Tresler has it. They call it politics, and as I said, he's a careful man."

Though many might not believe it, the most potent side of government resides at the local level in this state. Here things like contracts for picking up your garbage, downzoning and obtaining variances to do as you please on your own land can make you a millionaire, or a pauper, overnight.

Some county supervisors operate like feudal lords. They are untouched by the restrictions of term limits and largely ignored by the glare of the news media that is interested only in covering the A-list in Washington and the state capital. Supervisors in large counties in this state have constituencies larger than members of Congress. They reign over districts more vast than the Spanish land grants. And like the colonial dons of early California, some are in the habit of exercising unquestioned authority.

In a state where many citizens don't read, write, or speak English, where voters trudge through their daily existence like vassals, paying their taxes and asking few questions, a well-greased machine can maintain power for decades on nothing but its own perpetual motion. If you want your streets swept, your sewers unplugged, and the doors to your health clinic kept open, you'd better sign on to your local supervisor's oath of fealty. In some shining communities, it has reached the level of Stalin's utopian state. Here it no longer matters who votes. It only matters who counts the vote. It's the old ward system, alive and well in sunny Southern California.

"So our man Tresler is the common thread between Dana, Metz, and Fittipaldi. Their ticket to the arts commission. So what does it mean?" says Harry.

"Probably nothing," says Tolt.

"You don't think Tresler was in somebody's pocket?" says Harry.

"If it was anybody else, I'd say only up to his elbows," says Adam. "But Tresler doesn't need the money."

"The devil's got a corner on sin, but he still wants more," says Harry. My partner is a firm believer in the dark side of man.

"He's into power, yes. Taking bribes—you can look, but my guess is you're wasting your time. The fact of the matter is he had to appoint somebody. Why not the people who gave him money for his campaign? Sorry to say, but I have given in that cause myself," he tells us. "As well as a few others."

This doesn't surprise either Harry or me.

"It's hard to tote your load without greasing the skids," says Adam. "We all pretend it's not extortion, just the exercise of our First Amendment rights. Still there are times when most of us would rather not engage in that form of expression."

"Maybe we should see who else gave?" I say.

Tolt gives me a "What do you mean?" expression.

"Check Nick, Dana, Metz, our friend Nathan Fittipaldi. There should be disclosure statements filed someplace."

"My guess is it won't tell you anything you don't already know. Everybody who is anybody is likely to show up on Tresler's list," says Adam.

"All the same, we'll take a look."

It will tell me one thing: whether Dana gave in her own name. She told me that she didn't know Tresler. Now I want to know if she told me the truth.

Harry makes a note on the back of one of Adam's business cards, snatched from the little holder on his desk.

"What I can't understand," says Tolt, "is why Nick would enter into a business arrangement with Metz?"

I shake my head. "I don't know. But it does seem that Metz was obsessed with getting Nick on the hook for legal work."

This sets a few more wrinkles in Adam's forehead. "That's the part that bothers me most. It has a connection to the firm, and I don't like it. It seems to me this would only make sense if this business, this Jamaile whatever it was, was intended as an import-export conduit for drugs. In which case Nick's services would be a major asset."

He looks at me to see if I have any other theories. I don't.

"I like to think Nick got cold feet," he says. "That he thought about it and either decided not to, or that if he got involved, the better angles of his nature asserted themselves, and he wanted out."

"Maybe that's why they killed him?" says Harry.

"That was an accident, remember?" says Tolt.

"Oh. Right," says Harry.

The room falls quiet as we consider scenarios of what might have happened in Nick's life. Only the ticking of the antique regulator clock on the wall breaks the silence.

"There is a possibility," says Adam. He is still deep in thought, fingers now steepled, forefingers touching his lower lip as his brain tries to untangle the human equation.

"Of course it's only a theory," he says. "It wouldn't do to talk about it, especially right now with the question of insurance and accidental death in the air." He looks at Harry and me, looking for agreement on a vow of silence.

"What's one lawyer's theory, but a guess?" I say.

"Right. But consider for a moment. What if Metz was drawing Dana in, trying to get her involved, let's assume for the moment anyway, without her knowledge, in some extra-legal activity."

"To what purpose?" says Harry.

"In order to gain leverage over Nick," he says.

"She says she didn't know Metz that well. They'd only talked a few times," I tell him.

"Yes. But it would explain Nick's efforts to palm Metz off on you, wouldn't it?" he says. "To put some distance between himself and this man, while protecting his wife." Adam is a man well studied in human motivations.

"Go on."

"If the two men weren't getting along," he says, "Nick might threaten to blow the whistle. If that's what happened, Nick could have become a very real threat to them, to the people who killed them."

"You mean the people on the other end of the drug connection?" says Harry.

Tolt nods.

"I just don't think Nick would have ever gotten involved in drugs," I tell them.

"I don't like to think of one of my partners doing it either," says Adam, "but stranger things have been known to happen, human nature being what it is. And you have to admit, from all appearances, the Rushes must have been having some financial difficulties." He glances down at the spreadsheet from Nick's client trust account on the desk in front of him.

It's one of the unanswerable questions. Where did all the money that Nick made over the years go? Without an audit, canceled checks from his accounts, credit card receipts, we will never know.

Adam sits up from his brief reverie. "In any event, for the time being it wouldn't do to engage in too much idle speculation about victims. Especially now that a certain insurance carrier is getting ready to dip its pen in the ink pot and put its signature to a check."

"Point well taken," says Harry.

"What are we going to do about this other thing?" says Tolt. He means the forged trust account checks.

"Let me talk to Dana."

"Fine. Just don't take too long."

CHAPTER FOURTEEN

I take I-5 south from the Coronado bridge and acceler-
ate into the middle lane, past Logan Heights. At National, I take the freeway off-ramp and head east. In my
rearview mirror I can see the giant vapor lights from the
naval shipyard as they infuse their eerie orange glow into
the looming cloud deck that hangs over the bay.

It is nearly nine o'clock. Midweek traffic at this hour of
the night is light. A fine mist covers my windshield.

The streets are empty except for a few souls wandering
aimlessly. The only businesses lit up at this hour are liquor
stores and a few taverns.

It takes twenty minutes to find the street Espinoza mentioned during our last conversation at the federal lockup. I
have confirmation that at least this much of what he told me
is true.

The neighborhood exudes the kind of aura picked up by
a sixth sense that lingers and lifts the hair on the back of my
neck. It is not a place I'd want to walk my dog at night

unless the pup has sharp teeth, likes red meat, and can out-run a bullet.

I see lights at the next corner, so I slow down. As I get closer, I see some teenagers, one of them in a dark hooded sweatshirt leaning into the passenger window of a car stopped in the middle of the street halfway into the inter-section. The car is rocking to the beat of salsa jive from a sound system that vibrates the roots of my teeth whenever it hits bass.

The kid in the sweatshirt and his two friends check me out as I drive by. Maybe I'm a customer or maybe I'm under-cover. They lose interest as I head down the street.

I'm moving slowly, looking for street numbers. The driz-zle and the lack of streetlights make it impossible. I check the scrap of paper on the console next to me, the notes I'd made following my meeting with Espinoza at the lockup earlier in the week. This is the place. Espinoza was cryptic, but he did give up some information.

According to him, the man Jaime had an alternate hang-out whenever he was in town. He had gone there several times for meetings and on two occasions did not return at night. Espinoza told me that he drove Jaime to this place once, just before he left San Diego for Mexico. Espinoza dropped him off and said the number was either 406 or 408, he couldn't remember. But he told me that he saw the man that Jaime met. The guy was tall, over six feet, and skinny. Like a pole, according to Espinoza. The man was Hispanic and had a straggly dark beard, black hair, and wore a dirty gray felt hat. He watched this man talk to Jaime for a few seconds out in front of the house before the two of them went inside and Espinoza drove off. The only other thing he could remember was an older-model Chevy Blazer parked along the side of the house. He said he remembered it be-cause the large window in the back was smashed in and someone had covered it with a large piece of black plastic wrapped in duct tape around the window frame.

I drive past kids' toys on the sidewalk. Over the front door on a house near the end of the block, I see what appear to be three rusted metal numerals nailed to the frame in the shadows. I squint, trying to penetrate the darkness. It looks like 486.

I drive on, and this time I turn at the corner, pull a short distance up the cross street, and park at the curb, turning off my lights.

I had changed from my suit and tie at the house. I'm wearing an old pair of jeans, a navy blue slipover shirt, and a faded denim jacket I use for outdoor work. On my feet are a pair of running shoes.

I step out of the car, lock the door, then check my watch. It's almost nine-thirty.

It takes only a few seconds to make my way back to the corner and head down the street. I stop two doors down at the house where I saw the street number over the door. The drizzle has turned to a light mist, so in the dark I cannot see rain falling. Still I can feel wet pin pricks of moisture on my forehead and the back of my neck. I turn the collar of my jacket up and walk down the street. Moving slowly on foot, and being closer to the house, up on the sidewalk, I now have no difficulty making out the number over the door. As I approach the bottom of the steps, the tin numbers 486 are clearly visible above the front door. Even numbers are on this side of the street. Unless Espinoza has sent me on a goose chase, the house I'm looking for is on this side.

I hear the hot salsa and see the red taillights from the vehicle a block and a half down still stopped in the intersection. I move quickly down the sidewalk until I'm two doors from the end of the block, when suddenly a beam of light bounces off the wet pavement in the center of the street. The headlights are coming from behind me and moving fast. I skip across a damp patch of grass in front of one of the houses and duck under the front stairway. I have no desire to be silhouetted from behind for the crowd around the car, now just a little more than a block away.

I take a deep breath and settle under the stairs for a couple of seconds to get my bearings. Just as I'm about to step out, I look behind me. There on a door leading to a ground-level apartment is the number 406A. It is stenciled in faded block letters. I can hear the muted sounds of a television from somewhere inside, either upstairs or beyond the door behind me.

I step back out to the sidewalk and check the car with the salsa crowd still in the intersection at the end of the next block. Another vehicle has now joined them, pulling up behind the first car. The guys on foot have now divided forces, talking commerce through the open windows of both vehicles.

I look back at the house. There's a large bush against the front. Behind it partially concealed is a ground-floor window through which I can see the flickering translucent blue light of a television reflected against the pulled-down shade inside.

I look to my left at the house next door, and notice that there's a ground-level apartment under its front staircase as well. Running in from the sidewalk and dead-ending against this other house is a double strip of concrete each a little wider than the width of a car tire. Between them is a little gravel and what is now wet, packed hardpan with a light rainbow sheen of motor oil floating in the puddles. This driveway dead-ends into the front of what used to be a garage, now finished off as the exterior wall of a downstairs apartment.

I step across the two strips of pavement, through the grass and look at the door under the stairs of the second house. It is numbered 408A.

I walk back out to the sidewalk and check 406. There is no driveway on the other side. Here the long blades of grass on both sides of the stairs stick up like spikes. I'm not a gardener, but it doesn't take an expert to tell that these weeds and crabgrass have not been crushed under the wheels of a heavy vehicle anytime recently. Nor is there a ramp through the curb to the sidewalk.

If Espinoza was telling the truth, and his memory wasn't clouded as to the Blazer with its broken rear window and where it was parked, I'm betting that 408 is the address for the man with the beard and the felt hat.

I look over again. The downstairs apartment appears dark, as least as much of it as I can see through a small side window on the house. I back away, all the way to the sidewalk, and check the action in the intersection to my right one more time. There's a regular traffic jam there now. Enough cars that I can't count them all. A land office business, some coming, some going, music and the sound of voices, what passes for the commerce of the night in this neighborhood. I check my watch. It's now after ten.

Espinoza didn't say whether Jaime and the other man, the one in the felt hat, went up the stairs or underneath them when they went inside. Not knowing the layout, I could not anticipate the question or think to ask.

From the sidewalk I check the upstairs windows at the front of 408. On the first floor one of them shows the glow of a television. Another smaller window, perhaps a bathroom, has a light on inside.

On the top floor everything is dark. I walk down the sidewalk twenty feet or so and check the left side of the house. There are windows, but they're all dark. I go back the other way. One light toward the rear on the first floor. I can't tell how many apartments there are.

I check to make sure no one is watching from a window or one of the dark porches across the street. I would never hear the end of it from Harry if somebody called the cops and he had to come down and post bail on a peeping and prowling charge.

From what I can see, it looks clear, so I climb the stairs and find the mailbox on the porch. Underneath each slot is a name on a slip of paper slid into a groove, some of them typed, some written in pencil or pen. I take out my house keys. Attached to the key ring is a small light. I press the button on the side of this, and the muted red beam flashes on the names.

APT. A: JOHNSON
APT. B: HERNANDEZ

No initials.

APT. C: ROSAS, JAMES
APT. D: WASHINGTON, LEROY
APT. E: RUIZ, R.
APT. F: MORENO

Again no initials.

APT. G: SALDADO, H.

Using the light and a small notepad from my pocket I make notes with a pencil. Completing this task, I head quickly down the stairs. I retrace my steps to the car, and in less than a minute, I'm parked across the street half a block from the house with the driveway. I park between two other vehicles facing toward the house where I can see the front porch and the apartment underneath.

I check my watch. It is almost ten-thirty. Sarah should be getting home any minute. She has a key. I told her not to wait up. At fifteen, she is a good kid, straight As, and quiet. She is the one person I think about before accepting any cases I suspect might involve risk or before doing foolish things such as I am doing tonight.

I settle in, one eye on the cross traffic a block away. For some reason all of this business seems to approach in the perpendicular direction of the cross street. Why I don't know, but it keeps the approaching headlights to a minimum so that slumped down in the driver's seat it's not likely anyone is going to see me.

I snooze a little, one eye open. Every once in a while as business becomes thick at the intersection, traffic jams up, and a car will turn this way, forcing me to slide down a little deeper into the seat.

I don't know how long I've been dozing, but both eyes are closed when I wake to the sound of tires squealing on pavement. I open my eyes and try to quickly gain my bearings. The street vendors a block down have all disappeared.

All I see is the fading glow of taillights from the last car that turned and headed away from me. Within two seconds, they turn on another street and are gone. The intersection is now completely deserted.

I sit, slumped in the front seat, wondering what's happened. It doesn't take long before the answer arrives. It comes in the form of a police cruiser trolling slowly through the intersection, its light bar flashing disconcerting strobes. The cops inside use their spot to light up the bushes and the shadows against the house on the corner. They do a slow drive through the intersection and check the front of the house on the opposite corner. They keep moving slowly, and suddenly, as quickly as they arrived, the reflection of colored light is gone.

I continue to watch the intersection for several minutes. Nothing. No action. It appears the cops have scared them off.

Then all of a sudden, vehicle lights round the corner behind me. I slump down deep into the seat so that I am now mostly under the steering wheel, my legs folded at the knees up under the steering column. My head and shoulders are leaning off toward the passenger seat, so I am hunched down below the driver-side window.

The car approaches slowly. I hear its wheel crushing gravel on the pavement outside. Now I can make out the call signals on their police band even with their windows rolled up.

They strafe the three parked cars with the spotlight. Jets of streaking bright white flood through the windows, and suddenly the light bar comes on again. If they catch me lying on the floor, parked a block from Super Narco, they are likely to take every screw out my car looking for drugs. They will take my name off my license whether they find anything or not. Within twenty-four hours I'll be drawing curious glances from prosecutors and clerks in the courthouse. Judges will be peering into my eyes, looking for that glassy stare. God help me if I show up sleepy in court some morning, like tomorrow.

The patrol car stops next to the vehicle parked behind mine. A door opens. The police band is now loud enough that I can hear the static between calls. Footsteps outside.

He pulls on the door latch of the car behind me. It slips out of his fingers. Locked. He won't have this problem if he tries mine. It's too late to lock it. Besides I know he's looking through the window with a flashlight.

I get a mental image. He pops the door and finds me unconscious under the steering wheel. They have to call for the Jaws of Life to pry me out.

I can tell he is checking carefully now, looking through the windows with a flashlight. A beam moves around through my rear window.

"Jimmie."

"Yeah. I see him."

My heart is pounding.

A car door slams with a thud. Suddenly the engine hits on all cylinders. Tires screech next to my ear, just outside the door. In an instant, it's dark again, quiet. I hold my breath, waiting. It seems like an eternity. Probably fifteen seconds. I ease my head up, like a turtle coming out of its shell. I shimmy up past the steering wheel, wondering how I fit beneath it. The mysteries of adrenaline. My lower back is killing me.

Near the intersection of action I see the patrol car stopped, the light bar sparkling in its disorienting rhythm of red and blue. Spread across the front of the police unit is the kid in the dark-hooded sweatshirt. The hood is now pulled down so that a buzz cut is visible, dark stubble on his scalp.

One of the cops spreads his feet, then speed cuffs the suspect's hands behind his back. His partner is gingerly going through the guy's pockets.

The cop doing the search keeps depositing little discoveries on the hood of the car, poking different ones every once in a while with a finger, examining it under the glare of a flashlight like a miner checking for nuggets.

The other cop is down on his haunches now, feeling around the kid's ankles. Maybe looking for a gun.

Then suddenly, Eureka! I can almost hear him. When he stands up he's holding a roll of bills from inside the kid's sock, along with what appears to be some product, some little plastic packets. I can see them glitter in the beam of the spotlight that is now focused on the hood of the patrol car.

Another police car, a backup unit, approaches from the opposite direction. Within seconds there's a convention of blue standing in the middle of the intersection, light bars flashing.

They continue searching the kid. One of the cops comes up with a shoe in one hand and a sock in the other. He looks in the shoe and flips it on the ground. He starts shaking the sock. Little white packets fall out all over the hood of the car.

His colleague keeps shaking the sock. Things keep falling out. A regular horn of plenty. There are smiles all around from the guys in uniform.

Another patrol car pulls up. I'm starting to get nervous. They may camp here for the night, decide to go on a safari looking for the guy's friends.

Enough excitement for one night. I check my watch. It is now nearly one in the morning. The house across the street is pitched in darkness all across the front. The glow of the television in the upstairs window is gone. I'm wasting my time. Espinoza is jerking my chain. He's probably given me the address of one of his coyote caves, a place where he deposits illegals, part of the underground railroad to the promised land.

I watch as the cops put the kid into the backseat of one of the patrol cars. Ten minutes later, it begins to mist again, and the street party breaks up. Light bars extinguished, they head off in different directions. No doubt they figure they've chilled the action at the intersection for the night.

I reach for the key and I'm just about to turn the ignition, when I see the silhouette of a figure across the street.

He has stepped out of the shadows near the front door where I couldn't see him. He leans out, looks to see if the cops are gone. I can see him from the thighs up, as he leans against the solid three-foot-wall of the porch railing, both hands slipped into the pockets of his jeans. He is tall, slender, the dark outline of his head rounded to a point. He is wearing a hat to ward off the rain, a felt crusher with the brim turned down.

CHAPTER FIFTEEN

The next day I stumbled through an early morning court call downtown. Luckily it wasn't something that required mental dexterity. It was only a first appearance. I stood next to my client in the dock for a reading of charges and thumbed through my calendar to fix a date for entry of a plea. Between calendar pages, I wiped sleep from my eyes, having been up half the night looking for the man in the funny hat.

I have whittled down the names on the mailboxes to five possibilities. Given that Espinoza told me the guy was Hispanic, this is not rocket science.

Hernandez; James Rosas; R. Ruiz; someone with the last name of Moreno; and H. Saldado. Narrowing it beyond this, assuming the guy's name is even on the box and that he hasn't used an alias, will be more difficult. Then, assuming I can identify him, and assuming further that I trace some link between this man and the Ibarras down in Mexico, the two brothers Metz told me about, I might have something.

I'm laughing at myself. What I have is a pile of assumptions. I'm beginning to think Harry was right: I should forget it.

While I'm thinking this, I'm thumbing the white pages of the San Diego phone book. I find Hernandez, two pages of them. Without an initial, I'm left to check for the street address. Using a ruler to scan down the first page, I flip to the second. I'm actually surprised when I find it. "Susan." I scratch the name off my list. It might be easier than I thought.

A half hour later I have found James Rosas and R. Ruiz, first name Richard, both at the right address. I write down their phone numbers. There are lots of Morenos but none of them on the right street. Several of them show phone numbers with no address. Without a first initial, I draw a blank. I have the same problem with Saldado, even with the first initial H. Assuming it's a man, he either has no phone or he's unlisted. I flop the white pages closed in the middle of my desk, lean back in my chair, and think.

After a couple of seconds, I access my computer phone directory, do a search for a name, and when it pops up, I hit the auto dial. On the third ring, I get an answer. I grab the receiver off the cradle before she's finished saying: "Carlton Collections."

It's a woman's voice, raspy, with a lot of phlegm.

"Joyce?"

"Yeah, who's this?" Lisping like she has a cigarette dangling from her mouth.

"Paul Madriani."

"Ahh, my favorite lawyer." I can hear her wheezing on the intake. This is followed by a coughing jag, several wretched hacks, like a wood rasp working over a piece of pine.

I move the phone a couple of inches away from my ear to save my hearing.

"Hey, Bennie, it's Paul Madriani."

"Who?" I hear her husband in the background.

"Paul Madriani. You know, the lawyer."

"Don't tell me the fuckin' D.A. wants to talk to us again."

"No," she says. "He's just callin' to say hello."

"Tell him hello," he says.

"Bennie says to say hello. You are just calling to say hello?"

I tell her to pass greetings the other way. She does.

"So, what is it you want? A busy lawyer like you doesn't call just to chew the fat. Lemme guess. You got a deadbeat client you want us to find? Am I right?"

"Not exactly."

"Like I tol' you in court that day, my word is my bond. This one's on the house. Didn't I tell him that, Bennie?"

Joyce shouts this so loud I have to pull the phone away, but I can hear Bennie.

"Yeah. Yeah."

"Gimme the name, I'll draw 'n' quarter the bastard," she says.

Joyce and Ben Swartz own Carlton Collections. Where they got the company name I don't know. Probably off a pack of cigarettes. It sounded more WASPish than Swartz. This might be a plus if Joyce wasn't answering the phone.

The one thing I do know, phlegm or no phlegm, if you owe money, you don't want Joyce, her nose to the ground sniffing along in your trail of bad debts.

I have seen people suffer less who have had their knees capped by the mob. She will find you at your house, at your neighbor's, at your mother's, floating down the Merced River, in Yosemite, on your vacation. Your children will come home from school with notes in their lunch pails, telling you to pay up. If you go to a wedding, your name and the amount you owe will be printed in lipstick on the back window of the groom's car. Joyce views federal and state debt collection laws as a challenge. If she can't call you at your job, she will hire a skywriter to fly over your place of employment and print your name in block letters at five thousand feet, followed by the word "deadbeat" in pink smoke.

Most collectors have a series of dunning letters, starting with a polite request and ending with suggestions that your

kids may be sold into slavery. With Joyce, you get one polite letter. After that your ass belongs to her.

About a year ago, she pushed beyond the bounds when she
lowered the boom on a local church that was waiting for the
second coming to pay a printing bill. One Sunday at services
she showed up dressed to the nines, with a hat, and sporting
a name tag. She stood at one of the main doors out front, smiling at the gray-haired usher on the other side as he greeted the
morning congregation and wondered who the nice lady vol-
unteer was. Joyce handed out morning bulletins to a few hundred of the faithful.

When the pastor took to the pulpit, he couldn't figure
why members of his flock kept laughing every time he mentioned hell. Joyce had stuffed the bulletins with a dunning
letter for the printing bill, and it reminded the readers that the
devil is a deadbeat. They all stopped laughing when a sher-
iff's deputy showed up, armed with papers to do a till tap on
the morning offering. Unfortunately for Joyce, one of the
church elders was the chief deputy district attorney.

"So what's the guy's name?" she says. "This guy you
want us to find."

There is no client, I tell her. "The State Bar frowns on my
using your services for that."

"Why? They don't like us?"

"It's nothing personal," I tell her. "They make us arbitrate
any unpaid bills by clients."

"You're a lawyer. You telling me you don't win those?"
she says.

"Even if we win, it's usually suggested that we forget it.
It's bad P.R. Too many people already hate lawyers," I say.

"This bar, with an organization like that, it's a wonder you
can stay in business."

"Tell me about it."

"So wad is it you want?"

"I'd like you to check some names, see if you can get information on some people."

"What? Like their credit history?"

"Maybe. That might help."

"You wanna skip trace maybe?"

"Not exactly. I know where these people live. What I don't have in some cases is a first name, a telephone number, employment information if you can find it. Where they bank. Who their friends are." I give her the names from my list, and the street address.

"And so that you don't get in any trouble," I tell her. "This is not a neighborhood you want to visit. Only what you can get at arm's length, understand?"

"Hey. I don't go anywhere I don't take Bennie with me."

That's what I'm afraid of.

"What else have you got?" she says. "No social security number? Maybe a vehicle license plate?"

"No. Sorry."

"That's it? Last name—first initial? And you don't even got that for some of these people."

"And the street address," I remind her.

"You don't want much," she says.

"One other thing. The man I'm looking for. It's possible he deals drugs."

"Hmm. Well, now, that could help," she says.

"How is that?"

"This guy deals drugs, he's gotta have a pager, right? A cell phone? You ever seen a drug dealer doesn't have a pager and cell phone?"

"I don't know that many drug dealers," I tell her.

"Take it from me. They got pagers and cell phones. People like that they always do. Of course sometimes these belong to somebody else," she says. "That's the business to be in."

"What, cell phones?"

"Stealing them," she says. Knowing Joyce, I know she is only half kidding.

"So I guess we start by doin' the big five," she says.

"What is that? Jump in the air and slap hands?"

"Noo. Noo." Joyce has no sense of humor. "That's the high five," she says. "This is the big five. Different thing. These are the carriers. There's five major ones offer all the wireless in this county. I know. We collect for them all. So, this guy you're looking for. He's got a cell phone; I'll get his number. You want I should get you a copy of his monthly cell statement? Won't cost you any more, seeing as it's on the house."

"You can do that?"

She hesitates for just a second. "For you, sure. When do you need this?"

"Yesterday," I tell her.

"Gimme a day or so," and she hangs up.

CHAPTER SIXTEEN

I have put this off as long as I can. Adam Tolt is expecting a call from me before the end of the day. So this afternoon I call Dana and tell her I have to see her, here in my office. She asks if it's about the insurance. I tell her that's part of it in order to get her here. Then I tell her there is also something more serious we need to discuss.

It's a quarter after three, and she's late. When she finally comes cruising into reception, she's not alone. Nathan Fittipaldi is with her.

I am on the phone with a client, the door to my office only partly closed so that I can see them through the opening. They are both decked out, dressed like two college preppies headed to a party.

Fittipaldi has on a pair of tan slacks and a pullover shirt with Ralph Lauren's polo rider tattooed over one tit. The sleeves of a white sweater are draped over his shoulders and tied loosely around his neck. He is running a comb through dark hair, parting it in the middle, looking like some over-the-hill heartthrob off the cover of *Gentlemen's Quarterly*.

Dana is in a pair of white tennis shorts, tight enough that they leave little to the imagination, along with a blue sleeveless top that shows a lot of freckled and browned shoulders. She has on a white tennis cap, one of those visors with an adjustable strap and nothing but blond hair for the top. Her eyes are shaded in a pair of designer sunglasses that I suspect have set her back a good four hundred bucks.

She takes these off and holds one earpiece casually between her front teeth as she doffs the cap, drops it on our counter out front, and arranges her hair, holding a little mirror from her purse in one hand. "I must look a mess." She giggles.

"You look great," he says as he comes up behind her and snuggles.

When she turns this way, she sees through the crack in the door and spies me sitting in my office, phone to my ear, talking. To Dana this is an open invitation. Before I can tear myself away and close the door, she reaches it. Leaning over, smiling at me like she's playing peekaboo through the opening, she pushes it open all the way and waves, giving me the full benefit of her pearly whites beaming in my doorway.

Fittipaldi walks up behind her, standing a good foot taller than Dana and gawking at my office. He is buffed up, stretching out the shoulders and chest of his shirt, looking very fit.

"Paul, you know Nathan, don't you?"

With the phone in one hand, I hold up the palm of the other, letting them know that I like to finish one conversation before starting another.

"Oops." Dana laughs. Covers her mouth with one hand. Silly me.

She turns to Fittipaldi and mouths the words: "You two know each other," so that I can read her lips from across the room. Then she nods, a kind of self-assuring bob of the head to reinforce that I am part of the in crowd.

"Oh yeah, sure." He smiles, nods toward me, hands in his pockets now.

Deprived of the gene of discretion, Dana just wanders in. She waltzes around in my office with her hands clasped behind her back like Leslie Caron playing Gigi. She studies all the pictures on my walls, my license from the State Supreme Court, the framed wall certificates from the Southern District of the Federal Court, and one next to it from the Ninth Circuit.

While she's doing this, Nathan is standing in the open door, checking the place out. I sense from his expression that my office is not up to gallery standards.

"No, I understand. I know what you want. I don't know that it's possible, but I can try." I'm trying to keep the conversation with my client cryptic and confidential, a local businessman facing four felony counts of fraud and embezzlement.

Dana turns toward Fittapaldi and whispers: "I hope this isn't going to take too long." This is loud enough for me to hear, since she is standing only four feet from my desk. The woman waiting for a two-million-dollar insurance check, buying groceries out of her dead husband's client trust account, is in a hurry.

Then out loud she says: "It really is a beautiful car, Nathan. I just love it. I can't wait to get going." Knowing Dana, she wants the money. I can keep any bad news.

I'm forced to cup one hand over the mouthpiece in a futile effort to keep her voice from bleeding over the line to my client.

"Is somebody there?" he asks.

"Someone just walked in," I tell him.

She turns and looks at me. Motions with a finger back toward the other room, questioning the obvious, that I might like her to leave.

I shake my head. I'll have to continue the phone call another day.

Dana is flushed, her cheeks red, pixie hair turned to corn silk by the summer sun.

"Listen, I'm gonna have to call you back. Why don't I give you a call tomorrow? Are you going to be in the office?"

He tells me he is.

"I'll call you in the afternoon."

With a female voice in my office swooning over a car, he's afraid I might have better things to do, that I might forget, so he presses for a further commitment.

"Yes. No. I'll call you before three."

Before my receiver can hit the cradle, Dana bubbles all over my desk. "I thought you wouldn't mind if I brought Nathan along," she says. "We were just out for a ride. He was showing me his new Jaguar KX."

"XK," he says.

She laughs. "What do I know about cars? I mean, I just know it's beautiful." She turns to Fittipaldi as if to reassure him that he isn't riding around town in some pile of crap.

"You really have to see this car," she tells me. "It's a kind of midnight blue, brand-new."

Fittipaldi stands in the doorway beaming, as if he's just given birth.

"We came up the Strand with the top down. And let me tell you, this thing moves. Not like the Mercedes Nick drove." The way she says it makes it sound as if it's not only Nick's car that caused him to come up short against Nathan. "We were going to head up the coast for dinner. Nathan knows this great little place up in Del Mar."

"Really?"

The first word I've been able to get in.

"You really have to see this car. And feel the seats. I mean, I just sat there in the passenger seat and turned my face against it. It felt like a cloud." She says this all dreamy with her eyes closed.

About now, this is beginning to sound like a plan. Go outside, toss my lunch, and rub my face all over Nathan's fine upholstery.

"And I doubt if you'll believe this, but they're authentic jaguar," she says. "And sooo smooth." This time she adds a little motion to the words, rubbing her bare thighs just below the hem of her shorts with the flat palms of her hands. Of course this requires her to stick her little tush out. It's a kind of Marilyn move, which Dana has so perfected that she now owns it.

None of this is wasted on Fittipaldi as his eyes suck up the full motion.

"Not everyone could do this," she says. "But Nathan had it special ordered through a dealer in Manhattan. He had the interior redone by them."

She turns to look at him, dropping the dark glasses into her purse. "Where are they, darling? A block from your gallery back there?"

"Two blocks," he says.

"Really? I can't imagine a car dealership springing for the square footage in Manhattan. To say nothing of bagging jaguars to line their seats."

"Well, they're just down the street from Nathan's gallery."

He clears his throat a little. "The jaguars were killed and skinned near the Guatemalan border."

"Yeah, I didn't think they had any in New York," I tell him.

"They were taken by Mexican poachers," he says. "The government caught them."

"Lucky for you," I say.

"They're not usually sold." I assume he's talking about the skins, not the Mexicans. "But these were auctioned off for a good cause."

"Of course. To cover your seats."

He laughs, though I can tell by his look he's not amused. "To expand wildlife habitat," he says.

"And you should see how he did the dash," says Dana.

"I don't think Mr. Madriani would be interested," he says.

I have seen Dana enough times to know that she can project a dozen different personalities. She can change these with the frequency of her wardrobe and usually does. I have seen her do nothing but shrug a bare shoulder in a crowded restaurant and watch as a hundred guys run for sweaters.

Today she knows I have something more serious than insurance to discuss. So she has turned on just enough of the helpless bubblehead, probably hoping it will soften the delivery of any bad news and perhaps bring me riding on my steed to the rescue.

She gushes over the car for a few more seconds until she finally runs out of breath and is forced to confront the fact that this is not the reason I called and asked her to come in.

"Oh, listen to me going on," she says. "I suppose you want to talk about the insurance. This is about the insurance, isn't it?" Dana's life is one long quest in pursuit of gratification. Give me the good news first. Don't give me the bad news at all.

She drops into one of my client chairs, puts her tennis hat on top of her purse near her feet, then looks at her watch. Cocktail hour in Del Mar.

I glance toward Fittipaldi.

"Oh, you don't have to worry about Nathan," she says. "He knows all about it. I mean he's the only one I've been able to talk to. Besides you." She adds this as an afterthought.

"Wonderful." I smile

"I don't know what I would have done without him," she says. "I mean without the two of you, I'd be lost. You two do know each other?" Furrowed brows over her big blue eyes.

"We've met," I say.

"Sure." Fittipaldi offers me his hand and a smile. Welcome to Club Dana.

We shake.

"Well, what kind of an offer did they make?" she says. She is fishing through her purse, comes up with some lip gloss, and before I can answer turns to Nathan again. "Have a seat." She pats the arm of the chair next to her.

As he sits down, she turns back to me. "They did make an offer, didn't they? You said this was about the insurance."

"Only in part."

"What then?"

"I think it would be best if we discussed it in private," I tell her.

"I can just wait outside," he says.

"No." She says this in an emphatic way. It catches him starting to boost himself out of a chair that hasn't even gotten warm yet.

She's glossing her lips, holding up a little hand mirror. "Anything you can tell me, you can tell Nathan," she says as if it is a point of principle. She interrupts the glossing. "After all, he's been the only one who's stood by me through all of this. I can't tell you how many friends, or maybe I should say people I thought were friends, have deserted me since Nick died. You never know people until something like this happens. I mean they see me coming in a store, they ignore me. No. I want Nathan to be here, to hear whatever it is you have to tell me." She's back to the lip gloss now.

He looks at me, tilts his head and smiles as if to say, "her call."

"I don't think that's a good idea," I tell her.

"Why not?"

"To tell you that, I'd have to tell you what it was, in front of Nathan."

This has her thinking. She looks at me, trying to read my mind. Then she guesses wrong.

"They turned us down, didn't they?" All of a sudden the bubble and fizz are gone. She stops glossing her lips and puts the mirror and gloss on the edge of my desk.

"If it's bad news," she says, "just tell me." But she doesn't wait for an answer. "I get it. They don't want to pay." She looks away, having made up her mind that this is it. The sparkle in her eyes is replaced by a look of determination. "I knew it," she says. "I told you, didn't I?" This is directed at Fittipaldi.

She is up out of her chair now. He stays seated, looking

at me with a painful expression, like "How did I get in the middle of this?"

"Didn't I tell you, Nathan?" Before he can answer, she turns back to me. "I told him yesterday the insurance company would screw me over. I knew it when I first saw that man. That . . . that Luther guy. What's his name?"

"Conover?" I say,

"Yes. Conover," she says. "I knew when he looked at me that he didn't like me." The bubbly little pixie is gone. To Dana it is now personal. She starts pacing the office just behind the two chairs.

"The way he kept looking at me. Eyeing me up and down," she says. "I knew what he was thinking."

"And what was that?" I ask.

She looks at me. "You know as well as I do."

When I give her an expression like I don't, she says: "He was . . ." Now she has trouble saying it. "He was wondering why someone like me would be married to someone like Nick."

I give her another dense look, a little shake of the head, like I don't get it. I'm curious. I want to hear what comes out of her mouth.

"I think what Dana means is that the insurance company was critical because of their age difference." Nathan saves her.

"That's it," she says. "I know that's what he was thinking. That I was some tawdry gold digger," she says.

I'm thinking to myself that I would never use the word "tawdry" to describe Dana.

"Can you imagine how hurtful that is?" she says. I expect her at any moment to be reaching for the Kleenex.

Instead she says: "Fine, if they want to play hardball, we'll accommodate them. Those damages you told them about. The punitive ones. How much do you think we could get?"

Dana may know nothing about sports cars, but instincts of reprisal and vendetta seem to come naturally. "We can take them to the cleaners," she tells me. "We'll sue the hell out of them. Think they can screw with me." She's talking to herself now, pacing again—her right forefinger to her bottom lip, the long nail touching a lower front tooth and smearing the red lip gloss a little—contemplating just how far she should have me turn the wheel on the rack once I get the insurance company stretched out.

Then she stops. She turns this way.

Sensing that something more serious is coming, Fittipaldi turns in the chair so that he can see her, so that his back is to me now.

I can tell from Dana's darting blue eyes that some dark thought has suddenly stimulated them from behind.

"Are they going to pay her?" she says. The *her* she is talking about is Margaret.

"Dana. We need to discuss this in private."

"They are, aren't they? That's it, isn't it? Damn it. I knew it. They've decided to pay that bitch instead of me." She looks at Nathan. "Over my dead body," she says. "I was the one who was married to Nick when he got shot. I was the one putting up with him, putting up with his crap, not her. You are gonna sue them?" She looks at me like suddenly I'm the enemy. "Or did they buy you off too?" she says.

"Dana!" Fittipaldi, his voice now assuming a tone of command, gets her attention.

He shakes his head slowly, a signal that maybe she has said too much, gone too far, that she should calm down, watch what she's saying.

From the smooth pelt of jaguar to cold steel in less than a minute.

I say nothing, waiting to see if she's going to fire up again. But she doesn't. Instead she stands there looking down at the carpet, back to Nathan and then to me, trying, I suspect, to remember all the little poisonous items that spilled over the glossy bottom lip when the devil took hold. When it's obvious she's stopped, I finally step in.

"Nathan is right," I tell her. "You need to sit down. Calm down." She looks at the chair, but she doesn't move toward it.

"The carrier has made an offer," I tell her.

It's as if a pale light flickers on behind her eyes. The steel lips begin to bend toward a smile.

"But the reason I called you here today, what I have to talk to you about, has nothing to do with the insurance. At least not directly. It's . . . well . . . it's much more serious than that."

What can be more serious than two million dollars in cash? This seems to freeze her brain cells. The light of hope in her eyes suddenly vanishes. They glass over, so within a couple of seconds after the words leave my lips, Dana's eyes are two watery blue marbles. She stands there wavering back and forth on limp legs.

When she finally focuses, she is looking not at me, but at Fittipaldi, who is still turned toward her in his chair. It is fleeting. It lasts only an instant, the expression of dark apprehension that passes over her face like the shadow of a black cloud.

I can't see Nathan's face.

For a second it looks as if her legs might actually buckle, but Fittipaldi is out of the chair, grabbing her before she does. She stumbles through one step then catches herself, as he settles her again into the other client chair.

He huddles over her. "She's not herself," he says. "She's been under a tremendous strain."

"Yes."

"Do you have anything? A drink? Maybe some brandy?"

"No brandy," I tell him. "Soft drinks and some wine in the refrigerator in the other room."

"Just some water," she says. "I'll be all right." She's running the back of one hand across her forehead, her eyes still a little glassy. Unless she is awfully good, this is no act. Dana is white as a sheet.

"If you could get it?" he says.

I leave to get a glass of water. It takes me a minute or so to find a clean glass in the cupboard of the lunch room, knock some ice from one of the trays up in the freezer area, and fill the glass with water.

I'm almost back to my office door when I hear Fittipaldi's voice in hushed, low tones. "Don't say anything. We're almost through this. Just stay cool."

As he looks up, I'm standing in the doorway with the glass in my hand, smiling like the butler who's listened at the keyhole.

"Don't say anything about what?" I ask.

"Oh, we were just talking." He has one knee on the floor, next to her chair, holding her hand, looking at me, wondering how much I might have heard outside the door.

Dana pulls herself together, sits upright in the chair. She takes a deep breath, now the full-bodied flesh of her former shadow. Color back in her face. I hand her the glass and she sips a little water. She gathers a little condensation with two fingers from around the outside of the glass and wipes it gently across her forehead. Takes some more and hits her neck and chest just above the bodice of her blouse.

Whatever it was that sent her spinning, Nathan has pulled her out of it.

"I don't know what it was," she says. "I just felt a little faint." She sips from the glass again.

"What is it you needed to talk to her about?" Nathan suddenly seems to be in charge. "Is it something that can wait until tomorrow?" he asks. "I think maybe I should get her home."

"It's a serious matter," I tell him. "But if it has to wait one day, I suppose it can."

"Good," he says.

"I'll just have to call and tell them."

Nathan leans toward me, almost saying it but he doesn't: "Tell who?"

Dana's eyes glance up at me, as I pass her and walk to the side of my desk, where I stop and face her. Even in her withered state, she is a bubble of anxiety, filled with questions she doesn't really want to ask but is unable to resist.

"No." She takes a deep breath. "I'm feeling better," she says. "I'd like to know what it is." She's holding the icy glass of water to her forehead now.

"It has to do with the law firm," I tell her. "Rocker, Dusha."

She looks at me for a full second, then her eyes close and she expels a breath. When she opens her eyes to look at me again, I suspect she knows what I'm talking about. But the sideways glance she shoots toward Nathan causes me to wonder if he does.

To resolve any doubt, I tell her: "They have a few questions regarding some of the accounts that Nick managed before his death."

"Oh." Her parched lips open a little, head nodding slowly. "I see. I'm feeling better," she says. "Maybe you're right. Maybe we should discuss this in private. After all, it is business relating to Nick's firm." She leans toward Nathan who still has one knee on the floor beside her. "Would you mind?" she says.

Suddenly Fittipaldi is the man standing out in the cold. "Sure." What else can he say?

"You're a dear," she says.

"If you need me, I'll just be outside the door."

Probably on his knees with his ear to the wood.

She lets his hand slip slowly out of hers, and he leaves the office, closing the door behind him.

"Are you sure you're all right?" I ask.

"I'm much better," she says.

Instead of sitting in the chair behind my desk I move around front and settle one cheek onto the edge of the desk, looking down at her in the chair.

"What was it you thought I was going to tell you?"

"What do you mean?"

"What do I mean?" I smile. "When you went all light-headed on us and almost flattened my ficus bush behind the chair there."

She smiles at the little joke I've made. "I don't know. I just suddenly felt faint."

"You seemed to be feeling just fine a few minutes ago, ready to do battle with the insurance company. Until I told you that wasn't why I called you in here. That it was something else, something more serious. What did you think it was?"

"I don't know. I'm not sure." She looks at the wall in one direction, then the other. Her eyes everywhere but on me.

"But you know why I called you here now, don't you?"

"I'm not sure." She offers up a mystified expression, but she's sweating, the first time I have ever seen Dana perspire. She has the glass to her forehead again, hoping to cover it with condensation, while she licks the gloss off her lips.

"Think about it," I tell her. "Or maybe we should call Nathan back in?"

"No," she says.

"I thought so. He doesn't know about the trust account checks, does he?"

She brings the glass from her forehead to her lap, so that she has something to focus on down low, away from my searching stare. She shakes her head quickly as if this might make the admission less painful.

"Tell me, did you do the checks before or after you started holding hands with Nathan?"

She shakes her head, shrugs a shoulder. She doesn't want to say.

"You thought I was going to tell you that the police wanted to talk to you about Nick's death, wasn't that it? I suppose that would tend to move all the blood into someone's feet. I mean if the news seemed to be coming at you all of a sudden like that, and if you'd been thinking about the possibility for a while."

She looks up. "Why would they want to talk to me? They already talked to me, right after it happened. I don't know what you mean."

"Yes, you do. You thought they might be looking at you. Thinking about the youthful widow, married to a man who was married to his job, a lawyer who, according to you, even with the work ethic of a Puritan, wasn't doing all that well financially. You could see how the cops might be thinking about all that insurance money and how two million dollars might go a long way to soothe the loss of a loved one.

"Oh, I know what you're thinking," I tell her. "The police and their narrow little minds, always filled with distrust. But I'm afraid that's a genetic deficiency we will both have to deal with. It's one of the conditions of employment in the police force. And a real pain in the ass if you're in my line of work."

She looks up at me and smiles, the first note that I might be on her side after all.

"Still, anybody with a reasonable mind might wonder about all the ways a young woman such as yourself might find to spend that kind of money. That was it, wasn't it?"

"I don't know. I'm not sure," she says. "But you're right about the police. They're very suspicious about everything. Who knows what goes on in their heads?"

"But, why would they be thinking all those thoughts?"

"I don't know that they are," she says. "You're the one who brought it up."

"Guess I did, didn't I? Fine. Let's talk about something else."

A look of relief in her eyes, a different direction.

"Let's talk about what Nathan didn't want you to tell me."

"What do you mean?"

"When I was standing outside the door with the glass of water?"

This is not the direction she hoped for. "Paul, listen." Her soothing tone turns to honey, sweet and running fast, like something off a hot stove. "I'm really not up to this right now. I'm not exactly feeling well."

"Feeling faint again, are we?"

"Well. Just a little," she says.

"Want to try another subject?" I ask.

She nods.

"Let's talk about the law firm, Rocker, Dusha. They have a difficult decision to make now. What to do with all those client trust account checks that somebody else wrote, drawing down Nick's fees? Unearned fees," I tell her. "I mean, they may have to service some clients and not get paid, since somebody else already took the money."

"What else can they do?" she says.

"Well, let's see." I rub my chin as if this takes some thinking, which it doesn't. "I suppose they'd have a handwriting expert examine the signatures on those checks. From what I'm told, it looks like the same signature on all of them. So that won't be hard. Then they'd go hunting for suspects, get exemplars, signatures from those suspects. Well, you can see where this leads?"

"How would they find suspects?" she says.

"Well, they have the accounts where the checks were deposited. The bank tellers are likely to remember a face, even if somebody else's social security number was used."

She just swallows this, making me suspect that perhaps she used disguises.

"But, I don't think finding the person who did it would be a problem for them. In fact, I think they already know who it is."

"How?"

"The person wasn't that careful taking the checks out of Nick's drawer," I tell her.

Her eyes get big. This shuts her up.

"Then comes the hard part. They have to make a decision."

She's waiting, anxiously.

"One, they could take the money out of whatever source of funds this person might have. Say for example, some lucrative insurance settlement. You know, try to sweep the whole thing under the carpet. Avoid the embarrassment to the firm. That is, if they can move fast enough to keep the State Bar from turning it into an open investigation."

I can almost see her eyes do a little nod on this one, the corners of her mouth turning up just a little in approval.

"Or, number two, they could turn the checks over to the district attorney's office, file charges for forgery and theft, and leave it in the D.A.'s hands. Now that, that last one is the cleaner course of action. It's the one any good lawyer would probably recommend. That's the one that doesn't get them in any trouble with the bar. They just lose a little public face, some P.R."

Corners of her mouth down again.

"Of course, with all those suspicious little minds and nothing else to do down at the police department, it wouldn't surprise me to see an epidemic of paranoia sweep through the place if the D.A. were to get his hands on those checks, depending, that is, on who signed them.

"In which case, I suppose we might have to show a little understanding for those with wayward minds who might be misled into thinking that you had a reason for wanting Nick to die a sudden death.

"I mean, what with all those checks bearing Nick's name in somebody else's signature, the full-court press on the insurance company for a couple of million, and you riding around town next to Dudley out there, the two of you with the top down sitting on jaguar pelts. I mean you have to admit, it does beat grieving."

"You make it sound so . . ." she searches for the word.

"Tawdry?" I say.

"Selfish," she says.

"That's a good word. I mean not good, but, well, I think you understand what I mean. So. Now." I lift the other cheek onto my desk so that I'm sitting completely on it, my feet dangling a few inches above the floor directly in front of her. "Before I have to call Adam Tolt back and talk to him about which direction the firm might want to go, why don't you tell me what it was that Nathan didn't want you to mention when I was standing outside the door?"

She sits there wide-eyed, considering her options: door number one, carpet sweeping; door number two, some serious felonies for forgery and theft with some probable time, and some good points toward motivation on a double murder. Her response, which takes a nanosecond, tells me this is not a hard choice.

"We had been seeing each other," she says, "for some time. Nathan and I."

"I am stunned."

"I mean before Nick died."

"You mean before he was shot, killed?" I say. "There is a difference."

"Yes. That's what I mean." She corrects herself.

"If Nick died of pneumonia in a hospital with Metz in the bed next to him, the police wouldn't be looking under every rock for the people who shot them. They'd just figure God did it, and you'd be free to hold hands with Nathan as if nothing happened. You do see the difference?"

She looks at me with a bitter expression. "We didn't tell the police about it. We didn't think they needed to know. It was private."

"And now you're worried they'll find out," I finish the thought for her.

She nods.

"How? The two of you having been so discreet?" I say.

"Oh, stop it," she says.

"No. I mean it. Nathan's an expert on discretion. He even has the word printed on his business card."

She doesn't like this, looking at me through mean little slits. "Even you have to understand," she says. "My marriage with Nick was over six months before he was shot." Now that she's angry, she doesn't seem to have any difficulty saying the word. "He retained bragging rights, that was all. And he used them with his friends constantly. You should know. You were one of them," she says.

"Hey. He never kissed and told with me."

"All the same, it was an empty marriage. He knew it and I knew it."

"Then why didn't you divorce him? Or did you find an easier way of dealing with the problem?"

"You can't seriously believe that I killed him or that I had anything to do with it?" Now that she wants something, my feckless acceptance of her denial, Dana's eyes go all soft again and teary. She is able to turn this on faster than most kids can shoot a squirt gun.

"No. It's not your style," I tell her.

She smiles. There is palpable relief as the hard set of her chin goes smooth and round again.

"You'd probably use poison or a knife," I tell her. "But I can't be sure about Nathan. After all, he is fond of fast cars, and whoever shot Nick left a lot of rubber on the street."

"We had nothing to do with it," she says. "You have to believe me."

"So now it's we? You can vouch for Nathan?"

"He didn't do it. He couldn't do something like that."

"You shouldn't sell yourself short," I tell her. "Underestimating your attraction to men like that. It doesn't become you."

She should be angry, but instead another instinct takes hold. Looking up at me, she moistens her lips with her tongue.

"You don't believe me. What can I do to make you believe me?" she says. She's going all soft and feminine now, getting dangerous, trying to find her poison gland.

"It's probably not you," I tell her. "It's just the cynic in me. I sometimes have trouble accepting that the earth is round too. But I get over it. Still, let's get back to my initial question. If you didn't love Nick, why didn't you divorce him?"

"I don't know. I probably would have if I'd found the right man," she says.

"So Nathan wasn't the right man, is that it?"

"Oh, I like Nathan," she says. What she means is until someone better comes along. "I mean . . . he's very serious. I really don't want to hurt him. I don't want him to know about the checks."

"Yes. I can imagine how that might cause him to have some second thoughts on the relationship. I suppose he'd at least want to lock up his checkbook and credit cards in the vault at night."

"Neither of us had anything to do with Nick's death. You

have to understand I was desperate," she says. "Nick left me three months behind on the house mortgage. I don't know where all the money was going. All I know is I wasn't seeing any of it. The bank was threatening to take the car away. He wasn't coming home half the time at night. We were hardly talking. I think he knew about Nathan. But he didn't seem to care. Something else was going on," she says. "Maybe he had somebody else. I don't know."

"He didn't tell you anything about it?"

She shakes her head.

I slide off the edge of the desk onto my feet and walk around to the other side, settle into my chair, and scratch my chin, thinking. I sit there for a long time, maybe a minute, saying nothing, just looking at the wall under the row of licenses.

To Dana this must seem like a year, just sitting there sweating.

"What are you going to do about the checks?" She finally breaks the silence.

"Well." I take a deep sigh. "It looks like you're going to come up a little short on your end of the settlement," I tell her.

"Yes. I know. Fifty-seven thousand dollars," she says.

"No. It's going to be a little more than that." I walk her through the settlement terms, the fact that Margaret is getting two million on the deal or she's going to walk. In which case the entire settlement goes away, and Dana has an ugly conversation with the D.A. over some bad checks and probably much more.

I break the news to her that Harry and I won't be compromising our fees for representing her in the settlement. This will be a full third of whatever she gets, including the fifty-seven thousand she has to pay back to Tolt's firm.

Through all of this, she sits listening. She doesn't argue. Just your average block of ice as she calculates what is left to take home after being ravaged by lawyers. She doesn't like it, but Dana doesn't have a lot of choices.

"Is that it?" she says.

"Assuming Tolt hasn't changed his mind and the State Bar hasn't descended on his office."

She snatches her purse and the little tennis hat from the floor in front of her, gets up out of the chair, and turns to leave. Her little white fanny sashaying away.

"There is one more thing," I say.

"What?" She turns, standing halfway between my desk and the door. To Dana, she's now paid the price for the luxury of a derisive look, her expression filled with scorn as she eyes me, one hand on her hip above her golden thighs.

"Do you know who Grace Gimble is?" I ask.

"Who?"

"Grace Gimble?"

"One of Nick's lovers, I suppose?"

"You tell me," I say.

"I've never heard of her."

"What about Jamaile Enterprises?"

She shakes her head, dismissive now. "You asked me about that once before," she says. "I told you I never heard of it. Can I leave now?"

"Just one more question, in case the cops ask me. What did you tell them about Nathan? Did they ask you about him?"

"No. Not by name," she says. "They just asked the general questions. How was my marriage to Nick? Were we happy? What was I supposed to tell them?"

"You might have tried the truth."

"Oh yeah. My husband and I were barely talking. He wasn't supporting me. I was seeing someone else. I don't know who he was seeing because he wasn't coming home nights. Oh, and by the way, he was worth more to me dead than he was alive. Great legal advice," she says.

She has a point.

CHAPTER SEVENTEEN

It is late June and from all accounts the cops are no closer to finding out who shot Nick than they were two months ago. The double murder has all the signs of an investigation going nowhere.

I pull into the parking lot on Harbor Boulevard and find an empty visitor's space. Zane Tresler's county office is located on the top floor of the Hall of Administration, a Spanish art deco tower facing the bay.

I clear security on the ground floor and take the elevator up to the executive suites. At the far end of the marble corridor is a set of double doors, translucent etched glass framed in mahogany, the name ZANE TRESLER stenciled in gold letters across the glass. Tresler represents District 5, and Adam was right, he is now chairman of the board.

I jerk the heavy door open and walk in. Reception is its own museum. A floor-to-ceiling display case is situated in the center of the room like a pillar of ice. Inside are artifacts of an earlier civilization. If I had to guess, I would say Central or South American. They contain pieces of ancient pottery arrayed on shelves around a large stone tablet, covered in white plaster with figures etched into it. The printed card next to it reads:

SIXTH CENTURY MAYAN STELA

This magnificently preserved Mayan tablet, covered in limestone plaster and etched with hieroglyphs, is an ancient document and form of written expression used by Mayan scribes to record important events or religious ceremonies. The stela presented here was discovered in 1932 near the ruins of Tulúm on the Caribbean coast of the Yucatán Peninsula. It is believed to have been transported from an even earlier site somewhere in Central Southern Mexico.

My appointment with Tresler is for ten. I am a couple of minutes early. I step around the display case and hand my card to the young woman sitting behind the counter.

She picks up the phone and sends my name back, listens for a second, then hangs up.

"Someone will be out to get you in a moment," she says.

I turn to check the display on this side, behind me. Here there are pieces of pottery, dishes and a jug, some with hairline cracks probably dating back to the time of Moses. The card typed in neat print next to them says: TOLTEC: TENTH CENTURY. I'm wrong. Before I can read further, I am paged from behind.

"Mr. Madriani?"

When I turn, a young man is standing in front of me.

"Hi. I'm Arnie Mack, one of Supervisor Tresler's A.A.s." He shakes my hand under a guileless grin.

"The man has quite a display," I tell him.

"Yeah. One of the supervisor's passions. He's really into archeology and history. He's working to fund a museum for the area."

"Yes. I'd heard that."

"If you follow me, I'll take you back." He leads me past reception, a guarded door that leads to the inner sanctum.

We arrive at another centered set of double translucent doors, each etched with gold lettering across them.

ZANE TRESLER
CHAIRMAN OF THE BOARD OF SUPERVISORS

When the kid opens the door, there is a kind of musty odor. It's a familiar smell that seems to linger in government buildings dating to the depression, the WPA of the 1930s. I have often equated this damp scent with the smell of power.

He takes a few tentative steps into the cavernous office. "Excuse me, sir."

"What?"

"Your ten o'clock is here."

"Well, let him in."

"He's here."

Seated behind a desk twenty feet away is a bald figure, wrinkles climbing up his pale forehead, ending only as they begin to traverse the crown of his head. This seems aimed at me, like a well-polished bullet, as Tresler's attention is focused down on a prodigious pile of papers centered on the leather blotter in front of him, the only items on top of an otherwise clean desk.

He seems to possess the attentive powers of a mystic, as he neither moves nor looks up, as our shoes click and shuffle against the hard marble on our way to his desk.

Slight of build, Tresler is not what you would expect of someone possessing an estate in the billions and holding the reigns to a political dynasty, even if it's just a local one. He is wearing a short-sleeved rayon white shirt, buttoned right up to the throat, with one of those string ties that were popular in the fifties, this one sporting a sizable piece of blue-green turquoise in a silver setting just below his Adam's apple. If I didn't know better, I might expect him to get out the banjo and guitar any second. His nose is almost touching the papers as he reads.

The kid looks at me, not sure whether he should go or not. "Sir."

"Get out," says Tresler. "Get the hell outta here. Can't you see I'm reading?"

"Your ten o'clock, sir."

"I know. I heard you. You think I'm deaf?"

"Yessir." The kid figures I'm on my own. He heads for the door, ice-skating across the marble on leather soles.

"Have a seat. I'll be done here in a minute." Tresler still hasn't looked at me.

I sit in one of the leather armchairs in front of his desk, cross one leg over the other, and watch him. This goes on for a long enough period that I might wonder if he hasn't passed out, except that his nose is still suspended over the pile of papers. Every minute or so, one hand will come up from behind the desk, off his lap to flip a page over onto the finished stack.

After a couple of minutes of this, I clear my throat.

"What are you here for? Ramiriz send you over here to kiss my ass?"

The Ramiriz he is talking about I assume is Bernardo, the presiding judge of the county's superior court.

"Actually no. I'm here on my own."

He finally looks up at me, a quizzical stare, then he reaches over and picks up a single sheet of paper. I can see through it, lines typed on the other side.

"Says here you're with the county bar," says Tresler. "Court budget." He pushes his glasses back up toward the bridge of his nose and takes a long hard look at me.

I am guessing he is in his late sixties, maybe seventy. Ordinarily you would give the benefit to someone his age and assume that irritability overtook him about the same time as flatulence—and probably for the same reasons. In Tresler's case, I suspect he came out of the womb this way.

"What do you want?" he says.

"Adam Tolt set up the appointment," I tell him. "He did me the favor. That may be the reason for the confusion on your calendar."

"Ahh. You're a friend of Adam's?" he says.

"We know each other."

"How is Adam?" He puts his schedule back down on the desk, off to the side.

"When I saw him yesterday he was fine."

"That's good. Glad to hear it." Tolt's name seems to have the same soothing effect as a mild laxative.

"You got a card?" he says.

The kid was too frightened to hand him the one he had, so I get another from my pocket and hand it to him.

He examines this. "Mad-re-ani."

"Mah-dree-ahnee," I say.

"You say Tolt sent you?"

"No. He made the appointment. He didn't send me. Adam and I are acquaintances," I tell him. "He was kind enough to schedule the appointment since I didn't know you."

"I see. Worked on some cases with him, have you? Adam's a good lawyer." He takes his glasses off and squints at me now, so that I sense he can no longer see me. He feels around until he opens the center drawer of his desk, pulls out a small polishing cloth, and goes to work on each lens, exhaling a little warm breath on them as he works.

"Represented me on a couple of matters," he says.

"I didn't know that."

"Oh, yeah. It's been a few years," he says. "Back in the sixties. Some property issues."

"As you say, he's a good lawyer."

He puts the glasses back on, so he can focus again. The cloth disappears into the center drawer, everything in its place.

"So if it isn't the court budget, what is it you need to see me about?"

"I'm looking for information on some appointments you made to the County Arts Commission some time ago?"

"People I appointed?" he says. "Why? One of them do something wrong?"

"One of them was killed," I tell him.

"When was this?"

"Two months ago. I think you probably read about it in the papers. His name was Gerald Metz. He was shot and killed out in front of the federal courthouse, along with his lawyer."

He looks at me, makes a face. "I remember seeing the headlines. But the name doesn't ring any bells. I don't think I know him."

"You appointed him."

"I appoint a lot of people to a lot of things. Doesn't mean I know 'em. You have questions about this, you can get the information from my staff," he says. "You go out the door there and find my secretary, give her your name, and she'll get whatever information we have."

"You say you don't remember the name Gerald Metz?"

"That's what I said."

"I have two other names. Can I ask you if you know either of them?"

"Listen, I'm busy," he says.

"What I need to know is, if you didn't know them personally, were they recommended for appointment by someone else? And if so, who?"

"Why would you want to know that? Who did you say you worked for? Are you a reporter?" Fangs start to come out.

"No, sir. I'm a lawyer. I had a friend who was also killed. He was the attorney who was killed."

He nods soberly. "I remember the shooting. Saw it in the papers. A terrible thing."

"The client's name was Gerald Metz."

"Emm."

"You didn't know that one of the men who was shot in that incident was someone you had appointed to the arts commission?"

"No." He shakes his head. "No one told me that. I knew Mrs. Rush was on the commission," he says. "I take it her husband was your friend."

"You know Dana?"

"No. I can't say I ever met her. But I knew the husband."

"How did you know Nick?"

"Oh, I don't know. Met him somewhere. An event, a fund-raiser. We'd met a few times. He seemed like a nice enough guy. What was the client's name again?"

"Gerald Metz."

He thinks about this, shakes his head slowly. "No. I don't think I know that name. I'm not saying I didn't appoint him. I just don't remember the name."

"So you wouldn't know offhand why you might have appointed Mr. Metz to the commission?"

"I'm sure he was qualified. But offhand I can't say."

"Would there be documents anywhere that might show whether there were recommendations made by others to your office regarding these appointments?"

"Could be," he says. I get the sense that the answer to this might depend on what I want to use these records for.

"Can you tell me how Dana Rush, Nick's wife, got appointed?"

"Oh, that's easy," he says. "Her husband asked me to appoint her."

"Nick?"

"I assume that's the only husband she had."

"Then you must have known Nick pretty well?"

"As I said, over the years we'd met a few times. Now if you'll excuse me, I've got a lot of work to do."

"Where can I get the records for these appointments?"

"Talk to my staff," he says. Tresler is back to his pile of papers, trying to get rid of me.

"Can I ask you about one more name?"

"Who is it?" Now he's getting short.

"The name is Nathan Fittipaldi."

He thinks about this for a second, searches his memory quickly, then shakes his head. "Never heard of him."

"You appointed him to the commission as well."

"Like I say, I appoint a lot of people. If you have questions, talk to my staff," he says. "Now, get out."

CHAPTER EIGHTEEN

It has taken Harry less than two days to run down Tresler's list of campaign contributors. As expected, Adam Tolt shows up everywhere.

"The man's on everybody's list of givers," says Harry. Harry is sprawled in one of my client chairs, scanning the computer printouts as he summarizes his discoveries.

"Congress, half the state legislature, city council. Tolt gave to both candidates for governor the last time around. You'd think that would piss somebody off," he says. "Apparently not. The guy's name and address must come preprinted on everybody's Rolodex when they buy 'em. Remind me never to get involved in giving money," says Harry.

For some reason I don't think this is going to be a problem.

"Tolt gave to all five supervisors," he says. "No favorites. Two hundred and fifty dollars each. The max for individuals. He gave the same amount to Tresler." Harry figures we can use this as a benchmark to judge the others. "He's got a lot of money, but he gives in small amounts."

It is one of the urban myths, that high rollers by definition give large amounts. Even wealthy ones usually confine it to a few hundred dollars per candidate. They just spread it around more.

"Metz and Fittipaldi both show up," says Harry. "But again small. Metz gave a hundred. Fittipaldi a hundred and a half. What's interesting is they only gave to Tresler. My guess is they had a goal in mind."

"Appointment to the commission," I say.

Harry nods. "And while I don't like to disappoint you, Dana doesn't show up at all."

It seems she wasn't lying. Dana is nonpolitical, at least when it comes to politics.

"But there is a bell ringer," says Harry. "Guess who shows up as a major donor?"

"Nick."

"How did you know that?"

"Call it a hunch," I tell him. Tresler knew him. A politician with three hundred thousand constituents in his district isn't likely to remember your first name unless you fall in one of two categories: You have clout or you've done something for him recently.

"How much?" I ask.

"Maybe you'd like to guess that too? Pick a number."

"A thousand?" I say.

"Try ten," he says.

This sits me up in my chair. No wonder Tresler knew his name.

"And to get around the giving limits," says Harry, "he set up a PAC. Citizens for County Government."

Harry is talking about a political action committee, people with a common interest pooling their money for effect.

"They gave in five-thousand-dollar increments over two years. All of it to Tresler. Nick shows up as the treasurer. He gave to the individual max, two hundred and fifty dollars each year."

"Let me see that." Harry hands me the computer printout. I scan down the list. I don't have to go far to find the PAC. The donors are listed in the order of the amount given, large contributors at the top.

Harry can tell by my look that this is not something I had expected.

There are twenty names on Nick's PAC, a separate list for each year, but the names are pretty much the same. Some of them are out of county. Two are out of state.

"Did you ever know him to get involved?" asks Harry.

"Nick didn't have a high interest in civics," I tell him.

"That's what I thought. But I checked it anyway. He didn't give to anybody else. I looked for local, state, and federal, under donor names. Not a single hit for Nick, except on Tresler. So what do you think he was after?"

I shake my head. Not a clue.

"We can assume," says Harry, "that this would be a lock, ten thousand, to put his wife on this commission. But you'd have to admit it's a bit of an overkill. Especially for a guy who's missing house payments."

I settle back in my chair, still studying the list of names underneath Nick's.

"There was no hint from Tresler when you talked to him, right?"

"No."

"Maybe you should go back and ask him."

"He'd just tell me what every politician tells anybody who asks. 'I'm above all that. I never look.' He'd act surprised and tell me that Nick must have been a follower of his philosophy—senile belligerence," I tell him. "That's if I got through the front door. By now Tresler probably has my name on the list under 'cranks and the demented' with security in the lobby. Still he didn't try to hide the fact that he knew Nick."

"It's good to know that at least Nick's money bought him a little recognition, even if it was posthumous," says Harry. "We're no better off now than we were before."

The phone on my desk rings.

"Except now we have more questions." Harry finishes the thought as I answer the call.

"Hello."

"I don't know any other lawyers answer their own phone." I recognize the raspy voice on the other end. "Joyce here," she says. "I bet you thought I died and went to hell."

She tells me she and Benny checked out the neighborhood, the drug dealer's house last night. "But not to worry," she says. "Benny had his gun. Double-barrel shotgun, both of them loaded. We had to make sure of the address," she says.

"You didn't trust me?"

"We're professionals," she says. "Like to do it right."

I can see her up on the porch with one of those flashlights that takes a battery the size of a bread box, with a notepad writing down the names off the mailbox, while Benny sat in the car at the curb with his blunderbuss, ready to blow the shit out of the front of the place if anybody walked out the door. There are at least three felonies here that I can count. It's the problem with Joyce. I know mobsters with more discretion.

"What did you find out?"

"Your man. It's one Hector Saldado," she says.

"Are you sure?"

"Yeah. We got him dead," she says. "Trus' me."

"Just a second." I grab a pen and some Post-its from the holder on my desk.

"Spell it?"

She does. "Not only is he the only one with a cell phone lives there," she says. "You know, of the other names you gave me?"

"Yes."

"But he makes regular calls down to Mexico."

She can tell by the silence coming from my end that this is something of note.

"I thought you might be interested," she says. "There were a lotta them. These calls. At least three or four almost every day. None of them long. You know, a minute, maybe two. But how long can it take to order up some drugs? I mean, less time than a pizza, I'm sure. There's no special toppings."

"You have his cell statement?"

"I tol' you I'd get it, didn't I? You want it all? It's pretty long. You know, a minute here, two minutes there. A lot of the same phone numbers too," she says. "I checked it. The country code and area. Mexico," she says.

"Where? Do you know what part of Mexico?"

"Just a sec," she says. "Let's see, I got it here someplace."

I can hear her hand muffle the mouthpiece, papers shuffling.

"Here it is," she comes back on. "Cancún. Quin-tan-aroo? Is that right?"

"I've heard of it," I tell her. It's the area Metz visited when he did business with the two Ibarra brothers. "Listen. I have another job for you."

This afternoon I am pressed for time. I have a flight north at four, business in Capital City with an errand on the way. I should be at the airport by three, but I am stuck doing lunch, Adam style, in the private dining room next to his office. Tolt sits on one side, me on the other, a table the length of a runway. It is covered by a linen tablecloth and two candles in sterling silver holders. They match the silver chargers resting under the eggshell china dishes in front of us.

The firm retains a chef for special occasions, as well as a company that sends waiters in white livery whenever they are needed to work from the kitchen that is through another door. Everything you need to run a five-star restaurant.

"You handled it very well," says Adam. "Under the circumstances, I don't think anyone could have done better. You played the hand you were dealt, and you got a good result."

"For who?".

"For your client," he says. He reaches across with his butter knife and stabs one of the little squares in the dish, takes it back, and spreads it on a warm French roll that he's plucked from the linen-lined basket on the table.

"I know what you think, that I snookered you by using the settlement to cover the money she took. The fact is . . ."

"The fact is you recovered your money," I tell him.

"Right." He smiles. "What can I say? Sometimes things just work out," he says.

I have a feeling they work out for Adam a little more than they do for the rest of us.

The occasion is the receipt of the check in settlement from the insurance carrier. Dana has compromised her portion and authorized me to deliver payment, a check made out to Rocker, Dusha to cover the missing funds from the firm's trust account. All of this with interest. This now rests in an envelope on Adam's desk as we break bread.

"So that you know, she has no basis for complaint. I trust you told her that." What he means is with money in the bank instead of jail time over her head.

The waiter brings out the main course, poultry braised in red wine, with long grains of wild rice, a medly of roasted vegetables, and a new selection from the vintner, five different wines to choose from.

"Pièce de résistance," says Adam. Another waiter follows with assorted side dishes, stuffed mushrooms and asparagus in a glazed butter sauce, fare rich enough to give a poor man the gout.

"The pheasant is roasted in Madeira," says Adam. "I first tasted the dish on a trip to Portugal. I guess it was four years ago. I tried to get the recipe, but they wouldn't give it to me. So I had Armand call the restaurant in Lisbon. He's our chef and the chief chef at Marmande," he says.

"I guessed as much."

"They gave it to him. Professional courtesy. It's the same in every field," he says.

The waiter lifts the glass cover from the dish he has set in front of Adam. My waiter does the same. Adam slips his fork into the bird, burying it to the top of the tines. He cuts a small piece with his knife and tastes it as the waiter pours wine.

"Tell Armand he's outdone himself this time," he tells the waiter.

The guy smiles, neatly bows at the waist. "Is there anything else?"

Adam looks at me.

"I suppose we could do it reclining like the Romans," I tell him. "But if there's anything else, I can't think what it would be."

"No, that'll be all," says Adam.

They leave.

"I would have invited Harry," says Tolt. "You have a wonderful partner there. Good man. From the old school. I recognize it," he says.

For some reason, the two of them have hit it off. I would not have expected this, Adam the world traveler, confidant of the powerful, and Harry who irons his own shirts.

"I was impressed with the thoroughness of his research, the points and authorities you gave to the carrier. That was his work?" He looks up at me.

"Every bit of it. Harry has saved me on more than one occasion," I tell him.

"Every knight needs a good armorer," says Tolt. "I would have invited him, but I wanted to talk to you about something else."

Somehow I knew Adam wouldn't celebrate like this unless there was some other purpose.

"Some more wine?" he says.

"No thanks." I look at my watch.

"Not to worry," he says. "I'll have my driver take you to the airport."

"My bags are already in the trunk of my car," I tell him.

"You can park it in our garage. The driver will get you to the airport in ten minutes and drop you at the curb. That way you won't have to find a parking space. Give him your flight, he'll pick you up when you come back."

"I couldn't have you do all that."

"Nonsense."

"Keep it up. You're going to spoil me, Adam."

"That's the idea." He smiles and takes another bite.

"So, what is it you wanted to talk about?" I'd like to know what the charges are.

"I didn't ask you why she took the money. Dana, I mean. Mrs. Rush. I assume she was pressed financially. So I suppose no harm, no foul. But I would like to know one thing."

I'm sitting back, sipping wine, listening.

"The insurance, her taking of the trust fund checks. Did any of this have to do with Nick's death? I don't need to know any details," he says. "Whatever passed between the two of you in the confines of lawyer- client should stay there. And I will accept whatever you tell me. If you can't say anything, I understand. My concern regards the firm. I merely want to know whether we can expect more repercussions from this?"

"You want to know if I think Dana killed Nick?"

He makes a face. "I suppose. In a word," he says. "I've dragged my feet, covered some things. And I have my neck stretched out, just a little at the moment. I did it to protect the firm. But if there is something, and the police start looking, well, they're going to find the checks she forged. And then I'm going to have to explain to the bar, and possibly to the police, why I didn't report it."

"I understand."

"I thought you would."

"Unfortunately, I can't help you. Not because I don't want to," I tell him. "The fact is I don't know. She says she didn't have anything to do with it. She says Nick left her high and dry. That's the only reason she took the checks from his desk."

"Do you believe her?"

I laugh without doing it out loud. "I gave up trying to read those entrails long ago. She did know about the insurance. She had a copy of the policy. She told me she didn't find it until we spoke the first time. But to be honest, I don't believe her. She had to know Margaret's name was on the policy."

"So she lied to you."

"More than once."

"And the issue of double indemnity?"

"She didn't know what it was called, at least that's what she led me to believe. But she picked up the theory pretty quickly as soon as I told her Nick's death was an accident. I don't think this was news to her. She had to be reading the papers, following the investigation. The police were already speculating in public. Whether she might have talked to somebody else who gave her chapter and verse on a claim, I can't say."

"But your instincts. You've certainly developed those if you've dealt with criminal defendants. What do they tell you?"

I give him an expression like maybe I'd rather not say. But then I do. "My instincts tell me Dana is trouble. I'm not saying she killed her husband. I'm saying that you'd have a hard time trying to figure out what's going on behind those blue eyes at any given moment. Is she capable of it? I suppose. I don't mean pulling the trigger."

"You mean hiring somebody else?"

"It's been known to happen. But . . ."

"But what?"

"These people were professionals."

"How do you know that?"

"I was there. I heard the shots. If Dana hired somebody to kill Nick, it would probably be somebody she met someplace, in a bar, maybe a wayward lover she recruited. That kind of person usually doesn't have access to automatic weapons, semiautomatic maybe. But what killed Nick and Metz was a submachine gun. Nine millimeter. I saw some of the spent cartridges on the ground. They were ejected out of the car window when he fired."

"Hmm." Tolt sits back in his chair, chewing a piece of pheasant slowly as he considers this.

"So you don't think she did it?"

"I'm not saying that. She certainly had motive. And it's possible she's more resourceful than I think. She could have crossed the border. Flashed some money in the right places down in Tijuana, and you can probably find cops who will introduce you to people with Uzis, AKs, as well as the talent to use them. They might even do it for you themselves if you pay them enough. It's the thing about San Diego, the proximity to the southern border creates a whole new dynamic," I tell him.

"Then she could have done it?"

"It's possible."

"What you're saying is that anything's possible."

"That's what I'm saying."

"Unfortunately, that's not going to allow me to sleep much better at night," he says.

"It is what it is," I tell him.

We finish the main course and they bring on crème brûlée for dessert, along with coffee and a little cognac. He offers me a cigar and I pass.

"Nick used to love them. Smoked them like a chimney at the last Christmas party," he says.

"That's the difference between us," I tell him.

"Not the only one," he says. "I feel bad for Nick. I don't mean just because he's dead. He wasn't treated as well as he should have been while he was here at the firm. And I blame myself for that. I set the tone, and over the last year or so it's been one of not caring. But my wife was sick."

"I didn't know that."

"Yes. Cancer," he says.

"I'm sorry."

"No, it's all right. She beat it," he says. "But you never know how long you have to spend with those you love. So for the past two years, I've spent what extra time I had with her instead of here. And I'm afraid Nick—he was one of our newest additions—I'm afraid he fell through the cracks. I can't but think that maybe whatever he got involved with . . . Metz I mean . . . well, that perhaps it was the result of his seeing his potential here as somehow limited. You knew him best. Did he ever say anything?"

"He . . . ahh . . . well there's no denying he was disappointed," I say.

"So he told you. I knew it. And I have to blame myself. I was just too damn busy to pay attention."

"You can't help something like that," I tell him. "I know. I've dealt with it."

He looks at me, a question mark.

"I lost my wife to cancer six years ago."

"I didn't know."

"It's all right. I know what it's like. The time it takes. Your life stands still. But time doesn't. You stop living for a while. It took almost a year after she died before I could function fully again."

"Then you do know. Thank God I didn't have to go through that. But you live with the constant thought that maybe you will. And in the meantime, the firm kept going, growing. It's what happens when you get too big. You start going for quantity instead of quality."

"You're saying Rocker, Dusha is getting too big?"

"I hope not." He smiles. "All the same, Nick got caught up in that machine. No doubt he viewed his problems as a bad mix with corporate chemistry, that he didn't fit in. After all, he came here from a solo criminal practice. He may have fit better than he knew. But I wasn't around to tell him." At the moment Tolt is not looking at me as much as through me, to the wall beyond, taking personal stock, and not pleased with the picture he is seeing.

"Twenty-nine years with the firm. I'm sixty-seven years old. Pretty soon they'll put me out to pasture. And I suppose I should go gracefully. Still, I'll think about Nick and wonder whether if I'd been here he might still be alive."

"Perhaps you need to be a little more fatalistic," I tell him.

"What do you mean?"

"Lincoln had to get out of bed every morning knowing that before his day was out, he would likely have to review casualty reports. He considered himself lucky if these contained thousands of names, and not tens of thousands. After a year of this, he came to view the war as the result of God's hand at work, punishing the nation for the sin of slavery, and that he was just a tool. Lincoln came to believe that no matter what he did, or how he exhorted his generals, he couldn't end the war until God was ready."

"So you think I should be more like Lincoln?"

"Oh. I think everybody should," I say.

"You're not a fatalist, you're an idealist," he says.

"No. I'm a cynic because I know it's not going to happen. But I understand your feelings."

"I thought you would. You're different than Nick," he says.

"In what way?"

"You see what is practical, what's doable. Too many of the people here don't. I can't judge Nick, because I didn't know him well enough. So I won't. He and I may have been better suited than I'll ever know, because I didn't take the time or have the time. I don't want to make that mistake again. Life is too short not to know the people you work with. So I've been giving this a lot of thought," he says, "and I'd like to get to know you better. I would like you to come to work for the firm."

I look at him, shocked, round eyes.

"We'll double whatever you're making in your current practice. And we'll find a place for Harry. I have Harvard grads doing research for me. They could take lessons from him."

Harry in a place like Rocker, Dusha would be like a lit cigarette next to black powder.

"I don't think that would work."

"I don't want you to give me an answer right now. Think about it. Take it back to Harry. Get out your calculators and see what you both need to come on board. Think about it," he says. "I see no reason why the two of you couldn't continue to work together. We'll find adjoining suites, put you both under contracts, after a year, you'd both have an ownership interest, partners. You'd report directly to me," he says.

"I'm flattered," I tell him. "But I don't think . . ."

"Don't think about it right now. Give it some time. We can talk after you get back from your trip."

What can I say? I'm looking at my watch, time to go. Adam grabs the phone off the sidebar behind him, orders up his car and the driver, then walks me out the door to the elevator.

"Just press G-One, down to the garage, first level. My driver will meet you there, get your bags. Give him your keys, he'll move your car into one of the spaces in the garage until you get back. Give him your flight and he'll be out in front of the terminal to pick you up. Oh, and one more thing. Here, take one of these." He hands me one of the firm's newsletters, eight pages in four colors folded like a tabloid. "A little something to read on the plane," he says.

CHAPTER NINETEEN

With the roar of the jet engines, the kinetic drag of acceleration presses me back in my chair. A few seconds later, we lift from the runway and climb quickly to a thousand feet.

The pilot throttles back to cut noise, and we glide out over Ocean Beach, a few shimmering blue specks of back-yard pools, past Sunset Cliffs, and the rolling line of surf. The flight crew gooses the powerful turbines again and the Boeing 737 climbs rapidly, heading north up the coast.

We settle in at cruising altitude and I pull the attache case from under the seat in front, take what I want from it, and put it back. On the tray table in front of me is the newsletter from Tolt's firm, a file with Tresler campaign statements that Harry had collected, and Nick's small handheld device.

I settle back in the chair and open the newsletter. Just below the fold I see my name in bold headline type.

MADRIANI & HINDS
SETTLE CLAIM
FOR RUSH ESTATE

This is why Adam handed it to me. The story is not long, a few inches. It talks about the firm's key-man policy. Adam has taken the opportunity to boost this as one of the perks of partnership.

In two short sentences, the article covers Nick's death, the date, and the fact that he was caught up in a drive-by shooting while talking with a client in front of the federal courthouse. The last two graphs read like a promotional brochure for Harry and me.

"Those who knew Nick Rush will be happy to learn that even though Nick's death was tragic and untimely, local attorneys Paul Madriani and Harry Hinds of the Coronado law firm of Madriani and Hinds effected a sizable insurance settlement ($3.8 million) for Nick's family and survivors.

"The settlement was grounded on evidence that Nicholas Rush was the innocent and unintended victim of a drive-by shooting, thereby availing his heirs of insurance reparations under the life insurance policy's double indemnity clause for accidental death."

Lawyers, more than most, like to feed and water illusions of their own prowess. But I know that settlements like this don't happen unless insurance adjusters and the people they report to are operating under the influence, in this case of Adam Tolt.

I suspect Adam realizes, as well as I do, that it was a symbiotic relationship. We used each other. I wanted to maximize the dollar figure and get settlement as quickly as possible and get out of it. He wanted to dry clean the skirts of the law firm. If Tolt hadn't suggested his office as the location for a settlement meeting, I would have.

I assumed it would take several meetings and a few months to hammer something out and nail it down. Adam's reach may be longer, and his grasp more vital, than I had imagined.

The fact that he could get the carrier to open its purse so cheerfully and that they would allow Adam to publish the amount, which is what he really wanted, surprised even me.

While my partner was doing his legal research to justify whatever we would get, I was doing my own. I knew that Adam sat on a number of corporate boards.

Burrowing my nose into some publications, I discovered that the actual number was seven, unless I missed some, which I may have. All of these are large multinational businesses, with home offices in the U.S. Their boards include the usual list of corporate suspects, names you might recognize from government positions they've held in the past, or causes they've championed. These are people who make their living, to the tune of fortunes, just by being connected. They have developed a business celebrity. Corporations may wait in line to have them join their boards. Because they are on one board, they get on another. Because their name appears on those two, they pick up a third. Once they are there, competence is assumed. At the end of the day, they are sitting around the boardroom comparing handicaps on the back nine, making a million or more a year, and pocketing the company pens paid for by investors. It is not just in Hollywood where perception becomes reality.

What I learned by doing my research was that three of the Devon Insurance board members cross-pollinated with Adam on other boards. That was all I needed to know.

The settlement, and the publicity that now follows it, serves the purposes of Rocker, Dusha by bringing to an end any ugly speculation as to why Nick may have died. Confronted by client's questions at a cocktail party, Adam or his partners can now say, "Haven't you heard? Oh, yeah, Nick's death was an accident." To business clients for whom the exchange of dollars is like breathing air, the payment of cash is reliable evidence. The payment of nearly four million dollars by a sober and staid insurance company will be viewed as irrefutable proof that Nick was just another random victim in a violent world. Within a year, Adam will have most of his corporate clients trying to recall just how Nick died and thinking maybe it was lightning.

I'd like to hope that Adam has more respect for me than to believe I would be flattered by his article. Though I suspect if he thinks it would sweeten his offer for Harry and me to join the firm, he would see no harm in a little icing on the cake.

I scan the rest of the newsletter. Another office in the works. This one in Houston with an eye toward petroleum, gas, and oil ventures. All of the partners may not be happy, but Adam is still on the move, building his equity interest in Rocker, Dusha.

I stick the newsletter behind the flap in the seat in front of me and turn to the computer printouts of Tresler's campaign contributions that Harry has been working on. He has underlined two of the names from Nick's list of PAC contributors. One is a partner in the firm's office Washington, D.C. The other is one Jeffery Dolson, a partner in their San Francisco operation. Both men show up not only in the address book of Nick's handheld device, but also in the date book, which shows meetings in their respective cities with times and dates. Dolson, in San Francisco, met with Nick twice in the two months before Nick was killed, if the date book is accurate. The last time was only nine days before the shootings. It's the reason I am flying to San Francisco this afternoon instead of directly to Capital City.

Rocker, Dusha's offices in San Francisco are located at One Market Plaza overlooking the Bay Bridge and the waterfront. The location is pricey, but within grasping distance of the city's financial district. Here the firm occupies two floors on the upper levels, squeezed in between another law firm downstairs and a securities trading company above.

It is almost five o'clock, closing time as I step off the elevator onto carpeted floor and approach the reception counter.

A young Asian woman with a telephone headset is seated at one of the stations behind the counter. Two other women are gathering their things getting ready to leave for the evening.

The woman smiles. "Can I help you?"

I give her my card. "I'm here to see Jeffery Dolson."

"Do you have an appointment?"

"I'm afraid I don't. I just flew into town this afternoon and took a chance that he might be in."

"Just a moment."

Dolson heads up the firm's M&A division. Mergers and acquisitions is the place where lawyers capitalize on the laws businesses buy from Congress, the ones designed to ensure that wealth remains concentrated in as few hands as possible, usually by wiping out small investors. Talk to lawyers working in this field and they will tell you that corporate management getting rich when their companies go broke is just part of the normal business cycle. For people who believe the world is changing too fast, they should take comfort in the fact that a lot of money in America is still made the old-fashioned way, by stealing it.

The receptionist is talking through the transparent tube on her headset to somebody in the back or upstairs.

"I don't know. Just a minute. I'll ask him." She looks at me. "Can I ask you what it regards?"

"I had lunch with Adam Tolt in San Diego this afternoon, and I wanted to stop in and see Mr. Dolson." All of this is true, none of it responsive to her question. Just the same, Tolt's name does its magic. As the woman turns her back to me, she cups a hand over the end of the little tube, but I can hear her mumble into the mouthpiece. "Apparently, he's been referred by Mr. Tolt."

Open sesame. Three minutes later, I'm being ushered up the elevator by a secretary with my business card in one hand and a key to let us off the elevator on the executive level in the other. I follow her through the labyrinth of partitions to the far side of the building where the hallway is wide and the rosewood paneling is real. She knocks on the door at the end of the hall, the one with Dolson's name engraved in plastic on the wall next to it.

"Yes. Come in."

The door is opened, and I can see a large corner office with windows on two walls. One of these looks out at the cabled spans of the Bay Bridge. Through the other, I can see the single spire of the Ferry Building.

The man behind the desk is young. I would guess midthirties. He is straightening his tie, and from the look of his desk, with some papers sticking out of the partially closed top drawer, I suspect he has been cleaning up for my arrival. What the dropping of an important name can do to create a little anxiety.

Dolson shimmies around the partially open drawer that he has now given up on, and makes his way to my side of the desk. We shake hands as he looks at my card. "I understand you just flew into town?"

"Yes. A flight from San Diego. I had lunch with Adam Tolt today, and your name came up a couple of times. I thought that as long as I was coming north on other business it might be a good idea if we met."

"My name?" he says. "How is he? Mr. Tolt, I mean. I see him about once every six months or so. When some of the division heads get together to compare notes."

"He's fine. Doing great," I tell him.

"So did Adam, Mr. Tolt, send you to see me?"

"No. Actually your name came up in another context. I understand that you knew Nick Rush?"

His pupils float away from my face over to the wall of windows behind me and back again, as if they crossed the bridge and returned, all within less than a second.

"Nick Rush?" he says.

"Yes. Nick was a friend," I say. "And your name came up."

"Really?" This is an octave higher than his last statement. I can tell he'd like to ask in what context Nick might have mentioned his name, but he doesn't.

"It's terrible what happened to him," he says.

"I understand that Nick came up here to your office, to meet with you about a week or so before he was killed?"

Like he's been hit by a train. "Ugh? What?"

"I understood the two of you had a meeting here in your office?"

His lips are moving, sort of quivering, but nothing is coming out. "Oh. Oh that," he says. "Guess with everything going on I forgot about it."

How do you forget your last meeting with a man who is murdered nine days later?

"Then the police haven't talked to you?"

"Why would they want to talk to me?"

"They usually talk to anyone who had contact with one of the victims shortly before a murder."

"I couldn't tell them anything. How did Nick tell you . . . I mean why did Nick talk to you about our meeting?"

"Nick and I didn't have a lot of secrets."

"Oh. I see." Right now his eyes look as if they could swallow the couch I'm sitting on. His complexion has gone pale. "Tell me," he says. "How exactly do you know Adam Tolt?" Dolson is trying to put all the pieces together.

I open my briefcase and pull out the firm's newsletter. Hot off the presses in San Diego, it hasn't made its way to the colonies yet. I hand it to him, pointing to the story under the fold with my name in the headline.

"I did the settlement on the insurance for Nick's wife."

He compares the name on my business card with the headline. Then reads the article as if he is sucking the print off the page with his eyes. When he's finished, he looks at me. "Good result," he says.

This is the lawyer's equivalent of a high five after moon walking in the end zone.

"I understand Nick had a couple of meetings with you up here?"

I can tell by the look that he isn't sure whether I know, and if so how much. He's trying to regroup but has the look of a man struggling to fight off panic.

"It was social," he says.

"Excuse me?"

"My meeting. My meetings here with Nick. They were social." He says it with all the certitude of a guess on a multiple choice quiz.

I don't say anything. I look at him. What to do with a witness who's nervous. Let him talk.

"He just sorta dropped by from time to time. We talked. That's all," he says.

"So Nick came all the way up from San Diego just to socialize with you?"

"I didn't say that."

"But he came up specifically to meet with you?"

"Oh no. I don't think so."

"That's what his calendar says."

He looks at me. It's the kind of expression you might expect from someone who is swallowing his tongue. "His calendar?"

"Yeah." I don't tell him it was on a handheld and that I probably have the only copy.

"Nick put my name on his calendar?"

"That's what I said."

"You've seen this?"

"Uh-huh."

"This is his office calendar?"

"One of them."

"Then I suppose the San Diego office has seen it?"

"I'd have thought you might be more interested in whether the police have seen it?"

"Oh. Well sure. That's why you thought they might want to talk to me?"

"Sure. Why? Is there some other reason?"

"I told you. I don't know anything. Have they seen the calendar? The police, I mean?"

"Actually, I'm not sure."

"What do you mean you're not sure?"

"Well they could have things I don't know about. But I don't think they have it. At least not yet."

"Why are you doing this? What do you want? Is it money?"

"What makes you think I might want money?"

"Nothing. I don't know. It's just, this makes no sense. My name in Nick's calendar. I told you I don't know anything. I take it you haven't talked to Adam about this?"

"Tolt? No. Do you think I should?"

He doesn't say yes or no, so I turn the screws a little more. "But so that you know, you're not alone."

"What's that supposed to mean?"

"There are other names on the calendar. Meetings with other members of the firm. Dates and times."

He doesn't say anything, just looks at me.

"Why don't you tell me what the meetings were about?"

"So then Nick didn't tell you?"

"He would have, if I'd asked him. But somebody shot him first."

"The meetings had nothing to do with that. Besides, the article says it was an accident."

"Well sure. But then that was written by your firm. Of course they would want to keep their skirts clean. When a partner is killed, better an accident than something more sinister. Don't you think?"

"I think you should go now." Dolson has regrouped, gathered enough courage to convince himself that I don't know anything. "I think you should forget about the calendar or whatever it is you saw or think you saw."

"You can kid yourself if you want, but the calendar exists."

"You want to know what I think?"

"Sure."

"I don't think there is a calendar with my name on it. I think you made it up. Where is it? Did you bring it with you?"

"If it doesn't exist, how would I know the date of your meeting with Nick?"

"I think maybe that's all Nick told you. Or maybe you just

overheard it. As I said, it was social." He turns, heading for his desk. "I have work to do. I'd like you to leave."

Whatever it is, Dolson's fear is erecting a stone wall around it. He reaches his desk, and looks at me. "Are you going to leave or would you rather I call security?" He picks up the receiver like it's a weapon, his fingers ready to punch buttons on the phone.

"If that's the way you want it."

"I take it you can find your way out?"

He watches from the open door of his office as I leave, his eyes on me until the elevator doors shut behind me. The one thing I can be sure of, whatever Nick and Dolson discussed, it wasn't social chitchat.

It's only a few blocks, maybe a mile, from Dolson's office to one of the three addresses listed on the memo pad of Nick's handheld. The other two of these are in Washington, D.C., and New York.

By the time I find the address, it's getting late. Downtown San Francisco, like most big cities, is a disaster when it comes to parking, even after hours. It takes me ten minutes to find a space. It's after six, so I can ignore the meters. I lock up the rental car and walk two blocks back toward the address in the handheld.

The address is mixed in with some trendy restaurants, an antique shop with expensive Asian art in the window, a place some tony interior decorator might shop for well-heeled customers. The neighborhood is just off the Embarcadero but farther west than the RDD offices.

The building I'm looking for takes up about a quarter of the block, four stories and modern, a lot of smoked glass. But there is something strange; not a single light in any of the offices facing this side of the building. Usually in any business there is somebody working late, or at least a janitor.

I check the street name against what is entered in Nick's Palm device. I could have shown the calendar to Dolson, but it wouldn't have done any good. He would have accused me of making the entries in the device myself. It's the problem the cops would have at this point, unless of course Nick had synced the information in the device by copying it to his computer, which by now I'm certain he did not. The information in the handheld has been out of the victim's possession for too long a period to be credible. Anybody could have used a stylus to add or delete things. The verification for its authenticity is my word. A criminal defense lawyer, a friend of the deceased, who has withheld evidence in a murder case. Any testimony I offered would come apart like wet tissue paper.

It is the right street, so I head around the corner and up the block along what appears to be the front of the building.

This side faces the bay. Two blocks away I can hear traffic moving past on the Embarcadero in front of the wharfs with their cavernous arched doors and giant numbers on their overhead facades. I can feel a chilly breeze off the water and the smell of salt in the air. There are no lights visible on the upper floors here either, but I see what appears to be the front entrance about fifty yards up the street.

I turn the collar up on my suit coat, put my hands in my pockets, and walk as the wind whips the cuffs on my pant legs.

As I approach I see the street number over the front door, the same number that Nick entered in his memo pad. There is no mistake. It's the right address. But whoever Nick visited is gone. The place is empty. A large sign taped to the inside of the glass double doors in front reads:

AVAILABLE FOR LEASE

CHAPTER TWENTY

I t is mid-morning, Thursday, and as I pull into the underground structure at Susan Glendenin's downtown office, I recognize the large, dark blue, sixties-vintage Lincoln parked a few spaces away.

This car, the size of a boat, once belonged to Nick. Actually it would be more accurate to say that the car possessed him.

The Lincoln convertible with a folding hardtop that slipped into the trunk was an experiment by Ford. Only four of them were ever made, all handed out to high executives for testing. For whatever reason, production never got off the ground, with the result that the car and its innovations died on the drawing boards.

Nick picked it up in the early eighties as part of his fees from a client who got caught moving drugs under the folded hardtop in the trunk. This was before the government seized such property.

The car got more attention than most beauty queens. With the top down it looks amazingly like the presidential limo in which Kennedy was assassinated, and in fact it was used once in a major motion picture to re-create the scene. Nick was sure he had the only remaining vehicle of its kind still on the road. He worshiped it, shrouded and protected it like the Israelites with the Ark of the Covenant. For this reason, Margaret wound her lawyers up and took particular pleasure in stripping it from him in the divorce.

This I know because each time I met him over drinks or a meal he would revisit this like a slow-mo instant replay of some blindsided, bone-jarring hit in the Super Bowl. Of all the sharp and painful impacts of his domestic crash, the loss of these prized wheels seemed the sharpest and most painful of all. The worst part was that Margaret was driving his big blue baby all over town, refusing to sell it, parking it in tight spaces at the grocery store just to put dents in the doors, so the next time Nick saw it he could count them. Margaret is apparently already here waiting for me upstairs.

It took three days in Capital City to finish up my business while Sarah stayed with friends. Harry and I can't seem to let the old office go, so we have subleased most of the space out to two young lawyers and retained a single office for ourselves to share.

This morning when I get back, Harry is feeling somewhat self-satisfied, having done his measure of good works for the day. We have mailed a hefty check for Dana's fees, to Nick's daughter, Laura, along with a letter explaining that the money is from Nick's estate.

Harry is also gloating over an article that appeared two days ago in the *Trib*. It's a boiled-down version of Adam's newsletter, crediting us for settling with the carrier. It was the lead on a page-two story reporting that the police still have no suspects in the killings. Newspapers and two television stations have been calling the office asking questions and requesting on-camera interviews. Adam is making the most of the settlement. At this point the press will take anything to fill the news void in a double murder investigation that seems to be going nowhere.

So far, for some reason, the cops have made no effort to

question Espinoza. Why they would ignore him, after Harry's tip from his friend in the D.A.'s office, I don't know, but they would have to come through me to get to him, and no one has tried.

I have asked Susan Glendenin for a meeting with Margaret Rush this morning for one reason. It's possible that Margaret may have some answers to one of the more puzzling riddles concerning Nick's last year, his business dealing with Metz.

I take the garage elevator up to five. When I get there, the office air-conditioning is running on overtime. The city has been in the grip of a record-breaking hot spell for five days, with breezes wafting out of the desert like the Sahara.

As I enter reception with one finger hooked in the collar of my suit coat, holding it like a sack over my shoulder, I notice that Susan's door is closed. She is cloistered with Margaret, so after the secretary tells them I am here, I wait a couple of minutes before Susan opens the door.

She's cheerful as ever. She has facilitated this meeting out of natural graciousness and because it is the reasonable thing to do. Glendenin is the kind of lawyer who would make courts and judges obsolete if only her opponents would show the same levelheaded good sense.

"How are you, Paul?"

"Fine."

"Still hot out there?"

"Like a torch."

"How about something cold to drink?"

"Water sounds great."

"Come on in."

She orders up some iced bottled water from the secretary, then leads me into her office.

As I enter, Margaret is seated in one of the client chairs, facing away from me. She doesn't turn to look or greet me until Susan makes it obvious that to ignore me might be impolite.

"Margaret, I think you know Paul Madriani?"

She turns her head, looking down, a tight smile and a

nod is all I get. She immediately returns her gaze to the other side of the desk where Susan is now settling into her leather BodyBilt, with its high headrest and custom swivel arms. Lawyers now prize their executive chairs in the way they did their Porsches a decade ago, testing the levers of the air cylinder that control height and the tension of the back support for ride as if they are cruising at light speed toward the new world of geriatrics.

I take the other client chair and hope that Margaret's freeze will thaw before my ice water arrives.

"I have been meeting with Margaret," says Susan, "and discussing your request. She has agreed to answer whatever questions she can but with certain ground rules."

"I see."

"She does not wish to talk about the divorce or the property settlement agreement with her former husband. She would also prefer that we not discuss his subsequent marriage, if at all possible."

"I understand." Susan has been able to get this meeting only by telling Margaret that Dana was forced to compromise her position on the insurance settlement. This seems to have touched something profound and gratifying within Margaret: revenge.

If she knew that Dana forged checks from the firm's trust account, she would lay rubber with big blue, scorching the asphalt all the way up Broadway to get the news to the cops while it was fresh. No one knows this except Adam and me, along with a few minions in his office who have pledged an oath of silence, collateralized by their careers.

"Perhaps I should start," I say. The door behind us opens and the secretary enters with a tray, glasses, and three large plastic bottles of water from the refrigerator each sweating with condensation. I wait until she leaves to pick up the conversation.

"The questions I have regard what appear to have been business dealings that Nick had during the last twelve to eighteen months of his life," I say.

"Then you're talking to the wrong person," says Mar-

garet. She's still not looking at me. I have committed the un-
pardonable sin of being a friend of Nick's.

"Perhaps, but I thought you might have heard something,
maybe from others." What I am gambling on is that her
lawyers in the divorce turned over every rock.

"Fine. What do you want to know?"

"Have you ever heard of a business entity, a limited partnership or a corporation known as Jamaile Enterprises?"

She thinks about this, the features of her stern expression
softening as mental energy is diverted to firing up the memory cells. "No. I don't think so. No, wait a minute," she says.
"Yes, once. It was during the divorce." She breaks her own
rule. "My lawyers found out about it. They thought Nick was
using it to hide assets from the marriage."

"Was he?"

"No. I really didn't want to get into this," she says.

I look at Susan, who gives me a face, like she wishes she
could help but can't.

"At least they couldn't find anything in that company
when they looked at it."

"Do you remember when that was?"

"No."

"Do you remember during the court proceedings whether
they asked Nick any specific questions about it?"

"I thought we weren't going to talk about the divorce."

"It's an easy question," says Susan. "Either you remember or you don't."

"Fine. I don't remember," she says.

"Did you ever hear the name Gerald Metz used in connection with Jamaile Enterprises?"

"Wasn't that the man who was shot with Nick?"

I nod. She has to look over at me to see this, so we finally
make eye contact.

"Are you telling me they were in business together?"

"Apparently."

"Do the police know this?"

"They do. Did your lawyers ever look into Mr. Metz to

determine who he was and what this business deal might have been?"

"I don't know. You'd have to talk to them."

"I did. They wouldn't discuss it with me without your written consent."

"I'd have to talk to them about that," she says. Both Margaret and her lawyers are wary of anything having to do with the divorce and in particular the settlement agreement. They are probably worried that Dana might renew arguments that Margaret had no lawful claim to the insurance.

Susan raises a hand off of the arm of her chair, as if perhaps I shouldn't press on this any further, that maybe I should move on.

"Have you ever heard the name Grace Gimble?" I ask.

With this she looks at me, almost snaps her neck doing it. "What does Grace have to do with this?"

"You know her?"

"Yes. She's a friend," she says. "One of the few friends we both had. I mean one Nick and I both knew, who maintained a friendship with me after the divorce."

"Do you know where I can find her?"

"Maybe. But first tell me why you want to know."

"Her name shows up on documents creating this limited partnership. The one I told you about. Jamaile Enterprises. Can you tell me who she is? Why her name might be on those documents?"

She thinks about this for a second, quietly to herself, eyes studying the oak surface of Susan's desk, perhaps wondering if someone involved with Nick was a friend after all. "That's easy," she says. "After Grace retired from the government, she did some private secretarial work. Paralegal, they call it. To make a little money on the side. I know Nick threw some work her way from time to time, before he went to work for the firm. Before we were . . ."

"I see. Do you know where she lives?"

"I think so." Margaret fumbles in her purse and comes up with a small black address book, thumbs through it until she finds Grace Gimble's address. She reads this to me as I write it on a Post-it note from Susan's desk.

"Do you have a phone number?"

She gives me this as well.

"Have you talked to her recently?"

She thinks. "Not for at least a year," she says. "I suppose she was probably at Nick's funeral. I wouldn't know since I wasn't there."

"How did she know Nick?"

"She was his secretary at the U.S. Attorney's Office before he left."

I stop writing on the little slip and look at her. She can tell this is not what I had expected to hear.

"She retired about the same time Nick went into private practice. Nick told me she took some paralegal courses and worked out of her house."

This would explain her name on the documents forming Jamaile, especially if Nick, for whatever reason, didn't want them prepared using the clerical staff at the firm.

Before Margaret can say anything more, Susan's phone rings. Susan looks at me, rolls her eyes. "I told them to hold my calls." She picks it up. "Yes." Eyes looking at me, down at the desk, then she cups her hand over the mouthpiece. "It's for you," she says.

The only one who knows I'm here is Harry.

"Do you want to take it in the other room?" she says.

"No."

So Susan moves the phone a little closer and stretches the cord so that I can take it at the edge of her desk.

"Hello."

"Just a moment." It's Susan's secretary. A second later, Harry's voice comes on the line.

"Paul."

"Yeah."

"Listen, I thought you'd want to know. I just got today's mail."

"Can this wait? I'm in the middle of a meeting," I tell him.

"You're going to want to know what was in it."

"Fine."

"A substitution of counsel for Espinoza," says Harry.

"What?"

"I thought you'd be interested. Some lawyer named Gary Winston down in National City."

"When was this?"

"Almost a week ago. The notice just arrived in the mail. And that's not all. Before I wasted your time, I thought I'd check. See if Espinoza is in detention. He's not." Harry can tell he has my undivided attention from the silence coming from my end now.

"There was a bail hearing scheduled yesterday. Bail was set at a million dollars."

"Then it's probably all right," I tell him. "Unless I'm wrong, and he's more flush than I think, he couldn't raise the ten percent fee, the hundred grand for the bond."

"Guess again," says Harry. "He's been on the street since yesterday afternoon. Are you there?" Harry on the other end, listening to dead air from me.

"Yes. I'm thinking. Who put up the bond?"

"I don't know. Do you want me to see if I can find out?"

"Do it."

"They may know where he is. At least the address Espinoza gave them."

"Let's hope maybe a bondsman's watching him." If they knew what kind of a flight risk he was, they wouldn't have taken the fee unless they had some guarantee.

"And Harry . . ."

"Yeah?"

"See what you can find out about the lawyer, this Winston. Call me on the cell line as soon as you have anything. I'll be in the car."

I pocket the Post-it with Grace Gimble's address and phone number and apologize to Susan and Margaret for a hasty departure.

"There's nothing else you want to ask?" says Margaret.

"Not right now. I'll call Susan if I have more questions. Next time we can do it over lunch. My treat."

Margaret is not sure what to do with this, whether to say no now or later. She doesn't say anything. I tell Susan I'll call her, and I'm out the door.

Without more information, I am forced to make decisions based on assumptions. Whoever hired the lawyer to spring Espinoza also coughed up his bail. This is a chunk of change. Unless she won the lottery, it wasn't his wife. Whoever it is wants him out for a reason. And since they dealt directly with the man himself, it had to be someone Espinoza either met or had seen previously. Espinoza may know a hundred people that fit this bill, but the only one I know is the man in the felt hat, the man Joyce told me goes by the name Hector Saldado.

There's a little vibration against my leg. It's coming from the pocket of my suit coat lying on the seat next to me. It's my cell phone ringing. I fish it out.

"Hello."

"Can you hear me?" It's Harry.

"Yeah. Go ahead."

"I got ahold of the lawyer, this guy Winston."

"Yes."

"Says he never met Espinoza before he saw him in court, at the bail hearing. Catch this. The guy's been admitted to practice for only four months. Says he was retained by phone, a male voice. This person identified himself as Espinoza's brother. A check for the retainer came by courier a few hours later, along with a substitution of counsel already signed by Espinoza. The kid says he set the hearing. He called it a cakewalk. I got the sense it may have been his first time in court."

"Why?"

"He thought he was doing his client a favor with a million-dollar bail. Apparently he caught the deputy U.S. attorney, the one assigned to bail hearings that day, off guard. The prosecutor asked the court for a quarter million, then looked at the file and realized what he was dealing with. He immediately jumped it to a million, figuring like you that Espinoza couldn't raise it. The kid tried to knock it down, but the court said no. Espinoza told the kid on the way back to his cell not to worry about it. It wasn't gonna be a problem. The lawyer says he knows about the bond. He says somebody else must have arranged it."

My worst fears. "Did you talk to the bondsman?"

"He's out of the office."

I'm still hoping that maybe he's watching his investment, keeping an eye on Espinoza.

"Where are you headed?" asks Harry.

"South on I-5," I tell him.

"Are you coming back to the office?"

"No. Listen, what time do you have?"

"It's about eleven-twenty," says Harry.

"If I don't call you in one hour, do me a favor."

"What's that?"

"Call the police in San Diego and give them this address."

I give the address to Harry, so he can write it down and read it back to me.

"What's going on?" he says.

"Just do it."

"You want me to have 'em send a squad car?"

"More than one," I tell him. "But give me one hour."

"You got it."

CHAPTER TWENTY-ONE

I pull up to the curb under the shade of an old elm tree half a block up and across the street from the old house with its cut-up flats and sagging front porch.

The large two-story wooden frame house at 408 appears larger and more run-down in daylight. I also notice something that wasn't there on my last visit, an older model SUV parked in front. The body is boxy and beat-up, primed, but unpainted. Parked on the short gravel drive on the other side of the stairs, its front bumper is into the bushes against the house with the large, aggressive tread of the rear tires sitting halfway onto the sidewalk.

What catches my attention most, however, is the car's back window. It's covered by a piece of wrinkled black plastic, taped and wrapped around the window frame. This vehicle fits to a tee the Chevy Blazer that Espinoza described on my visit with him at the lockup.

I sit and watch for a few minutes. Signs of life in one of the houses, the one at 408. The front door opens, the screen door pushing out.

Tall and slender, carrying a suitcase in each hand, I recognize the build. It's the Mexican I'd seen that night, the one Espinoza had described, but without the hat this time. If the name on the mailbox is real, and Joyce's information is accurate, this is Hector Saldado, who makes calls daily on his cell phone to the area around Cancún.

Saldado carries the suitcases down the stairs to the back of the beat-up Blazer, where he swings the rack with the spare tire out of the way and lifts the hinged rear door with the plastic-covered window. As he tosses the suitcases inside, another figure comes shooting out the door. Running barefoot, half naked, carrying a child in her arms, she makes it to the top step when Saldado turns and sees her.

She tries to get past him on the stairs, but he reaches out and grabs her by one arm, almost ripping the child out of her hands.

She tries to pull free, and he swings her around so the baby is nearly propelled from her arms by the centrifugal force.

The Mexican is powerful, wiry. With his hands gripping her upper arms from behind he lifts her, the child still sheltered in her arms, off her feet. Quickly he has her back up the stairs, inside the door, and beyond the shadows, where he stops, turns, and looks, making sure no one has seen him. I slide off to one side behind the wheel. Then he disappears.

The entire episode took less than twenty seconds. Anybody watching would consider it overly aggressive for any husband to treat his wife in this way. Some might call the cops, though I wouldn't want my own life to hang on that slender thread. What she is doing here I don't know, but Robin Watkins, Espinoza's child-wife, is in serious trouble.

I grab my cell phone and dial nine-one-one. The operator comes on.

"I want to report domestic violence."

"Is this an emergency?"

"It is."

"Is the act occurring at this time?"

"Yes." I give her the address, my name, and cell number.

"We will dispatch a car."

"How long?"

"It may take a few minutes," she says.

"How many minutes?"

"I can't give you an estimate. We don't have any officers in the area at the moment. As soon as a unit is available."

I hang up, take a deep breath, and step out of the car. From the backseat I grab my old attache case, Samsonite, hard-sided and heavy. I close the car door and step back to the trunk. Inside, under the spare, I find the tire iron, a half-inch steel rod, about eighteen inches long, straight with a chisel point at one end for fitting into the jack, and curved to a forty-five-degree angle with a welded tire lug socket on the other end. This state now has two yammering U.S. senators who would strip every implement of defense from the hands of its citizens. That they haven't banned lug wrenches and hammers is only a question of time.

I take the documents and files out of my briefcase and lay the iron diagonally inside, the only way it will fit, then close the briefcase and slam the trunk. As I head across the street, I hit the auto-lock button on my key ring and listen as the doors lock. The heat is oppressive, the sun beating down, reflecting up off the street's fractured concrete.

At the top of the stairs I check the mailbox. Saldado, H. is still listed as residing in apartment G.

I pull open the screen. The front door is still open, so I step inside. It's cooler here, dark, with a current of air drifting down the hallway from the back of the house.

The apartment at the foot of the stairs directly on my right is lettered "A" in dented brass, screwed into the top cross brace of the old three-panel door.

There is another door directly across the hall to my left; apartment B. Farther on, there are two more doors on that same side, apartments D and E. Apartment G, Saldado's, has to be upstairs.

I climb the stairs two at time, watching where I step, trying to make as little noise as possible. Near the top, my eyes come level with the floor of the hallway on two. This traverses the second story directly over the hallway below.

I continue my climb until I see the door on the right just beyond the top of the stairs: G.

From the layout of the building, Saldado's apartment appears to be larger than the other flats. With only a single door on the right because of the open stairwell, his unit spans the entire length of the building, front to back on that side.

I press my ear against the soiled plaster of the wall just above the level of the floor. I am still standing six or seven steps from the top as I listen. What sounds like noises from a television inside, voices followed by canned laughter.

I check my watch, hoping to hear the screeching tires of a patrol unit pulling up out front. Instead what I hear is the cry of a woman, a single wail, followed by a dense thud as something or someone slams up against the wall on the other side. The vibration against the walls causes me to pull my head away. It is followed by a muted scream and what sounds like sobbing.

Quickly I open the attache and take out the tire iron. Feeling the weight of it in my hand, I scramble to come up with a plan, some diversion, a distraction, something that will take Saldado's mind off of the woman if only for a moment to give the cops time to get here.

Ahead of me down the hallway, past the door to his apartment, a small section of the wall juts out, maybe two feet square. In a larger building this might be the wall covering a steel I-beam, part of the interior structure. In this case, my guess is it's a plumbing or electrical chase installed when they carved the old house into apartments.

I look at Saldado's door again. I can't slip inside his apartment unnoticed, but my business card can. Quickly I jot a note on the back of one of my cards, climb to the top of the stairs, and carefully set the briefcase in the center of the top step, so anybody coming or going can't miss it.

Quickly, I move down the hall until I'm standing directly in front of Saldado's apartment door. There is a security hole

for viewing, one of those round fish-eye lenses in the door.
I can't be certain, but from the angle I am guessing that anyone looking from inside won't be able to see far enough
down the hall to glimpse the abandoned attaché.

I take a deep breath, then slip the business card under the
door, and pound as hard as I can on the door, twice.

There is one quick sob from inside. This is instantly muf-
fled. Before it stops, I am ten feet down the corridor moving lightly on the balls of my feet, in the opposite direction
from the empty briefcase.

I huddle behind the plaster column formed by the chase,
barely deep enough to conceal my body with my back
pressed against the wall.

Several seconds pass. I listen.

The voices from the television inside suddenly become
more faint until I can no longer hear them. Then, nothing. I
stand listening, what seems like an eternity. Beads of sweat
form on my forehead and upper lip, while my sweating palm
grips the tire iron. I strain to listen. Nothing. Seconds pass
to a minute. I check my watch. The cops should be coming.

Then I hear it. The sign of life given up by every old
building, the universal groan from one of the aging floor
joists as someone walks over it. Someone is moving slowly
near the front door just on the other side, probably looking
through the peephole. I visualize what is happening inside.
A man, tall and wiry, scruffy dark beard peering through the
hole, seeing nothing. Then picking up my business card and
reading the message.

"Mr. Espinoza: I have a $5,000 cash refund for your unused
fees since you hired another lawyer. A friend gave me this
address and I'm trying to find you. Paul Madriani"

Saldado may not be welcoming visitors, but five thousand in cash?

Several more seconds pass, then footsteps inside. I hear
crying. This time it's the child. Then hobbled footsteps. A
man's voice, something in Spanish. The sounds getting

closer to the door. I tighten my grip on the tire iron in my right hand. The dead bolt is turned on the inside, and the door opens. I press my back against the wall.

"Who's there?" It's a woman's voice, scared, faltering. "Who is out there?"

They listen for a second. Saldado's probably looking through the peephole, while he holds a pistol to her head.

"See who it is." A whispered, harsh voice, accented. "And remember I have your baby in here. The door closes for a second. Then I hear the security chain slide off, and it opens again. He pushes her out into the hallway and closes the door behind her quickly. I hear the dead bolt snap closed and the security chain slide back in place.

I peep, one-eyed, around the corner of my hiding place. She doesn't see me. Robin Watkins already has her back to me as she focuses on the only visible item out of place in the hallway, my abandoned briefcase on the stairs. I had hoped Espinoza would go for this, giving me a one-time shot from behind with the tire iron.

Instead Watkins stands at the top of the stairs looking down. "Hello. Are you there?"

No answer as I hide in the alcove. If she sees me, with her child held by Saldado inside, I'm afraid she will panic and give me up. She starts down the stairs, slowly, calling out as she goes.

As she nears the bottom, I lose the sound of her footfalls, periodically picking her up from the sound of her voice as she calls out. I hear the squeak of the front door, followed by the wooden screen as it opens and slams closed.

If the cops drive up now, there is no telling what she will do; run to them or run back upstairs to the apartment to save her baby.

But it doesn't happen. I check my watch. The cops are taking their time. A few seconds later I hear the doors down below again, first the screen then the front door closing. Her footsteps moving, not up the stairs but down the hallway below, toward the rear of the building. She is checking carefully, every place I may have gone, calling out. I hear the back door open and close, then silence. I wait and listen, wondering what Saldado is doing inside. Probably looking out the windows. If a patrol car pulls up, all hell could break loose.

For a few seconds, I wonder if perhaps fear hasn't overtaken maternal instincts, causing Watkins to take off through the backyard. I hear the baby crying inconsolably inside. Watkins can no doubt hear this as well.

Just about the time I think she has taken off, I hear the rattle of the knob at the back door, not down below this time but at the back porch on the second story, five feet away and down the hall to my right. I press back as deep as I can into the shadows as I hear the door open.

She is coming. Back to the apartment. Watkins will have to walk right past me to get there. The door closes behind her. I hear her breathing, sniffling back tears, her feet shuffling on the old wooden-planked floor. Her face is bruised, one eye closed from the swelling. Her nose is bleeding. I can't tell if it's broken. Her gaze cast down at the floor, she doesn't see me until she looks up.

I put a finger to my lips, gesture of silence. Robin looks toward the door down the hall, then back to me. She sees the tire iron in my hand and shakes her head quickly. Robin Watkins knows what lies behind that door. Knowing this, she has little confidence in me or the weapon in my hand.

Before she can say anything, I reach out and grab her, pulling her toward the wall.

"My baby's in there," she whispers.

"I know. Besides Saldado, how many are there inside?"

She looks at me like she doesn't recognize the name or understand the question.

"The man inside with your baby, is he alone?"

She nods slowly, in a trance. I'm wondering if she's drugged or just in shock.

"Where's your husband?"

She points toward the door.

The child is crying again.

"My baby. I need to get my baby," she says.

I have to hold her by one arm to keep her from going. "Does he have a gun? The man inside?"

She shakes her head, shrugs. She doesn't know. "A knife," she says. "It's all I saw."

"We have to figure some way to get him to come out," I tell her.

She shakes her head and tries to pull away again.

"Listen, if you don't help me, I can't get your baby out of there."

This seems to focus her attention.

We don't have much time. Saldado had to hear her when she opened and closed the back door. He'll be watching through the prism right now, wondering what she's doing out of view.

"Walk past the door as fast as you can," I cup my hand over her ear and whisper. "Get the briefcase and take it back to the apartment door. When you get to the door hold it up for him to see. He'll be watching you through the peephole. Tell him I went to my car to get some papers for your husband to sign, but the money is in the case. Understand? The money is in the case. Then put it on the floor right outside the door. Whatever you do, when he opens the door, don't go inside."

"My baby's inside."

"I know. I'll get your baby for you. Do you understand?"

She turns her head and looks up at me. I'm not sure she does.

"Will my baby be all right?" She almost says it out loud. I put my hand over her mouth.

"I'll take care of your baby. When he opens up you just step to the other side of the door and stay out of the way."

She nods.

Before she can ask another question, I send her on her way. She looks back at me over her shoulder, now clearly in the visual compass of the prism. I motion for her to look the other way. She does it, making it appear as if someone is pulling the strings on a marionette. She is in shock. My fear is, after she gets the briefcase and returns to the door, she will have forgotten everything else.

But before she gets there, she stops in front of the door. I hold my breath. If he opens the door and pulls her in, there is nothing I can do. My mind wants to send her telepathic messages to move.

I hear the chain slide on the door from the inside. I start to move, trying to close the distance to the door. The noise from the chain seems to jar her back to reality. Her feet begin to move, a kind of slow shuffle on down the hall toward the stairs and my attache case.

I take a deep breath and settle into my hiding place. I can pray that Saldado is alone and without a gun. If not, he's gonna be pissed when he gets the drop and finds out I only have sixty bucks in my wallet and some change in my pocket.

She picks up the briefcase and turns this way. Robot in a trance. I'm nodding, motioning for her to come this way, back to the door.

She walks like a zombie. She is in shock. She could be suffering a concussion from the blows to her head. She carries the empty briefcase in her left hand. When she gets to the door, she turns and stands there looking straight ahead at the blank wooden door.

Saldado has to be watching her through the prism right now. I motion to her, grip one wrist with my hand, and raise the other hand still holding the tire iron. "Lift the briefcase and show it to him." I do everything but say the words.

Finally she does it, hesitates for a moment, then says: "The money's inside."

I hear the security chain come off. Then he pauses. "Where is he?"

She shakes her head a little. Clears the fog. "Went to his car," she says. "Some papers to sign."

He thinks about this for a second. Then the dead bolt turns. Open sesame. I work my way around the pilaster, and hugging the wall with my back, I'm at the door in three long sideways steps. Watkins is still standing there in front of it holding the briefcase. She's in a daze.

Holding the tire iron in both hands, I motion with my head for her to move aside. She doesn't see me or it doesn't register.

The doorknob turns. There's no time. With my back against the wall I raise my left leg, put my foot against her arm holding the briefcase, and push as hard as I can with my foot. The briefcase comes out of her hand and drops. Watkins sprawls to the floor six feet away down the hall. An instant later, the door opens a crack.

I throw my body against it, shoulder first, and push with my legs. I trip over the briefcase, lose traction, leather soles on a wooden floor.

The door opens halfway before Saldado knows what's hit him, his eyes wide, two black olives floating in a sea of white. I get just a glimpse of his face before he reacts. Quick as a cat, he throws himself against the other side of the door and stands me up straight. Suddenly the momentum shifts. Leaning, he has leverage. He reaches around the door, something in his hand, shiny and flashing, a straight razor. He swipes at me, catches my right arm, and slices the thin sleeve of my cotton shirt as if it were tissue paper.

In the instant it takes me to regroup, he has the door closing like a mountain has fallen on it from the other side.

I push with everything I have. I'm losing. The door is closing inch by inch, until it hits something hard and stops. I look down. Robin Watkins, bleeding and bruised, is huddled at my feet. She has jammed my briefcase into the opening.

I throw my shoulder against the door and it budges. Saldado knows he can't win. He can push, but he can't close the door. He tries kicking at the case, but Watkins is holding it in place with both hands.

He tries to reach out with the blade again. This time I deflect it with the tire iron, catching his knuckles with the lug end of the steel. He pulls his hand back in. For a few seconds, he holds me. I throw myself against the door, once, twice, three times. Each shot transfers the blow to his body on the other side. He absorbs several more of these, then suddenly steps back and the door flies open.

Saldado retreats to the center of a small living room. He backs up and nearly falls over a low, flimsy coffee table. He flattens one of the legs and kicks the rest of it out of the way. Splintered pieces of wood fly across the room. The tabletop crashes into a large package wrapped in plastic and lying on the floor by the end of the sofa.

The Mexican crouches, knees flexed, holding the razor blade out in front of him, his eyes fixed on the tire iron in my hands.

Off to my left is the child, a little boy sitting in soiled Pampers on the couch, wide-eyed, staring at me. For the moment, his crying is stopped by the surprise of my entry. He has one little fist wet with saliva in his mouth.

I look at Saldado, and the thought reaches both of us at the same instant. He makes a move toward the child. I lash out with the iron, missing him by a few inches, but it's enough to make him step back and to his left. As he does I move into the breach, circling to my right, putting myself between him and the boy. He continues this circular dance of combat and forces me farther to the right. He's looking at the open door and Robin Watkins kneeling on the floor. I'm where I want to be, and I don't budge. He has the blade, but I have greater reach with the iron. If he slashes at me and misses, I'll break his arm. If I get lucky, I might nail him in the head.

Saldado studies the situation, dark pupils darting back and forth between Watkins kneeling in the doorway and her child on the sofa. Either one of them will do. He feints toward the mother and catches me leaning. I lash out. Nothing but the swish of air. He goes the other way toward the child. The tire iron cuts a figure eight through empty space.

He backs off, smiling at me. "Not so easy, uh?" He wipes perspiration off his upper lip with one arm.

I'm watching his eyes. He's gauging the distance of my reach, my willingness to risk the blade.

He looks at the child, then back at the mother. Obvious moves now, leaving me to wonder which one he will go for, his focus never far from the tire iron. He looks quickly at the child, takes a half step in that direction.

This time, I don't go for it. Instead I move my head in that direction, my feet planted firmly. When he reverses field toward the door, I'm ready for him.

Saldado is committed. Momentum carries him. Just enough time for a quick hitch with the iron for a back swing. I lay into him like a left-handed batter with a Louisville slugger. The lug end of the tire iron catches him full force, low along the left side of his chest—a deadening thud and the cracking of bone.

"Unnnnnhhhh." It knocks the wind out of him. Saldado staggers backward. Surprise and pain, followed an instant later by anger—all the emotions of adrenaline flashing across his face in less than a second. Before I can follow up with another blow, he lashes at me, a halfhearted effort, but enough to keep me away, fight or flight.

He comes at me again. The blade slashes under the iron. I bend at the midsection, leaning back, and the straight edge of the razor misses my stomach by an inch.

Looping the iron, I catch the back of his hand on the follow-through, but without enough force to do any damage.

Saldado is holding his side with one hand now—glancing under his arm, feeling the pain, and assessing the damage. There's blood on his shirt. He looks at it, then realizes, as I do, that its not where I hit him.

There is an arc of tiny red splotches up high on his shoulder as if someone swung a loaded paint brush in his direction.

Breathing heavily, in pain, he connects the dots before I do. He smiles. "You're bleeding, *señor.*"

I glance quickly down. There is blood dripping off the end of the tire iron and onto the floor.

While I'm distracted for an instant, Saldado tries for an opening. I check him with my eyes, catching him leaning and freeze him in place. Having felt the bite of the steel in my hand, he has no desire to offer up a second course.

My right shirt sleeve is red from the elbow to the buttoned cuff where he slashed it with the razor through the door. Adrenaline has killed the pain. Either that or he's severed a nerve.

His movement is slower now. So is mine. He positions his injured side away from me, protecting it, still holding the bottom of his rib cage with one hand, as he waves the blade slowly back and forth, stirring the air in front of my face with the other.

He tries to get me to swing at the blade, moving it closer. I refuse to take the bait. He would move in behind my swing and catch my arm coming back. In the meantime, the razor would be free to do its work.

"Man, you keep this up," he says, "you going to end up like your friend on the floor there."

"Yeah, you do a real good job beating on women," I tell him.

"No. No. Not that one. Your other friend. Over there." He gestures with his head in the other direction. "I let you keep the money. Take it and go. I give you your life," he says.

I glance over quickly and realize he's talking about the package wrapped in plastic and lying on the floor.

"Espinoza?"

He nods slowly, smiling at me.

"What about the child and the woman?"

He shrugs, offers a disarming smile. "What are they to me?"

Watkins must have seen him kill her husband. I can't believe he would let her go.

"I've already called the police," I tell him.

"You lie."

"Stick around and find out."

He waves the blade at me. "How long you think you can bleed like that, man, and still stand up? Huh? Why don't you go?"

His eyes tell me that the second I move toward the door he'll come with the blade.

"Let her take the child and go."

"Sure."

"Robin?"

She looks at me but doesn't say anything.

"Get your baby," I tell her.

She looks at the child, then back at me.

"Get up and get your baby."

The Mexican is smiling. He knows if he can take me down, he can catch the woman and her child before they can get to the front door.

She stands up. Takes a few tentative steps into the room.

"Come behind me," I tell her.

The Mexican smiles at me. He could grab her in a second, force me to drop the iron, then cut her throat and kill me.

She moves behind me, grabs the child, huddles him in her arms.

"Go," I tell her.

She moves to the door, then turns and looks at me.

"Go!" I turn my head and take my eyes off of him for a fraction of a second.

In that instant he comes at me. The blade comes underneath. He reaches up with the hand of his wounded side and grabs the action end of the iron before I can swing.

I trap his arm with the razor under one elbow against my side.

"Go!" Between clenched teeth. It's all I can do to keep from biting my tongue as Saldado's body crashes into me, his shoulder coming up under my chin, forcing my head farther to the right.

With terror etched in her eyes, clutching her child, she disappears down the hall.

Saldado, with the razor hand trapped under my arm, tries to maneuver his wrist to cut into my back. I feel the blade scraping against the cotton fabric of my shirt, and I pull him, twisting, whirling to keep him off balance.

I leverage the weight of my body and let physics do the rest. Centrifugal force sends us hurtling across the room until our feet hit an immovable object, Espinoza's body, and gravity takes over.

I cuff my hand around the back of his neck and, on the way down, give him a hard shove, accelerating his fall and driving him onto his chest.

I hit the floor on one shoulder. The crushing contact knocks the wind out of me.

Saldado takes it on the chest, landing directly in front of my eyes. He expels a mist of vaporized blood from his nose and mouth, propelled by breath from a punctured lung. The hand with the blade slaps the floor and the razor clatters across the old hardwood planks.

For several seconds neither of us moves. Crumpled on my side against the end of the couch, unable to breathe, I listen to his wheezing punctuated by occasional groans.

My brain is beginning to go blank, vision blurred like someone has poured water over a sheet of glass in front of my eyes.

I see him lift his head, the frothy bubbles of blood dripping from his mouth and nose.

My own breath comes slowly, shallow, my head as light as helium.

He struggles onto to his hands and knees, his eyes glazed with pain and pitted with anger as he looks at me and weaves on all fours.

I focus on the shining blade across the floor.

He turns his head and sees it.

I try to move, but my body won't obey. My feet are cold, vision dimming; audible illusions begin to fill my ears, sounds of buzzing.

When my eyes return to him, Saldado's attention is no longer on the razor across the floor. Instead he is struggling to his feet, holding his side, his dark eyes directed toward the front of the building. As my vision fades, I recognize the sound, somewhere beyond the walls of the room, the electronic harmonics of a siren.

CHAPTER TWENTY-TWO

I reenter the world of the living from a haze, a foggy view of the plastered ceiling in the Mexican's apartment.

Flat on my back for some reason, I'm feeling no pain. The hard floor is gone, replaced by something softer. I try to sit up, but I can't. I am strapped to a gurney. I start to raise one hand toward my head, and somebody reaches out and grabs my arm. "Stay still. You're gonna pull the needle out."

Guy in a blue uniform taping a needle down on the back of my hand. He has one knee on the floor, working over me, adjusting a little plastic wheel on a tube from a bag of clear fluid that is running down through the needle, and into me.

"How you feelin'?"

I try to talk. "Like I got a chip of wood in my throat."

"Don't talk. Lieutenant. He's startin' to come around."

The bag for the I.V. drip is being held by another EMT, standing over him. The needle is in my good hand, the left. My right arm is bandaged, gauze and tape all the way from the wrist to the elbow. My arms are laid across my chest, like they were getting ready to put me in a box.

"You lost a lot of blood."

Through the frog in my throat, I talk. "I can't feel anything."

"That's the pain meds." The words come from another voice. "Don't worry, in the morning you'll feel like shit." The face finally comes into view, familiar, but I can't place it. He's in shirtsleeves and tie, wearing dark glasses and carrying a notepad in one hand and a can of Diet Coke in the other.

"Let me sit up." The straps hold me in place.

"No. No. Stay there." The EMT is not going let me move.

"Right. So you can fall on your ass and sue the city." The Diet Coke still has the icy sweat of chill on the can.

"I'd offer you one, but then you'd puke all over the crime scene. Some fucking lawyer'd find a way to use it against us in court. The vomit defense. Then we'd never be able to solve that." He motions off to the side with the can in his hand.

I roll my head in that direction and see Espinoza. The top of his body, anyway. Most of it still wrapped in plastic except for his head and upper torso where the sheet has been sliced and peeled back like the husk off a cob of corn. His complexion is white. A narrow crease of dried blood, the thickness of dental tape, runs across his throat.

I roll my head back to look at the guy in the dark glasses. "Do I know you?"

"Oh, yeah." He takes the glasses off. "Lieutenant Ortiz." He gives me the pearly whites, skin so tight over the bone structure of his face that the dental feature could be part of a naked skull. "Remember? Had that nice conversation in your office. I did the monologue. You claimed privilege. Talked about your buddy Nick Rush, Gerald Metz. You do remember?"

I nod.

"I couldn't be sure. All the drugs they're putting in you

from that bag. Probably almost as good as the shit Metz was selling. What do you think?"

I don't answer him.

"What, no opinion? OK, fine. We'll let that go. What do you think about this?" He wags his head toward Espinoza's body. "You think it was an accident? I understand Rush was an accident. Read it in the paper," he says. "Oh, yeah. Wandered into the path of a cruising bullet. It's like they say, speed kills." He looks at me, leaning over again.

I don't respond.

"What, nothing to contribute? Jeez, for a fuckin' mouthpiece, you don't have much to say. And I was led to believe you were the mastermind behind that insurance coup. Well, that's fine. You save your voice. We can talk tomorrow. Besides, one dead body at a time. Which leads us back to this one. You didn't happen to see it when it happened, did you?"

I shake my head.

"I shoulda figured that. What can you tell me? Let's see. We know he's dead. What did he use, a scalpel?"

I turn my head the other way, toward the floor across the room. It's gone. I look back at Ortiz. "A straight razor."

"Aw. That what he cut you with?"

I nod.

"A name?"

I have to clear the frog living in my throat before I can get the word out. "Saldado."

"Ah. I take it somebody you didn't represent this time. Good for you. He's the one lived here, right?"

I nod.

"Man has a funny way of treating visitors," he says.

One of the EMTs checks the bandage on my arm, and I wince.

"You can roll him out in a minute," says Ortiz. "I want to talk to him just for a sec."

The guy checks the I.V. quickly, then moves away to gather his equipment.

"For a lawyer, you don't seem to get it," says Ortiz. "You're supposed to hand out your business cards to the injured, not the dead." He's holding my card in his hand. The one with the note on the back to Espinoza.

"You wanna tell me what this was all about?"

"I used the card to get in. He had them."

"Who?"

"The mother. The child."

"The nine-eleven call. Domestic violence."

I nod.

"I see. And who gave you the cape and tights? Why didn't you wait for us?"

"No time. Where are they?"

"They're all right. She's gonna have a shiner in the morning. But she's alive. More than we can say about her uglier half over here." He motions toward the dead body on the floor next to me.

"Must say she's taking it pretty well, considering. Then again, it probably wasn't a picture-perfect romance. Who beat her up? Saldado?"

I nod. "You get him?"

"No. We got here, he was already gone. But we got people out looking, checkin' every house, looking in the sewer. Everyplace we can. He'll turn up."

"Don't think so."

"What, you know something?"

I shake my head.

"Trust me. We'll get him."

If they didn't snag him coming out of the apartment, they won't find him now. People who do what Saldado does for a living move without suitcases and call signals without a huddle. They would have a dozen contingencies worked out before the cops came knocking, holes they could dive into or pop out of, places to hide, be picked up from, or dropped off at. In a few hours, after dark, if I hadn't shown up, Espinoza, his wife, and baby would have each been gift wrapped, dumped in the back of the dark Blazer, and probably headed for a shallow grave somewhere in the desert east of the city. Unless I miss my bet, Saldado or whatever his real name is, is long gone, probably on his way to Cancún.

Ortiz breaks from note-taking to inspect my arm and head, then adds a few entries for his report. "He sure as hell did a number on you."

"Like they say. You shoulda seen the other guy."

"What did you do, serve him with process?"

"Broke his ribs."

He looks down at me smiling, incredulous. "With what, your finger?"

"Tire iron." I point under the front edge of the sofa.

Otriz pushes the couch a little until it slides a few inches, exposing one end of the tire iron.

"Jack. Something over here you missed."

One of the evidence techs comes over, hands in surgical gloves.

"Did Saldado touch it?" says Ortiz.

I nod.

"Dust it for prints, then tag it," he tells the tech. "You'll need to get his prints too, to eliminate 'em. And blood," he says. "See if you get any traces. We might get lucky. DNA for an I.D. Our man here says he broke a few ribs with the thing there."

I cough, clear my throat to get his attention again.

"What is it now?"

I tap the front of my shirt, on my chest on the other side, away from my cut arm.

"What are you saying?"

"His blood."

Ortiz comes down for a closer look. Where the Mexican coughed it up when we hit the floor. There is a fine mist of tiny specks, little dots of dried blood like bits of rust across the chest of my white shirt, some on the side of my face.

"Jack. Get a pair of scissors."

A second later the evidence tech comes back. A few snips and he cuts a four-inch-square swatch out of my shirt.

"You become more cooperative somebody sticks you with a knife. I'll have to remember that next time I come to your office for an interview. Anything else you have?"

I shake my head. "That's good for now. You're lookin'

a little peaked," he says. "You guys want to get him outta here?" To the EMTs now, "That arm's gonna take some stitches. If I call ahead to the E.R. and tell 'em they got a lawyer on the way, I'm sure they can find their biggest needle." He smiles at me.

"Fine idea," says the evidence tech. "Tell them to get that fuckin' harpoon they use to close on autopsies. That'll give him something to talk about when he rolls up his sleeves at bar meetings."

"Thanks."

"Don't mention it." Ortiz, now wearing his dark glasses again, is smiling. "You want me to call your partner?"

I nod. I try to form the words, but nothing comes out. I try again. "My daughter."

"You want me to have him call her?"

Quick nods.

"They're gonna hold you at least overnight. For observation," he says. "And we're gonna talk some more tomorrow, hmm? So that you know, don't try and tell me there's no connection between your friend here and the other client, Mr. Metz. Cuz I know there was."

I shake my head.

"Don't bother," he says. "I'm also going to assume you're gonna tell me about it, when you're feeling better, like tomorrow?"

Before I can respond, Ortiz has turned around to talk to one of the uniforms. "I want a hold put on him. Material witness," he says. "He doesn't get a release from the hospital until I sign him out. Personally. You understand?" Then he looks down at me and winks. "See you in the morning."

Espinoza's murder is all over the front page of this morning's paper, along with pictures of Saldado's apartment building fenced off from the street by yellow tape. Harry has brought copies along with a change of clothes to my hospital room at County General. Security is sitting outside my door, making sure I don't leave.

"Even made the evening news," says Harry.

"When do I get out of here?"

"Relax. It could be worse."

"You want to tell me how?"

"You could be sharing a room with someone else."

"I am. With you."

"You could be here under a managed-care plan."

"There you have me."

"Try turning on the soaps." Harry points to the overhead TV. "Take your mind off of things."

"That'll take my mind all right."

"Relax. At least Saldado didn't cut a nerve," he says.

Harry is right. My arm is hurting like hell this afternoon, throbbing all the way to my armpit, from there to my brain right behind my eyeballs, like little strikes of lightning.

"One of the few times I agree with the cops," he says. "Tell them what you know, and let's get back to work for the American people," says Harry.

"What do I know? Espinoza's dead." Harry has brought me slacks and a clean shirt, so I change as we talk. Gingerly I roll the sleeve down over my bandaged arm and button the cuff at the wrist.

"Looks like you're going to be writing with your left hand for a while."

"I take it they didn't find Saldado?"

Harry shakes his head. "They're still checking the neighborhood, talking to people. My guess is they're wasting their time. You had a stiff in your living room, would you stick around?"

I don't answer him.

"Me neither," he says.

"With a broken rib, could you run like that?" I ask.

"Depends what I was running from," says Harry.

I've got one foot up on the side of the bed trying to tie the shoelace with a stiff arm.

"You want me to do that?"

"When I start drooling, you can put me in St. Florence's home for extended living. Until then I can tie my own shoes," I tell him.

"Fine. Just trying to help."

"How long can Ortiz keep me here?"

"Tell you one thing. Wouldn't want to be your nurse," he says.

"Harry?"

"What?"

"How long can Ortiz keep me here?" Harry looks at me, shrugs a shoulder. If I have to depend on my partner to spring me from the hospital, I may as well take up squatter's rights.

I bring up the other shoe, place it on the edge of the sheet where the mattress meets one of the side rails, and go to work on the laces. That's when I hear voices outside the door. A second later, it opens. I stop with my foot on the bed and look up.

Ortiz waltzes through the door, this time with his partner, the blond linebacker.

"As we speak," I say.

"What did I tell you, Norm? Give a lawyer a day with his ass stretched across a bedpan, and he'll smile when he sees you."

"In case you haven't looked, this one isn't smiling," I tell him.

"Listen to this. Off the happy juice for a few hours and the first part of him that works again is his mouth. You remember Sargeant Padgett?" says Ortiz.

"How could I forget." Padgett has a pad and pencil out, ready to take notes. "How you doin'?"

"From the looks of it, better than you." Padgett slumps into the other visitor's chair next to Harry.

"Don't tell me you write?" says Harry.

I look at him. "Be nice."

"Listen to your partner," says Ortiz. "He wants to go home."

"I'd shake hands, but both arms hurt," I tell him.

"Knife in one, all-night drip in the other." Ortiz describes my injuries to Padgett with a smile.

"I'm ready to leave now."

"You haven't finished tying your shoe," he says. "Then you have to tell us what happened."

"What happened! I got stabbed. I'm a crime victim."

"Yes, but what were you doing there? And don't tell me you were looking for a client."

"I was."

"Don't tell me that. I don't want to hear that. Espinoza wasn't your client. Not anymore." Ortiz looks at his partner. "Clarence Darrow here slides a business card under this guy's door, telling him he's got five grand in cash to give to his dead guest."

"Sounds like an invitation to become a pin cushion," says Padgett. "They teach you that one in law school?"

"It got me in the door."

"Why did you hustle him? Espinoza?" says Ortiz. "From what we see, you're not hurting for clients. The wife tells us you came to her apartment and wanted to represent her husband."

They have a lot of the answers already. I don't say anything, and Padgett contributes a little more.

"You left him in the can. At federal detention. We understand your partner here went into cardiac arrest when he called, found out Espinoza was on the street. Anybody ever tell you when you take a client you're supposed to provide legal services?"

"Who are you working for, the bar?" says Harry.

"We talked to the first-year law student who got him out," he says. "And seeing as you didn't collect a fee, you weren't in it for the money."

"So tell us," says Ortiz, "why was everybody so interested in Espinoza?"

"You want to tell him or should I?" says Harry.

"Oh, good. A lawyer with a brain." Ortiz looks at Harry.

"We heard that Espinoza might know something about the shooting in front of the federal courthouse." I talk before Harry can.

"And where did you hear this?"

"From your people," says Harry.

Ortiz shoots him a look.

"Our people?"

"What are we supposed to do? People talk. Some of them work for the government. OK. They're not supposed to. Still, they talk; we listen."

"You have the names of these people?" says Ortiz. Padgett is sharpening the point on his mechanical pencil, turning it for some new lead.

"I don't think they ever mentioned their names," says Harry.

"Agencies?"

Harry shakes his head. "That either."

"I see, anonymous phone calls to your office."

"Something like that," says Harry.

"It's an open investigation. How would you like to have a deputy D.A. ask you under oath, in front of a judge?" says Padgett. "Maybe spend some time in the bucket for contempt?"

"They have rooms like this, you won't hear me complaining. TV, three squares. Probably pick up a few clients in the day room. Sounds like a vacation," says Harry. "To say nothing of the publicity. Lawyer goes to jail to protect his sources."

"That's reporters," says Padgett.

"Yes, but it's such a good cause," says Harry. "I think they'd stretch the rule."

"That's right, I forgot. The settlement kings," says Ortiz. "Accidental death. Let's talk about that. Who was it you were representing? The wife, the new one, what's her name?"

"Dana," says Padgett. "You remember, good looker. Blond. Sassy little thing. Diamond-studded fangs."

"How could I forget? What did she get, a million, million and a half?" asks Ortiz.

"Something like that," I say.

"And you," says Padgett. "How did you take your fees? A check? Or was there some other arrangement?" He cracks a grin. "You know we can always find out."

"Do that."

"We understand she's seeing somebody else," says Ortiz.

"Besides who?" I ask.

"Give him a break," says Padgett. "Maybe it was just a momentary lust."

"Maybe it was business" I say. "Tell me, what do you think of his car?" Padgett's face gives it up, the kind of expression that doesn't have to say a word to make a confession. They have been following Fittapaldi. "Yeah, I know. I'm not partial to Jags either."

"Maybe it was a three-way twist," he says.

"You mean tryst, don't you?"

"Twist, tryst. The three of 'em together."

I turn to Ortiz. "I know this is a stimulating conversation. But can we go now?"

"Not until you tell me about Espinoza," he says.

"What do you want to know?"

"For starters, why did you go looking for him at this guy Saldado's apartment?"

"I had Saldado's name. Espinoza gave it to me when I interviewed him at the lockup." It's a little white lie, but this way I keep Joyce's and Bennie's names out of it.

"How did they know each other, Espinoza and Saldado?"

"I don't know the connection. Not exactly."

"What do you know?" Padgett's pencil working on the pad now.

"You remember the visas that were stolen a year or so ago? The van down in Tijuana?"

"Why the feds had Espinoza in custody," says Ortiz.

"Right. I saw the arrest in the paper. Espinoza's name came up in my interview with Metz, before I handed him back to Nick."

This catches the two cops where they live: in the curiosity department.

"What did he say?"

"He gave me the name. Said Espinoza was a go-between with some people he was doing business with down in Mexico."

"What people?"

"Two brothers."

"Names?" says Ortiz.

"Ibarra. Arturo and Jaime."

"So these brothers, they were dealers?" says Ortiz.

"Who knows?"

"That's your business. That's why you wouldn't do Metz, isn't it?"

"He told me they hired him to do some construction work. That's all I know."

"But you didn't believe him," says Ortiz.

"What I believe doesn't matter."

"Sure it does. That's why you gave Metz back to your friend. That's why he's dead. And that's why you keep nosing around. Or did I miss something?" Ortiz is quick.

Harry claps a couple of times from his chair in the corner. "Now can we all go home so my partner can get the therapy he needs, and the rest of us can get on with life?"

"So when Metz got shot and this guy got arrested, you remembered the name?" Padgett is trying to get his notes straight.

"I told you."

"Tell me again," he says.

"Slower this time, so he can get all the stick-people pictures a little bigger," says Harry.

"Fuck you," says Padgett.

"If you think you can spell it, put it in your book there."

When Padgett doesn't write anything, Harry says: "That's what I thought."

"You saw it in the paper?" Padgett tries to ignore him. "Or you got wind that there was somebody in the federal lockup might know something? Which is it?" says Padgett.

"Both."

"Both? How can it be both?"

"Somebody told him about Espinoza's arrest, so he went looking in the paper," says Ortiz.

"Maybe you should be taking the notes," I tell him.

"Then you checked the name and remembered that Metz had mentioned it in the interview, is that it?"

"Yeah."

"That still doesn't answer why you picked up Espinoza as a client," says Padgett. "Why you didn't call us."

"I did."

"When?"

"Yesterday. Nine-one-one. You were late getting there."

"Cute," he says.

"So what doesn't fit?" says Ortiz.

"What do you mean?"

"What is it that ruffles you about Metz and your buddy Rush?" says Ortiz. "You don't think Rush was capable of doing a drug deal?"

"It's not a question of capabilities. It's a question of judgment."

"I see. He was too ethical."

I smile. "He was too smart. Nick was a former prosecutor. He did major drug cases. Why, after all these years, would he become a player?"

"Maybe he needed the money. We've looked at his bank account," says Padgett. "The cupboard was getting a little bare. Besides, you think cops and prosecutors never turn to the dark side?" says Padgett.

"In your case, I'd make an exception," I tell him.

What is bothering me is not that Nick was above reproach, but that he was no man's fool.

"Besides, Nick would never get involved in a drug deal with a client. That would be like serving candy to you people. Tell me your mouth doesn't salivate at the thought? Nailing some defense attorney caught up with somebody like Metz. Hmm?" Ortiz gives me a face of concession. "Now tell me, have you found any drug connection in this thing? With either of them?"

"You just gave us one. The two brothers down in Mexico," says Padgett.

"I didn't say it was drugs."

"But that's what you thought."

"And maybe that's where we're making our mistake."

"So what do you think it was?" says Ortiz.

I take a deep breath, blow out some air, look at Harry, about to cross the Rubicon. "Ever heard of something called Mejicano Rosen?"

Ortiz looks at his partner, who shakes his head. "What is it?"

"We don't know. According to Espinoza, it's what these people in Mexico were dealing."

"Maybe something new. Manufactured," says Padgett. "I can check with the narcs, DEA. They mighta heard of it."

"I've made phone calls," I tell them. "Nobody who does narcotics cases in California has ever heard of it. I don't think it's narcotics," I tell him.

"So what is it?" says Ortiz.

I shake my head. "I was hoping to talk to Espinoza and find out."

"We know who paid to spring him. Hired the lawyer and posted the bail," says Ortiz. "Three guesses. The first two don't count."

"Saldado."

"I figured he must have picked him up from outside the facility. He wasn't going to let him go far."

"Is that his real name?" says Harry.

"We don't know. We're checking prints from the apartment. If he's ever been booked in the states, they should have something. We may get another name."

"More than likely, you'll get twenty of them," says Harry.

"We couldn't find a driver's license under Hector Saldado. So there's a good chance it's an alias," says Padgett.

"What about the car?" I ask.

"What car?"

"The one out in front. The rusted-out Blazer."

Ortiz looks at me like I'm speaking Farsi.

"Broken back window. Black plastic."

Ortiz looks at Padgett, who shakes his head.

"There wasn't any car." By the time Ortiz looks back at

me, he knows there was. "Where the hell did it go? You didn't happen to get a number off the plates?"

I shake my head. "It was there when I went in. You're telling me it was gone before your people got there?"

"We know he didn't take it." Padgett's up out of his chair now, worried that somehow he might have let it slip through his fingers. He had the outside detail.

"Check with traffic. They cordoned the area around the house," says Ortiz.

"Maybe it wasn't his?" says Padgett.

"Espinoza told me about it. It's how I found the place. The way he talked, he thought it belonged to Saldado."

"Then who took it?" says Ortiz.

I don't have an answer.

Ortiz turns to his partner. "Check the other tenants in the building, see if anybody besides Saldado is missing. Now," he says. "Use the phone outside. And get a description out on the car."

I give them details about the black plastic over the back window.

"That should make it easier to I.D.," says Ortiz. "Get somebody on the horn. Find out who's over there. We still have somebody on site?"

Padgett is not sure.

"See if any of the neighbors have anything on the plates. One of them might remember. And Norm—" Padgett is already out the door. He sticks his head back in. "Call down to the border. Have 'em put a stop on the vehicle if it tries to cross."

CHAPTER TWENTY-THREE

This morning Adam Tolt calls. He wants to meet for lunch. I suspect he wants an answer on his offer to join the firm.

Just after noon, and I find him at a table on the terrace of the Del Coronado, sitting under one of the large umbrellas and looking over the top of his menu toward the blue Pacific. It is one of those days that makes everyone want to move to San Diego.

"Sorry I'm late."

"No problem." He already has a drink. "What can they get you?"

I order one of the boutique brews on tap, and the waiter goes to get it. I slip my coat over the back of the chair and sit.

"It must be casual Wednesday," I tell him. Tolt is sans the suit and tie today, wearing slacks and a polo shirt.

"A few times a year I swing through the other offices unannounced. Just drop in, little inspection, see how things are going, talk to the partners, that sort of thing. I take the

Gulfstream since it gets me there quickly, and I may as well be comfortable," he says.

"Must be nice."

"Leaving tonight. It's why I wanted to talk to you."

There is a pause. "I read about what happened in the papers," he says. "This fellow Espinoza." He takes a sip from his tumbler, scotch on the rocks. Adam wants to know what's going on. Why I didn't tell him about Espinoza before this.

"You have a more exciting practice than most of us," he says.

"What? Does this mean the firm is no longer interested?"

"Did I say that? I didn't say that. Why? Have you made a decision?"

"I haven't talked to Harry, but I don't think it's gonna work."

"Then you haven't thought long enough. Take some more time. We can take Harry for a ride in the Gulfstream. Let him play with some of the corporate toys."

This could be dangerous. Harry has a fascination with the high life and would happily take the jet for a test run to Monaco. I decide to keep silent about my partner's weak spot.

"No need to decide now. Pick your moment."

Adam doesn't want to take no for an answer.

"The arm?" He motions to the bulge under my right shirt-sleeve, puffed out by the bandage. "I assume that's where he got you, the other guy. What was his name?"

"Saldado."

"You could have told me about Espinoza." Adam looks hurt.

"At the time I couldn't."

"Lawyer-client?"

I nod.

"The papers are saying he was connected with Nick's shooting."

"There's a lot of speculation," I tell him. "Actually, Espinoza was out of the country at the time."

"I assume you're trying to get answers?"

"I admit it wasn't a good way to go about it. Harry warned me."

"Harry must be the better half of the partnership. The part with judgment," he says. "Did you learn anything?"

"Espinoza was killed before I could."

"You weren't troubled by the possibility of a conflict? Representing him?"

"You sound like my partner."

"He has a point."

"Why are you so interested in this?" I ask him.

"I have an interest in protecting the firm," he says. "Yours, I assume, is driven by some perceived obligation you feel toward Nick?"

I look at him, but I don't answer.

"You don't have to explain. I understand. It's why I called. I assume you're up a dead end."

"Looks like it."

"What do you know about this other man, the one who attacked you?"

"Not much. I got a good look at him."

"Did Metz ever mention him?"

"No."

Adam sits back in the chair, looking at me, wondering, I suspect, if I've told him everything. "There is something else," he says. "But before I tell you, I have to know. Is there anything else, anything you haven't told me?"

"About?"

"Nick's death."

"No. I don't think so."

Adam looks at me from behind the dark glasses, a pair of expensive aviation shades with gold rims, trying to mind meld with me. Lawyers know there is always a little something every other lawyer holds back, if for no other reason than to corner the market on secrets.

"So what is this revelation?" I ask.

"I shouldn't tell," he says.

"You came all the way over here for you not to tell me?"

"All right. Fine. I'll tell you, but I want your word it doesn't go beyond this table."

"You got it."

"It's a letter. It was mailed to Nick at the office. It arrived two days after he was killed."

He lifts the large linen napkin that has lain folded neatly in two even halves on the table in front of him since my arrival. Underneath it is an envelope. He hands this to me.

There is a mailroom stamp from the firm on the envelope, showing the date of receipt on the outside.

"One of the secretaries found it. Somehow it got sorted off into a box downstairs. Never made it to Nick's office from the mail room. Everything being in chaos after he got shot. The police got some of the stuff from his office, but it seems they never checked the mail room."

"When did you get it?"

"This morning," he says. "One of the secretaries going through the box found it. As soon as she saw Nick's name and the cancellation date on the stamp, she brought it to me. So naturally I opened it."

"Naturally."

"It was sent to the firm." Adam is a little defensive on this point.

There's a foreign stamp up in the corner, something in Spanish. Adam is up-front about the date.

"I've checked it. The man is real. Quite prominent. According to my information, he owns a chain of banks and resort hotels in Mexico."

I open the envelope, remove the letter, and unfold it, heavy parchment. It is typed, written in English, and dated four days before Nick was killed. The letterhead is embossed, a seal, what looks like an ancient warlord's helmet and under it a phone number, a single digit area code (9) followed by three numbers and a dash, two more numbers, another dash and two numbers. I have seen this particular sequencing of phone numbers before. They were on the cellular telephone statement of the man Saldado, sent to me by

Joyce the collector, though there they included the country code for Mexico.

There is what appears to be an address: something called Blvd. Kukulcan, Km. 13 Z.H., and a city, Cancún, Q. Roo, Mexico, C.P. 77500.

The letter itself is brief. Two short paragraphs.

Dear Mr. Rush:

I am given your name by associates. I have been told you are a prudent man of business, a lawyer. I write so that you will know that I am informed of the recent activities of my sons. As a father I am not pleased with their undertaking. I wish to take the opportunity to assure you that they will not be permitted to continue. So that you know, I am pledged to this.

I assure you that I will deal with my sons in an appropriate manner. I would ask that as a man of judgment you consider this with regard to any future actions you might wish to take.

Yours truly,

Pablo Ibarra

I finish reading, study the letter for a moment, then read it again, trying to capture the import of the message.

"What do you make of it?" he says.

"I don't know."

"It sounds to me like he's trying to get Nick to back off from going after his two boys. The part about assuring Nick that he will deal with his sons in an appropriate way. Sounds to me as if he's trying to say there's no need for you to do it. I'll do it. Doesn't it to you?"

I read it again. "It's possible."

"If he was . . . I mean if Nick was in some fashion going after the sons, it's possible they could have killed him."

I concede the point with a look.

"That's why it's important that you tell me everything you know about this man Ibarra."

"What makes you think I know anything?"

"Because you knew Nick. You interviewed Metz. You're the only one who may know how the pieces fit."

"What pieces?"

"Is there a drug connection? You don't have to be prescient to read the signs. The letter comes out of Mexico; the sons are in some kind of trouble. Nick's expertise is in narcotics cases. Connect the dots," he says.

"Have you told the police about this, the letter I mean?"

He shakes his head, almost ignoring me, occupied with other problems at the moment. "I wanted to talk to you first. Avoid getting blindsided."

"Wonderful." I drop the letter and let it float like a leaf onto the table between us.

"What's the problem?"

"The problem is my prints are now all over the letter."

"Yes?"

"You can be sure the cops will dust it for prints when you turn it over," I tell him. "Something like this coming to them late in the game, they're sure to. They'll want to know where it's been all this time, and who's touched it."

"I didn't think of that. So what do we do?"

Two lawyers sitting at lunch in a swank restaurant trying to figure how to cover their tracks on a piece of concealed evidence in a homicide case. Not exactly a question you'd want to see on the bar exam.

"You can tell I don't do criminal work," he says. "But we're in the soup together. I touched it too."

"Except that your prints will be easy to explain. The letter came to your firm. You had to open it to see what it was. Whether it was covered by some client confidence. Now the cops are going to want to know why you brought it to me."

He takes his glasses off, puts them on the table. Looks at me as he rubs his chin with one hand, contemplating the problem. "We could wipe it with a cloth or something."

"Not a good idea, Adam."

"No, I suppose it's not." I can tell Adam would have rather I'd come up with that idea. It's the kind of questions you see in transcripts of hearings before the bar, before they suspend your license. "And who suggested this course of action?"

"It's the problem with physical evidence," I tell him. "Sometimes it's not what's there, but what's missing that gets you in trouble. We'd end up taking Ibarra's prints off the letter. They'd wonder why they weren't there."

He looks at me, a pained expression.

"It's all right. We'll just tell them the truth. You knew I'd be curious. I was a friend of Nick's. You wanted to know if I knew anything about it. So you gave me the letter to read. It just means the cops are going to have a lot more questions for me."

"Yes. I suppose that's always the best approach," he says. "The truth. So, do you?"

"Do I what?"

"Know anything about it?" He picks the letter up from the table in front of me, this time carefully handling it from the edges, and gently folds it, putting it back in the envelope. All the while looking at me, waiting for a response.

"The letter, no. I've never seen it before."

"I assumed that much," he says. "Otherwise you would have told me, right?" What he means is just like I told him about Espinoza.

I dodge the question by taking a healthy swallow of ale, filling my mouth.

Adam is shrewd. Whether he'd thought about my prints on the letter or not, he is determined to screen every piece of information that comes his way so that none of the dirt flies up and hits the firm. He also guesses that I am holding back, as I assume he is.

"Have you ever heard of the guy before? This Pablo Ibarra?"

Now it would require an affirmative lie. "I've heard the name. Tell me, how long have you had the letter? Really?"

Adam smiles. "What difference does it make?"

"The cops will want to know."

"I got it this morning," he says.

"Tell me you didn't go down and sweep the mail room the night Nick was killed?"

"Who's asking, you or the police?"

"Maybe I don't want to know."

"Trust me, you don't," he says. "Where did you hear the name? This man, Ibarra?"

"Gerald Metz gave it to me."

"Metz?" He thought I was going to say Nick. Now it comes out of left field.

"During my initial interview with him. He'd done some work with the sons. Said it was a construction job."

"Right. Did he ever mention the father?"

"In passing."

"Did Metz know him?"

"It depends on whether you believe Metz. According to him, he only knew the name. He'd never met him."

"You didn't tell me this before."

"I didn't tell the police, either. Like you with the letter." Touché. "Piece of advice," I tell him.

"What's that?"

"If you're going to take it to the cops with your story, I suppose your secretary will verify it?"

"Absolutely."

"You might want to make sure she touches the envelope at least."

He smiles. Adam's already made a mental note.

"What else did Metz say about them?"

"He also said the father was upset about something. That's why his deal fell through. If anything Metz said was credible."

"Go on," he says.

"That's it."

"If the papers get their hands on this, they'll crucify us. They'll be crawling all over the firm, demanding to know what Nick was involved in. Wanting to know if we're being investigated, whether we've been shredding documents. Legalgate," he says.

"I don't know about you, but I'm thinking the answer

lies in Mexico. I've booked a flight for tomorrow, the earliest I could get there. I want some information. I'm not going to wait for it to come to me."

"If you want to talk to Ibarra, you could just call him on the phone."

"I thought about that. The problem is, for all we know, he may have killed Nick himself. I don't mean pull the trigger. But he might have hired somebody. If he didn't, he may come to the same conclusion we did, that his boys are involved. You think he's going to talk to me about something like that over the phone?"

"Probably not."

"I don't think so either. Besides, if I call him, even if he's willing to talk to me, he's going to want me to come down there, and he's going to want to set the terms and conditions, no doubt a meeting on his turf."

"I want to get to the bottom of this as much as you do. When people start asking questions, I want to be able to tell them Rocker, Dusha and DeWine were not involved in anything illegal. If anyone says we were, they're going to be looking at an action for business disparagement that will take their house, their dog, their wife, and their retirement, not necessarily in that order.

"I'm coming with you. The Gulfstream is already fueled, at the airport," he continues. "It would take us about four, four and a half hours flight time. We can leave tonight. In fact, there's a firm we do business with down in Mexico City, security and investigations. I've used them before. I could arrange to have their services available. One of the biggest drug rings in the world operates out of the Yucatán Peninsula. Hell, I've read that half the resorts in Cancún were built with drug money. Given the kind of people we are dealing with, I think it would be wise to have some extra 'insurance.'"

This sounds good but incredibly expensive. "I don't want to cost the firm a ton of money."

"Nonsense. I may not be as adventuresome as you are, but I like to have an edge before I go sticking my nose in."

He looks at his watch. "I think Cancún is Central time zone. We wouldn't be able to do anything down there until tomorrow anyway. Say we meet at the airport in Carlsbad at nine o'clock tonight. McClellan-Palomar, that's where we keep the plane. Do you know where the field is?"

"I'll find it."

The waiter brings our lunch. Adam picks up the envelope with Ibarra's letter so it doesn't get splattered with soup.

"In the meantime, I'll have the secretary touch this a few times and have it delivered to the police by courier in the morning, after we're gone."

CHAPTER TWENTY-FOUR

Three hours in and the sleek Gulfstream is knifing through the night sky on its way south. I gaze out the tiny oval window and listen to the drone of the twin jet engines as we skim above humid thunderheads, wondering where we are and what is beneath us.

Adam is asleep on the couch across from me, a seat belt loosely draped over his midsection and buckled on the outside of a blanket that covers him. Shoes off, his stocking feet are sticking out beyond the end of the blanket.

He is a man grown accustomed to the finer things. It's what a life of privilege can do. He has no sense of airport security lines that look like a scene from *Gandhi*. If I told him they stopped serving meals on trays with real silverware, I don't think he would believe me. If you suggested that security now prevents even the use of plastic utensils on airliners, his first question would be, "How are you supposed cut your steak?" Man out of touch with the world.

His mouth is open, sleeping like a baby. I suspect he is

snoring, though with the sound of the engines, I can't hear it.

I look at the stars, holes in the dark sky, and finally doze off.

The next thing I know, Adam is shaking me by my good arm. Fully dressed, his shoes back on, he is straightening his tie.

"We're descending toward the airport in Cancún. You might want to freshen up."

Twenty minutes later we're on the ground, rolling down one of the taxiways toward a hangar with its yawning door open, all lit up inside. The pilot pulls right in and shuts the engines down.

As he does, three large SUVs, dark and gleaming under the bright lights, drive up and park in an arc around the wing on Adam's side. I start to get my bags from the back.

"You can go ahead and leave the bag," says Adam. "They'll get 'em for us."

I follow him to the door. Adam slaps the pilot on the arm. "Good flight. Very comfortable. Now, you guys are heading back to San Diego, as I understand it, tonight."

"Right. Be back here tomorrow night. Then we'll be on the ground here 'til Sunday evening."

"Great," says Adam, and he heads down the stairs with me right behind him. Before I get to the ground, he is already shaking hands, smiling at two men who have gotten out of one of the cars. He motions me over.

"Julio. Like you to meet Paul Madriani. Paul. This is Julio Paloma. Julio'll be our guide while we're down here. I hope you don't mind. Our firm has used Julio's company for security on trips down here before. I took the liberty."

"Not at all." We shake hands. Julio is a big man, I'd say six-foot-five, a broad grin, white even teeth, and a hand that swallows my own. Neck like a bull, shoulders like an NFL lineman, he's the biggest man I've ever seen except for the one standing next to him.

Adam introduces me to Herman Diggs, an African-American mountain who I am told is from Detroit. I look up at him. His top front tooth is chipped like a jagged piece of ice. I don't ask how it got that way. I'd like to have my hand back. Both of them are decked out in slacks and dark blazers, enough cloth to sail a good-sized ship, each with a patch sporting a company logo over the breast pocket.

Adam tells me they are specialists in corporate security. They conduct some small talk with Adam while their minions gather our luggage.

We head toward the second car in line, followed by the Julio and Herman show, guys with our bags taking up the rear like a safari. These they pile into the back of the last car in line while they huddle to call signals on the best route to wherever it is we are sleeping tonight.

"You sure you have enough vehicles?" I ask Adam.

"Never be too careful down here," he says. "Julio can tell you. He chauffeured me around Mexico City last time I was down. That was about two years ago, wasn't it?" His voice goes up a notch to be heard over the blast of a jet throttling up off in the distance. He turns to look at Julio, who is too busy at the moment, making arrangements for travel, to hear him.

So Adam turns back to me. "May as well get in," he says.

Oversized tires with lots of aggressive rubber. We could use a ladder to climb up into the backseat of the huge Suburban. We settle in and find the seat belts. Adam closes the door to keep the air-conditioning inside. The engine is still running.

"Anyway, it was a meeting on gas and oil leases for one of our clients." Adam's going on with his story even if nobody is listening. "And son of a bitch if somebody doesn't try to grab one of our briefcases. Two kids on a motorbike."

"Really?"

"That's what I mean. You've got to be careful."

"Did they get it?"

"Hell, no," he says. "Herman there saw it all in his sideview mirror. He opened the driver's door just as they were accelerating. Made a real mess. Blood all over the inside of the door, broken bones. Nobody killed, so I guess it could have been worse."

"Yeah. They could have run into Herman," I say.

Adam laughs, takes off his glasses, and wipes them down with a handkerchief. The car's air conditioner is working overtime with one of the front doors still open.

"Beginning to fog up. I hate the humidity down here." Adam checks his watch, then taps it with a finger. It's stopped. He takes it off and taps it gently against the metal frame around the inside of the passenger window, then listens to it close to his ear to make sure it's going again.

"This old Hamilton's an antique," he says. "Like me. It keeps great time, but it doesn't like humidity. Makes two of us." He wipes perspiration from his forehead with the handkerchief. "What time have you got?"

"It's a little after one-thirty."

"Add two hours," he says. "Central time. We'll sleep in the morning. Otherwise we'll be wasted."

Herman and Julio finally get everything together and we head for town, Herman behind the wheel and Julio riding shotgun.

Out of the airport, within two minutes we're on a dark four-lane highway traveling at high speed for a few minutes before we reach an overpass. We turn off and head toward what looks like open water behind flat terrain covered by low jungle foliage. A few miles on, and we start to see lights, a few pedestrians walking along the sandy shoulder of the road, and small businesses. Another mile, and now there's a sidewalk and the lights are brighter.

"You ever been here before?" Julio sitting sideways, looking at me from over the front seat.

"No."

"All jungle, *un pantano,* in English ah, 'swamp' until maybe," he has to think about this, "twenty years ago. Then the government they decide they want resort. Here." He smiles, gestures toward the floor in the front seat, as if the government would plant their resorts at that location. "And poof, like that, resorts all over. Meliá Cancún, La Piramides,

Royal Solaris Caribe. Like Las Vegas," he says. "You been there?"

"Not for a number of years."

"Disneyland, huh?"

"That's what I hear."

He starts pointing out the attractions. By now the properties are abutting one another, palatial grounds with manicured lawns to make French aristocracy envious. These are lit up by banks of floodlights, some of them in color with water effects, fountains shooting spray skyward. He tells us that the name of the busy boulevard we are on, two lanes in each direction with traffic lights, is Kukulcan.

Adam disconnects his seat belt, and slides forward, leaning over the back of the front seat to be heard better. "This is the street where this man Ibarra has his office?"

"Yes, sir. We'll be coming to that right up here. Beyond Kukulcan Plaza. I will show you."

"Anything on the two sons?" asks Adam. "Ibarra brothers."

"Ah, yes. Bad people. Very bad," he says. "Emm, south. They are south, near Tulúm."

"What he means, they got property down there," Herman tries translating as he drives, glancing back over the seat occasionally to make sure he can be heard. "Word around is they trying to develop it. You ask me, I think they doin' something else."

"Drugs?" asks Adam.

"Could be."

"And the father?"

"Mystery man," says Herman. "Told he and the boys don't get along."

Adam settles back in the seat again, leans over toward me. "Sounds like confirmation of what we've heard. Father and sons not getting along. And drugs."

"Metz told me that the brothers wanted heavy equipment to develop a project on the coast, some property they wanted to sell for a resort. It could be true."

"Did Metz send any equipment?"

"No."

"There, you have your answer," says Adam. "But perhaps part of his story was true."

"What's that?"

"Fact that the father and sons are at each other's throats."

"Here it is." Julio turns and leans over the seat. "This building right here is the plaza. You hotel is here, but we go on to Ibarra's?"

"Yes. Yes." Adam motions for them to keep going. He wants to see where Ibarra's office is.

"Dats an indoor mall, you need anything," says Herman. "Lotta shops, restaurants, air-conditioning. Hangout for the ugly Americans wanna say they been to Mexico but didn't sweat. This area's called the Zone. Zona Hotelera."

"Zona Hotel-aaaara," says Julio.

"Hey, whad I say? Listen, I do the white man talk, you do the spic shit and everything be fine. Stay cool."

"Enough, guys. You're making Mr. Madriani nervous," says Adam.

"We just kiddin'," says Herman. "Hotel-aareeya."

"Aaara," says Julio. He's packing a bulge under the front of his coat that, when he sits forward and turns, swings open to reveal the metal clip slid into the handle of a heavy semi-automatic, all of which is cinched up high under his armpit in a worn leather shoulder harness.

Herman turns his head toward us and leans back again. "Ibarra's office, just up ahead here a ways."

We go about a half mile and off to our right is lush greenery the size of a golf course, a carpet of velvet grass rolling into the distance and, beyond it, an immense resort hotel in the shape of a pyramid, ten or twelve stories high, what the pharaohs could have done if they'd had smoked glass and twinkling lights. Out in front a Mexican flag the size of a runway rolls in slow-mo, undulating waves from the top of its pole, animated by the gentle Caribbean breeze.

"The old man own that?" says Adam. He sounds as if he'd like to pick up Papa Ibarra as a client.

"Perhaps," says Julio. "Bet he has partners."

"I'd like to be one of them," says Adam.

"His office is on the top floor. The penthouse," says Herman. "And nobody gets up there 'less they have an escort and appointment." Herman sounds as if he's tried. "Man's a regular Mexican Howard Hughes," he says.

"Who is this Joward Jewes?" says Julio. "You keep talking Joward Jewes."

"Hughes. Hughes." The sound whistles as air passes over Herman's chipped front tooth. "Read my lips, you stupid spic. Why don't you learn how to speak English?"

"Because we speak Spanish here," he says. "No black jive."

"Jive?" Herman's voice goes up an octave. "You never heard no jive from me, cuz I be speakin' the Queen's English."

"Which queen es that?" says Julio. "The one dances at the queer bar downtown?"

"Hey, man, now you gettin' personal." Julio leans over the seat and smiles at me, taps me on the knee. "Don't pay attention to us. We do this always," he says. "Besides, you no have to worry unless I pull this thing out and point it at his head." He gestures toward the gun under his arm.

"What? That thing? Last time you try to pull that teeny weeny thing out, got caught in your zipper," says Herman. "Had to fill his mouth with Kleenex, keep him from screamin' free willie."

"Don't believe him," says Julio. "He just jealous cuz I get all the good-looking women."

"Right." Herman ignores this. "Word 'round town is your man Ibarra's strange. Lots of money but nobody ever sees him. Know what I mean? Just lets his money talk for 'im."

Julio is on the small walkie-talkie now, communicating with the other drivers, something in Spanish, then listening, one finger to his ear, holding in the earpiece.

The lead car suddenly does a U-turn, and we follow, three dark vehicles, like a train in the middle of the boulevard. There's a cop settled back on a motorcycle half a block up, his arms folded over his chest, one foot on the ground balancing the cycle. He sees us, looks, reaches for the handlebars. Then thinks better of it. He doesn't move. His arms go back, folded against his chest.

You get the feeling that vehicles like this, rolling black power with smoked windows, driving on each other's bumper, might be carrying some high government official, or worse, some patron who owns a chunk of the country. One look and the traffic cop has decided he will get his quota somewhere else tonight.

We drive back a mile or so and turn into a private driveway that snakes uphill. Finally we come to a stop under a canopied entrance to a small hotel.

Herman jumps out and opens the door. He can move for a big man. Adam gets out. I slide across the seat and follow him.

It's like a blast from a sauna and into a refrigerator, as the automatic doors open and close behind us. Adam and I stand around in the small lobby while Julio introduces himself and does business at the antique, carved-oak desk just inside the door.

It's a small European-style hotel. Adam tells me it used to be a private mansion, thirty-nine rooms of marbled luxury. Lost in a sea of glitz, large tourist resorts, their glittering lights with acres of gardens and lawn, no one would notice the Casa Turquesa, its gleaming floors and circular staircase tucked in along the beach and huddled up against the mall.

A few seconds later, Julio is back with room keys.

"You both on the top floor. Adjoining rooms. Herman will have the room on one side, I the room on the other. Two of my men will be down here, the others will stay with the cars.

The manager, accompanied by four bellmen, one for each bag, leads us to the elevator, and we head up.

Three minutes later, I am alone in my room, door closed with the air conditioner humming.

I close the curtains. I'm too tired to enjoy the view, and right now the king-sized bed looks more inviting than the pool down below. I take a shower, and a half hour later, I'm asleep.

CHAPTER TWENTY-FIVE

A few minutes before nine in the morning, the lobby of the Casa Turquesa is empty except for a girl at the small desk by the door.

"Buenos días." She smiles and asks me if I want to take breakfast at the restaurant out by the pool deck.

Instead I order a cab.

Twenty minutes later, the driver drops me off in an area of old Cancún, on a street called Tankah Calle. Here the shops are not as glitzy as out near the beaches in the hotel zone. The buildings are mostly two and three stories, dingy.

Cancún is now a city of a million people and has the feel of a quiet, rustic town that may have grown a little too fast. There are modern shops jammed in between stucco buildings that look as if they date to the forties. The streets are crowded with cars, most of them honking horns, the Mexican equivalent of brakes.

I look for an address along the sidewalk and then realize the number I'm looking for is on the other side of the street.

I hustle between cars and take a few honks crossing over, and then I walk half a block.

I see the name on a sign hanging out over the sidewalk before I see the number. ANTIQUITIES BIBLIOTECA.

Nick had misspelled it in his little handheld. I had gotten up early and checked the Cancún phone book this morning, suspecting that I would probably find it. The telephone number in the book matched the one in the memo pad of Nick's device, if you ignored the international code for Mexico.

From out on the sidewalk I see an "open" sign hanging on the glass door, so I head for it. I can see a woman inside at the counter talking to a gentleman, his back to me.

My hand is nearly to the doorknob when he turns to give me a profile.

I pull my hand back in and walk quickly past the door and continue on until I find a newspaper rack three shops down. I drop a few Mexican coins in the slot and grab an edition of a Cancún paper I can't read. I sit down on a bench and open it.

Six minutes pass before Nathan Fittipaldi comes out of the front door of the antiquities shop. He comes this way, so I hold the paper up in front of my face until he passes, crosses the street, and then I follow him.

Two blocks down, he enters a parking garage, walking down the ramp and disappearing into the shadows. I stand across the street from the exit with the newspaper and keep an eye. A minute or so later, a large Lincoln Town Car rolls up the ramp with a driver in the front seat. The back windows are tinted, but the driver has to stop to pay the charges at the exit booth.

Through the windshield I see Fittipaldi sitting behind the driver in the backseat. Next to him is a woman, blond hair and dark glasses, snuggled up to him. It seems Dana has found the time to vacation in Mexico.

By ten-thirty I am back at the hotel where I find Adam in the restaurant having breakfast.

"Where were you? I called your room, but there was no answer."

"I decided to take a walk, get a little exercise."

"How was it?"

"Good."

"Listen, I've thought about our schedule here. We don't have a lot of time," he says. "Unless you want to hold over and take a commercial jet back."

I have to be back in the office on Monday, I tell him.

"Then I think it might be best if we use today to scout out the brothers down on the coast. What do you think?"

"I thought we would talk to the father."

Herman and Julio are at a table far enough away so we can talk and not be overheard. The cabana, restaurant, and bar by the pool are empty. Adam is wearing a pair of heavy tan pants and boots with a light nylon slipover shirt.

"I thought it might be wise to wait until Friday before talking to Pablo Ibarra. I had my office call his and tell him I was coming down on business. I told them to keep it vague. He knows I'm with the same firm as Nick was. We have a tentative appointment for tomorrow evening. Now, if you want to change it, I can."

"No. That's fine."

"I suspect that the answers ultimately lie with the old man," he says. "But I am also afraid that if we hit him dead on, not knowing more, that Pablo Ibarra will stonewall us. He has nothing to gain by talking to us, unless he thinks we know more than we do."

"How do we do that?"

"You read his letter to Nick," he says. "What do you think he was trying to say?"

"He was telling Nick to back off."

"Right. To leave his sons alone. Nick had something on the sons or they were doing something that the father didn't like. We have to make Pablo Ibarra suspect that we know what that was."

"I'm listening."

"We need to take a look at their operation. At least have some clue as to what they're doing."

Adam's plan seems to make sense.

"I had Julio's people scout the location down on the coast."

"When?"

"When I called and told them I needed them to meet us here. I was trying to figure how to use what little time we had the best way we could. Two of his people took one of the cars yesterday, went down the coast, and checked the place out. They found it."

"Then why don't we go?"

"That's what I thought."

An hour later we're headed down the coast, back past the airport.

In the sunlight the terrain looks different. The resorts are like alabaster palaces set against the turquoise waters of the Caribbean.

The water is so clear I am told that divers swear they are peering through air. Through breaks of jungle and rises in the highway, I can see rolling waves, white beaches, the shoreline dotted with coral inlets and reefs of basalt.

Traffic on the road moves at a clip, in places narrowing to two lanes, then opening again for passing. There are very few vehicles, just an occasional tourist bus, mostly empty, and a chartered van for scuba divers on their way to a remote beach.

Overhead the sky is clear and bright. But in the distance above the jungle to the south, it is leaden. Every few seconds I can see tiny threads of fire as lightning strikes the jungle floor fifty or sixty miles ahead of us.

Large land crabs scurry across the road, moving like giant spiders from jungle to jungle, across the strip of pavement separating them from the sea.

Adam fills me in on the two Ibarra brothers, Arturo and Jaime. He has a thin file compiled by Julio's firm, pulled together and faxed from the home office in Mexico City this morning.

"Took a quick look at it this morning when I got up," he says.

"Three years apart in age," he says. "Arturo is the mover, shaker, the businessman, if you want to call it that. Jaime is muscle, all the way to the area between the ears. He has a bad reputation for temper. He killed a man in a fight four years ago in a private club and got off on a theory of self-defense. He has a few minor convictions, but an extensive arrest record." What Adam is saying is, "What you would expect for the wayward son of a wealthy man?"

"It starts as a juvenile with auto theft, graduates two years ago with attempted murder. It seems the old man's money has been able to keep him out of the slammer thus far. Though that may not work much longer if what we hear is true, that there's a falling-out between father and sons."

"Any narcotics?" I ask.

"Eight years ago," says Adam. "Let's see." He licks his thumb and turns a page. "Here it is. Both of the sons were arrested. It was dismissed for lack of evidence. Federal Judicial Police believed they were into cocaine, growing it out in the jungles down in the area we're going to today."

"Anything in the states?"

He looks, peruses the record in the file for several seconds, and turns some pages. "Doesn't look like it. There is a credit report. It shows they have bank accounts in several foreign countries, Belize and the Caymans, nothing huge, but continuous activity."

"So they're making money doing something," I say.

"It would appear," says Adam. "They applied for a loan about four months ago, listed assets including the last major deposit. That was about eight months ago, just shy of three hundred thousand dollars, U.S. So they've got something going." Adam takes a deep breath, closes the file, and we settle in for the ride.

An hour on and we see large signs along the road for something called Xcaret. Julio explains that this is a water theme park built around Mayan ruins. Families come for the day. For a fee they can swim in the natural lagoon or play in the artificial waterways constructed by the developers with the blessings of the government.

The Mayan Riviera has its moments, incredible natural beauty and undisturbed jungle, with pockets of tourist wealth. We pass a number of these. Most of the resorts are closed off behind iron gates, with armed guards in kiosks out in front.

From what I can see, the tourists who stay in the resorts pass along the road in air-conditioned comfort, only coming and going.

Real life is out here. Traveling at seventy miles an hour, we come upon periodic migrations along the shoulder of the highway. Groups of men walking along the road dressed in shirts and jeans four sizes too large for them.

"There must be a town," I tell Julio.

"Ah, villages. All over," he says, "in the jungle."

"Where are they going?"

"They look for work," he says.

Every few miles there's another band, trudging along the sandy roadside in cast-off athletic shoes, some of them trailing wives and children, little kids, scrubbed and carried by their mothers, with their older brothers and sisters walking along in the dust. Like their parents, looking for a way to feed themselves for another day. I cannot help but think of Sarah at home, and what she would think, looking at kids her age unable to go to school, having to scratch the soil to eat.

Adam leans over and says: "Even for this, the natural forces of the economy have an answer." I begin to think he can read my mind.

"And what's that?"

"It's why it didn't make any sense that the Ibarras would be talking to Metz, trying to bring heavy equipment down here. There's your answer." He points off in the distance, a mile or so ahead, a bald part of the landscape where something has hacked away at the jungle. As we draw closer I recognize it: a construction site.

"That's where they're all going," he says.

The place looks like an Egyptian tomb-building scene

out of the *The Ten Commandments*. A vast anthill of men, too many to count, wielding shovels and pushing wheelbarrows, not a single piece of heavy equipment anywhere in sight. Even concrete is being mixed in a series of large tumblers on location, no modern cement trucks.

"It's what didn't make any sense when you told me about the story Metz gave you. When labor is plentiful and cheap, why would you bring bulldozers and backhoes?" says Adam. "Besides, the government down here doesn't favor it. You don't get to depreciate your equipment in Mexico. You're expected to hire your countrymen. Give them jobs. Did you notice the hotel staff last night?"

"What about them?"

"Veritable army," says Adam. "It took three of them to lead each of us to our rooms, one to lead the way, one to carry our luggage, and one to follow along, I suppose to make sure we weren't ambushed from behind. Mexico is learning how to avoid revolutions," he says. "You have to admire them for the effort."

"You sound like you travel down here regularly."

"Enough. I like the people. Friendly. What you see is what you get."

"Then why all the security?" I ask.

"I'm a humanitarian," says Adam, "not a fool." Something catches his eye. He leans forward and talks into Julio's ear over the seat in front.

When he settles back, he looks at me and points off to our left. "That's Puerto Adventuras up ahead there. It's a resort. Has a fleet of good fishing boats. Have you ever done any deep-sea sport fishing?"

"No. I've had clients that are into it, though."

"You should try it sometime. We're going to stop there on the way back for dinner. We may spend the night, depending on how late it is."

"I didn't bring a change of clothes, toothbrush, or anything else."

"Don't worry. We'll go native," he says. "Besides, anything we need we can find there."

We pass several signs with the word *Cenote,* each of these
listing kilometers. I ask Julio about these.

He tells me that the Mayans considered them sacred watering holes. They worshiped at these caverns in the limestone under the jungle where large quantities of fresh water
gathered, sometimes running in underground rivers.

"There are many of them in the jungle down here. Some
of the Indians take their water from them even today. You
want to be careful, though," he says. "Watch out for ah . . .
how do you say? *Caiman."*

"Gators. Big ones," says Herman. "What he's tellin' you
is, you get off the road, you wanna watch where you take a
drink."

I make a mental note, not that I'm planning on drinking
anything that doesn't come out of a sealed bottle.

A few minutes farther up the road, and Julio is looking at
a map spread open on his lap. He's talking in Spanish into
the handheld wireless again. *"Aqui. No, no, no, no, aqui."*

The lead car throws on its brakes and suddenly turns left
across the highway without a signal. The car doing at least
forty. We all follow, a Mexican intersection.

We bounce along on a sand-strewn road into the strip of
jungle between the highway and the coast, my body buck-
ing in the seat belt. We travel for a few miles.

As we approach a rise in the road, Julio issues orders for
the cars to slow down. Finally we stop. He marks the place
on the map with his finger and confers with Herman, who
seems to agree. Then Julio gets out of the car and runs up to
the lead vehicle. The man in the passenger seat of that car
gets out, and the two of them take off up the road, on foot.

They are gone for about five minutes, when I see Julio
coming back toward us, a few steps and a skip as he hustles
down the road. He finally reaches the car. Adam pushes the
button, rolling down his window.

"This es the place." Julio is out of breath, perspiration
running down his forehead and cheeks, dripping from his
chin. "You will want to take a look."

Adam closes the window and gets out. He tells the driver to keep the motor running and the air-conditioning on.

I climb out on the other side while Julio opens the back of the car and fishes around for something. He comes up with a bottle of water, takes a long drink. *"Señor?"* He offers it to me.

I pass.

Then he finds two pairs of field glasses, large Bausch & Lomb's, twelve power, fifty millimeters. He hands one to me and the other to Adam, then leads us back up the road.

It takes three or four minutes uphill and around a bend before we reach the crest where Julio's helper is still standing, looking toward the sea in the distance. As we approach, he's crouching, blending into some low jungle foliage at the side of the road.

He speaks to Julio in Spanish and holds up two fingers. He points off in the distance. *"Dos hombres fuera de la casa."*

Adam and I settle in next to them. I can see that from this point the jungle declines gently toward a cove and some rocky bluffs on the coast about a mile away. A little to the north, perhaps a half mile from where we stand, is a sizable clearing in the jungle, red clay and naked limestone scraped clean, like a bald spot in a sea of green. I would guess it is several acres in size. Parked on it is an assortment of trash, wrecked-out vehicles and abandoned tires, some larger trucks, old Fords and Chevys, one with a rusted crane on the back that looks like it could be an antique.

The ground is spotted with empty fifty-gallon drums corroding in the sun, some of them dented and tipped on their sides. Splotches of darkness spread from the yawning open ends of these into the soil, the last contents leaking out onto the ground.

On the far side, closest to the bluffs and the sea is a construction trailer, white sides and a flat metal roof with an air conditioner on it, ripples of heat rising from this.

Out in front of the trailer, a few large truck tires laid on their sides with pieces of plywood thrown over them form a crude wooden deck in front of the door that faces this way.

Julio finishes talking to his assistant, then swivels around on his haunches to translate for Adam and me.

"This es a road they don't use," he says. *"Otra.* Over there." He points. "The other road. They use."

I lift the field glasses to my eyes and adjust them. On the other side, farther to the north, a winding stretch of brownish red soil wends its way back into the jungle and disappears around a curve.

"My man says two of them are outside the house. The trailer. They are armed."

I bring the glasses back to my eyes and check it out. I see nothing moving around the trailer. The cars parked closest to it appear to be empty. With the sun now behind us, anyone outside is likely to be around in back of the trailer, in the shade, where we can't see them.

"We'll stay here for a few minutes," says Adam. "It's getting hot." He takes off his hat, one of those floppy safari things with a broad canvas brim, then crunches it up and uses it to wipe his forehead.

Julio hands him a bottle of water. Adam uncaps it, takes a drink, and immediately spits it out. "It's hot," he says.

Julio shrugs as if to say, "That's all I've got."

Adam pours the rest over the back of his head and lets it drip down onto the jungle vegetation at his feet, then opens the hat up and puts it back on his head.

"There."

When I look, Julio is back over my shoulder.

I bring the glasses back to my eyes and train them at the trailer. From the back side a man walks this way, what looks like a short assault rifle of some kind slung from one shoulder, muzzle pointed at the ground. Just as he rounds the corner on the front side of the trailer, the door opens and another man steps out onto the plywood step in front.

I squint into the glasses to make him out. He turns his body away from me just as I focus, awkwardly closing the door with one hand. I notice there is no arm coming out of the other sleeve of his shirt.

When he turns around again I realize why. His arm is bandaged up against his body, shoring up the broken ribs I gave Hector Saldado when I hit him with the tire iron.

CHAPTER TWENTY-SIX

"Are you sure?" says Adam.

"In the flesh," I tell him. "I was watching the sharp edge of the razor most of the time, but I'm not likely to forget that face anytime soon."

Adam takes a look and I hand my field glasses to Julio, who focuses on him and watches, then hands the glasses back to me. "He lose an arm?" he says.

"In a manner of speaking." I watch as Saldado steps down from the plywood platform, wrestles a cigarette one-handed from a pack in his shirt pocket, then lights it with a lighter from that same pocket.

Then he ambles to one of the vehicles out front, a large van with back doors open, and calls two of the guards to come over.

He gives them directions, pointing inside the van. One of them gets in, while the other one, his rifle slung over his shoulder, tries to pull something out of the back. He's not having an easy time.

Saldado calls several more of them from behind the trailer. Six of them finally muscle the thing out of the van.

"You see that?" says Adam.

"Yeah."

Whatever it is, is about six or seven feet long, wrapped in a cotton bed sheet that has twine tied around it. The six men stagger under the load. They lift it up onto the platform in front of the trailer, and then through the door inside.

"What do you think it is?" Adam lowers the glasses from his eyes and looks at me.

"I don't know."

A few seconds later, Saldado comes out of the trailer, gets in the van, and drives off, headed for the dirt road on the other side of the property.

"Well we've confirmed one thing. The brothers were involved with your man, Espinoza," says Adam.

"I'd like to know what that thing was they were carrying."

"We could try and take a closer look."

"How?"

Adam talks with Julio who in turn speaks in Spanish with the other man. He motions off toward the other road with his hand. When Julio comes back he says: "You can get much closer to the trailer from the other road. He says there are some larger windows in the back, a sliding door. They walked in yesterday, and with field glasses they could see people inside."

Adam thinks about it. "You want to try?"

"Why not?"

Fifteen minutes later we've collected ourselves, cooling down in the air-conditioned cars, back out on the highway. We backtrack less than a mile and turn off on another dirt track toward the sea. Julio says something into the handheld as we drive. A minute or so later, I look back through the rear window and realize that the other two cars in our caravan have suddenly disappeared.

"Don't worry," says Adam. "Julio's people know what they're doing."

"Yeah, they be gettin' the fuckin' artillery out," says Herman. "Case we get our asses caught." Herman doesn't like what we're doing. "Ya want I get you the bullet-proof vest from the back," he says. "Da one wit da bull's-eye got all the holes in it."

"Herman, cut it out," says Adam.

"Yessir." But when I look in the rearview mirror, Herman is still smiling, winks at me, chipped tooth looking like a broken picket on a fence.

"It will be all right," says Julio. "If they stop us, I will tell them that you want to talk business. That you are down here looking for property for a resort. I will also let them know that we have people out on the road," he holds up the walkie-talkie, "other cars. They are not likely to do anything. They would have no way of knowing what they are confronting."

Adam smiles at me. "This is why you hire people."

The Surburban rumbles down the road, bouncing over washouts from the last hurricane. Suddenly Herman hits the brakes, skidding tires throwing up dust. He's turning the wheel, trying desperately to avoid plowing into the pickup that is parked across the road. We end up off the side, with the nose of our car in the jungle undergrowth.

"Man on the road," says Herman. One hand is off the steering wheel; when it comes back up, it's clutching Herman's big stainless forty-five automatic.

"Herman. Put the gun away," says Adam. "Julio."

Without another word Julio is out of the car, slamming the door behind him, his hands out in front of him, showing anyone who is looking that they are empty. He holds them above his shoulders, spouting Spanish a mile a minute.

The dust begins to settle and I see a man, faded running shoes, dark pants, and a yellow shirt. He is pointing a rifle at Julio's chest. Another one pops out of the jungle on the other side of the road. When I turn, two more are coming out of the bushes right next to our car, one of them with an AK alternately pointing at my window and then sweeping the back of Herman's head.

Fortunately Herman has reholstered the forty-five, both hands now on the steering wheel.

"Everybody stay cool," says Adam.

The conversation seems to go on for a long time. Julio with his hands up, the other guy with his rifle pointed. After what seems like an eternity, Julio makes a tentative move with one hand toward his belt. He reaches very slowly down and lifts his walkie-talkie out of its carrying case. He holds it up so the other guy can see that this is not a weapon, then talks into it, the other man watching and listening. Finally, the other man nods, waving the muzzle of his rifle in the direction of travel.

Adam takes a deep breath. "Well at least it looks like they're not going to shoot us here."

Julio comes back to the car and gets inside, his face shimmering with sweat. "It's all right." He is breathing heavily, wiping his face with a handkerchief from his pocket. "I have been told that we are to follow him."

The pickup pulls back and clears the road.

Herman starts backing out of the bushes, tires sliding on green vegetation, pulls back onto the road, and drives past the truck.

We slow down for a second, just long enough for another vehicle, a beat-up rusted-out Toyota pickup, to pull out in front. Two men are riding shotgun in the back, rifles laid across their laps pointed in our direction. They are sitting up on the side wall, one hand on the rifle's grip, finger in the trigger well, while they hold on with the other hand and the truck bounces along the road.

"What did he say?" says Adam.

"Private property," says Julio.

"All that talk for two words?" says Herman.

"Yeah, well. Next time you can do the talking."

"You did fine," says Adam. "You kept us alive. Better than your friend pulling out his goddamned gun." Adam pats Julio on the shoulder.

He kept us from getting our asses shot off, and Adam knows it.

A few seconds later, we pull into the sunlight, a big open area. From here the clearing is much larger than it appeared from the jungle road up above. Herman and the driver in front instinctively swing off to the left in a wide arc that ends up skidding to a stop in front of the trailer.

"Un momento." Julio is out of the car before it can stop, his hands in the air again, talking to the man in the yellow shirt, who has climbed out of the passenger seat of the Toyota. The two gunmen from the back jump out and train their weapons on our vehicle. They are soon joined by three more who seem to materialize from out of nowhere. One of these, the closest to the window on my side of the car, is pimple-faced, a boy, maybe fifteen or sixteen years old.

The man in the yellow shirt holds up a hand, palm out, the universal gesture to stay put, talking to Julio.

He calls to the trailer, and a couple of seconds later the door opens. My vision doesn't penetrate the shadows inside. Whoever it is talks from there.

"Por favor, señor." Julio is now interceding, his hands still raised. I can make out a few words. *"Norteamericanos, hombres de negocios."*

Questions from inside.

"Sí." Julio nodding his head. *"Sí."*

Then silence. Julio stands there, sweating in the sun.

The kid outside keeps waving the muzzle of his assault rifle past my head.

More conversation between Julio and whoever is inside, Spanish too fast for me to comprehend much of anything, though I make out the words: *pueden entrar.*

Julio comes back to the car. He opens Adam's door and sticks his head in. "Both of you can go in," he says. "We must remain here. They will want to search you. You have no weapons?"

Adam shakes his head.

"No," I tell him.

Julio holds the door while we get out. I slide across the seat and follow Adam out his side to avoid Pimples with his cannon standing beside my door.

They do a thorough frisk on both of us, all the way down to the ankles, smalls of our backs, and crotches. They take the folder notebook out of Adam's hand and check to see if anything is in it besides paper and a pen. They give it back to him, then one of them moves us toward the door, pushing with the rifle in my back. We step up onto the plywood platform and toward the door.

As Adam walks inside, I can feel a rush of cool air escaping from the rooftop air conditioner running at full bore.

The second I clear the doorway, it slams closed behind me. I feel another set of hands checking from under my arms down to my belt, another quick check for weapons.

Instinctively, my hands go up. Then whoever it is pulls the wallet from my back pocket.

Inside the trailer it is dark as a cave, small windows with venetian blinds pulled closed. One small floor lamp in the corner. Coming in from the brightness, I can't see much of anything for several seconds.

The guy behind me moves around to the front. He is older, harder, an edge to his face that the kids outside have not yet earned. Even in the shadows, I can see that his face is pocked by acne.

Across the room in the corner a man sits behind a desk, slick dark hair, shirtsleeves, and a tie. I am guessing in his mid-thirties. He is leaning back in an old wooden swivel desk chair that groans as he moves. His hands are coupled behind his neck, feet planted in the middle of the desk, on top of the blotter with papers and ripped-off slips from an adding machine underneath his alligator loafers.

There is a tumbler of what looks like whiskey and ice at the edge of the desk.

He watches with cool disinterest as his man finishes checking Adam, pushing hard enough that Tolt is wobbling around with his hands in the air. He finally finds what he is looking for, Adam's wallet. Then he steps away.

The guy behind the desk says: "You can put your hands down now." Perfect English. "So you're American businessmen. You have business cards?" Acne flips him both wallets and he catches them on the bounce off his desk, one of them landing in his lap.

He opens one wallet and looks inside. "Paul Madriani." He looks. I nod. Then the other wallet. "And Adam Tolt."

My eyes are on the large blanket laid over the object lying on the floor against the wall two or three feet from where I'm standing.

He starts fishing inside the wallets and comes up with business cards. "Both of you are lawyers. What can I do for you gentlemen?"

"May I ask who you are?" says Adam.

"You can. You may." But he doesn't offer a name.

"We, ah, we're down here scouting properties for development," says Adam. "Real estate along the coast. The Riviera between Cancún and Tulúm. Looking for opportunities."

"I see. What everybody wants, a good opportunity. Have a seat. Where are your manners, Jorge? Get the gentlemen a drink." He is still picking through our wallets as he chides his subordinate for his lack of hospitality.

Adam takes a seat on a hard wooden chair across from his desk. I try the couch a few feet away, nearer the window. Through a crack in the blinds, I can see Julio outside chatting it up with one of their guards. Herman has lifted the rear door of the Suburban and is sitting in the back with his legs dangling over the bumper, his arms folded, sweating with his jacket on, one hand not too far from the automatic under his coat, assuming they haven't lifted it from him.

From here I can also see a small corner of the item on the floor where the blanket is folded back. It is white and looks like gypsum, rough edges like stone.

"What would you like to drink? We have bourbon." He pulls a few more items from our wallets, what look like driver's licenses, and checks these against the business cards already out.

"Sounds like it'll be bourbon," says Adam.

"And you?" He looks up at me.

"The same."

Jorge leaves to get the drinks.

The man behind the desk fixes Adam with a stare. "You gonna stick with this bullshit?"

"What are you talking about?"

"The real estate bullshit?"

"I assure you . . ."

"You can keep your fucking assurances," he tells Adam. "What I wanna know is what you're doing here."

"I'm telling you we're looking for property." Adam is holding a leather folder with a pen and paper for effect.

"Fine. You want to talk about property. We got property. We got a nice cliff over here, goes way out over the ocean. Maybe you like to see it? Lot of rocks at the bottom."

"We were thinking perhaps a nice beach," says Adam.

"I'll bet you were."

"I'm telling you we represent investors, a consortium up north."

"That's right. A company called Jamaile Enterprises," I say.

I can feel a palpable wince from Adam as I say the words. If looks could kill, I wouldn't have to worry about the man behind the desk. But I figure we have nothing to lose. I want to see if I get a rise, but he doesn't seem to recognize the name.

I'm guessing this is the business side of the brothers Ibarra, Arturo, who is threatening to drop us off a cliff, which leaves me to wonder about Jaime, the one Metz called the Neanderthal.

"To buy land down here, you need a Mexican partner."

"We know that," says Adam.

"I have had enough American partners to last me a life-time," he says. "They never seem to work out. Last ones got cold feet. Left us high and dry."

"How did you deal with it?" I ask.

He looks at me, makes a face, and glances at Jorge who has now rejoined us holding two glasses, bourbon on the rocks. "We had to sever the relations, you might say." He smiles, thin lips, tight and sinister.

"Well, I can assure you that that would not happen here," says Adam.

Jorge deposits one of the tumblers with iced bourbon on the desk in front of Adam and hands the other one to me. Then he takes a seat at the other end of the couch, staring at the back of Adam's head through dark, dead eyes. Occasionally he glances over at me with the affability of someone measuring you for a coffin.

"I told them you might want to take them over and show them the cliff." Ibarra is talking to Jorge. "Of course, we let them finish their drinks first."

"I'm telling you we're just exploring for property." I can hear the strain in Adam's voice as he tries to convince him. A man of influence, suddenly without any.

"Esploring," he says. "That's a good word. It looks like you are esploring all right. You come here with men who are armed." He nods out toward the cars, toward Julio and Herman, leaving us to wonder whether Ibarra's men outside have taken their weapons.

Someone raps on the door from outside.

"Yeah, what is it?"

One of guards comes in. It's the man in the yellow shirt, a rifle slung over his back. He crosses the room to the desk and leans over, whispering something into Ibarra's ear.

The loafers come off the desk and Ibarra sits up straight. There's a quick conversation in Spanish, whispered and hushed tones. Then Ibarra waves the man away with the back of his hand. The guard leaves.

"I am told you have other cars with more men out there somewhere. You say you come looking for property, but it sounds like you don't trust me. That's not good for business."

"One can't be too careful," says Adam.

"No. You want to call these people, tell them to come in here so we can all sit down and talk?"

"I don't think so." Tolt smiles at him.

"I didn't think so." Ibarra is left to figure his next move.

"*Salud.*" Adam lifts his glass and takes a drink.

The Mexican joins him and I follow. The whiskey is smooth, something expensive, just warm enough to give that amber glow as it spills down my insides, anything to keep the joints at my knees from clattering against each other.

Ibarra continues to finger our wallets, pulling every scrap of paper out. He takes his time. My eyes wander to the slab of stone, with its gypsum edge exposed, leaning against the wall across the room. Then something hits the window outside near where I'm sitting.

Jorge hears it and pulls one of the blinds with a finger to look outside.

"*Qué es?*" says Ibarra.

"*Nada.*" Jorge lets the blind close, then looks at me.

I shrug.

As he turns to look at his boss, I sneak a peek over my shoulder out toward the cars.

Julio, who sees my eyes through the slit of the blinds, gives me a furtive gesture, head nodding and a thumb below his waist, pointing vigorously in the direction of the cars.

An old model Buick is stopped in a cloud of dust just this side of the black Suburban. Two men get out. One is Hector Saldado.

"If you're finished with us, we're gonna go."

"You're gonna go when I tell you," says Ibarra.

I look at my watch. "You've got less than a minute and our people are gonna be in here. Make up your mind."

Adam is looking at me, wondering what I'm talking about.

I walk over to the desk and pick up the two wallets along with our licenses and papers Ibarra has spread around on top of it. He doesn't try to stop me.

"Come on, we're leaving." I head for the door. Tolt gets off the chair and follows me. I hear footsteps on the plywood platform outside, the voices of two men speaking in Spanish just beyond the door. Another second and Saldado will be inside with us.

Jorge is off the couch. When I look up, he has planted himself like a boulder between us and the door. He looks at

Ibarra for direction. Arturo hesitates for a second, looks at us, little slits, then nods to Jorge. He steps out of the way and opens the door.

In the time it takes him to do this, I reach behind me like a relay runner grabbing for a baton and take the folder out of Adam's hand. I raise it to my face just as Jorge opens the door, shielding my eyes from the sun, and my face from Saldado's view.

"Jaime, *cómo esta?*" Arturo Ibarra is greeting the other half.

As I step out onto the platform, I glance down and see two feet in pointed cowboy boots directly in front of me. I step around them.

"Excuse me."

Adam follows along.

By the time we step off the platform, Julio already has the car door open. Herman is inside behind the wheel with the engine running.

Without looking back, I duck my head inside and scurry across the seat. Adam is right behind me as Julio slams the door closed and jumps into the front passenger seat.

None of us says a word until we've covered at least a mile on the dirt road, and then Adam explodes: "What the hell happened? We could have been killed. Why didn't your men stop Saldado out on the road?"

CHAPTER TWENTY-SEVEN

The best that Julio's people can figure is that Saldado returned to the trailer by a different route. Besides, they were looking for a van, not the Buick he returned in.

"Son of a bitch," says Adam. "Why the hell do you people think I hired you? So I could get my ass shot off?"

"We thought we had it covered," says Julio. He is looking straight ahead, out through the windshield, avoiding eye contact with Adam, who is furious. Tolt is bouncing up and down on the backseat, leaning forward, his face six inches from the back of Herman's head.

"You thought. Did any of you think to scout the road? To see who's in the vehicles as they go by? No. Your man up there on the other road with us. He got a good look at Saldado through the glasses. He knew what he looked like."

"How they supposed to look in all the cars come on that road?" says Herman.

"That's their job," says Adam. "That's what it means to

be a professional. You can't do the job, then you ought to
find another one."

"I do my job just fine," says Herman.

"Don't you talk back to me."

Julio reaches over with one hand just above the seat and
nudges Herman to shut up.

"If I wanted to get my ass shot off, I could have tied myself to a tree and let you take shots at me with that blunderbuss under your arm. Not that you could hit anything. Damn
near got us shot out on the road going in, pulling that thing
out."

"Calm down, Adam. Nothing happened," I tell him.

"Nothing happened," he says. "Where the fuck were you?
And what was that crap about Jamaile Enterprises?"

"We didn't get a rise on Jamaile," I tell him.

"You sure as hell got one out of me. Son of a bitch. You
could have gotten us killed."

"They would have killed us no matter what we said if it
hadn't been for the other car out on the road."

"He's right," says Julio. "They wouldn't believe us until
I permitted their man to talk to my driver on the radio."

"You screwed up," says Tolt. "Admit it."

"If it makes you feel better, fine," says Julio.

"It's not his fault," I tell him.

"Bullshit."

"Adam."

"What?"

"If Julio hadn't recognized Saldado when he did, you and
I would have been sitting there sipping bourbon when the
Mexican walked in and started peeing in my glass."

"That's true," says Herman.

"When I want your opinion, I'll ask for it," Adam tells
him. "And as for Julio, if he'd done his job right, we
wouldn't have had to worry about Saldado. I have a half a
mind to call the office in Mexico City and have them send
somebody who knows their job."

"And as for you." He looks at me. "How the hell did you
know he'd let us go? Forcing the issue like that. He could

just as easily have had that muscle-bound idiot shoot us. We could be lying back there dead right now."

"If Saldado had come in and seen me, we would be dead," I tell him.

I can see the chip in Herman's tooth through tight lips in the rearview mirror as he grips the wheel with both hands and looks at me, thankful that there's someone else to share Adam's tongue-lashing.

"Take me to Cancún. I'm paying a fortune for these two idiots," he says.

He sits back, quietly steaming for several seconds, arms folded, his face turned away from me, looking out the side window. Then the second rush. Adam starts doing what every angry lawyer does best, cross-examining everybody around him, demanding answers that don't exist.

"Where did he go when he left? Tell me that."

"Who?" Julio turns to look at him. He shouldn't have asked.

"Who? Who the hell do you think I mean? Saldado."

"How would we know that?" Julio turns to the front again.

"Of course not. That would be too fucking easy. Have one of your men follow him."

"Adam, give it up. We didn't even know he was going to be there," I tell him.

"Why didn't you watch him?" Adam ignores me. "What did he do, just reappear? Apparition out of thin air?" This is addressed to the back of Julio's head as the Mexican sits there silent, his face increasingly red until it looks like a beet. The veins along the side of his neck resemble surgical tubing. "If you worked for me, I'd fire your ass."

Adam's executive style splashes all over the inside of the car as we drive, anger and ugly insults.

As I sit and listen, I wonder whether Nick had ever been treated to this. It is one of those watershed moments that tell you more about someone than you ever wanted to know. Julio is sitting there taking the worst of it, Herman gripping the steering wheel, looking straight ahead, gritting his teeth and trying to project himself into some other dimension.

It may be far too charitable, but Adam's anger is motivated in large part by the afterglow of fear, the sudden realization that, but for the fates, the world could at this very moment be without one of its favorite sons: himself.

"Take us back to Cancún," he says. "Now." Adam slams his back into the seat again and folds his arms across his chest, his steely gaze again out the side window.

The trip back is like a ride in a deep freeze. Herman and Julio sit up front like two stone idols, trying not to breathe so Adam won't notice them.

By the time we pull up in front of the Casa Turquesa, it's dark. It seems Adam has gotten over his rage. "I want to freshen up a bit. How about some dinner, say half an hour in the restaurant downstairs?"

"Good."

"Julio. You and Herman can join us as well." Adam gets out of the car and heads inside.

"What's that, a fuckin' imperial command?" says Herman.

"Quiet. The man's going to hear you," says Julio.

"What the fuck do I care? Hope he does." Herman leans over the steering wheel. "Who's he think he's talkin' to like that?"

"He was scared. So was I."

"Yeah, but you didn't act like that," says Herman. "That don't give him the right to show us that kinda disrespect. I mean, I'd tear somebody's tongue out for less than that. I'm a professional," he says. "I've taken bullets for people worth more than that shithead."

"Calm down," says Julio. "You don't need this job. I do. I cannot afford to be fired because you can't keep you mouth shut. Take a swim in the pool, watch a movie on the cable. Cool off."

"Can't. Gotta be at supper half an hour. You heard the man."

"Then go take a cold shower." Julio gets out of the car,

slams the door, and walks toward the hotel, leaving Herman and me sitting there.

"Ain't worth it," says Herman.

It was an ugly incident, but I'm not going to pour fuel on the flames with Herman. Instead I get out of the car, stretch my legs, arch my back, and I see him coming down the stairs toward me. The stress of the day is worse than I thought. I'm seeing things, until Harry looks at me and says: "What took you guys so long?"

Inside, Harry and I head to the bar. I'm strung out like a wet noodle, sitting on one of the stools while the bartender makes a margarita and pours it into a glass the size of a tropical fish tank. I usually stick with wine or beer. Today I make an exception. Harry is on the stool next to me.

"He didn't tell you I was coming down?"

"Not a word."

"Probably got busy and forgot. He told me he only thought about it at the last minute."

"What are you doing here?"

"I came down to see if I could help," he says. "I've been worried."

"What about?"

"The conversation we had. The one about you getting killed and me getting on with life."

I look at him but don't say anything.

"I thought about it. And well, it might not be as easy as I thought. Besides, if anything happened to you, I'd have to divide up everything in the partnership and deal with Sarah. She'd skin me."

I smile at this, nudge him in the ribs with my elbow. "So when did you come down?"

"This afternoon. Adam called."

"When?"

"Last night."

"We didn't get in until after three in the morning."

"It wasn't that late when he called. Time difference I suppose. Still, he got me outta bed. Said the plane had to go back

to San Diego, to deliver one of the other partners on a quick
flight somewhere early this morning. That it would be coming back down here this afternoon. He asked me if I wanted
to take a ride. I had nothing up on Friday. So here I am.
Adam had a car pick me up at the airport.

I suck some margarita through a straw, feeling the tequila
score my stomach like etching acid. I remember now why I
stopped drinking the hard stuff.

"I think Adam lives in a different world from the rest of
us," he says. "What did you think of the plane?"

"Forget it. It's not in our budget."

"We could park it and live in it," he says. "Use it as a flying office. I think I could get used to it." Harry as part of the
jet set. "It might take a while, like an acquired taste. You
know. Fly around some. Go to Bimini. Las Vegas."

"You don't even know where Bimini is," I tell him.

"Yeah, but the pilot could find it," he says. "You don't
think these executives give 'em coordinates when they get
on board, do you? No, they just tell 'em they wanna go,
drop a load on a crap table someplace, and an hour later
they're in Reno at the Mapes . . ."

"Harry."

"What?"

"The Mapes was torn down two decades ago."

"Really?"

"Yes."

"Fine. They're in Las Vegas at the MGM. Use your imagination. Speak of the devil," says Harry.

Before I turn on the stool, Harry is up. "Adam. Want to
tell you that plane is nice."

"You liked the ride?"

"What's not to like?"

Tolt is shaking his hand. He has changed, put on a pair
of slacks and a clean shirt, wearing sandals and looking comfortable and relaxed.

"Glad you could make it." Adam's voice is back to a normal tone.

"Yes, he did." I swing around on the stool and look at Adam.

"What's with you?" he says. "I thought it would be a nice surprise. The plane was coming back empty. We were getting near the weekend. Why should we have all the fun?"

"He's right," says Harry. "In fact, I think I'm gonna have one of those." He points at the fish bowl in front of me on the bar.

"Why not? Bring a margarita for my friend here," says Adam.

"How was your flight?" He and Harry head for one of the tables.

Adam is one of those luminaries who floats through life buoyed by the ether of his own celebrity. I suspect the fact that he lost control in front of me has injured his sense of divinity. He latches onto Harry, and they stroll to the table to talk about airplanes and the finer trappings of private flight.

"Bring your drink and join us," says Adam.

"In a minute." I notice Herman coming in the door heading my way.

"What's goin' on?"

"Getting shitfaced," I tell him.

"Good to know one of us knows what's he doin'. Fuckin' Vesuvius still spoutin' lava?" Herman's talking about Adam.

"I think it's gone dormant for the moment."

"So why don't we eat and get it over with, so I can be accused and go back to my room?" he says.

"To get the bulletin on that, you'll have to talk to the tour director." I nod toward the booth.

"Who's he talkin' to?"

"My partner."

"What's he doin' here?"

"I don't know. Adam's full of surprises. Take a load off. Sit down. Have a drink."

"Hey man, not me. I'm on duty. I don't do that. Uh-uh. That's *all* I need. Man report me for drinkin' on duty, the mood he's in. Get my ass fired, be flippin' burgers back in Lubbock by Monday."

"Few minutes ago, you were ready to quit. Besides, I thought you said you were from Detroit."

"Way of Lubbock," he says. " 'At's when I lost my scholarship. Fucked up my knee and ended up down here."

"Football?"

"Uh-huh." Herman steals a furtive glance toward the booth, making sure it's safe to talk. "Fire-breathin' shithead scorched all the hair off the backa my neck. Lucky I didn't take us head-on into one those scuba-flippin' taco-tenders comin' the other way with all their shit up top. He be lookin' like jaws about now, fuckin' metal tank stickin' outta his head."

"Where's Julio?"

"He's hidin' out. Be down in a minute. You notice there ain't no courtesy bar in the room and no vending machines. This place looks like a fuckin' tomb. Off season," he says. He reaches over and grabs a handful of bar napkins from the waitress station, since there is no waitress on duty, and wipes beads of sweat from his forehead and neck, and drops them all wet and rung out on the bar.

"We ain't had nothin' to eat since breakfast. No lunch, no supper. Contract says we get a break every two hours. You seen any fuckin' breaks?"

"Take a break. Have a drink." A drink might calm him down. I'm afraid if Adam opens his mouth again, given Herman's mood, he might find the big man's foot in it.

"You tryin' to get my ass in trouble, man? Besides, I wanna eat. I'll drink later when it cools down. That shit ain't good for you in the heat." Herman's obsession at the moment is his empty stomach. I can hear it growling.

The bartender comes over to clean up the pile of napkins Herman has left on the bar, and Herman starts complaining to him about his constitutional right of access to a vending machine.

"No hablo inglés."

"Yeah. I bet you'd talk some fuckin' English if I slapped a fifty on the bar and told you to put a round of drinks up."

"Qué?"

"Kiss my ass."

The bartender scoops the napkins into a trash can on his side, smiles, and moves away from the angry dark mountain next to me.

"This shit ain't cuttin' it. I want something to eat." He turns toward the table and Adam. "Hey you, boss man. Tell me, we gonna eat or what?"

Adam, who has his back to him, turns around, blinks a couple of times, then smiles. "Sure. You hungry, Herman? Good idea. Go get Julio. We'll have some dinner."

The conversation between Adam and my partner hasn't been entirely about the history of flight.

"He told me what happened this afternoon." Harry spreads a little butter on a hot flour tortilla as he talks. The empty margarita reservoir is on the table where he left it. Harry is feeling no pain.

"What is it, best two out of three falls, you and this guy Saldado?" he says. "How many chances are you gonna give him?"

"It wasn't my idea to go visiting this time."

"You know, Adam, I assumed when you told me you were coming down here, and that with security and all, everything would be covered."

I look at him. Harry keeps talking.

"But I guess even with that, things go wrong."

"Let me get this straight. You talked with Adam before we came down here?"

Harry looks at me. "Did I say that?"

"Yeah, you did."

He gives me a sheepish look, then turns to Adam. "Knew I shouldn'ta had that drink," he says.

"Paul, it's no big thing. Harry was worried about you," says Tolt. "And he had good reason, after what happened at Saldado's apartment."

"And so you called for lunch, and it just so happened you were taking some vacation time."

"Well, all right, so we conspired a little."

"A little."

"We weren't going to let you come down here alone," says Harry.

Now I understand how Harry got here. Empty plane, my ass. Adam sent it back to get him since one of us had to be in the office on Thursday.

"He has a point," says Adam.

"And look what happened," says Harry. "Even with the precautions. Security and all. You know what I think? I think maybe we should all take a nice swim, lay in the sun tomorrow morning, have a nice lunch, and then hop on Adam's plane, say *adiós,* and fly on home."

"I'll vote for that," says Adam.

"Haven't you forgotten? We have a meeting with Pablo Ibarra tomorrow evening."

"Forget the meeting with Ibarra," says Harry. "You met with the son today, the one who talks and whose knuckles don't drag on the ground, and what did you find out? Nothing."

"Not exactly."

"What? Tell me what you found out that you didn't know before," says Harry.

"We found out that the sons are connected to Saldado."

"Excuse me. I stand corrected," says Harry. "Besides that revelation, which they nearly engraved on your headstone, what else?"

"We know Saldado killed Espinoza and that Espinoza was the link to Gerald Metz. We also know that the brothers had American partners in a prior deal and that the arrangement didn't work out. What were the words he used? They had to sever the relationship?"

Adam nods. "Something like that."

"You knew that before you came down here," says Harry. "When people kill their partners, it's usually due to some dissatisfaction in the arrangement."

"No. What we had before was conjecture, guesses. Now we have Arturo Ibarra in his own words telling us, filling in the gaps. If you want to go home, go. As for me, I'm going to talk to Pablo Ibarra, then I'll go home."

"Listen to him," says Harry. "You haven't had enough of these people? You talk to him." He turns to Adam and lays his linen napkin on the table next to his plate.

Adam takes a deep sigh, picks up his wineglass, and takes a sip. "First, I should apologize. I admit I lost it this afternoon. I've had all the excitement I want for a while. Julio, Herman, I want you to understand I didn't mean what I said today. And Paul. Well, I think you know. I've never been quite that close to a near-death experience before, and it unnerved me. I didn't handle it with much grace."

"You got up and followed me out the door," I tell him. "That's all the grace required, given the circumstances."

"I don't mind telling you I nearly tossed everything on his desk when I turned around and saw him holding the wallets. I thought he knew for sure we were lying."

"I suspect he did. What he didn't know was where the other cars were, how many men were in them, and how they were armed. You don't go to war unless you know where the enemy is."

"That was Julio's idea," says Adam. He raises his glass in a toast to the Mexican, and Julio smiles, looks down, embarrassed. He is starting to lighten up.

I ask him what he threw at the window to get our attention.

"A coin," he says. "I think it mighta been a ten-peso piece. I don't know." The value of this is less than a U.S. dollar.

"Who's counting?" says Adam. "Put it on the tab."

We all laugh.

"Damn." Adam's looking at his watch again, takes it off, and taps it on the edge of his plate. "Thing keeps stopping."

"It's all that cold sweat," says Harry. "It's probably frozen."

"What time is it?"

I look at my watch. "Seven-twenty."

Adam sets it, winds it, and listens with the crystal up to

his ear. "I want to collect my messages. See if anybody called."

"That reminds me. I almost forgot," says Harry. "You had some messages, voice and e-mail. I had Marta listen and make up a list off the phone and print out the e-mails. I've got them in my briefcase upstairs."

"Anything important?"

"Oh. I almost forgot. Grace Gimble."

"What about her?"

"I talked to her. It's what we thought. She did the corporate papers for Nick on Jamaile, but she doesn't know what it was for. She said that Nick just asked her to put 'em together. She signed as an officer just to get them filed."

Another dead end.

"And Joyce from Carlton called. Left her home number, said to call her back. And your friend Blakley from New York. He sent you an e-mail on Wednesday. He checked the address from Nick's little handheld. It was a vacant office building, just like . . ."

I cut him off with a look.

"The other one . . ." he says. "What? What did I say?"

"What's this about Nick?" Adam is looking up at him, strapping the watch back on his wrist.

"Nothing," says Harry.

"Nick had a handheld PDA?"

Harry has already stepped in it.

"Yeah. What did they call it?" I look at Harry.

"A Handspring. I think that's it," he says.

"Yeah."

"How did you hear about it?"

"Actually, Nick left it behind at the coffee shop the morning we talked, on his way to see Metz."

"What, and you found it?"

"Paul saw it on the seat and tried to catch up with him," says Harry. "But he couldn't get there in time."

"So he had already been shot?" says Adam.

"No."

Adam stares at me, one of those acid-like analytic gazes, a Tolt mind probe.

"I have been wondering all this time why," he says. "The death of a friend, sudden and violent, I understand that. But that's it, isn't it?"

"What?" Harry looks at him, wondering what he has missed.

"Forget the PDA," Adam tells him. "What your partner is saying is that if he'd been able to catch Nick, to stop him out on the street, Nick wouldn't have been standing there when they drove by to get Metz. That is it, isn't it?"

"I don't know what you're talking about."

"There's no maybe about it. I can see it. It's written in your eyes. What stopped you?"

"What do you mean?"

"I mean the reason you're down here, looking for answers," he says.

"Now you're starting to sound like Harry."

"What is it?" he says.

"Let's talk about something else," I tell him.

"Fine. Then let's talk about Nick's electronic address book. Did you turn it over to the police?"

"No." Harry gives Adam one of those looks that pass between lawyers whenever they discuss the stupid things clients do. "He wanted to see what was in it first."

Adam rolls his eyes. "Surely you've had enough time to do that?"

"I don't think Nick had it that long. He was just beginning to play with it. Trying to figure out how it worked."

"So there was nothing in it?"

"Just a few items. Some names, addresses, a few dates. Nothing of significance."

"This address in New York?"

"A dead end."

"I see." Adam is miffed, another secret I didn't share. But there is something else I haven't considered until now.

"Let me ask you, did you bring this thing of Nick's with you?" says Adam.

I shake my head. "It's back at the office."

"That's too bad. You know, if you'd let me take a look at it, there might have been something in it I might have recognized. After all, Nick did work for the firm."

Touché.

Adam is tired. He wants to get some sleep. "We can relax around the pool tomorrow, during the day, meet with Ibarra in the evening, find out what he knows. I'll get the plane fueled and we can leave tomorrow night, as soon as we're finished. Sack out on the Gulfstream and be home early Saturday, be fresh for work on Monday morning. How does that sound?" Adam looks at the two of us.

"Agreed."

Julio smiles. Almost done.

CHAPTER TWENTY-EIGHT

The sun at this latitude starts to bake concrete at sunrise, so by the time we arrive on the patio behind the Casa Turquesa, Harry is hopping across the pool deck in bare feet before he slips into the water.

"How is it?" says Adam.

"It'll be fine as soon as the skin grows back on my feet."

"I mean the water."

"Feels good." Harry ducks under, comes back up, and shakes some of it out of his hair. Then he starts doing laps underwater. For a man who once smoked, Harry defies all the odds. He has the lung capacity of a blacksmith's bellows.

Adam has already made arrangements so that a table is set under one of the two large canvas cabanas near this end of the pool.

He has given Julio and Herman the morning off, letting them sleep in after the long drive up the coast last night. One of Julio's lieutenants is watching the cars, and another is sitting in the lobby, reading the paper and keeping an eye.

"It's hardly worth staying open," says Adam. "The place is empty."

He is right. Harry is alone, swimming in a pool the size of a lake. According to the clerk, the only other guest besides our party checked out this morning. Larger groups are clustered at the big resorts down the road where they cater to tour groups and trade conventions. But any way you cut it, it's definitely not the high season in Cancún.

Tiny ultralights, their engines buzzing like lawn mowers, fly by every few minutes, heading north up the beach trailing banners trying to peddle anything that the few tourists might be willing to buy. This one has a sign that reads: PAT O'BRIEN'S—CARIBBEAN LOBSTER TAIL.

Harry climbs out of the pool, but not before he splashes some water on the concrete. He grabs a towel from a stack on one of the chaise longues, then toe-dances over the hot pavement to the island of shade under the cabana. He puts one foot up on the chair, drying himself off and looking out toward the ocean.

"You know, I been thinking." Harry is trying to clear water out of an ear with one finger, using a corner of the towel. "If the three of us were able to piece this together— Espinoza, Saldado, the Ibarras—why haven't the cops?"

"It could have to do with the fact that we're palming some of their cards," I tell him.

"Like Nick's PDA," says Adam.

"And the letter from Pablo Ibarra," I say.

Adam smiles. "Point taken."

"I know that," says Harry. "But you gotta figure there's only three of us. The cops have an army, a ton of resources, computerized crime histories, forensics lab, snitches on the municipal payroll. By now they've gotta have Saldado's fingerprints from his apartment."

"Which means?" says Adam.

"Which means they probably know more than we do—his real name, for starters. It couldn't take that long to check with the Mexican authorities."

"So what's your point?" says Adam.

"So if Saldado has a record in Mexico, it would show associations, people he ran with. You'd think the cops could connect the dots."

"Maybe they're just a little slower off the ball," says Adam.

"That and a lack of motivation," says Harry.

"What do you mean?"

"Paul and I have talked about it. Nick wasn't the kind of crime victim that brings on waves of passion in the breast of law enforcement."

"You don't really think they're sitting on the case?" says Tolt.

"One thing we know they don't have is a Gulfstream to wing their way south," I tell him.

Adam's eyebrows arch as he looks at me.

"Not that I'm unappreciative. It's a fact. Unless they're flying down here to pick up a suspect, or question one already in custody, that kind of travel takes time to work its way through the bureaucracy."

"I hadn't thought of that," says Adam. "Then you think they might be on the trail?"

"I don't know how they could miss it," says Harry. "The trail to the Ibarras couldn't be more clear unless we hung signs. You gave the cops their names at the hospital."

Adam's expression is one of approval, nodding as his eyes gaze down at the table, some restoration of faith in the system.

"And they'll have the letter from Ibarra by now. I know because my ears have been burning for the last day," says Adam. "That lieutenant, what's his name?"

"Ortiz," I say.

"He's gonna be on the warpath when I get back. Wanting to know how long I had Ibarra's letter. It's why I haven't called the office. I don't want anybody there to have to say they talked to me, or that they know where I am. Better if I'm able to say I was out of touch until I got back."

"Then what are you gonna do?" says Harry.

"Hunker down, take some official abuse I suppose. What can they do?"

"If they can prove you were sitting on the letter, plenty," says Harry. "If it's all the same with you, I'd just as soon be back in San Diego tonight, watching the Dodgers kick the crap out of the Padres on the tube. Instead we're goin' to see some guy, who if he's anything like his kids, is probably gonna have his people kick the crap out of us. That's if we're lucky."

"We'll be home tomorrow," I tell him. "You can read the box scores in the paper."

"Which one, the Padres or us?" says Harry.

"That reminds me." Adam is looking at his watch, holding it up to his ear again. "What time have you got?"

"A couple of minutes past nine," I tell him.

"Oh, shit. My watch says eight-forty."

"You should get that thing fixed," says Harry.

"I've got to go, call the pilot and make sure he doesn't drink anything at the bar today. Have him fuel the plane or we'll be here all night." Adam is out of his chair, halfway to the stairs, talking to us over his shoulder as he goes.

I watch him climb the steps, taking them two at a time, moving like a man in his twenties, all the way to the top as he disappears like a flash through the door to the lobby.

"Guess if the pilot drinks, we won't be flying tonight," says Harry.

"Looks like it."

"How much do you think it takes to fill one of those things up?"

"Oh, I'd have to think a fifth of vodka would put any pilot I know on his can."

"Be a smart ass," says Harry smiling. "You know what I mean. The plane?"

"How would I know?"

"You think they have to wait in line? Get out the credit card?"

"Go ask Adam."

He thinks about this for a second. "No. The steps are too

hot. Besides, if I go back inside the air-conditioning, I'm done for the day." He looks at the pool instead. "Think I'll go back in the water. Why don't you at least sit on the side, put your feet in?"

"Why not?" I grab my dark glasses off the table and slip off my running shoes.

"Besides, the sun might cook some of that lip off you," he says. "A fifth of vodka."

Harry is right. The water feels good. The pool is shallow, slightly more than three feet with little signs all the way around in feet and inches to keep their northern guests from diving in and breaking their necks. If you want anything deeper, the Caribbean is just down the steps and across the beach.

Another ultralight buzzes by towing its sign. Harry pops up in the center of the pool just in time to see it.

A few seconds later another one comes over, this time from another direction and maybe thirty feet above the rooftops, close enough that I can see the wire struts and hear the nylon fabric on its wings flapping as it buzzes past. Its shadow flashes over the deck and the pool and then is gone almost before I see it.

"Isn't he a little low?" says Harry.

"Just a little."

Harry, with a line of sight out toward the beach, has one hand up shading his eyes, watching as the plane heads out over water.

"Must be giving rides," he says. "He had a passenger."

I look up, but the building next door blocks my view. When I look toward Harry, he is back underwater.

There is a breeze off the sea, flushing some of the hot air from the patio. I wet my hands in the pool and prop them behind me on the hot deck, leaning back. I'm getting hungry, wondering how long Adam is going to be.

Out on the water the parasail boat comes by again, its engine winding up and then dropping RPMs like a Mixmaster as it bounces its way north against the chop. Behind it, nearly invisible at this distance, is the thin steel cable curving up toward the parachute, its rider, looking like a dot in the sky, hanging underneath.

I watch the parachute as it sails slowly past in the distance. Splashes in the water in front of me, sending up a spray. Harry's throwing gravel. Wasps whine past my ear. I flick them away with the back of my hand. There's a spark from the pool's concrete coving, and something hits my cheek. I rub it. There's an instant before the synapse in my brain fires after I see blood on my hand.

An image out of the sun, diving toward the plaza from over the roof of the Casa Turquesa behind me. It projects a shadow that crosses twenty yards of terraced foliage and the deck around the pool, before I can even turn my head. Kaleidoscopic silhouette—raptor racing across the ground. An instant later, the high-pitched whine of the ultralight engine—fleeting images of color, it fills my frame of vision for an instant and is past me almost before I hear it.

It sends me sprawling, rolling onto my side across the hot concrete. A rip of reports as it passes, jets of spray in the pool, shattered tile at the edge. A second later, a shower of spent brass cartridges hits the water while others click across the concrete at the far end.

As the plane wings out over the beach and pulls up, gaining altitude and losing speed, I see the pilot, both hands on the control stick, looking straight ahead. The plane is nothing but an open frame, the pilot's feet in a set of stirrups. I can see him push one of these as the ultralight makes a slight turn to the right and climbs.

His passenger is in a kind of jump seat up behind him, sitting higher, the propeller pushing from behind. He is looking back to assess the damage, a set of goggles strapped to his head, shielding his eyes from the wind. In his hands, I can see what looks like a dark snub-nosed machine gun, moving it around, working at something. Then I realize he's loading a magazine with fresh rounds.

I look for Harry, but I don't see him. What I do see is the vaporous hue of blood drifting in the water out near the cen-

ter of the pool. I track it to a dark shadow on the bottom, and
before I can think, I'm in the water, kicking off the side,
pulling with my arms.

Before I'm there, I fill my lungs with air, and on the next
stroke I pull under the surface toward the shallow bottom.
Silence, only the pounding of my pulse in my head and
chest. Snagging Harry under the arms, around his chest, my
feet under me, I shoot us to the surface. I can't tell if he's
alive. His body is limp, chin resting on his chest. I grab his
hair and pull his head back, look at his face. His eyes are
closed.

Backpedaling with my feet on the bottom, I push through
the water, towing Harry toward the stairs and the hotel.

In the distance, the ultralight circles in a broad arc out
over the surf, turning, dipping its wing, wheeling around.

I'm concentrating on the plane when my feet hit the steps
of the pool and I fall backward, end up sitting on the next
step with Harry in my lap. I hang onto him and try to get up.

I see the waiter in his white linen jacket, facedown, hugging the tiled floor just inside the sliding door to the restaurant on the pool deck. But he's not looking at me. He's
looking at the plane as it approaches.

I yell and wave for him to help.

Instead he gets on his feet and runs toward the kitchen.

I look down and see Harry's blood on my shirt. The back
of his head, his hair is matted. A head wound. Not good.

When I look back, the ultralight is bearing down, making speed with its tail now into the onshore wind. With nothing but adrenaline, I heave Harry and myself up onto the
pool deck and drag him, heels across the concrete until I
reach the canvas cabana, and lay him in the shade. I turn and
look toward the stairs up to the hotel, but there is no one
there.

The plane is approaching the beach. I grab the table and
flip it on its side in front of Harry's prostrate body. I reach
for a towel to wrap his head, anything to stop the bleeding,
but there is no time. The pitch of the engine changes as the
plane noses down, gaining speed.

I step out from under the cabana and see the plane coming straight at me, maybe two hundred yards away. I run along the pool deck toward the other end, closing the distance between us, shortening his target time.

Like radar, the gunman's attention is drawn to the moving object. Bullets shatter the glass in the windows and the French door to the thatched-roof bar overlooking the beach. Then I hear the sound of the shots.

The gunman fires in controlled bursts. Half a second, twenty rounds. I see light puffs from the muzzle and the trail of brass as it glitters in the sunlight, the plane dropping cartridges like rain.

I sprawl onto the concrete, knees and elbows sliding, as bullets rip into the stucco wall just above me, walking a pattern into the low hedge at my feet. The sound of the burst follows an instant later. It is almost lost in the whine of the engine as the plane races by, over the pool, followed by its winged shadow.

The gunman swings around to fire another burst, but the pilot is forced to pull up, in order to clear the roof of the hotel. The rounds go high, ripping into the thatched palm-frond roof of the bar as the ultralight disappears behind the Casa Turquesa.

Where the hell is Julio and his security? I glance at my watch. The second hand is still moving. I figure ninety seconds, maybe two minutes, depending on how wide they take the turn, if they come back.

I run back to the cabana where Harry is lying on the concrete, grabbing a towel on the way.

Down on one knee, I place my ear to his nose and mouth and feel for a pulse. Shallow, but he is breathing. I reach around the back of his head, searching with my fingers for the wound, feeling for a depression in the bone through the hair. Nothing, just blood. I fold the towel into a long strip and wrap it as tightly as I can around his head, tucking it under like a turban on his forehead. I grab cushions from two of the chaise longues nearby, as well as a stack of towels. I put the towels under his feet to elevate them. Maybe not a good idea with a head wound, but I think Harry is in shock. I cover him with the cushions. It's all I can do for the moment.

Then I step away from the cabana, this time to the other side of the pool, putting distance between myself and Harry so they won't be tempted to spray bullets through the blue canvas top.

On this side there is a small mushroom-shaped kiosk bar with a thatched roof, right up next to the pool.

My eyes race over the area, looking for cover. In the corner of the patio forty feet away, near the low wall looking over the beach, sits a white metal bench, a bronze statue taking up a third of it. Larger than life, a solid hunk of metal, feet planted firmly on the ground, the figure's head is turned toward the north, staring pensively up the white strip of sand. It has one arm raised to shoulder height, holding out a hand with a cigar clenched between two fingers.

In the water beyond the beach, the tow boat, its bow slapping in the chop, is pulling its cargo in the parachute again, oblivious to what is happening a quarter mile away. The driver is doing a large circle, a horseshoe of white water at his stern.

As I am looking, the whine of an engine cuts the silence in the distance, just for an instant. Then it's gone, dampened by the high structures around me. I scan the roofline of the hotel, then the tops of buildings on either side. My eyes continually return to the southwest corner of the plaza, the gap between the hotel and the building under construction next door, where the ultralight came from the last time.

Then suddenly it's behind me, coming north up the beach. I drop down, my body flexing, flinching, waiting for the bullets to hit as I pivot on one knee. It takes an instant to connect sight and sound when I see it, a half mile to the south moving this way, an ultralight lumbering up the beach, towing a long sign behind it.

My head is pounding when I hear sirens somewhere in the distance. Another couple of seconds and I hear them again, out on the highway, moving this way.

There is no sign of the plane. I take a deep breath. Then my attention turns to Harry.

Some of the hotel staff have gathered near the rear of the lobby, up the stairs from the pool. I can see their heads peeking from around the edges of the large plateglass door.

I wave with one arm, motioning for them to come down and help. As the door opens and the manager and another man start down the stairs, half of the liquor bottles in the kiosk behind me explode. Splinters of wood from the shelf under them fly up like toothpicks before I hear the sound and look up.

Flying into the quickening current of air off the ocean, the ultralight is suspended nearly motionless in the sky just above the top of the hotel roof.

Its wings wobbling, the pilot struggles to hold the platform still as another series of puffs rise from the muzzle of the gun, his companion firing over his shoulder.

My body heads toward concrete with the force of gravity as something hisses and cracks past my ear.

When I look up, the pilot is tapping all his skills, beginning to inch forward as the breeze slackens.

I retreat across the concrete on my hands and feet and huddle on my knees behind the kiosk.

On the next burst, a few of the bullets hit metal inside the kiosk with a dead thud. The rest blow right through the little building, flashing like electricity, one of them fragmenting as it hits the cement a few inches from my hand.

This drives me out into the open. A quick glance.

The gunman has the muzzle pointed up, slamming another magazine in. He pulls the bolt and lets it slide closed before he sees me. He slaps the pilot on the shoulder.

It's a footrace for cover.

The plane noses down to pick up speed. I can hear the engine as it closes on me from behind, sliding in like a roller coaster, riding the currents of air over the palm trees.

The winged shadow overtakes me in less than a second as bullets slam into the concrete, a procession of them chasing me across the concrete deck.

I throw my body into a headlong dive. I hit the low wall overlooking the beach with my shoulder. I carom off it like a billiard ball and roll under the bench, curling into a fetal position beneath the sitting bronze figure.

Bullets spark as they hit the bench with a ping. A few of them, finding openings in the filigree, slam into the concrete, taking divots. Chips of cement, bits of copper jacket pepper my face.

The plane flies right over the top, the gunman pouring fire down on me as he passes. Bullets hitting bronze, turning into mushroomed metal until the last few hit the low wall on the outside.

I claw my way out from under the bench and kneel, peering over the top of the balcony out toward the sea.

The ultralight wings out over the surf, climbing for altitude. The gunman looks back, craning his neck, trying to get a glimpse around the flashing propeller and the tail section, to see if he got me. When he sees my head above the balcony, he slaps the pilot on the shoulder, frantically motioning for him to come around again.

I feel something warm dripping on my shoulder. I reach up, and there is blood dripping from by earlobe, where I've been nicked.

I watch the small plane. The gunman wants him to turn around. The pilot can't, gesturing with his hands toward the other ultralight flying across his path, heading up the coast trailing the sign: SEÑOR FROG—FREE T-SHIRT WITH DINNER.

The gunman, his arms waving, gestures in frustration in the jump seat. The pilot powers down. I can hear the whining engine drop to a purr, as he gives the other plane plenty of room to pass.

They clear the trailing end of the sign, and he throttles up, dips his nose, and lowers a wing for speed in the turn. I can see the pilot clearly now, looking this way, trying to get a quick fix on me.

I stand so he can see me.

The gunman points, using his arm, flexing it at the elbow, back and forth, directing the course of attack.

As soon as I see this, I move laterally across the plaza, running north along the balcony over the beach. I keep my eye on the plane until I reach the spot. Then I stop and turn toward him.

Like a game of dodgeball, the pilot has to guess which way I'll go. He is focused, eyes riveted on me. He adjusts his course a little to the left, lowers the nose for more speed, closing fast now, hunched over the stick, both hands and feet on the controls.

He is focused on me and does not see the cable just a few yards away, tethering the parasailer to the tow boat. The force of the impact throws him forward with enough force that I can see the tubular frame supporting the wing over his head actually bend. The left wing crumbles like brittle paper, fabric tearing as the fiber frame twists around the cable.

A good three hundred feet above them, the rider in the parachute gets an unexpected thrill, being jerked and dragged thirty or forty feet through the air by the impact.

The driver of the tow boat sees what's happened and cuts the engine, his bow dropping down into the water.

I watch as the ultralight spins out of control, its motor now racing. The propeller hits something, and I flinch with the impact as the plane comes apart in the air.

What is left of the wing separates. The frame, its engine, and passengers, drop like an anvil, plummeting into the water just beyond the surf.

Pieces of the wing and tail section trail after it as they float and tumble like leaves. They splash one after the other into the sea.

The parasailer glides down, settling smoothly into the water, the tow boat swinging around to pick him up.

When I look back, everything from the plane is gone except a sheen on the surface as it rides the undulating deep blue just beyond the waves.

My body shaking, hands trembling, I turn and look toward the hotel where Harry is still lying motionless under the cabana.

CHAPTER TWENTY-NINE

Within minutes after arriving, the paramedics have Harry stabilized, an I.V. in his arm, bandages around his head, and an oxygen mask over his face.

With cops crawling all over the hotel, some of them with guns drawn, the medics carry Harry up the stairs and wheel him on a gurney through the lobby. It is crowded with police and a few people who have wandered in off the street to see what has happened.

I look for Julio's security man. I don't see him. No sign of Julio or Herman.

I consider using the house phone and calling Adam in his room. But the gurney is moving too fast. I want to be with Harry at the hospital in case something happens.

Outside, they collapse the gurney and roll Harry into the back of the ambulance. I pile in behind the attendant, and as soon as the door closes, we roll down the driveway leading to the boulevard out in front. Another crowd has gathered here, but two traffic cops are holding them back. They have cordoned off the driveway and move some traffic cones to let us by.

The paramedic tells me that the hospital is not far, a few miles.

Everything is a blur as I notice the fingers of Harry's left hand move, then his right arm. He opens his eyes, blinks, searches the ceiling of the ambulance, then sees me.

"You're going to be all right. Just stay still. We're almost to the hospital," I tell him.

He smiles, tries to say something, but he can't with the mask over his nose and mouth.

He nods, but I don't know if he believes me.

Four minutes later, they roll Harry out of the ambulance and into the E.R. A nurse in scrubs with a paper mask down around her chin screens me, peeling me from the side of the gurney as we enter the emergency entrance. She gets some basic information, then tells me to go to the lobby, to the admitting desk. The swinging door closes in my face.

The lobby is crowded. People sprawled in chairs, some of them looking as if they've been here all night. Kids are playing, crawling on the floor.

I wait in line twenty minutes, then fill out forms and get in line again. It takes another half hour, leaning against the counter and answering questions on medical insurance, the health policy from the firm. I give them a business credit card to guarantee payment. This from the soggy wallet in my hip pocket. Harry's watered-down blood all over the front of my shirt.

When I'm done, I spend another forty minutes standing and pacing, occasionally looking at my watch. I have called the hotel twice. Nobody answers at the desk. Mass confusion.

All the chairs in the waiting room are taken. People looking at me, blood on the shoulder of my shirt from the nick on my ear. I look at my watch again, wonder what's taking so long, knowing that with each passing minute the chance of bad news increases.

Then a voice. "Anybody here with Mr. Hinds?"

I turn and see a young Hispanic man in green operating scrubs standing by the counter.

"I am."

He has one of those faces you can't read, the only apparent emotion being fatigue.

"I'm Doctor Ruiz." He looks at my bloody shirt. "Are you all right?"

"I'm fine. How is he?"

"Mr. Hinds is resting comfortably. We did an X ray looking for fractures, bullet fragments, chips of bone from the skull in the brain. We didn't find anything. It appears that the bullet only grazed the skull."

"So, he's going to be all right?"

"He has lost a lot of blood. It took a number of stitches to close the scalp. I cannot say for sure. We will have to watch him for the next twenty-four hours, to make sure there is no swelling of the brain. We're going to hold him at least overnight. We'll see how he is in the morning."

"Can I see him?"

"For a moment. He needs to rest. Right now he is sedated for pain. He's going to have quite a headache when the meds wear off." He tilts his head to my right and looks at my ear. "Do you know you have been wounded?"

Absently I reach up. Touch it. "Yeah. It's nothing."

"If you like, I could have one of the nurses clean it."

"It's all right. I can take care of it when I get back to the hotel."

He leads me down a hall and through a set of double doors to one of the emergency trauma rooms. The door is open. Harry is lying on a gurney in the center of the room, a blanket covering his body, his head bandaged.

The doctor tells me they will be moving him to a room upstairs in a few minutes. I thank him and he heads to his next patient.

I walk over and look at Harry. His eyes are closed. I touch his arm. He opens his eyes and looks at me.

"How are you feeling?"

"Great." Gravely voice. "Maybe they'll gimme a prescription for whatever they pumped in my arm. Right now I'm feelin' just fine. What happened?"

"You don't remember anything?"

"Who are you?" he says.

He reads my eyes. "Just kidding. Last thing I remember is a shadow on the water, just before the mountain fell on me. What was it?"

"We'll talk about it later. You rest. They'll be coming to take you upstairs to a room in a couple of minutes."

"No. No. I want to go with you." He starts to get up off the gurney.

"Harry!"

"Oh shit." Hand to his head, he settles back down on the gurney. "My head feels like it's gonna come off."

"If you don't lie still, it probably will. The doctor says you're going to be feeling some pain when the medications wear off. For the time being, you rest. I'll stop by again later tonight." I squeeze his arm and head to the door.

"Paul?"

"Yes."

"Where's Adam and Julio?"

"That's a good question."

I flag a cab in front of the hospital and head back to the hotel. By the time we get to the intersection leading to the driveway up to the Casa Turquesa, the crowd out in front is gone. A motorcycle cop is standing at the driveway entrance, screening traffic in and out.

The sun is searing. I glance at my watch. It's nearly two o'clock. I'm feeling nauseous. I have a headache. I haven't eaten since last night. The blood from my ear is dried and caked, but the sweat running down my face in the cab, which has no air-conditioning, causes the salt to burn in the wound.

The cop at the gate will see the blood all over the front of my shirt as soon as we pull in, and the inquisition will start before I can get out of the cab.

Rather than go up to the hotel, I have the driver go past the entrance and take a left behind Kukulcan Plaza.

Up on the bluff behind the shopping center, overlooking the beach, are apartments and condos. Julio's firm has rented space in one of the less expensive condos so that they could park the big Surburbans in the underground garage. The rest of Julio's team, when not on duty, has slept in the condo upstairs. Herman pointed it out to me on one of our trips.

I have the cab driver drop me off in front of the place.

The two-story building houses a half dozen units with stairs out in front leading to the units on the second story. Each of the units look the same.

As we drive up, I see the driveway to the garage, a concrete ramp at the side of the building leading down underneath. So I head toward it and down the ramp.

I am looking for Julio's man, the one who's supposed to be watching the cars, hoping he has a radio to contact his boss. If not, maybe there is a phone in the condo upstairs. I can call Adam and find out what's happening in the hotel, have them bring me some clean clothes. If I'm lucky, by now Adam and Julio will have answered most of their questions. I can fill in a few blanks, get a meal in my room, and nap before we meet with Pablo Ibarra; that is, assuming the meeting is still on.

After the events of this morning, I've become a convert to Harry's way of thinking. As soon as I button Adam, I plan to lay heavy hands. When Harry is ready to travel, we should hop on the plane and hightail it home. It's one thing to look for answers as to who killed Nick. It's another to meet them.

Even though it's dug into the earth like a bunker, the underground garage is warm and humid.

I turn the corner and see the cars. Two of the Surburbans are there. One is out. The one on the right has its engine running, fouling the garage with fumes.

The man watching them is sitting inside, listening to music, with the air conditioner running. I hear the muted vibrations of low notes, pounding out a bass in a monotone. I'm waiting for the car to sprout hydraulics and start jumping in place.

As I slide up along side, I see the familiar five o'clock

shadow in the side-view mirror. I've been looking at it for two days in the car. Julio sitting behind the wheel. I tap on the glass of the window behind him, but he doesn't hear me. I open the driver's door.

"Where were your people . . ." The words aren't out of my mouth when I see the splatter on the windshield like rust-colored stucco. Spider-legged fissures in the windshield fan out from a crater in the glass a few inches above the steering wheel.

The side of Julio's face is an ashen shade of blue, cyanotic. His eyes are half closed in a death daze. In the center of his forehead is the exit wound the size of a quarter, the edges swollen, already congealed with blood. This has run down his face in rivulets around his nose, covering large areas of his shirt and pants.

I stand there with my mouth open, the sweet metallic taste of monoxide in my throat. The mind-numbing music and the fact that I'm standing inches from a dead body in a foreign county tends to focus the mind. Quickly I scan the garage to make sure I'm alone.

I search through the pockets of my shorts for a piece of cloth, paper, anything. I find a folded cash register receipt still damp. I open it up and using it between my thumb and forefinger, I carefully reach under the steering column, find the key, and turn off the ignition. The deafening silence causes me to flinch, look around, make sure I'm still alone. Then I close the car door, wiping the handle with the tail of my shirt.

It takes me five minutes to make my way back up the hill. I cross the empty street behind the plaza, take off my shirt, and drop it into a trash can at the curb on the other side. I enter the shopping center through a door on the back side. The cool, dry atmosphere of the air-conditioned plaza washes over me as I catch my breath inside. Except for the blood on my ear, I look like a tourist who forgot his shirt back at the pool, shoes without socks and beads of sweat.

Against the wall just inside the door is a pay phone. I

fumble with Mexican coins, trying to figure which one to use for a local call. I end up dropping a ten peso piece, then dial the hotel. A few seconds later, I get the front desk.

"I'd like to speak to Mr. Adam Tolt. He's a guest."

"One moment."

I hear voices. The clerk speaking in Spanish to someone else. I hear him say 'Señor Tolt,' a rubbing sound, his hand covering the mouthpiece, the word *Inglés*. Then another voice comes on the line. "Hello, who is this?"

"I'm trying to reach Mr. Tolt. Adam Tolt. He's a guest at the hotel."

"Who is this?" The voice speaks with the tone of authority.

A half hour ago, before finding Julio's body, I would have given him my name, crossed the street, and talked to the cops. Instead I don't say another word. I hang up.

The hotel has a small desk with a single phone. If I call again, the clerk will recognize my voice.

At a counter a few feet away, there's a young girl offering sample scents of perfume from some atomizers. I step over and tell her I've had a little accident, pointing to my ear. I ask her if she wouldn't mind placing a phone call for me in Spanish. It would only take a moment.

She smiles and steps around the counter. I drop another coin in the phone and dial again.

"I want to talk to one of their guests. An African-American gentleman. A black man. His name is Herman. I'm afraid I don't remember his last name, but there are only a few guests at the hotel."

When the clerk answers, the girl speaks in rapid-fire Spanish. They go back and forth a couple of times. Finally she hands me the phone and smiles. "His last name is Diggs. Herman Diggs. They are ringing his room now."

"Thanks." I take the phone, listening as it ringing. Three times, no answer. On the fourth ring, "Hello."

I recognize Herman's voice.

"Herman. Paul Madriani."

"Well, shit, 'bout time somebody called. Where the hell

are you? I been lookin' all over. Go to sleep, wake up, and everybody's gone. Startin' to think somebody called an audible and I missed it. Can't fine Julio, any of the rest of the crew. And some clerk downstairs says your partner got shot. Some shit about airplanes."

"Herman!" I have to raise my voice to stop him from jabbering.

"What?"

"Go find Adam Tolt. I tried to call him a couple of minutes ago and the cops cut me off."

"No shit, Sherlock? Tolt's gone."

"What do you mean, he's gone?"

"Vanished, disappeared, vamoosed, gone. I went to his room. The place is all fuckin' tore up. Cops are down there wrappin' the place early for Christmas. All kinds of yellow tape across the door. It was Ibarra 'n' his bro. They snatched Tolt right under our nose. This morning while their fuckin' air force was busy shootin' up the pool."

"How do you know?"

"Cuz the brothers turned Tolt's room upside down lookin' for somethin'. When they didn't find it, they took Tolt and dropped me a note. They want a meeting tomorrow morning early. At dawn. At some ruins. Place called Cobá. Some temple. Just a second, I get it." He leaves the phone to get the note and comes back.

"Here it is. Something called the Doorway to the Temple of the Inscriptions. I looked on a map. Cobá's in the middle of the fuckin' jungle. They holdin' Tolt as collateral for this Rosen shit, whatever it is. So I hope you got some. Otherwise they gonna be sending your friend back a piece at a time."

"Do the police have the note?"

"No. It was slipped under my door early this afternoon. All they know is Tolt's gone and his room's a mess."

This sends a lot of silence from my end of the line.

"Hey. You there?"

"I'm here, Herman."

"Tell me. Where exactly is here?" he says.

"I'm across the street in the plaza."

"What the fuck you doin' there?"

"I don't have time to explain. Can you get out of the hotel without the police seeing you?"

"Yeah right, six-foot-five, three-hundred-pound bro', I'm gonna slip through the lobby unnoticed like Tinkerbell."

"There's gotta be some way."

"Yeah. I can do it. It won't be easy. First tell me why?"

"I'm going to need your help."

"Take me a minute to get dressed," he says. "In my Skivvies."

"I've got some bad news," I tell him.

"What?"

"Julio is dead."

Silence on the other end. "What you talkin' 'bout? Ay don't believe ya. Bullshit."

"I just saw him. He's sitting behind the wheel in one of the Surburbans down in the garage with half of his head gone. Do you know where the rest of your people are?"

Nothing but the sound of his breathing on his end.

"Herman?"

"What?"

"Where are the rest of your people?"

He hesitates for a second. "Ay don't know. Called the condo four or five times. Nobody answers."

"Then we have to assume they either bought them or they're dead. And one of the cars is gone. Do you know where it is?"

"No."

"Do you have keys for the other two?"

"Got keys for all of 'em."

I tell him to meet me in half an hour on the sidewalk behind the plaza. Then I hang up.

I buy a pair of pants, a couple of shirts, some underwear and socks at one of the men's clothing shops in the mall, then head for the men's room. Inside I wash the blood off my neck and clean away some of the crusted blood from my ear, being careful not to reopen the wound. Then put on one of the new shirts.

Out in the mall I wait inside, watching for Herman through the glass doors I had entered forty minutes earlier. A few seconds later, I see him hoofing it up the sidewalk and coming this way. He's wearing black high-top shoes, a pair of black chinos, thighs bulging, and a tee-shirt, stretched in every direction. Around his waist is an oversized fanny pack on a thick web belt sagging from the weight of the forty-five and the clips of ammunition inside.

Carrying the shopping bags with my clothes in them, I head out and meet him on the street.

"I don't believe you, man. Fuckin' shoppin' at a time like this," he says.

"I had blood all over my clothes."

"Oh. That's different," he says.

"Everything I brought with me is locked up in the room, including my passport."

"Looks like you gonna be talkin' to the powlice before you go home," he says.

We head down the hill.

Five minutes later we're standing in the garage under the condo, Herman with the leather pouch on his left side unzipped. His right hand is in it under the flap.

The Suburbans are parked where they were when I left, the smell of exhaust still lingering in the air.

"Which one's Julio in?"

"One on the right."

"Stay here."

"Herman."

"What?"

"Leave it. Don't touch it."

"Can't just leave him here," he says. "Besides, my fingerprints are all over that car."

"There are things besides fingerprints," I tell him. "There's nothing we can do. As soon as we get the other car and get out of here, we can stop and call the cops from a pay phone. Tell them some kids saw the body in a car in the garage. Give them the address and hang up. They'll take care of it."

"I at least want to see him," he says.

"I understand. Look, don't touch."

Herman goes up and looks at Julio through the driver's side window. "Fucker did this is dead," he says. "Now I gotta go tell his wife and kids."

"He was married?"

"Yeah. Gal named Maria. Nice lady. Three kids. Two boys and a girl."

"I'm sorry."

"Yeah. So am I."

"We need to go," I tell him. "Do you have the keys to the other car?"

"Yeah."

"Then we should go."

"Not yet." He turns and walks back the other way, right past me.

"Where are you going?"

He doesn't answer.

"Herman!"

"You wanna go, go," he says.

"This is crazy." I follow him.

He leads me through a door and up two flights of stairs, man on a mission. Herman has to use a key from his pocket to unlock the door upstairs. Once inside, he heads down a hall, past several doors. He holds out a hand for me to slow down, pops the snap holding the handle of the gun in the fanny pack, and pulls the stainless automatic out, holding the muzzle up toward the ceiling, the gun near his right ear.

He stops in front of one of the doors and puts his ear to the wood, listens for a second, then slips a key into the lock. Motions for me to stay where I am in the hall. A second later, he is inside.

I wait outside listening. Nothing. A few seconds later, Herman swings the door open. "They're gone. And all their stuff. Like they checked out. Bags, everything."

"Why?"

"Sold out's what I figure. Otherwise, Ibarra's people killed 'em, their stuff would be here. The way business is done down here," he says. "It's either buy you or bullets. There ain't no other way."

Back at the car, Herman fishes for the key in his pocket, then steps around to the passenger side window and, without opening the door, looks across toward the driver's side of the front seat.

"What are you doing?"

"There's things besides fingerprints," he says. "There's things besides bullets too." Then he opens the door, pushes the button that unlocks the other doors, goes around to the driver's side and pulls the latch to pop the hood. It takes a minute or so, looking around the engine block, then underneath before he's satisfied.

"Where you figuring on going?" he asks.

"The glass pyramid."

"See Papa Ibarra?" he says.

I nod. "I assume he's the only who can tell us what this Mejicano Rosen is and help us find Adam."

"And who killed Julio." Herman walks to the back of the car and opens the back hatch. He finds a key on the ring and slips it into a key slot in the floor, turning it. The entire section of carpeted flooring lifts out. Underneath is a rack with three long guns and something that looks like a short machine gun.

"Can you shoot?"

"I've fired a gun before."

"Not what I asked. Can you shoot?"

"I don't know."

"Here, you take the shotgun." He hands it to me. "You slide the pump underneath each time you shoot. Like this. Then shoot again. This little thing. This the safety. Keep it off when you're shooting. Think you can handle that?"

"Yeah."

"Just don't point it anywhere near me." He grabs a box of shells and hands them to me. "I'll show you how to load it inside." Then he pulls the little machine gun from the rack and gathers up several magazines of ammunition, each one with a gleaming, round copper bullet protruding from the forward side of the open end.

"We're not going to go in there with these?"

"Watch me."

CHAPTER THIRTY

In the car I slip on a pair of long pants from the shopping bag in back and put on socks while Herman drives. A block from the glass pyramid, we stop near a restaurant and I use the pay phone to call the police and tell of the location of Julio's body. Then I hang up.

Herman doesn't want to talk about it. Man on a mission, he turns onto the private lane leading to the glass pyramid. The road is lined with palm trees planted in the thirty-foot strip of grass that forms the center divider.

We wind along this toward the hotel. He parks in a space out in front.

"Go inside, get us a room, high up. Close to the top floor as you can get."

"Why?"

"Just do it. Bring the key back here."

A few minutes later, I'm back in the car. "Eighth floor. Is that high enough for you?"

"It'll do."

"Now what?"

"Sit tight." He backs out of the space and pulls around the hotel, ten stories of smoked glass on an angle, reflecting sunlight like a solar generator.

Herman drives through the parking area, edging his way around the building until he finds what he's looking for: dumpsters and service vehicles, a small electric cart with canvas bags filled with dirty linen in the back.

"This place." He parks the car.

"What now?"

"You just sit here fo' a second." He gets out and goes over to the cart. Hands in his pockets, he stands, looking around, ultimate stealth, your usual seven-foot dark mountain. Then he grabs a folded canvas linen bag from the back of the cart and returns to the car. This time he gets in the backseat.

"What are you doing?"

"Tol' ya, just sit tight." He leans over the backseat into the rear compartment, grabbing the guns, the pump shotgun, and the stubby little machine gun, making sure they're loaded, the magazines are in, and the safeties are on.

"Now. In a minute I'm goin' over there." He talks while he checks the guns. "Do you see that door?" He nods in the direction with his head.

"Yes. I see it."

"In a second I'm goin' in there. What I want you to do is just sit right here 'til you see me wave from that door." He gathers up the extra ammunition and puts it in the laundry bag, unclips the web belt from around his waist, and drops the fanny pack with the forty-five into the laundry bag too.

"Then I want you to get out of the car, walk over there. Don't run, just walk. And bring this shit witcha."

He hands me thirty pounds of canvas with sharp edges sticking out everywhere. "You got that?"

"I got it."

He reads my expression, one filled with doubt.

"Hey, fuckin' Tolt, he's your friend. I don't care they cut his ears, nose en balls off, hang 'em on a charm bracelet. But this man upstairs, this Pablo Eyebarra. Far as you and I are concerned, he be the fuckin' Wizard a Oz. Man with all the answers. Now we can either go talk to him or we can go home. I don't know 'bout you, but I ain't goin' home 'til I get the answer to at least one question. Who the fuck shot Julio? So you in or you out?"

"I'm in," I tell him.

"Good. I thought so. Den let's do it." Herman smiles through his chipped tooth, opens the door, and seconds later he disappears into the service entrance at the back of the hotel.

After letting Saldado practice his meat-cutting arts on my arm and becoming gunnery target for the Ibarrian Air Force, I am in no position to question Herman's judgment. Whatever he's missing on that score, he makes up for in loyalty. The difference between us is he's more direct.

Before I know it, he's back, waving at me to come.

I get out of the car with the bag over my shoulder, Santa Claus with an arsenal. I walk quickly toward the door. When I get there, Herman takes the bag and pulls me inside like a rag doll. I follow him down a short corridor. I don't have a lot of choice; he has me by the belt towing me along. I see some guy in whites and a chef's hat cross the corridor in front of us, passing from the kitchen to another room across the hall. He doesn't see us.

Herman opens a door and pushes me into a dark service closet, then closes the door behind us.

"Gotta find the fuckin' light," he says.

We stand in the dark for a couple of seconds until I hear the metal beads click on the light over our heads. Herman with the string pull.

"Here. Put this on." He hands me a white linen smock, the kind waiters in posh restaurants wear. .

"Would you like to tell me what we're doing? Or is that a surprise?"

"Probably best you don't know the details. That way you free. Know what I mean? Adapt to the circumstances. What my main tai chi man says. What you don't know can't fuck witch your brain."

"Inscrutable."

"What ya say?"

"Nothing.

I slip on the smock and button it up to the tunic collar.

In the meantime, Herman is going through a bag of soiled ones, trying to find a tunic big enough. He finally settles on one. He has to leave three of the buttons undone high up around his chest and neck. It fits him like a rubber coat, the bottom barely reaching his belt.

"Don't worry. Man's gonna be in no mood be doin' fashion reviews. Be too busy with his ass pucker lookin' down the barrel your gun."

"We aren't gonna shoot him?"

He doesn't look at me.

"Herman."

"Depends what he has to say. He tells me he sent somebody over to shoot Julio, you can expect to find little bits of him stuck in the holes I'm gonna be making in his wall with little emma gee in the bag there."

"No. I don't think so."

"Think what you want. But you gonna be thinkin' it in the dark by yourself in about ten seconds." He grabs the bag with the guns, pulls the string on the light overhead, then opens the door a crack and peeks out.

"Show time," he says and steps out into the hall, the linen bag over his shoulder looking like the Pillsbury Doughboy after a bad day. I watch as he latches onto a rolling stainless steel cart against the far wall.

There's a linen tablecloth over the top of it and a warming compartment underneath. He checks to make sure there are no lit sterno candles inside the compartment, then slings the bag with the guns inside, and closes the stainless steel door.

I look at my watch. It's ten minutes to four. Adam and I weren't scheduled to meet Ibarra until six-thirty.

"You comin'?" Herman's looking at me.

"He may not even be there."

"Then we'll flop down on his nice furniture and wait."

I push the cart out into the corridor. "Let's hope the man has nothing but good things to tell us," I say.

"Good. There you go. Positive thinkin'," he says.

We take the service elevator. It stops three times along the way, to pick up a maid on five and drop her off on seven, and once again on the eighth floor.

A maintenance man with a bucket in his hand stands in the doorway looking at us.

"*Abajo?*" he says.

Herman holds his fist out with his thumb pointing up.

The man shrugs his shoulders and starts to get on anyway.

Herman moves his bulk in front of the door. "Elevator'll be right back down, bro'."

The man looks up at him. I don't think he understands a word Herman said, but he comprehends the body language. He stays where he is, and the doors close.

We ascend the last two floors undisturbed. When the doors open again, we are in a small pantry area, dishes stacked on shelves against the wall in front of us, crystal glassware, towels and linen napkins, everything arranged in a neat order. To the left is a door leading out into a hallway. To the right, another wall. A large double refrigerator, zero clearance built into it, with silverware and serving utensils on shelves and hooks on each side of it.

Herman puts his thumb on the open-door button and holds it as he leans to his right and looks toward the hallway, then nods, giving me the all clear.

I push the cart out into the pantry, and Herman steps out. The elevator doors close behind us, point of no return. This is Pablo Ibarra's private lair. Offices and living quarters and, if Herman's plan is star-crossed, his own personal army.

I step to the front of the cart and peek around the door leading out into the hallway. I snap my head back in quickly just as the guy sitting in the chair twenty feet down the hall turns and looks this way.

Herman's big dark eyes stare at me like two dots under question marks.

I hold up one finger and point in the direction down the

hall. Then I make a sign, a circle with my thumb and finger. I look through it and pretend that I am turning a crank. Then I point to the ceiling.

Herman nods. He turns and looks at the wall behind him. Quietly he lifts a large soup ladle from a hook on the wall and takes a towel from the shelf. He wraps the ladle tightly in the towel with the handle facing the end of the cart near his hand.

Then he goes to the refrigerator and opens the door. He looks around without touching until he finds what he wants. When he turns around he's holding an aerosol can of whipped cream.

I look at him like, "What're ya gonna do, give the guy a sugar high?"

He ignores me, nods toward the door that we should be going now.

Before I can even think, he pushes the cart with me in front of it out into the hall. I turn around and take my end as if I'm pulling with my back to the guard sitting in the hall.

I look over my shoulder and get my first good look at him. He's wearing a blue serge suit, sitting in a straight-back chair against the wall. He has one leg crossed over the other, reading a newspaper. Just beyond him is a set of double doors, heavy polished teak.

He hears the clatter of the cart, as the wheels rumble slowly over the thick carpet, and looks this way. Lean face, dark eyes, and no mirth, he checks us out, then turns back to his newspaper.

"Like I was sayin', chef tells me sauce is not the thing," says Herman. I look like, "Maybe they might be expecting Spanish."

He ignores me. "Sauce is out. Now the French, they got their sauces down. But it's the Eyetalians can cook. And they don't put sauce on nothin'. You can't cook, you need sauce." Herman is pushing the cart with one hand, talking with the other.

As we approach, the man in the chair puts his newspaper down on the floor and gets up. He leans a little and looks at the cart, first one side and then the other, from a distance. Herman pushes the cart until my back is almost right into the guy. The guard is trying to see around me to the side with the compartment.

"As I was sayin', you really wanna learn how to cook . . . Why don't you step outta the man's way, so's he can do 'is job?"

I shuttle sideways to the other side of the cart.

"I was sayin', you lookin' to buy perfume, you talk to the French."

The guard leans down.

"You wanna cook . . ."

He reaches for the stainless steel door to the warming compartment.

"You gots to talk to the . . ." Herman wacks him with the heavy end of the ladle, backhand along the side of the head without even looking, "fuckin' Eyetalians," he says.

The man hits the floor like a sack of cement.

Herman grabs the aerosol can of cream off the top of the cart and runs to the other end of the hall. By the time he gets there, the cap is off the can. He reaches up and sprays whipped cream all over the lens of the security camera, covering it with white foam until some of it is dripping on the floor.

I open the compartment and take out the bag.

Herman jogs back, rolls the guard over, and frisks him on the floor. He comes up with two pistols, a semiautomatic in a shoulder harness, then a small revolver strapped to the man's ankle. "Put 'em in the bag." He tosses them to me.

"Gotta move before that shit melts." Herman's talking about the cream. "After that they be seein' us, only difference is gonna be two whities. Besides, they be sendin' somebody from maintenance up here any minute."

"That's if they weren't looking at the screen when you nailed him."

"That case," says Herman, "they be carryin' somethin' besides buckets."

I take the shotgun out of the bag, check the safety, holding my finger along the outside of the trigger guard.

Herman strips the belt off the guard's pants and hog-ties
him, hands and feet pulled up behind him.

Then he grabs the pistol pack from the bag, straps it
around his waist. He quickly checks the machine gun, pulls
the bolt and cycles a round into the chamber, and checks the
safety one more time.

He hands me the bag with the extra ammunition. "If you
be thinkin' positive thoughts, be thinkin' we not gonna need
that shit," he says. "We do, it means we in a fuckin' Mexican bullet fiesta."

He tries the handle on the door. "Shit. It's locked." We're
standing in a dead-end corridor, armed like terrorists, not
knowing whether Ibarra has a task force coming up the elevator for us at this moment, and all we have for cover is a
food cart half the size of Herman's ass.

I go to the guard's pants pockets as he's lying on the floor.
Nothing but change and a pocketknife. I feel a lump in his
suit coat pocket, reach in, and find a large ring with a single
key on it.

Herman takes it. It slides into the lock and turns. He looks
at me and takes a deep breath. Then he inches the door open
and peeks through. "We're in business."

Quietly he opens the door, then lifts the cart so the wheels
don't make any noise, and uses it to hold the door open.
Then the two of us grab the guard under the arms and drag
him inside, closing the door behind us.

We are in a kind of entryway. A partition wall directly in
front of the door, with a large oval mirror hanging in the center and a low credenza with some books and a plant on it
forming the centerpiece underneath it.

The partition extends ten or twelve feet up. Overhead, the
ceiling is glass, rising on the diagonal toward the apex of the
pyramid. On both ends, the partition is open.

Herman goes to the right. I do the left. When I peek
around my end, I find myself looking across a large room to-

ward a wall of slanting glass that becomes the ceiling as it rises overhead.

In the center of the room is a large desk on the Mexican tile floor. There is a man seated behind it with his back to us, typing, hunt-and-peck style, on a computer keyboard.

I look along the partition and see the edge of Herman's forehead taking in the same picture I am.

There is a door to another room on Herman's side. Nothing on mine but more glass. For the moment, the other door is closed.

We pull our heads in, backs against the partition, and look at one another. Herman gives me a strange expression, shakes his head, and shrugs. How do you figure, drug lord at the keyboard? It's as if neither one of us wants to be the first to shatter his serenity. Man lost in his own thoughts.

But time is running. We step around opposite ends of the partition at the same moment. Herman clears his throat.

The man at the computer stops, lifts his head, and turns. When he sees the guns, his eyes widen. He reaches for the desk.

Herman lowers his muzzle on him. "Not 'less you wanna be changing out all those nice windows behind ya." The man leans back in his chair and raises his hands above his shoulders. Whether he understood Herman or the gun isn't clear.

"Se habla inglés?" says Herman

The man doesn't answer.

"Shit," says Herman. "How's your Spanish?"

"You got mine beat."

The man behind the desk is small, slight of build, no more than five-foot-six. His black hair is graying at the temples; I would say he's in his mid-sixties. His dark eyes are wide at this moment, taking in Herman and the submachine gun.

"Listen fuckhead, you better start saying somethin' I can understand or I'm gonna shoot ya," says Herman.

"I speak English," he says.

"Good for you. I wasn't lookin' forward to callin' an in-

terpreter. Where's that door go?" Herman sweeps the closed
door with the muzzle of his cannon.

"To living quarters."

"Who's in there?"

"No one."

"You wouldn't be bullshittin' me?"

"Perhaps a maid. I don't know."

"Anybody likely to come through there?"

He shakes his head. "I left instructions not to be dis-
turbed."

"Good, cuz if somebody comes walkin' in that door unexpected, they gonna be gettin' one hair-raisin' shock. And
it ain't gonna be doin' your wall no good either. You Pablo
Ibarra?"

He doesn't answer, just looks back and forth at Herman
and me, my shotgun pointed at the floor.

"Who sent you?"

"Why, you expecting someone?" says Herman.

He doesn't answer.

"I ain't exactly sure who sent my friend over there. But
you might say whoever the god is handles revenge had a
hand dispatching me."

"Herman."

He looks at me. "What?"

"Let the man talk."

"I'm tryin'. Fucker keeps askin' questions," says Herman. "Where I come from, one's gots the guns gets to ask
the questions. Motherfucker lookin' down the barrel's the
one's gotta answer."

The Mexican in the chair is looking back and forth as we
argue, probably wondering if we're high on something.

"What do you want to know?" he says.

"Your name for starters. Make sure we get it right on the
headstone," says Herman.

The man hesitates.

Herman clicks the safety off on his spray gun.

"Herman. That's enough."

"Maybe we take him outside, see if he wants to do some window washing," says Herman.

"I am Pablo Ibarra," he says. He closes his eyes as if waiting for the impact of the bullets.

"Father of the two assholes in the trailer down in Tulúm?" says Herman.

He opens them again. "They are my sons. Did they send you?"

Herman gives me a look. "Must be a cordial fuckin' family. Can't wait to meet the mother of your children."

"My wife is dead," he says.

"Oh. Sorry. Natural causes or did one of the kids shoot her?"

"Cancer," he says.

"Too bad, but that ain't the death I'm here for right now. Why did you kill Julio?"

"Who?"

"Don't you make like some fuckin' Mexican owl to me. You know who I'm talkin' about. Julio Paloma. Big guy. Used to have a forehead without a hole in it."

"I don't know this man."

"You may notta met him, but you sure as shit had him shot."

"Why would I do this?"

Herman looks at me. Rolls his eyes. "See? Keeps askin' more fuckin' questions." He has his finger inside the trigger guard.

"I have never heard of this man." Ibarra looks at me. "Please. I don't know who you think I am. But I have never had anyone killed. I am a businessman."

"You wanna ask him about this Rosen shit before I shoot him?"

"Calm down, Herman."

"You calm down. Right now I'm worried about how many keys been given out to that door behind us."

"Mr. Ibarra, my name is Paul Madriani."

"Yes." His eyes latch onto me like I'm a lifesaver.

"I was supposed to have a meeting with you tonight, at six-thirty. Myself and a man named Adam Tolt."

"Cut to the fuckin' chase," says Herman.

"We talked with one of your sons yesterday. Arturo."

"Yes?"

"This morning Mr. Tolt was taken from his hotel room and a note was left, telling me that unless I appeared at a place called Cobá tomorrow morning with something called Mejicano Rosen, Tolt would be killed."

"Why are you telling me this? Why don't you go to the police?"

"Because I think you know what Mejicano Rosen is."

Ibarra looks at Herman, then at me.

"Enougha this shit," Herman goes over and grabs Ibarra by the back of the collar, nearly lifting him out of his chair.

"What are you doin'?" I ask.

"No," says Ibarra. "I will tell you."

"Fuckin' A, you will. And you," he says to me. "No wonder costs an arm and a leg to hire a lawyer. Ask a couple a questions, takes forever. Coulda shot the fucker, been outta here by now. But, nooo. You wanna talk. So you wanna talk? Consultation room's this way," he says.

CHAPTER THIRTY-ONE

With his forty-five making a dimple in Ibarra's back, and the long guns in the linen bag, Herman marches Ibarra to the service elevator and pushes 8 to go down.

We drop two levels. Herman takes a quick look out. We brush by a maid on our way out of a service area and out onto the eighth floor.

Each level forms a kind of open terrace, hanging gardens of Babylon, looking over a vast atrium that forms the interior of the pyramid.

Halfway down the hall, a young couple comes breezing out of their room.

Ibarra sees the open door. His thought is nearly palpable, and for an instant I freeze, afraid he is going to run for the room and Herman will shoot him.

Herman nudges him with the gun. "Don't even think about it." He has a towel over the pistol, draped across his arm as if he should be carrying a finger bowl in the other hand.

As soon as we are past the couple and out of earshot, he talks to me from the corner of his mouth. "Be easier just throw the fucker off the balcony," he says. "Score him on his swan dive in the lily pond down there."

"Herman, we don't know that he killed Julio. And even if he did, it's a matter for the police."

"I didn't." Ibarra waddles in front of him with the gun in his back.

"You gonna be walking with your ass on your shoulders, you don't shut up," says Herman.

A few doors down I find the number that matches the one penciled on the little envelope with the key card I got when I checked in downstairs.

I slide it through the lock and hear it click.

Inside with the door closed, Herman checks the bathroom and the closet, then pulls the curtains closed on the window and pushes Ibarra backward onto the bed. "Now I wanna hear you talk."

"You have met my sons?" he says.

"Only one of them. Arturo. The other, Jaime is it? He wasn't there."

"You are probably lucky. Jaime has a bad temper. They have been involved in activities for which I am ashamed."

"And I suppose they did this all by themselves?" says Herman.

"I admit at times I have done things for which I am not proud. But I didn't want my sons to grow up this way. I have tried every way to stop them. Even gone to the authorities. But you know what Cancún can be like."

"Here we go," says Herman. "Fuckin' mistakes been made. Next he be tellin' us he got religion when he seen the light coming outta the little hole at the end of my gun."

"Believe me. I have tried to stop my sons, but they will not listen. All they want is my money, to finance their schemes. When I refused, they found other sources."

"Narcotics?" I ask.

"For a time. But that stopped. I was able to influence certain people."

"Your children cuttin' into your profits, were they?"

"I do not deal in drugs. I do not allow them on the premises of my hotel."

"You wrote a letter to a lawyer in San Diego, a Mr. Nicholas Rush. What was that about?"

Ibarra looks at me, puzzled. "How do . . ."

"Never mind that. What did Mr. Rush have to do with your sons? And who or what is Mejicano Rosen?"

"Then you know about it? It is pronounced Roseton. Not Rosen."

"What is it?" I ask.

"Roseton means Rosette in Spanish. The French under Napoleon, when they found it, they named it the stone of Rosette after the name of the village in Egypt where it was discovered. The English called it Rosetta."

"What's this shit?" says Herman.

"The Rosetta Stone," I say. "It's a fractured slab of rock found by Napoleon's forces when they invaded Egypt. It was engraved with ancient Egyptian hieroglyphs along with a Greek translation. It allowed archeologists for the first time to understand the language of pharoahs."

Herman has a dense look on his face. "Wait a minute. You lost me. You tellin' me this 'bout some rock from Egypt?"

"No," says Ibarra. "The Mejicano Roseton in your language is the Mexican Rosetta. It is the last remaining key to the ancient hieroglyphs of the Maya."

"Do you have it?" I ask.

"Unfortunately no."

"Where it is?"

"I cannot be sure, but I know that it exists and that it is priceless. My sons have been trying to acquire it."

"Is that what Nick Rush was after?"

He nods. "He had been doing business through another man."

"Gerald Metz?"

"How did you know that?"

"Never mind. Go on."

"This man Metz had done business with my sons previously."

"What kinda business?" says Herman.

"My boys were looting archeological sites. At first they were simply buying a few trinkets from the Indians who found things in the jungle, small figures carved in jade, sometimes trinkets in silver or gold. My sons would then sell these items to dealers in your country or in Europe. Wherever they could be paid the most. Occasionally they would find something more valuable.

"Then Arturo and Jaime began locating sites that were still covered by jungle. They are easy to spot if you know what you are looking for. In the Yucatán, the jungle floor is flat. Any rise, a small mound, what looks like a hill, is very often the remains of a Mayan structure overgrown by trees and vines. They learned how to find these. They hired laborers and destroyed sites, looking for treasure."

"Didn't your government try to stop them?"

"They tried. But it is impossible. There are too many locations, not enough guards. Your government demands that we control the flow of narcotics through our country. That is the priority. The sale of looted artifacts is a huge business. Thousands of items are taken every year from Mexico and Guatemala and sold on the black market. Some of these people are drug dealers. They make more selling artifacts than they do selling drugs, and there is less risk. You do not go to prison for life for stealing Mayan relics."

"Who would buy them?" I ask.

"There are people who deal in such things. They sell the items to wealthy Americans, so their wives can have figurines made into earrings and tell their friends where they came from. The larger, more expensive items are another matter."

"That's what we saw at the trailer," I tell Herman.

"What?" says Ibarra.

"It looked like a large slab of stone, like a headstone, only taller. We couldn't see it very well. They had it covered with a blanket."

"Tell me. Did you see white paint on it?"

"On a corner, under the blanket. It looked like white-wash."

"A stela," he says.

"What estella?" says Herman.

"A stela. It is a stone sign used by the Maya for historical and religious purposes. They would cover the stone in white limestone plaster. Then they would carve their hieroglyphs into this softer material. There are maybe thirty or forty of them that we know of, and most of them cannot be read. The jungle moisture has destroyed the writing. I had heard that my sons had found one."

"So they'd sell it, right?" says Herman.

"Yes."

"How much they get?"

"If the one they have is legible, tens of thousands, perhaps a hundred thousand U.S. dollars. If what is on it is important, if it reveals unknown information about Mayan rulers, their civilization, it could be worth much more."

"And this ain't the Rosetta thing you was talking about?"

Ibarra shakes his head.

"That be worth more, right?"

"You cannot put a value on the Mejicano Roseton."

"Tell us about it?" I say.

"I take it you have never seen a picture of the Mayan codices?"

"Uh . . . ah . . ." Herman looks at him.

"They are books made of tree bark that has been flattened and covered with a lime paste, like the stelae. The pages are folded like an accordion and painted in vivid colors with hieroglyphs.

"There are only four of them known to be in existence. They are located in various museums around the world: Dresden, Madrid, Paris. One is in the hands of a private collector. They are the only remaining books of Mayan history written by the original scribes. All of the others were destroyed by Spanish missionaries. The books were believed by the Spaniards to be tools of the devil.

"A Franciscan missionary, his name was Diego de Landa, he burned hundreds of the Mayan books in the great auto-da-fé in 1562."

"What the fuck's a auto dafay?" says Herman

"The Inquisition. The Spaniards burned the books, along with the Mayan scribes who wrote them, so that the books could not be re-created."

"What's this got to do with this Rosetta thing?"

"I am getting to that. Before de Landa burned all of the Mayan books, about forty years earlier, a group of Spaniards were shipwrecked in the Caribbean off the coast of what is now Mexico. They were washed up on a beach on the Yucatán not far from here, and they were captured by the Mayas. All of them were put to death, except two. A man named Gonzalo Guerrero and a shipmate named Jerónimo de Aguilar. These two survived. They lived with the Maya in captivity for eight years, until the Conquistador Hernán Cortés, the man who conquered the Aztecs, heard about them and paid a ransom.

"De Aguilar went back and became the translator for Cortés. He became very important in the conquest of the Mayas."

"The other man, Guerrero, did not go back. He had married a daughter of one of the Mayan rulers and became a Mayan warlord."

"He went native," says Herman.

"Yes."

"And he taught the Mayas the battle tactics of the Spaniards. Leading a Mayan army, he defeated the Spaniards at a place called Cape Catoche. When the Spanish government learned of this, they wanted him dead."

"But what's this got to do with the Rosetta?"

"This man Guerrero lived and fought the Spaniards for twenty years until they killed him in 1536. They shot him with an harquebus, a kind of primitive musket. Guerrero knew that sooner or later the Spaniards would kill him. He also knew that they would destroy Mayan civilization as he knew it. So he had the scribes prepare a secret codex. A great Mayan book of hieroglyphs. This not only told their history and listed their rulers, but it also described the various city states that existed before the Spaniards came and how they interacted with one another.

"But the important part, what no one had ever done before, because they could not, was that Guerrero translated the hieroglyphs into Spanish. He included this translation as part of the codex."

"The Mexican Rosetta," I say.

"Yes. People have been able to work out a majority of the hieroglyphs, but they cannot be absolutely certain they are correct. And there are still twenty maybe thirty percent of the hieroglyphs that remain a mystery. These are the more complex and important ones. They may reveal things about the Mayas that have been lost and forgotten for centuries."

"You know a lot about this," says Herman. "Why?"

"I have been trying to purchase the Mejicano Roseton for three years. Without success. I have made a great deal of money constructing buildings and doing business. I wanted the Mejicano Roseton to remain in this country. It is part of its heritage."

"So who has it?" I ask.

He shakes his head. "For years it was believed to be in the possession of Indians in Chiapas. The Mexican government has been dealing with a kind of indigenous independence movement there for some time. About ten months ago, I was told that it had been sold, to raise money for arms and food. The Mexican Army was closing in on the Indians. They did not want it to fall into the hands of the government, where it would be put on display in Mexico City. So they sold it."

"And you don't know who bought it?" I ask.

"No. But I believe that my sons may have it."

"That don't make any sense," says Herman. "Why the note telling you to bring it?"

"Herman, let him finish."

"What note?" says Ibarra.

"Never mind. Go on."

"It is just that I found out that my sons were negotiating with this man Metz to deliver the Mejicano Roseton to an American buyer. According to the information I had, this buyer was represented by Mr. Rush."

"That's why you wrote the letter?"

"Yes. I wanted him to know that I knew what was going on. And that I intended to stop it."

Nick's only contact to the world of art and collectibles was through Dana. And the only one she knew with connections sufficient to peddle something on the scale of the Rosetta was Nathan Fittipaldi.

"But something of the scale of the Mexican Rosetta would be impossible to display in a museum. Even a private collector would have to hide it," I tell him.

"Private collectors, people who have that kind of money, often have private collections; they show a few trusted friends and keep it as a secret. There are those who would be willing to exercise patience, to hold it and wait. A museum might possibly take it."

"They'd never be able to exhibit it. The Mexican government would be all over them."

"Probably. But it would come down to a legal claim," says Ibarra. "The museum would probably say that the Rosetta had been in a storage crate for decades. I have heard that such things happen. It shows up as an indistinct item on an old bill of lading. The document may date to the nineteen twenties."

"Meaning that the item was found in an earlier expedition?"

"Exactly. Museums have warehouses filled with such items. They might not catalogue them for decades. Who is to say it wasn't there? They simply claim that they did not realize its significance until they opened the crate and examined its contents. Of course my government would demand its return. But it is unlikely that they would succeed. The Indians of Chiapas might complain and tell the world that they sold it only months before, but who is going to listen to them?"

"So you think your boys got it?" says Herman.

Ibarra shrugs his shoulders. "I believe it is a possibility."

"Maybe we should go down and ask 'em." Herman looks at me.

"The last time we went down there, we had three cars and six men with guns. This time it's just you and me."

"Yeah, but last time I wasn't motivated," says Herman. "Besides, people at that trailer look like they just crawled outta mud huts. The brothers wouldn't be able to trust 'em in the jungle with bullets. Their guns probably all rusted up."

"I don't know. The one they had pointed at the back of your head looked pretty good." I turn my attention back to Ibarra. "What do you know about a place called Cobá?"

"It's an archeological site. Very large, more than seventy kilometers square, I believe. Maybe two hours south of here, in the jungle. Why?"

"Does it draw a crowd, many tourists?" I ask.

"No. Very few in fact. Most of what is there remains to be discovered. It is still covered by jungle. They don't expect to uncover it all for perhaps another fifty years."

"That's why they picked it," says Herman.

"Who?"

"Your sons, if they're to be believed," says Herman.

"Have you ever been there, to Cobá?"

"Yes. Two or three times."

"Do you know a place there called the Doorway to the Temple of Inscriptions?"

He thinks about this for a moment. "The tourist literature, they give all kinds of names to these ruins to get the tourists excited. You know, get them thinking about men with whips and fedoras in leather jackets so they will visit."

"What else did the note say?" I look at Herman.

"Place had painted walls or something."

"Oh, you mean Las Pinturas. Yes, I know where that is. A stone structure with a small room on top. Inside of this room there are columns with painted hieroglyphs and inscriptions carved on the walls. They retain some of the dyes and stains put on by the Mayas."

"Could you take us there?"

"I suppose I could." He looks at Herman, probably thinking that a trip to Cobá is better than getting shot.

"You got any people can help us?" says Herman.

"What, to kill my sons?"

"No, no. They show up, I do that. Less you wanna help. I'm thinkin' maybe drive cars, play lookout. I mean somebody ain't gonna sit and stare at whipped cream on a camera all afternoon."

"I have people," says Ibarra.

"Yeah. Seen your people." Herman slips his pistol back into the fanny pack and drops it in the bag. "Still I suppose we better go back upstairs, wake up ladle-head. See if he figured how to undo his belt buckle yet."

CHAPTER THIRTY-TWO

We pull out of the parking lot at the glass pyramid just after four in the morning, nearly two hours before dawn.

Herman is scrunched up on a couch that runs the length of the passenger compartment along one side of Ibarra's stretch limo.

We left the black Suburban in a private area of the hotel's underground garage. The cops in Cancún and probably the Mexican Federal Judicial Police will be looking for the two Suburbans that are now missing from the scene of Julio's murder. Residents in the condo are sure to have seen the three vehicles parked there together.

In the front seat are Ibarra's driver and another man, not quite as large as Herman, broad shoulders and a steely look.

Behind us is another vehicle with four security men. Three other vehicles with security left the hotel a half hour ahead of us. We are slated to meet at a point along the highway, at which time I will transfer into one of the other cars and drive by myself to the parking area at Cobá.

Herman, Ibarra, and his people will approach the archeological site from a different direction along back roads. If all goes according to plan, they will be in place around the structure Ibarra calls Las Pinturas before I arrive. Some of his men are equipped with high-powered rifles and laser scopes to pick up heat signatures of people hiding in the bush. Ibarra has assured me that they are qualified marksmen.

We are unable to go to the police, since Pablo cannot be certain that his sons have not bribed some of the local authorities. Even if they haven't, it is likely that the police would hold me for questioning well past the time set in the note, in which case Ibarra's sons would kill Adam.

Sitting in the seat next to me, Pablo Ibarra tries to brief me on the terrain and what I will find when I get there. I can tell he is worried, a father on the verge of a violent collision with his sons, taking no joy in what he must do.

"I hope and pray that they are not there," he says. But I can tell that the note that was shoved under Herman's hotel room door, telling me to bring the Rosetta to Cobá, leaves little doubt in his mind.

"What I do not understand is why they think you would have it," he says.

"I don't know."

"Unless perhaps it is because of your association with this man Rush. Did my sons know about this?"

"I didn't tell them."

"None of it makes any sense."

When I told him about the aerial attack at the Casa Turquesa, Ibarra scanned early editions of the local newspapers. He was looking for the names of the two men in the ultralight to see if he might recognize them. The brothers used ultralights over the jungle to look for ruins. Divers pulled the two bodies from the water late yesterday. But Ibarra didn't recognize either name.

He has put together a package wrapped in cloth and tied with twine. Covered, it could pass for the Maya's ancient book unless you had specific knowledge of its dimensions, which we do not. Once its cover is removed, however, not even the untrained eye would be fooled by the two plywood boards with paper between them.

I try to catch some sleep as we roll along the highway that connects Merida, the old Spanish Colonial capital, with Cancún.

I doze. It seems like only a few minutes when I feel a bump and wake up. We are rolling slowly, maybe twenty miles an hour, through a village along the highway.

"What is it?"

"Nothing," says Ibarra. *"Topetóns.* Speed bumps. They put them on the highway coming into the villages so that people slow down."

We come to another one, more like a hill than a bump. The long limo is now forced to come to a near stop to keep from dragging its rear end or losing its suspension. Herman sleeps right through this. I look at my watch. I've been asleep for twenty minutes.

The road to Merida is two lanes, one in each direction. Even at this hour, before five A.M. there are a few people moving about in the small settlements off the highway. Lights are on in some of the tiny cinder-block houses with their corrugated metal roofs. I have seen buildings like this before, on the islands of the Caribbean. They are fashioned to withstand hurricanes and tidal surge. The walls will stand. You can find your roof later or pick up someone else's.

Except for the areas hacked out for human habitation, the low jungle engulfs everything within view. The even, verdant canopy is unbroken but for the occasional banyan tree that pokes through toward the sky and the indomitable microwave towers with their red lights blinking in the distance. To the east the faint glow of morning is already beginning to define the clouds.

"Do you have children?" says Ibarra.

"One. A daughter. She's fifteen."

"It is difficult."

"Yes." I have thought about Sarah and wondered what

she will be doing in a few hours. Mostly I have been wondering whether I will ever see her again.

To think I could unravel the reasons behind Nick's death was arrogant. To risk the security of the only family that Sarah has left was foolish beyond belief. If I were divorced perhaps, but I am not. I am widowed.

Harry was right, a single parent has no business doing what I am doing. And now it's too late. By my actions, I have placed others in jeopardy: Harry in the hospital and Adam now in the hands of Ibarra's sons. There is no turning back.

We turn off the highway at a place called Nuevo Xcan and head into the deep tropical forest. Here the road narrows, with vegetation nibbling at both edges of the asphalt. The road runs like a ribbon through jungle growth that becomes visibly more dense and taller with each kilometer.

The leafy green is impenetrable. It rises up like a wave in a sea of darkness on both sides of the car. We rocket along at seventy miles an hour, gliding over slight undulations only to find more road stretched out in front of us, a seemingly endless thoroughfare to nowhere.

The long springs of the limo lift us over a slight rise. On the highway ahead I see the taillights of two cars parked in the middle of the road blocking it.

"It's all right." Ibarra sitting forward in the seat. "It's my people."

The limo comes to a fast brake, the security car right on our bumper. Herman slides forward on the seat and finally wakes up.

"What's goin' on?"

"Time to switch cars," I tell him.

"Shit, we already there?"

"Not quite. How far is it?" I ask Ibarra.

"Just a few miles. You will turn off to the right. You can't miss the road. There should be a sign to the archeological zone."

The limo rolls to a stop behind the other two cars in the middle of the road, and we get out. The trailing security car pulls up behind us, and two men dressed in camouflage fatigues get out and stand near the open doors, surveying the road behind them and occasionally glancing into the jungle overgrowth alongside the road. One of them is holding an assault rifle.

Up in front, Ibarra's people are standing around on the road, two of them looking at a map spread out on the hood of one of the cars. The car doors are open, and some of the men are taking the chance to smoke a last cigarette before going in. They are wearing flak jackets, and two of them are holding scoped rifles.

Herman is walking next to me. "Rifles ain't gonna be much good in the jungle," he says. "Less they get an opening in the brush. I knew I shouldn't a listened to these people. I shoulda brought the shotgun, the MP-5."

"I think it'll be all right. They look like they know what they're doing."

"Yeah."

Ibarra waves me forward, toward one of the cars with an open door.

I start to walk.

"Hey."

I turn and Herman is looking at me.

"Ain't you gonna say good-bye?"

"I wish you were coming with me."

"I could get in the backseat, lie down," he says.

"Right. They wouldn't see that. Besides, I have to go a ways on foot. Their people would pick you up before you could follow me thirty feet."

"Probably. Here. You better put this on." He's holding a lightweight green jacket in his hand.

"I'm not cold."

"I know. Just trust me. Take it. White shirt you got on is gonna light you up like a lantern out there in the jungle."

I take the jacket and slip it on.

Herman zips it up, almost jerking me off my feet, pats the collar down, paws like a bear. "You don't wanna give 'em nothing makes a target on your chest."

"Right."

"There's a little something for ya in the pocket," he says. I reach in.

"Other side."

I dig it out. It's a small gun-metal blue semiautomatic pistol.

"My backup piece. Figure you're gonna need it more than me. Walther PPK .380. Six shots, so don't get carried away. And don't go shootin' at nothin' beyond ten, twelve feet. Waste of time, besides you just draw attention to yourself. Little switch on the side. You hit it, it turns red side out. Then it's hot."

He takes it, checks the clip, slaps the back against his hand, making sure the bullets are properly seated.

"What if they frisk me?"

"They won't."

"How can you be sure?"

"They won't let you get that close. What they want, you gonna be carryin'. That book. My guess is, they just gonna shoot you and take it."

"Why?"

"Trust me. Your friend, he's probably already dead."

"We don't know that."

"No. But I got a feelin' something ain't right. You take this." He hands the gun back to me. "Use it if you have to."

I slip it back inside the jacket pocket. I hear Ibarra calling to me. "They're waiting. Gotta go." I hold out my hand to shake his.

"Shit I don't want that." Instead he reaches out, grabs me by the shoulders, and gives me a hug, an embrace like a grizzly.

"You take care," he says. "You still be in one piece when this is over. You understand?"

"I'll do my best."

"Shit, you gonna have to do better than that," he says.

We both laugh.

"See ya."

"Take care," I answer.

I turn and head for the car.

When I get there, Ibarra has the mock Rosetta under his arm. He places it across the front seat on the passenger side.

The keys are in the car.

"There is one last thing," he says. "Do you have a scrap of paper, anything small, something to write on?" He has a pen in his hand.

I fish through my pants pockets and come up with two wrinkled and tattered scraps of pink paper. I give one of them to Ibarra.

He flattens it out on the hood of the car, turns it over to the blank side, and starts drawing, small fine lines. "When you drive in, you pass the restaurant. A white building with a flat roof. You turn left into the parking area. The visitor's entrance is here." He puts an X on the map. "There are some large trees. There will probably be a rope across there. You just go under it.

"Once you are inside, you will have to be careful or you will get lost. It is like a maze. There are many paths, some of them going off into the jungle."

He draws my attention back to the diagram. "You will walk maybe a hundred meters from the entrance and the path goes to the right. You stay on it," he says. "A little ways beyond that, you will see some ruins called La Iglesia, it means church." He marks it on the map. "There will be stone platforms at different levels in front of it and stairs going up. You pass through the plaza. You will see buried ruins all around you. Here you go left, go maybe fifteen, twenty meters, and on your right you will see the opening to the ball court. It is a flat, open area, long and narrow with slanting walls of stone on each side. There is a stone hoop sticking up out of the walls. You pass through the ball court, and you will come to an area where there are bicycles parked." He circles it on the little map. "Tourists rent them to ride the paths. Don't take one. Just walk, otherwise you will get there too quickly. We won't be in place. When you get to the bicycles, there will be paths going in different directions. Three, maybe four." He draws these with the pen. "You must take the path that goes to your right." He points with the tip of the pen to the junction. "That will take you to Las Pinturas. It is maybe three or four hundred meters. You will see the ruins, a small pyramid with a square stone structure on top. There are palm leaves over the roof of the structure. You can't miss it. Do you understand?"

"I think so."

"Here, you take this." He hands me the slip of paper, then I climb into the car behind the wheel and roll the window down.

"What time have you got?" he says.

We check our watches.

"You have plenty of time. Remember," he says, "you give us at least ten minutes head start before you leave from here."

"Got it."

He closes the door. "We will be there," he says. "Good luck." Then he turns and runs back to the other cars.

Car doors slam one after the other. Then the tires of the two sedans and the limo grind gravel, racing by me on the road heading west.

Within seconds, their taillights disappear around a curve.

I sit with the window down, listening to the sounds of dawn in the jungle, the chirping and screeching of some distant animal, the humming wings and clicking of insects.

I take another look at the little map on the pink paper, fold it in half, and slip it into the pocket of my jacket. I give them twelve minutes just to be safe.

Three miles up the road, I see the sign with an arrow pointing to a turnoff, white letters on a blue background: Villas Arqueologicas Cobá.

I take the turn to the right. After a few miles, the road turns to dirt, and moments later I see the restaurant, a two-story building with a flat roof and a second-story veranda. Jutting out from under the railing on the veranda is a slanting palm-covered roof sheltering outdoor tables and chairs.

Straight ahead is a large body of water, a lake, with high grass along the edges. Ibarra has warned me, if I have to move quickly into the jungle, to try and stay clear of any

wetlands. Mexican crocodiles may be an endangered
species, but they have been known to eat dogs and small
children and, on a rare occasion, tourists.

The road curves left in front of the hotel, and a few hundred feet up I pull into the parking area. It is flanked by a few
small structures, mostly stucco, small curio shops, and next
to it a small square building with a palm-thatched roof, the
ticket booth at the entrance.

Beyond this, a path leads in to the archeological area. It
passes between two large trees, curling bark hanging from
gnarled trunks that look as if they might have been standing
when the last Mayan ruler walked between them and turned
out the lights. There is a rope suspended between them.

I pull up and park in front, turn off the engine, and check
my watch. I have twenty minutes to get to the area around
the Las Pinturas. By now Ibarra and his people should be
getting close, checking for Arturo's men hiding in the bush
and taking up positions on them.

I pick up the wrapped package from the seat, get out and
head toward the entrance, quickly slip under the rope, and
head up the path.

The walkway is uneven. Ruts in the sandy soil, crossed
by ridges from shallow-rooted trees, force me to watch my
step. What little light there is at this hour is filtered through
the foliage overhead.

I pass a display under a thatched roof to my right and
climb a small rise. Then the path heads down, a gradual
slope, and goes to the right. On either side of the path are
symmetrical mounds, gentle rises with small stunted trees
and saplings growing out of them, sending up shoots like
hair on a beast. These are busy laying down more shallow
roots, some of them winding like snakes into the crevices of
rock outcroppings.

Under the trees and on the sides of the mounds, the
ground is littered with stones, their edges rounded by ero-
sion, their shapes too balanced to be formed by nature.
Everywhere I look, I can see small hills, bumps in the jungle, Mayan ruins still buried.

Thirty feet on, I come to an opening, the plaza, what Ibarra called La Iglesia. It is a large pyramid with several terraced levels in front and steep crumbling steps leading to the top. As a tourist attraction in the U.S., it would be a lawyer's dream.

I pass through the plaza and go left. Suddenly I'm lost.

I stop and find the pink paper diagram in my pocket and peer at it in the dim light. Ibarra has written the words "ball court" in tiny letters.

I turn slowly, a one-hundred-and-eighty-degree pirouette. Then in front of me, against the sharp edges of stone, I see the silhouette of a curving shape in the distance. It is a stone hoop on the diagonal wall of the ball court.

I check my watch, pick up the pace, and jog through the court, an amphitheater of smooth stone on each side.

Sixty yards on, through the dim light the path levels out and opens into a wide area under a grove of larger trees. I see twenty or more bicycles parked here, some of them leaning against the trees and others lying on their side, a few of them upright with kickstands down.

So far everything on Ibarra's little diagram is accurate. I keep walking and shift the package under my arm to the other side. As I do this, I rub the fabric over my jacket pocket and feel the hard edges of the pistol inside.

I am hoping that I won't need it. Still the heft from the metal tugging at my pocket offers the possibility that I can defend myself if I have to.

"Señor."

CHAPTER THIRTY-THREE

The voice coming from behind stops me dead in my tracks. My heart pounding; if he doesn't shoot me first, I will still lose half a year of life.

In the dim light I turn, no time to reach for the pistol in my pocket. Half lost in the shadows behind a tree, I can see the slight figure of a man sitting on what appears to be a large tricycle. It has two wheels in front with a small seat over them and a single wheel in back.

He pedals out of the shadows. His eyes seem to be riveted not on me as much as the cloth-covered package I am carrying under my arm. He gestures with a hand toward the seat in front of him, an invitation for me to get on.

I shake my head. "No thanks." I start to turn.

"Señor." This time he is more insistent. The message is clear. There is a reason he is here at this early hour. He has been sent to collect me.

He is wearing a thin cotton shirt and jeans, worn running shoes, sockless where I can see his brown ankle above the foot resting on one of the pedals.

If he is armed, he has hasn't shown it, and there are no bulges in his clothing. Ibarra warned me not to take a bike to the site. But by now he and his men should have had plenty of time to get in position.

I could simply turn and walk away, take my chances. But from the look in his eye, I suspect he would follow me, clattering along behind on the bike like a cowbell telling everyone in the bush where I was. No doubt they have paid him for the ride, probably more than he makes in a week pedaling tourists through the jungle. Now he feels compelled to perform the service.

"Why not?" I step toward the contraption.

He nods and smiles, gesturing toward the seat as I climb up and sit down.

I hold the package in my lap as he pedals through the clearing, picking up speed on the slight downgrade, then takes one of the paths to the right, stands up, and his legs begin pumping in earnest.

We bounce along the trail, level as a tabletop, not quite as smooth, listening to the balloon tires as they crunch over the decomposed limestone. The tricycle splashes through a puddle of standing water, and one of the tires sprays muddy water up onto the seat. I try to shield it with an arm but too late.

He laughs and says something in Spanish, but I don't understand him.

"Just a second. Hold on a second."

He continues pedaling.

"Stop." What's the word? *"Pare."*

"Qué?"

"Pare."

"Sí."

Slowly he brings the bike to a halt as I feel through my jacket pocket for the slip of paper with Ibarra's diagram. I unfold it and try to make out the squiggles and lines in the dim light. Then I see the words "far right."

"We went the wrong way."

"Qué?"

"We took a wrong turn. Back there." I wave with my arm back over his shoulder. "We were supposed to go to the right. The far right." My voice projects volume to compensate for the lack of language skills. I turn all the way around on the seat and point back over his shoulder. "The other way," I tell him.

"Donde?"

"There."

"No," he says. *"Por aquí,"* and he points down the path in front of us.

"The Door to the Temple of the Inscriptions is that way," I tell him.

"No." He shakes his head, stands up, and starts pedaling again. *"Por aquí."*

"Stop."

He ignores me.

I try to step off, but he picks up speed so that one foot drags on the ground.

"Señor." His voice is harsh now, angry.

I look back over my shoulder and he shakes his head at me. *"Por aquí."* He nods in the direction we are going.

I get the message. He's saying it's this way. Whoever has sent him has given him precise instructions. I could drag both feet, stop the bike, and get off. Use the pistol to get rid of him if I have to. But then I would never find Adam. They would kill him, if they haven't already. Of course they will kill both of us the minute they open the package and see what's in it. Ibarra's plan was never to allow them to get that close. I was to see Adam. Have them bring him into the open. One of their marksmen would take out whoever was holding him, and at that same instant I was to throw the package into the underbrush and follow it.

In the confusion, Ibarra's men wearing flak vests were to grab Adam and pull him behind cover.

Now I grind my teeth as we ride. The only certain security is the tiny Walther in my pocket. Each turn of the wheels puts more distance between Pablo Ibarra's men and me. Herman was right. Whoever planned this planned it well.

. I look down at the pink scrap of paper folded over in my hand. It's one of the telephone slips Harry brought down from the office. On the form-printed side is the message. I recognize Marta's handwriting.

It's strange how in moments of crisis, familiar things offer the illusion of comfort.

I'm rumbling through the jungle on a three-wheeled bike, sitting in front of a crazy Mexican who is probably delivering me to my death, and all I can think about is Joyce Swartz, the name on the line. I can hear Joyce's raspy voice over the phone, the muddle of her words, the cigarette dangling from her lips as she talks.

I stare at the slip in a daze, reading words, unable to decipher the message as the vibration of the bike shivers my vision and rattles my teeth.

Suddenly the rhythm of the wheels begins to slow as he stops pedaling and coasts. I look up and we roll to a stop in the middle of nowhere. The white limestone stand of the path narrows into the distance ahead, then disappears around a curve. He has covered at least a mile, maybe more, from where the bikes were parked. Now he motions for me to get off.

"Where? *Donde?*"

"*Aquí.*"

"Where am I supposed to go?"

"*Aquí.*"

"Here. You want me to stay here?"

"*Aquí.*" Then he motions down the path with one arm, as if he's waving me away.

I pick up the package and step off the bike.

He swings it around in a wide arc, turns, and heads back.

I stand in the middle of the path, watching him until I can no longer hear the rattle of metal. I lose him as the bike recedes into the distance, swallowed by the edges of jungle as the path disappears.

I turn and look the other way. There is nothing but a narrow strip of white in both directions, like a single thread running through a cloth of green. The man on the bike pointed in that direction, so I begin to walk, staying along one edge of the path near the underbrush to make myself no more of a target than necessary.

Tucked under one arm is the package. Suddenly I stop and look around. Every bush and tree along the path looks like every other one. Still it's better than delivering a package of empty hopes to men with guns.

I break a branch from one of the bushes to mark the spot, and then I set the package behind an outcropping of stones a few feet off the road. Its absence and my knowledge of its location give me something to bargain with, if only to kill time in hopes of finding an opening. If they don't see it on me and they're smart, they won't shoot me at least until we talk.

I step back out to the path, still carrying the little slip of paper in one hand. There's no way to tell the distance to the spot where Pablo Ibarra's men are waiting since the diagram conforms to no scale. Besides, having ridden through curves and around bends on the front of the bike, I have no sense of direction.

I'm about to ball up the note and toss it into the brush when my eye catches a word on the other side. The word "Capri." Without the jarring motion of the bike I read the cryptic message written by Marta and handed to Harry, along with other messages, in an envelope.

"Joyce says Jamaile owned one piece of property. The land under the old Capri Hotel."

I stand there for a moment, my eyes on the slip of paper, weary, unable to focus. I start to walk slowly down the path, thinking Nick owned Jamaile and Jamaile owned the Capri, the greasy spoon downtown where we had coffee that morning.

I look up and step a little closer to the bushes on one side as I walk. What does it mean? None of it makes any sense. If Nick owned a chunk of land downtown, why didn't Dana know about it, or Margaret in the divorce? Nick was broke. What was he doing looking at empty offices in San Francisco and New York, dealing with Metz and the Ibarra broth-

ers to broker a piece of history worth millions? Certainly he
would get a fee, but . . .

Suddenly I stop. My heart skips. I turn and start to walk
quickly in the other direction. A few steps and I start to run,
looking back over my shoulder, headlong down the path.

The broken branch pointing the way to the package is just
ahead, when he steps out from the green foliage on the other
side of the path ten feet in front of me. Adam is holding a
pistol pointed at me.

"Where are you going in such a rush?"

I stop, look at him breathing heavily, then bend and put
my hands on my knees to catch my breath.

"And here I thought you were coming to save me," he
says.

"You killed them. Nick, Metz, Espinoza, Julio."

"No. No. There you go, jumping to conclusions. Actually
I didn't have anything to do with Espinoza. I didn't even
know about him until you told me. In fact the sheer volume
of things I didn't know overwhelms me.

"And as for Nick and Metz, I didn't pull the trigger if it
makes you feel any better. Though you could say I did set
matters in motion. Some people out of Tijuana actually. The
world has become an awful place. For enough money they
don't even want to know who you are. I have to say they did
a better job than the two idiots in the airplane. I didn't like
that whole idea, but they insisted. By the way, if you don't
mind my asking, how's Harry?"

"He's going to be fine."

"I see. That could be a problem. You see, I couldn't be
sure how much he knew, so I thought it would be best if he
were invited to join us.

"You actually came here thinking you were going to meet
the two brothers. I must say I did a bang-up job in a short
period of time. You like the outfit?" His clothes are covered
in dirt, one knee is torn out of his pants, and there's a bruise
on the side of his face.

"All part of the preparations," he says. "You can imagine
my panic when Harry dropped that bit about Nick's hand-

held computer over dinner. We probably would all be getting on the plane about now, flying back to San Diego if I hadn't heard that."

"Why?"

"Why don't you turn around get down on your knees? Now," he says.

I do it.

"That's it. Now put your hands out in front of you on the ground and lie down. Spread your arms and your legs and don't move. That's good."

Adam steps forward, presses the muzzle of the pistol into the small of my back, and starts patting me down.

"Hell, I couldn't be sure what was in Nick's little computer. And you kept keeping secrets from me."

He feels along my side, the small of my back, then the other side. "God knows what other little morsels you know that I don't. It wouldn't do to get us all home and have the police suddenly find some piece left behind by Nick that sends their magnetic dial pointing in my direction."

He feels up and down both legs and then steps back. "You can get up now."

I get to my feet.

"Tell me, is that the thing over there? This Mejicano Rosen. I saw you put the package behind the rocks and break the branch. I was going to follow you, and then I heard you coming back."

"Why don't you look?"

"I don't think so. You're a little too anxious. What is it, tear gas? Something to stun whoever opens it? Don't tell me Pablo Ibarra actually had the stuff?"

"Actually no."

"I'm dying to know. What is it? I don't mean the package. I mean this Rosen thing?"

"You don't know?"

"I don't have the foggiest."

"Then why did you write the note telling me to bring it?"

"I had to have some reason to get you here. I mean it would have looked a little funny if I'd sent a note from the brothers just telling you to come here and pick up Mr. Tolt. But I have to say curiosity is killing me. Why don't we walk while we talk," he says. "It's not far. Besides it puts a little more distance between us and anybody you might have brought along. You did bring someone along?"

I don't answer him. We start down the path, Adam behind me with the pistol six or seven feet, judging by the sound of his voice.

"So this Rosen thing. Something Nick wanted?"

"It looks that way."

"What?"

"An ancient text of the Mayan language."

He laughs. "You have to be kidding. Nick? What was he going to do with it, sell it?"

"Actually he was going to trade it."

"For what?"

"For a height variance on a piece of real estate he owned."

"What are you talking about?"

"It's a long story."

"Yeah and I'm afraid you don't have that much time."

We walk for several minutes until we come to a clearing in the jungle dominated by a huge mound of stone, a pyramid eroded on the edges by time and weather. Facing us is a steep set of stairs rising all the way to the top, capped by what appears to be a small stone structure.

"I hope you brought your climbing shoes. Go on."

We cross the clearing and I start up the steps. They are steep and there is nothing small about them. Most have a rise of two feet or more and a narrow tread, with nothing to hang onto except the steps above.

Leaning forward, we climb hand over hand. I have my hands on the stairs two or three above where my feet are. Adam manages to keep his gun hand free, with the muzzle pointed at me. For someone in his sixties, he has amazing dexterity.

The humidity off the jungle floor is beginning to heat up as the sun rises. It is light now, and as we climb I can see the top of the jungle canopy laid out like a green blanket all around us with mauve-colored peaks jutting through it in several places, the remnants of Mayan architecture stripped of their jungle cover.

"So what's it going to be, a shot to the back of the head like Julio, or will it be an accident this time?"

"I thought we could decide that when we get to the top."

"That's a little dicey, isn't it? When they find my body, either with a bullet in it or at the bottom, and you up at the top, the Mexican authorities may be asking you some pointed questions."

"Of course they will. And I'll have all the answers. How the Ibarra brothers held me hostage, without food and water. You like my costume? How they beat me, trying to find out about this Rosen thing. The fact that I knew nothing about it. After they shot you, or you went off the edge depending on how you want to do it, seeing as I'm flexible, the brothers, or more likely their hired guns, panicked and left me up there. It's a harrowing story," he says. "Of course, blindfolded I wasn't able to see a thing. I've taken the liberty. The blindfold's in my pocket, along with a little duct tape for my hands and feet. I don't even have to tie any knots, just rub a little dirt into the tape and twist my wrists a bit like I've been struggling to get free. I think that should satisfy them."

Adam's got it all figured.

"Did you know it's the highest Mayan pyramid on the Yucatán Peninsula?"

"I'm honored."

"Actually if you look over there." He gestures with the pistol. "Just off the stairs to your right, it's more of a cliff."

"I can see that."

"I thought that would be a good place for us. They call this the Nohoch Mul. The big mound. According to the book, it's a hundred and thirty-six feet high. Twelve stories. One hundred and twenty steps."

"Maybe we could start over and I could count them."

"I don't think so. Just keep going."

Tolt constantly maintains his distance, always two or

three large stone steps below me, just out of kicking distance.

"I assume you brought help? Let me guess, Herman?"

I nod.

He laughs. "That man is an absolute pain in the ass. Always smiling through that damn chipped tooth. Though I have to admit he did give me the idea for disarming Julio."

"Herman's pretty upset about that."

"Yeah I suppose they were pretty close."

"Why did you have to kill him?"

"I had to have something to demonstrate the violence of these people, their desperation in dealing with you."

"Shooting up the hotel pool wasn't enough?"

"Well, they weren't just going to snatch me and leave my bodyguards, were they?"

"What did you do with the rest of Julio's people?"

"I made an executive decision. I called Julio that morning, before you and Harry got up, and told him that I wanted him to go up to the condo and to stay there until I came up. When I left the pool later in the morning to make my urgent phone call, I grabbed his man in the lobby and we both took a cab up to the condo. I'd already trashed my room before I came down. At the condo, I told Julio to send the rest of his men back to Mexico City, that we wouldn't be needing them. Of course, he was happy to comply. He figured the job was over."

He stops for a second, wipes his brow with the bottom of his shirt. "It's getting warm. Anyway they packed their bags and ten minutes later Julio's people were gone. I told Julio to take me back to the hotel. He got in the front seat. I got in the back, and I asked him for his gun."

"Just like that?"

"No. I told him I didn't want any more gunplay of the kind that Herman had engaged in the day before when he damn near got us shot. Pulling his pistol out like that was stupid. Julio agreed. The fact was, he was still stinging from the ass-chewing I'd given him in the car the day before. He just handed it over. It's the thing about authority. Most people never question it."

"Except people like Nick, is that it?"

"Well, I didn't spend thirty years building the firm to have Nick Rush come along and tear the whole thing apart. He was out talking to my partners, making them offers, telling them he was going to come up with cash to capitalize a new firm with offices in every city. What would you do?"

"I wouldn't have killed him."

"Well, you're younger than I am. You have some years ahead of you yet. I wasn't looking forward to a solo practice or sitting on a porch somewhere in a rocking chair. I had a name, a reputation. I'd built something. People in politics, entertainment, business, the people who count, they know the name of Adam Tolt."

"Is that it? Your identity was caught up in it?"

"Damn right. After all is said and done, what else have we got?"

Adam's life was the firm. He knew that without it people wouldn't return his phone calls, blue ribbon committees wouldn't ask him to serve, politicians wouldn't go out of their way to cross a crowded room to shake his hand. And to Adam those were the things that made life worth living, that and the private jet and high-rise corner office overlooking the bay. People have killed for a lot less.

"Who else came along besides Herman? Don't tell me it's just the two of you?"

"A few others."

"I knew you would bring backup." We're getting near the top. He stops to take a breather, so I stop too. "No, no, you just keep moving. I'll be right behind you."

He takes off his hat and wipes his brow with the brim. "Of course, they would all be slinking around in the bushes about a half mile from here. Over there, I think." He glances off to his left, keeping the gun pointed at me.

"Yeah, if you look you can see it. Get up there a little ways ahead, I'll let you take a look. That's it." He shuffles to his right, so that I remain in his line of sight as he looks over his left shoulder.

"See that little building poking up through the jungle? What was the name again, something about a door?"

"The Doorway to the Temple of Inscriptions."

"That's it. I think that's it. Coming by the trails on foot, it would take them at least ten, fifteen minutes to get here. By then, I'm gonna be long gone. I'll bet they briefed you on that area until you knew every pebble on the ground."

I don't answer him.

"It took me a while, digging around in a bookstore after I shot Julio, to find a map of this place with names of the ruins so I'd know where to send them while I dealt with you."

"That was a nice touch, Adam."

"I thought so." We continue climbing. "One thing I do need to know," he says. "Where exactly is Nick's little hand-held?"

"You don't really expect me to tell you?"

"I suppose I could look for it myself. You said it was in your office last time we talked. Which reminds me, how much does Harry know about all this?"

"Nothing. Harry doesn't know a thing."

"Now, you know that's not true. He knew about the hand-held. I wish I could believe you, but you're just a constant disappointment. This is getting entirely too violent. Still I suppose people do die of infections and accidents in hospitals."

I reach the top of the pyramid.

Adam stops on the steps below me.

My body is covered in sweat. Breathing through my mouth, my throat is parched. The sun is now hitting us on an angle out of the eastern sky, beginning to heat the stones, reflecting off the rock around us. Through the canopy from the jungle floor, steam clouds drift up like inverted cones of smoke.

In front of me centered on the top platform is a rectangular stone structure with a single door. The interior is lost in shadows. Carved into the exterior near the top of the corner stones at the level of the roof are two human figures suspended upside down.

"Step over there."

I look at Adam. He gestures with the gun, toward my left as I face him. He is breathing heavily, sweat dripping from his chin, his shirt soaked through.

Ten or twelve feet away, the stairs disappear and it's a sheer drop with a small ledge about halfway down.

I move toward it.

Adam approaches. He keeps one eye on me, along with the pistol, while he looks over the edge, surveying to see if the fall is going to be enough. Then he looks back and smiles at me. Apparently he's satisfied.

"Now if you'll just step over this way."

"You don't expect me to just jump off?"

"Don't worry, I'll help you."

As the words clear his lips, there is a tinny sound of metal clattering somewhere below us. Adam takes a quick step around to put me between himself and the sound.

I see a bicycle rattling over the uneven ground as it enters the clearing from the path. The figure riding it appears to have his knees hitting him in the chin with each pump of the pedals.

He stops in the middle of the clearing, puts his feet down on both sides, sitting on the seat, the bicycle dwarfed beneath him, and looks up at the top of the pyramid.

"Dat you, Adam Tolt?" Herman shades his eyes with one hand. "You know I figured you for a son of a bitch. But you outdid yourself. And so you know, Julio didn't think much a ya either. And I'm certain his opinion ain't come up none since you shot him in the back of the head."

"You try and come here, and I'll kill him." Adam puts the pistol up to my head.

"You know," says Herman. His hands now on his hips, still sitting on the bike. "That thing's not gonna do you a god damn bit a good against me down here. You see, I know Julio's Glock don't shoot for shit. You'd been more than a foot away from him, youda missed the back a his head. Kept tellin' him to get the sights fixed."

"Well I'm not likely to miss Mr. Madriani here."

"Yeah but I got a question for you. After you shoot him, how you gonna get down here without coming through me? My forty-five shoots a little better than that piece a shit, and the bullet's bigger to boot."

"He doesn't seem to put much value on your life," says Adam.

"Well, I warned you that he was pissed about Julio."

"So what are we going to do about this problem?"

"It's not my problem," I say.

"It won't be if you're dead. Tell him to go or I'll kill you."

"He says to go or he's gonna kill me," I say.

"Don't change his situation none. Few minutes Ibarra's people gonna be here with rifles. Then they gonna start bouncing bullets off the rocks up there. And it's gonna get mighty hot. Don't suspect you brought any water witcha?"

"No, we didn't think about it."

Adam presses the gun against my head. "Shut up."

"It sounds like it's your move."

"Let me think."

"You could let me go."

"That son of a bitch is just crazy enough to try to kill me anyway. You said it. He's angry over Julio. I shoulda shot him instead."

"Well we all make our mistakes. And I should warn you. Herman's confidence in the Mexican justice system is just a little higher than his respect for the modern American version."

"Meaning what?"

"He's probably gonna shoot you."

"I'm getting tired waitin' down here. You want I shoot a couple a rounds your way? Maybe I get lucky," says Herman. "And the noise is gonna bring Ibarra that much faster. Or maybe I just come up there and kick your ass, throw you off that fuckin' thing." Herman gets off the bike, drops it on the ground, and starts marching this way.

"What's he doing?" says Adam.

"I don't know."

"You tell him to stop, or so help me I will shoot you here and now."

"Herman. Stay there. Don't come up."

Herman doesn't listen. He just keeps coming, talking to himself, muttering under his breath. I can hear him all the way down at the bottom of the steps. He starts climbing, taking the two-foot steps in stride like they were built for him.

"Herman, *stay there*."

He keeps coming.

"Crazy son of a bitch," says Adam. He points the gun at him, takes aim.

I hit his arm with my shoulder just as he pulls the trigger. The snap of the round, the explosion next to my ear, sends a ringing vibration through my head.

A thousand birds lift out of the jungle. Flitting black specks like bugs on a windshield, they fill the sky.

Herman stops on the stairs and looks up. "Now you fuckin' did it." Herman unholsters his automatic, the sun glinting off the polished stainless steel.

Adam tries to push me over the edge. I push back, the rubber soles of my shoes gripping the stone, my toes right at the edge. He tries to twist for leverage, one arm around my neck. We struggle at the edge of the stone precipice.

I slip his grip and end up landing on my butt on the hard stone platform behind him.

Adam points the pistol at me, and then out of the corner of his eye he sees Herman still coming, charging up the stairs. Adam turns and aims, both hands this time on the Glock, taking a careful bead on Herman's bulk now only ten or twelve steps from the top. He fires, and I hear the bullet as it hits flesh.

Herman stops, looks down, puts his hand to his chest, and staggers. Then he looks at Adam and starts coming again.

I reach for the pistol in my pocket, and it snags on my jacket.

Adam aims and fires again. I hear the same thud as the bullet hits home. This time Herman goes down on one knee. He drops his pistol and it clatters down several steps. I can see Herman's face pumped with blood, the veins bulging on his neck. He's holding his side with one hand.

The small Walther is out of my pocket. I pull the slide and cycle a round into the chamber, aim at Adam, and squeeze. Nothing.

The safety is on. I bring it back, fumble with the tiny lever, click, and it shows red.

Adam has the Glock up, taking careful aim at Herman's back as he struggles to reach for his pistol on the stairs.

I squeeze off a round. The little Walther torques in my hand and the bullet catches Adam in the arm, jerking his body just as he pulls the trigger. His shot goes wide.

He turns and looks at me, his eyes like two eggs sunny-side up in a platter, wondering where I got the gun. Adam missed it when he frisked me. The small pistol was underneath, inside the pocket of my zippered jacket as I lay on the ground. He failed to check the front when I got up.

He has the Glock lowered at his side, the muzzle pointed down at the stone as he stares in disbelief at the gun in my hand.

If he raises the Glock, Adam knows I will shoot him again. Instead he looks at me, smiles, then shakes his head as if he is daring me to do it. He turns toward the motion on the stairs.

Herman is reaching for the automatic.

Adam takes aim.

This time, with the crack of the Walther, it barely moves in my hand. Tolt's head snaps sideways as a tiny red dot appears on his temple, followed by blood like someone tapped a barrel. His knees buckle. His ass hits the stone. For an instant his torso sits upright. Then gravity takes it sideways. When I blink he is gone, over the edge of the platform.

Harry is out of the hospital, his memory and faculties intact, and Herman is in.

Surgeons removed one bullet that lodged in the muscle of Herman's chest, up high near his clavicle. The other passed through his side, piercing what Herman called one of his love handles. He is talking about decorating it with a diamond stud, a conversation piece for the ladies that he can flash above his trunks whenever he struts the beach.

As for Adam, a Mexican medical examiner picked up pieces of him with a sponge from a rock outcropping five stories below the top of the Noche Mul. I suppose you could say that Adam was a victim of his own management style.

Adam had wounded Nick's ego in ways he probably never understood. Some lawyers, unhappy in their position at a firm, might take a client or two, like candy from a dish, on their way out the door. But not Nick. He wanted it all, right down to the gold ashtrays and Persian carpets.

Nick was making a run, trying to peel off partners like a monkey stripping fruit from a tree. His plan was not only to

take the best part of Rocker, Dusha's talent, but as many of
the firm's major clients as he could scoop up in a single
pass, swinging from the branches. A new firm with his own
name on the letterhead's top line.

Like every palace coup in the making, this one could ruin
careers if those on the move were caught in the act. The
other players, some of the partners upstairs, key people in the
other offices, stayed in the shadows while Nick set the mu-
nitions at Rocker, Dusha for self-destruct.

Adam's obsession with empire, his constant expansion
onto turf for more offices, was cutting into his partners' take-
home. These were fertile grounds of discontent for Nick. He
planted the age-old seed of every revolution: Nick offered
them a better deal.

When he was killed in what looked like an accident, a
drive-by aimed at a client, there must have been some damp
carpets in the firm's executive suites—and it wasn't from
crying. The people involved in his coup had to wonder what
careless notes Nick might have left behind.

He was the one taking all the chances. Of course, he had
nothing to lose and the most to gain, the kind of odds Nick
would like—managing partner, overnight, in one of the
largest firms in the state. It was the kind of edgy action that
would give a normal person peptic ulcers. To Nick it was the
etching acid of independence, the stuff of which new be-
ginnings are made. Revolution in a banana republic.

What he needed to pull it off was a source of ready cash.
Partners in an established firm don't jump ship en masse, unless somebody with a healthy line of credit is standing ready
to bankroll the new venture. It was one thing to move to a
new office. It was another to give up your Lexus.

Where was Nick going to get that kind of money? Actually, he told me, that morning over coffee, but I wasn't listening. It was one of Nick's character flaws, unfortunately
not his worst: the irresistible compulsion, if not to crow, at
least to hint of victories, before they were won.

The money would come from the old Capri Hotel itself,

Nick's watering hole with its coffee shop in the dismal basement where he and I had our last conversation.

The hastily formed limited partnership, the seemingly
defunct Jamaile Enterprises had only one asset. It owned
the property on which the hotel sat.

All the pieces snapped together like a puzzle. Nick had
leveraged the purchase of the hotel with a multi-million-
dollar mortgage. He would have amortized this over a
short term. He didn't plan on holding the property for
long. It was where all of Nick's money went, the hefty fees
he was taking home from the firm, the money Dana was
no longer seeing to pay for the house and the car, to support her in the style to which she had become accustomed.
Nick was busy plowing all of it into servicing the debt on
the mortgage for the rundown hotel, meeting the payments
each month like a miser, while he plotted revolution.

How do you maximize an investment like that? Nick re-
vealed that as well. But again, I was tuned out.

It was easy. First you buy the land. Then you get a variance to build above the current height restrictions. Suddenly
the land was worth three or four times what you paid for it.
Nick had it all figured. There was nothing to prevent him
from going higher, except the whim of local government.

And who had the power to grant such a variance? The
joint powers of authority, the same authority that controlled
most commercial property downtown: the super-zoning
kingdom chaired by Zane Tresler.

It was why Nick's name showed up so prominently on
Tresler's list of campaign donors. Not because Nick thought
he could buy the man. Tresler wasn't for sale, at least not for
money. Adam was right about that. Nick gave generously for
one reason only, to get Tresler's attention, to buy access.
The closer on this deal would come later, after the Mexicans,
the two Ibarra brothers, delivered on their part.

That was where Metz came in. His name on the limited
partnership documents, coupled with the mortgage on the
hotel property in the name of Jamaile, was a critical part of

Nick's plan, one that he couldn't have been comfortable with, but over which he had no control.

I could never figure how a streetwise lawyer like Nick could be so slow as to do business on paper with a client who turned up a player in a criminal probe. What I didn't realize is this: Metz's name on the partnership was the required security the Mexicans demanded before they performed their part.

The Ibarra brothers had done business with Metz before. They trusted him. For a decade, they had been looting archeological sites in the Yucatán, southern Mexico and Guatemala, selling their finds to rich gringos and posh galleries in Europe and the U.S.

It was why they needed the stolen visas found by the feds in Espinoza's closet when they searched his apartment. These would be valuable in bringing carloads of artifacts across the border.

Metz provided a convenient cover with his construction company. He also offered an outlet for laundering money. This is what the feds turned up, thinking they had drugs. Looting ancient sites was beginning to pay better than narcotics—and with less risk. Even if you got caught, you generally didn't do life in a penitentiary for stealing someone else's cultural heritage.

Under Nick's scheme, Metz would take a chunk from the profits of the Capri property once the variance was granted and the land was sold to some got-rocks corporation. Metz would then pay off the Ibarra brothers.

It was why Nick tried to palm Metz off on me, to handle the arraignment. Since he was doing business with the man, an appearance next to him in court would only serve to heighten Nick's profile. Figuring the feds were checking Metz for drugs, as soon as they realized this was a dry hole, Nick knew they would settle for a fine to cover the cost of their time, this on the illegal transfers of cash into the country by Metz. They would slap his hand. A deal like that would be a cakewalk, even for Nick's buddy Paul who shied away from drug cases.

By then everybody would be happy. Metz would have more cash than he'd ever seen in one place before. And Nick would have the money to finish the law firm coup, Rush and Company, no doubt with a flashy new corner office for himself overlooking the bay and the blue Pacific.

And how was Nick going to get the variance? What do you give to someone who has everything? What gift, what token can anyone offer to a man like Zane Tresler; what would lock him in? Nick had that answer too. You give him something to occupy a place of honor in the white, chambered nautilus, modeled under all that glass in his office. You give him the key to a lost language. You give him the Mexican Rosetta.

But Nick never got that far. He never saw the shadow looming up in front of him: the austere figure of Adam Tolt. Adam was not the kind of man to spend his life building a law firm and then allow Nick to steal it.

The relationship between them was one born of convenience and, I suspect, more than a little bad karma. In the end, Adam had to see Nick as his worst nightmare.

Initially he liked the fact that Nick made Rocker, Dusha a full-service firm. The addition of low-visibility, criminal law services fleshed out the partnership. He liked the money, and he was satisfied with the occasional advice Nick offered on cases. But most of all he liked the Chinese Wall Nick provided around the firm's respectability. It kept everything clean and tidy. Whenever business clients ventured into crime land, or found themselves there by unhappy circumstance, Adam could banish them down the elevator with a friendly pat on the ass and still keep the revenue flowing. In this way, the firm's most valued clients, the ones who didn't have a grand jury giving the smell test to their stock transactions, wouldn't have to wrench their backs, rubbing up against the expensive finish on Adam's paneled hallways while trying to avoid contact with Nick's untouchables.

As for Nick, he got to tie his wagon to a brighter star, a

major firm about to go supernova, with all the prospects that this seemed to present.

I say "seemed," because my guess is that within a year, Nick realized it was an illusion. His position with Rocker, Dusha was a dead end. They'd put him downstairs for a reason. To keep his clients from sullying the dignified atmosphere of the real firm. No doubt Adam planned to move Nick lower once Rocker, Dusha expanded enough to inhabit the entire building. Nick could have his own private hell next to the furnace in the basement, where his clients could get credit for time served in purgatory. Adam made it clear. He didn't want Nick doing anything other than criminal cases. The path to growth was blocked.

Even for someone like Nick, with an uncanny sense for the human condition, it couldn't have taken long before Tolt started hearing murmurs. With a firm full of nervous partners, there had to be some who wanted to place bets on the back line, trying to cover both sides in case Nick came up short.

I can only imagine Adam's state of mind when he started picking up the scent. A man closer to the end of his career than the beginning, with no place as lofty to land, facing an assault from a direction he'd never anticipated: the basement. His first thought must have been that Nick was out of his mind. Somewhere in the recesses of Adam's frantic brain must surely have passed the thought that this was also history's verdict of Hitler and Stalin, not a comforting thought given their initial success and the carnage that followed. Things must have looked even worse when he considered his options.

For a man with a Rolodex full of heady phone numbers, no doubt with the private line to the Oval Office topping the list, a man who had reached the zenith of a career most people would envy, all Adam could see were the stunning heights from which he could fall. Sure he had a name, a solid reputation of accomplishment, almost all of it in earlier decades. Important people would take his calls, as long as he was the senior partner at Rocker, Dusha.

As any enduring dictator will attest, when faced with the skirmish line of rebellion, the first rule of survival is to hang the leader. Adam must have stayed up nights trying to figure ways to force Nick out of the firm. But he had a problem. He was missing some vital information. He couldn't be sure how long Rush's revolt had been going on or how many of his partners had already signed on. It wouldn't do to call Nick on the carpet and can him, only to find himself voted out of the firm the next morning.

Plan B wouldn't work either. Adam couldn't just pick up the phone and start calling partners, trying to divine if they'd been talking to Nick behind his back, measuring Adam's throat for a good cutting. To do that would be to admit that he'd already lost control. Whether Nick won or lost, the partners would smell blood. Adam would be voted the position of partner emeritus, given a broom closet for an office and a book of crossword puzzles to occupy his time.

He could have waited for the revolt to erupt and then taken Nick and the rebels who followed him to court. But as every law firm knows, the last thing any client wants to hear is that his lawyers are all suing each other. The clients would bail and Adam knew it. What good is it to be a bull and own a field, if there are no cows and no grass in it?

Adam may have been the senior partner, but he wasn't senile. It didn't take him long to confront reality. He was a lawyer. Nick was a kamikaze pilot. If need be, Nick was fully prepared to bring himself down in flames, all over Adam's finely polished decks. What tends to occupy your mind when you think about doing battle with someone in Nick's situation is a lot of blood, most of it being your own.

Confronted by the situation, it is easy to imagine the desperation that might drive someone like Adam to excess. In Tolt's mind there had to be a way, something more direct, with a quick and certain result, some action he could take, and finish, before his partners started running for the doors. Even to those with mental powers not nearly as subtle as Adam's, there is little in life more definitive than death.

The opportunity presented itself in the risky nature of

The federal government has flexed its muscle. It has exercised its powers of eminent domain and condemned an empty lot with its cavernous hole that was once the site of the old Capri Hotel.

The General Services Administration announced yesterday that it plans to build a new federal courthouse at this location.

I lower the newspaper, close my eyes, and hold my breath. Sitting here motionless, I listen, and I can hear it. Faint as a distant whisper, it lingers in the air, just at the edge of the human auditory frontier. The familiar pitch that became the signature finish to a thousand yarns of combat in court. Somewhere beyond my mortal horizon, I can hear Nick, and he is laughing.

COMING SOON IN HARDCOVER

Double
Tap

STEVE

A PAUL MADRIANI NOVEL

MARTINI

PUTNAM

Nick's practice. It might have been any of a number of Nick's seedier drug clients who could have gotten the nod, to be standing next to him on the street that morning.

It requires surmise to plug a few of the gaps, but I suspect that Adam picked Metz for a reason. Lawyer's intuition tells me that Margaret, Nick's ex, had lied to me when I talked to her with Susan. She had known about Jamaile Enterprises. Her lawyers would have turned it upside down, looking for hidden assets during the divorce. But timing is everything in life. Nick was lucky. He was still working on the loan papers to buy the hotel.

Adam would have been cultivating Margaret in hopes of gathering dirt on Nick's vices, even the ancient ones. She turned out to be a wellspring of information. She told him about Jamaile, Metz.

Adam must have thought he'd found the grail. What better to get the cops salivary glands going in the morning than a criminal defense lawyer gone bad, turned to the dark side and doing business with one of his own drug clients. It was a prosecutor's wet dream. Adam had to figure they would look neither hard nor long at any other theories or, for that matter, waste a lot of time chasing after the shooters.

Tolt had no idea what Jamaile really was or what Nick and Metz were up to in Mexico. It is only my guess, but I think Adam actually believed Nick was involved in drugs. If nothing else, it would have served to cement his resolve, convinced him that he was fighting the good fight, and provided the consolation that no matter how dark his deed, he was doing it for the firm, saving it from the devil. If he had looked more thoroughly at Jamaile, he might have picked someone other than Metz as the patsy. Had he done that, it is likely no one would have been able to connect the dots and find Adam hiding at the end, all the pieces lacking, as they were, reference points like the hieroglyphs of the ancient Maya.

And so Nick Rush left the firm, feet first. Adam's gamble very nearly paid off. With no general to lead it, the troops scattered, and the coup died with Nick, so by the time I started nosing around, it was history. Why would anyone place their career in my hands, confiding to me their part in a revolution that never happened? It was why Dolson didn't want to talk when I met with him in San Francisco and why the office building at the address in Nick's handheld was empty, available for lease. Nick was looking for new office space. It's what you need when you're opening a firm.

Even if the thought had dawned on any of Adam's partners that Nick's move might be the motive for murder, there was absolutely nothing on their radar scope to link Adam to the shooting. After all, the cops were all looking under other rocks, assuming, as I did, that Metz was the target.

If that wasn't enough, there was the rock-solid evidence that Nick's death was an accident, with an insurance check approaching four million dollars conceding that fact. I will never know how many arms at the insurer's home office were twisted off at the shoulder by Adam on that one. What I do know is that he used every opportunity to boast about my victory, especially in the firm, even to the point of putting out his piece in the firm's monthly newsletter and making sure it got dropped on every partner's desk.

It was the thing that started me thinking. Why? It was unlike Tolt to go out of his way to embarrass a carrier after what everyone agreed was a generous settlement. It was also Adam who single-handedly fought off their demand for secrecy regarding the amount paid, a virtually uniform secret in every such settlement. I couldn't figure what his reason was. How better to cover your tracks? An insurance company doesn't pay that kind of money unless they are sure it was an accident. Adam's partners would know that. It would kill any suspicion that might be lingering in their minds.

This morning, as I lean back in my chair and read the paper, my loafers crossed on top of my desk, I can't help but smile at the story Harry has circled on page three. Not because it is news. I heard it on the radio in the car last evening on my way home, one of the local stations.

It is the final touch, the ultimate irony that even Nick, at his most calculating, could not have anticipated.

STEVE MARTINI

COMPELLING EVIDENCE
"Rich, cunningly plotted...remarkable."
—*Los Angeles Times*
0-515-11039-6

THE SIMEON CHAMBER
"A fine foot-to-the floor thriller!"
—*New York Daily News*
0-515-11371-9

THE LIST
"A commanding voice."
—*New York Times Book Review*
0-515-12149-5

CRITICAL MASS
"Double crosses galore and an ingenious ending."
—*Publishers Weekly*
0-515-12648-9

Available wherever books are sold or to order call:
1-800-788-6262

B089